A

**"Once we sta... , "there's really no way back."**

Abby clung to him. "I don't want to go back, ever! Not to England, not back to *them!*"

Duke lifted his head to gaze down, narrow-eyed. That wasn't exactly what he meant, and yet it was. He hesitated, actually afraid now. She was more to him than just a stiff, snide woman who had blossomed on board ship and come to full bloom in this raw land like a sun-struck morning glory. She was his Abby Rose, and she moved him to his very soul.

But she did have to go back. She could never really be his, he mourned. Not as helpmeet and companion and wife throughout the struggles that lay ahead. He was just endangering both their futures here.

Yet if she wanted this and came to him, he thought, he could not hold back. Kissing her, pressing closer, he made his decision to love her now even though he might lose her later.

Dear Reader,

The new year is here, and not only are we bringing you some terrific new books to read, we also have some very exciting news in store. In fact, it's *so* exciting that I don't think I can wait before delivering it. Next month we're going to be bringing you *four* Harlequin Historicals every month instead of only two. Your enthusiasm has been so great and your welcome to our authors so warm that we couldn't resist answering your requests for more top-notch historical romances every month. In months to come, favorite authors such as Heather Graham Pozzessere, Patricia Potter, Bronwyn Williams, Lynda Trent and more—as well as talented new authors we've found for you—will be coming your way. I hope you can't wait to read all the Harlequin Historicals we'll be bringing to you in the months and years to come.

But let's not forget this month, when Caryn Cameron and Nicole Jordan bring you New Year's reading to delight and entertain. There's always something good going on here at Harlequin Historicals!

Leslie J. Wainger
Senior Editor and Editorial Coordinator

# Braden's Brides

## Caryn Cameron

# Harlequin Books

TORONTO • NEW YORK • LONDON
AMSTERDAM • PARIS • SYDNEY • HAMBURG
STOCKHOLM • ATHENS • TOKYO • MILAN

Harlequin Historical first edition January 1991

ISBN 0-373-28661-9

BRADEN'S BRIDES

**Books by Caryn Cameron**

Harlequin Historicals

*Dawn's Early Light* #11
*Silver Swords* #27
*Liberty's Lady* #39
*Freedom Flame* #49
*Braden's Brides* #61

---

## *CARYN CAMERON*

is a former high school and college English teacher who now writes full-time and is the author of best-selling historical romances under her own name, Karen Harper. She is a lifelong Ohioan who, with her husband, enjoys traveling and family genealogy. She also plays the piano and keeps in shape with Scottish Highland dancing.

My gratitude and appreciation
to my sisters-in-law
for their support and friendship

# Chapter One

*February 25, 1835*

"**I** simply must get out of here!"

The small tan and white spaniel, nicknamed H.M., barely stirred at her mistress's outburst. The wailing wind and shifting ship were even too much for her otherwise lively dog, Abigail Anne Rosemont thought. Abigail was tired of hearing and watching her leather-bound trunks slide back and forth, back and forth, on the floor of her small private cabin. Today was entirely too rocky to read or sketch the afternoon away, and everyone she might have talked to was indisposed. She just had to escape this nine-by-twelve-foot cubicle before she went mad.

The other cabin-class passengers Abigail had become acquainted with were temporarily ill. As Captain Gates put it, after one rough day across the broad mouth of the Bay of Biscay, they were "green at the gills from that old villain, mal de mer." Abigail felt fine but for cabin fever after these six days out; the journey from London to New South Wales would take four months in all. Let the others keep to their bunks or hang their heads over their necessary pots. Abigail was not going to miss one moment of this adventure! A heady sense of anticipation still beat in her veins like too much rich claret.

As ever when she ventured out, even to breakfast in the cuddy—which was what the ship's dining hall was called—she was gowned properly and well, down to her veiled poke bonnet with its tulle ties. She had brought no maid of her own, but had a suitable arrangement for sharing the services of the captain's wife's girl to help her dress. No cause to let down standards here or have someone later tell the cousins she was traveling to visit, the Godfrey-Bennetts of the Grange, near Sydney in New South Wales, that she had been anything but stylish or proper en route. From the excited letter that had acknowledged Abigail's acceptance of the family's invitation for a lengthy holiday, she could tell that her hostess was keen on current fashions. So Abigail had spent a fortnight in London before she sailed, buying gifts and modernizing and refurbishing her rural wardrobe. After all, she had once been the very picture of Georgian fashion, but then, when the tragedy occurred, she'd forgone all that for quiet country things.

"But there will be quiet country things in New South Wales for us, too," she comforted herself as she patted H.M. She wrapped her heavy, dark blue burnoose cape around her, draping its hood carefully over her hat. Then she left her cabin and made her way to the dim, deserted dining hall.

Ordinarily, Abigail spent lamp-lighted evenings here with the other cabin-class passengers whose cubicles opened onto the cuddy near the stern. Most every evening the captain's wife or Abigail had played hymns or waltzes on the warped pianoforte; the two old scientists pored over their botanical texts or played backgammon; the sober Scotswoman nodded in her chair; and the newlyweds, the Wainwrights, shy and enamored as two turtle doves, took early to their cabin.

What the intermediate-class passengers in their even smaller cabins on the lower deck, or those steerage passengers crowded in the forecastle, did at night, Abigail had no notion, though she did see them during the day exercising in their forward area. The less she thought about all those steerage-class women and the strange men with them the better. Still, she would have liked the chance to sketch them with her pen and ink if she could somehow get closer unseen.

Out on deck, the clip of cool breeze suited her mood. Matching her strides to the sway of the ship, she walked briskly. It had taken great courage for her to leave behind all that was familiar and beloved in the orchard-studded estate of Fairleigh, her grandfather's legacy and the fortune he'd left her. Old Lord Sinton's heiress, they had called her in those thrilling, now tarnished days of her single London season. "Old Lord Sinton's eccentric and reclusive heiress, what's been hiding out in the country for nigh on ten years," she'd heard one seamstress whisper to another just last week when she went for a final fitting.

It would have been so easy to remain forever in those well-loved surroundings of Kent with her memories for company. There she would still be riding across the gently rolling land on her beloved roan gelding, Windsong, sketching lovely vistas and the familiar faces of country folk—and keeping at bay the shame and sadness of a man's brazen betrayal. And to think, a Gypsy fortune-teller at Windsor Castle had once declared before the royal family that she would wed a prince or a duke! Now she was a twenty-six-year-old spinster, who had been well enough content in exile until her beloved Janet had died and—

A wall of wind smacked her the moment she cleared the protection of the main-deck structure. Momentarily stunned by the force of the blast, she spun her back to it. A wave spanked high by the bouncing prow speckled her with spray. Stinging saltwater blinded her. The blast lifted her, ripping at her heavy cloak and gown. A fist of breeze punched up under her bell-shaped skirts and snatched her hems up, up, far above her ankles, whipping yards of material like great flapping wings to fly about her face.

It all happened so fast. The wind yanked away her hood and Abigail's bonnet went sailing. Her extra looped plaits of fashionable false hair were tugged loose of their tortoiseshell combs and pins she had labored to arrange with-

out a maid's sure touch. She stumbled backward into
something hard, to bounce once off her crescent-shaped
bottom bolster, which shoved clear around to the side of her
left hip. She clawed at her streaming, shoulder-length, curly
red hair to see. She grabbed for the rope banister on the
companionway that led below decks. At the next pitch, the
stairs rose, then tilted at an angle. She gasped for air, but her
restrictive corsets and the tight belt around her narrow waist
were hardly made for breath to fight the elements.

Bent over, half-blind, she lunged for the shelter of the
companionway. But everything disoriented her: the sudden
shock of wind, the slide of hull, the stinging salt in her eyes.
And the deep, masculine shout somewhere nearby. She
reached in the direction she thought the rope banister was
strung but grabbed someone's muscled arm instead. A man
coming up the stairs, the captain, a crew member—she did
not know or care. She gave one desperate yelp as hard hands
seized her waist—below her ravaged cloak and skirts that the
winds had hoisted as the crew did their sails. Both grateful
and horrified, she clung desperately to her unseen rescuer,
who pulled her down several steps into shelter.

"Hang on, then!" was the first thing she heard him say.
"What in heaven's name is the likes of you doing up like this
now anyway?"

She couldn't catch her breath. For one dizzying moment, the only thing separating this man's hard, warm
hands from her skin was a thin linen petticoat. Then he
helped her tug the layers of garments down. He looked both
intrigued and annoyed at the package he unwrapped.

"Oh! Oh, I—oh, sorry!" she gasped out when she saw to
her abject consternation who her companion was. That
forbidding man who herded that harem of young women
about on the lower-class promenade deck above the forecastle! The one who was often accompanied by that strange-
looking man Captain Gates had told her was an aborigine
from New South Wales. This man before her was the one
who never wore a top hat and seemed to glare at those on the
private cabin-class deck with eyes she had thought must be

dark and demonic! Now she could see they were an icy blue that pierced right through her. "Oh!" she managed again. His gaze probed as if she still had her skirts hiked shoulder high—and for his crude pleasure only!

She was dismayed to think how she must look to him. The displacement of her false bottom made her look mis-shapen, and her false hair hung ludicrously by a thick, single strand. Her own natural hair had now gone as frizzled as if she had dashed miles through the rain. Worse, where the man's warm hands had touched her momentarily, under her skirts, she still felt his handprints like burning brands that matched the heat of her cheeks and throat.

Despite the roll of the vessel, they stood now on opposite sides of the narrow companionway down to the man's deck. The late-afternoon sun brought cold, shifting light to their shared shelter as the ship continued to rear and plunge. They eyed each other warily while Abigail struggled to smooth her clothing—and her utterly disheveled demeanor—back in place.

"We—we haven't been introduced," she stammered like a ninny, she who had once been the darling of the London season before everything hit her and spun her around so she fell apart, just like this. Even that flash of painful reminder almost devastated the tattered remnants of her poise.

"A bit late for proprieties now!" he said tersely through hard, thin lips that looked, like the rest of him, disapproving and cruelly judgmental. Again, that triggered her worst inner fears. It made her draw herself up haughtily and purse her full lips and wrinkle her smooth brow. It made her want to strike out at this man and run to the refuge of her tiny cabin. But Abigail only stared back at him as coldly as she could.

He, leaning nonchalantly—insolently even—against the oak wall, continued his appraisal of her. She could hardly bolt down the steps or to her cabin, however, until she settled her garments and herself. She noticed from the few words he'd spoken that the man's voice had some strange, quick pace to it, unlike any Irish lilt or Scottish burr she'd ever heard. Every bit the savage, like that aborigine of his, she thought. He had no doubt never worn a proper top hat in his life, for his face was deeply browned and he had auburn hair streaked with sun-struck blond. Then, too, his hair was a bit long in back, below proper collar length; his side whiskers, conversely, were a bit shorter than most men wore. Straight coffee-colored eyebrows slashed his broad forehead and shadowed those sharp, assessing eyes. His nose was straight and narrow. Molded shoulders bulged his mahogany-hued frock coat and dark striped waistcoat, though he seemed to possess a certain lithe grace. A strongly muscled neck and square jawline—despite the lack of attention to what should have been a crisp collar and correctly tied cravat under it—commanded attention. She was five feet five inches; he stood a good deal taller. But most of all, she noted, he emanated an intensity that seemed tightly coiled inside, controlled by an iron wall of will. Appalled to be caught staring so openly, she made a grab for her wayward tail of false hair and tugged the rest of her own pinned tresses loose in the process.

"That will teach you," he observed, not budging, as a gentleman would have, to give her more room.

"Teach me not to walk in the wind, sir? I both walk and ride in it at home whenever I so please."

"Teach you, I mean, not to go about here in all that false padding—that hair, those ribbons and ruffles, that bottom roll and so many petticoats that you almost took off like a bird—"

"I'll thank you not to comment on such, such private things!"

"Which almost became public enough a moment ago! And I was erroneously thinking your thanks would be for helping you."

"Yes, well, I am relieved you happened along."

After that quick exchange, silence stretched between them. Appalled that she could not patch her hair together better while he kept staring so rudely, she abandoned that task and gave her ravaged skirts a final flounce. Gathering her burnoose tightly in front of her to stop his prying gaze, she started up the steps.

"Wait! Better to walk down through here and go up closer to your cuddy entrance," he warned and caught up with her to take her elbow.

She shook him off. "No, I couldn't go that way," she blurted before she realized it sounded as if she would not deign to set her cabin-class foot anywhere near steerage. She hadn't actually meant that at all, but only that she had no intention of plunging into the dim depths with this man. "I mean," she floundered, "I'll be just fine now that I'm pre-pared for what's out there. And I do thank you, sir, for keeping me from toppling down the stairs." *But not,* she wanted to rant at him, *for the way your hands touched me as familiarly as your eyes!* Holding her skirts tightly, she bent quickly into the slap of cold wind.

For a good ten minutes after the woman left, Duke Braden stood at the top of the steps watching the wind billow the sails and churn the gray, rolling sea. He'd only come up from the intermediate-class cabin he shared with the queasy Kulalang to get a breath of fresh air and a glimpse of sunlight before he visited his ladies down in steerage. And here he'd ended up with as good as Samson's Delilah in his arms. No doubt, just like all the rest of those haughty, touch-me-not-type ladies, she'd like to put him in his place and clip his wings if not his hair. If she blew into the sea on her way back to her precious, pompous fellow folk on the main deck, so much the better, he assured himself. He knew her class and he knew her type, and that was that. Yet there was some-thing about her that rattled him on a deeper level and in a different way than most other fancy women did. But maybe, he thought, it was just her distinctive looks.

Her hair was a radiant red like the sun setting through the shimmering eucalyptus haze of the Blue Mountains at home. Her tresses were curly on their own with a resilience a mere slosh of spray and rip of wind could never weaken. She was tart-tongued, but he admired her sea legs, her steely stare and the iron in her backbone. She wasn't the sort of pretty face he favored—too pinched with no pert tilt of nose tip or soft, sweet curve of mouth. He doubted she ever smiled. She probably sniffed that classic nose disdainfully at everything. But those thick-fringed hazel eyes were alluring—a combination of all the natural hues he loved in the Parramatta Valley—green and blue and brown all swirled together.

Despite the fussy laces and fancy flounces, the body her blown cloak and skirts had revealed seemed sweetly rounded, as his brother, Earl, would put it. But then, Earl would probably have throttled that spoiled little snob.

But not Duke Braden. He was a man who knew that a cool head got better results than an angry hand—most of the time. And right now he had his hands full with the six women downstairs who really needed his help, and that red-haired little prickly pear was not worth another thought. He'd been watching her parade under her ruffled parasols all week on the cabin-class deck, and now he knew damn well what she was really like—inside and out!

Yet as he went back downstairs, he rubbed his hands together where he'd grasped her warm, firm flesh through the last layer of clothing that had saved her dignity. His palms tingled to touch her again. It took all six of his charges chattering at him at once before he put the little snip out of his thoughts for good.

The next day, when the seas—and Abigail's heart—had somewhat calmed, the barque *Challenge* started southward around the western tip of Spain. That evening, cabin-class passengers came back to partake of cuddy food once again, served by the two table servants who also tended to the needs of the four cabins opening onto the cuddy. Everyone chatted pleasantly enough over what the captain's wife, Gwendolyn Gates, announced was the last of the smoked ham before their steady diet of salt beef and salt fish began. "But we'll have the occasional chicken in the pot from that flock in cages up on deck," she assured them, and nodded so her long salt-and-pepper curls bounced. "Too bad those six sheep in the hold are breeders or we'd have ourselves a leg of mutton now and again. They belong to that same intermediate-class passenger as those six women going along to find a mate, you know."

Abigail nearly splashed her spoon in her curried broth. "That man with all the women—he's a farmer, and those sheep are his?"

"Indeed, though there's no doubt much more to say about him, isn't that true, my dear?" Mrs. Gates prodded her husband in his place at the head of the table.

"I suppose so," was the only rejoinder.

Mrs. Gates seemed to dote on gossip and bemoaned the lack of it so far out here, but that didn't budge her spouse to further details while he ladled soup into his mouth. Abigail and his wife, seated at either side of him, both waited for him to say more, while the other five passengers along the linen tablecloth clattered away with their silver on bone china.

"It seems only appropriate," Mr. Jervis Crombie, one of two elderly botanists aboard, remarked wryly in the awkward silence, "that a man concerned with breeding sheep should be escorting those brides to New South Wales on that new bounty immigrant program."

His companion, Michael Saxon, peered over his spectacles and bobbed his agreement with a grin. There was even the hint of a smile on Captain Gates's lips at that subtle jest.

"Thing is," Mr. Crombie went on, "the fellow's the only half-civilized soul from New South Wales on board we could chat with a bit about the flora we can expect to find and preserve on our botanic mission. Perhaps we should ask him up for dinner some night if the captain and Mrs. Gates wouldn't mind."

"Of course not," Mrs. Gates assured them. "There's a thing or two I'd like to ask him. As long as he doesn't bring along that Negro valet of his—"

"Native aborigine, Mrs. Gates," Captain Gates put in. "We are hardly headed for darkest Africa, you know, but a civilized English colony much like the mother nation herself.''

Abigail almost choked at the idea of dining with that sheep farmer after what had happened. But she forced herself to finish her soup before the bowls were cleared for the meat course. On a long voyage, where water was rationed at only one gallon per day for all one's needs, she had to down her liquids even if her stomach was now rolling at this conversation. She dreaded being stared at from close range by that man during an entire evening. He might even tell the others how much he had seen of her and make a joke of it, though she could hardly imagine laughter on the face of the stern man she met yesterday. Why, whoever knew if that grim mouth of his sported teeth or fangs! Still, she had been hoping to speak to someone from New South Wales and question them about everything she could expect to find there, and she could hardly ask that pagan he traveled with.

"What say, Lady Abigail?" Jervis Crombie was asking.

"Oh, I'm sorry. What was that, Mr. Crombie?" Abigail replied.

"Just admiring your iron constitution to be able to sleep at night and eat like a soldier when the rest of us were down with the Biscay Bay rough-sea woozies, that's all.''

Everyone laughed at the way he had put that, Abigail included. Even the shy newlyweds, Mary and Percival Wainwright, and the dour Mrs. Graham from Edinburgh, going to Sydney to join her military adjutant husband, tittered a bit. But now Abigail sympathized with their former seasick plight more than they knew: last night after that appalling situation with that man, she had not slept one whit and had avoided breakfast, too, as past memories and future fears assailed her. Had she made a mistake to leave behind all that was dear and secure in Kent? Was she being reckless to long for some sort of great and grand adventure before, God forbid, unexpected death took her as it had Janet? And with Phillip Godfrey-Bennett, her hosts' son in New South Wales, newly widowed and of like age as she, was she being foolish to agree to live there, when she never intended to become one bit involved with a man ever again? Realizing she was woolgathering, she forced herself to dig into her ham and parsleyed potatoes.

Abigail usually managed to hold such agonizing at bay. But now that man had triggered a torrent of memories. Somehow those few moments with him up on deck had made her feel lonely when she'd thought she was doing just fine. And not just lonely for her departed family, or her friend Janet, or even for the home she'd left behind, but lonely for really living!

Though Abigail Anne Rosemont had grown up an only child, she had never felt lonely in her youth. There had been distant cousins about on holidays and visits; she'd had a mother who doted on her, and a dear maternal grandfather, too. After her mother died, her grandfather, Lord Sinton, saw that she was properly, even elegantly, presented in society where she met many charming acquaintances among the noble sons and daughters of the land. But more than any of those "friends," she had always had her maid, Janet.

Janet Jones was of the same age and the same size and the same heart, as the two of them used to say. Though Janet's mother had been Abigail's mother's lady's maid, the girls were always together. Abigail passed on to Janet what she gleaned from her tutoring. Janet learned to ride when Abigail did. Janet sat and embroidered nearby while Abigail sketched the outdoor vistas they loved. They shared girls' secrets almost as if they were sisters—as if the wide chasm of class did not separate them at all in the countryside of Kent where they grew apace to womanhood. And Janet was the only one who ever called her Abby.

Grandfather had never called her aught but "my dear" or "dearest girl." She had lost her father in the Napoleonic Wars when she was four and recalled no more than a handsome face and bright red uniform when he lifted her on his horse and smiled up at her. Mother had called her Abigail Anne before she died of fever several years ago, because of a broken heart, some said. When she heard that, Abigail mourned both the loss of her mother and her own failure to be enough for her to live for.

Even when Janet became Abby's lady's maid on her fourteenth birthday, the difference in their status barely came between them. Rather, they shared and giggled over everything as Janet's skillful fingers did up Abby's long, crimson tresses or hooked her gown. Even when Abby went out without Janet on visits or rode to the horn with Lord Northurst, the girls still shared everything later. It was only death that came between them.

Last year, the very month before Janet was to wed—with Abigail's encouragement and blessing—Fairleigh's chief groom, the young maid had died of a ruptured appendix. So sudden, so painful, so unfair.

But it was not just losing Janet that had shaken Abigail to her core.

"Abby, Abby," Janet had gasped as her stunned fiancé Jedidiah sat on the far side of the bed, holding her other hand while Abigail bent over her. "I hate leaving you and Jed, but you know what I hate almost more?"

"It's all right, Janet. Please don't strain to talk—"

"No, listen. I was just thinking I haven't seen things. You know," she rasped and drew a shallow breath, her eyes so bright with pain and fever, "things much outside of your friends' homes or London or Kent. Fairleigh's beautiful, but there's a big world out there. I'm not ungrateful or greedy—but you know—you know what I mean—"

Abigail Anne Rosemont did indeed know, though the full impact of what Janet had imparted in the last conscious hour of her short life did not fully strike her until after the funeral. Abigail knew she had lost a dear friend, and became determined to lose no more time. The one who had been closest to her and called her Abby was gone, but she had given her a challenge to live by.

And that was why she could not bear to bring along another maid as companion on this voyage of discovery. It would have been like betraying Janet, however much Mrs. Godfrey-Bennett had hinted that British servants were worth their weight in gold in New South Wales, where people had to "scrape by" with convict help. Abigail's loss of Janet and that deathbed confession of regret were the real reasons Lord Sinton's heiress had decided to accept the long-standing invitation. She would travel to someplace called the Parramatta Valley, eight miles outside of Sydney, New South Wales, on the other side of the world. She had vowed to see and experience as much as she could—the far-flung, the exciting, the exotic things Janet had secretly longed for.

That hardly included experiencing at too close range that man with all the women hanging about him and that frightening aborigine of his. She might find a way to sketch them from afar, but no more. That man's look and demeanor reminded her too much of things she'd prefer to forget. And yet she could not shake his voice, his words, even his touch. Other voyagers might have suffered from so-called mal de mer yesterday; she was suffering from mal de man and she didn't so much as care if she ever learned his name!

Abigail lay awake yet a second night, listening to the liquid laughter of ladies on the sea air. Their voices, drifting through her single porthole on the rush of wind from forecastle to stern, haunted her. It had to be those six women with that man; there were no other females aboard but Mrs. Gates, Mrs. Graham and young Mary Wainwright. Abigail was glad no one had mentioned that man's name at table; she did not want to know! But right now she thought she heard his deep voice mingling with the women's laughter at the raucous, if improper, good time they were all having so late at night.

She turned over in her narrow bunk again and bumped the dog at her feet. H.M. just resettled and went back to heavy sleep, but Abigail got up and fumbled with a sulfur match to light her whale oil lamp. For a moment she wrapped her Persian-blue wool robe around her shoulders and then discarded it. Somehow, despite being at sea in February, she felt warm and hoped she was not courting a

fever. She sat down on the flat trunk she kept by the single
tiny table and propped up her drawing board with her half-
finished sketch. She had been watching those women while
they strolled about their promenade deck today—two
blondes, one redhead and three brunettes. Three were short,
three were tall, all wore rather faded, old-fashioned pe-
lisses. Not one sported the burnoose that had been so stylish at home ever since Napoleon's Egyptian defeat by the
British. But none of that really mattered now. What stuck
in Abigail's mind—and what she had begun to sketch—was
that the women were all having such a good time together.

And *he* was there with them, escorting different ones,
pointing things out as if there had really been something to
see but endless rolling billows and the distant gray coast of
Spain or Portugal on the horizon. Once again today, the
man wore no top hat; the wind tossed his hair. Why, even
the old botanists had rigged chin straps for wearing their
hats on deck, and still managed to tip those hats to her every
time she took her promenade on the stern.

The man with the women seemed to nod her way more
than once, though she couldn't be certain and was hesitant
to respond in any way. Who knew what he was telling those
women of how she'd looked with her skirts up? She'd
learned the hard way about gossip and scandal and never
intended to go through anything like that again. But she
couldn't very well exile herself to her small cabin where she
would go quite mad in no time at all. Or, she was afraid, the
next time she fell asleep, she'd have that dreadful nightmare she hadn't experienced for years where she was naked
before a staring group of people and they were all whispering and pointing at her.

She lifted the silver lever on her precious ivory fountain
pen to release the flow of ink. Usually she sketched with
various-sized quills, but the pen served her better when the
sea rolled like this. The sketch she had begun was of two
clusters of women, all so happy and lively. She had drawn
them in ornate, fashionable garments—unlike those of her
unwitting models. Her mind drifted as she added more de-

tails to their tresses and skirts, their expressions and their stances. As she listened to the distant voices she concentrated on reproducing what her mind's eye saw. But she still couldn't bear to place the man in the space she had left for him in the very center of the drawing.

She was afraid he might turn out to look exactly like that New South Wales sheep breeder. She hated to admit she was insatiably curious about him, despite her instinctive distrust of him. And, worse, each time she began to draw him, the image in her mind kept blending with that of another, whose face brought back the bitter memory of her ruination.

She had once believed Tremont, Lord Northurst, to be everything she envisioned her love would be: handsome, solicitous, polite, thoughtful, titled. He was the first and only man she had ever trusted and adored. He dazzled her; he filled her heart the first time she saw him at the cotillion, her second dance after being presented at the court of King George IV. They rode together in Hyde Park and through the Kent countryside. He loved horses, too. With her chaperon and friends in tow, they attended the races at Newmarket and rode to the horn, though she did not care for hunting. But Tremont did, so she gladly went along. He asked her grandfather for her hand and proposed to her at the end of her first social season. Grandfather wanted them to wait a year, even two, but Tremont was impatient in his rush to possess her. Abigail became impatient with Grandfather, too.

"But I would not have been presented if I weren't ready to be wed, Grandfather," she had protested to him in his dim, leather-scented study one night while Janet waited just outside the door. "After all, the ton is a sort of marriage mart."

"You're too young to know men, my dearest girl, that's all."

"I don't wish to know men, sir. Just my beloved Tremont."

"But he is older, more worldly. 'Tis a common thing, I know, to wed young to one's elders, and yet, the North-ursts have invested heavily in shaky endeavors lately, and I don't mean to suggest it but—"

But her young, fervent heart had not wanted to hear of investments or worldliness. The only investment she longed to make was to entrust her life to the dashing Tremont and his exciting world. To make her happy, Grandfather finally agreed. But then Tremont's world came crashing down around her, only one week before the great wedding they had planned in the Gothic chapel at Fairleigh.

"'Pon my word, can't wait till all this folderol is over and I can just get to her," she overheard Tremont declare to a friend that terrible night. She stood on the far side of a tap-estried screen set up to ward off drafts from the large hall at Fairleigh, where Tremont, his parents and several ever-present friends had come to stay for final wedding prepa-rations. Abigail blushed hotly at her betrothed's fervor to bed her. He had hinted at it several times to her, but to boast of it to his friends! She felt her flesh tingle beneath the neckline of her satin gown.

"Never know about females breeding young as Abigail. Sometimes it takes a while to catch," Tremont's friend re-plied matter-of-factly, and several others agreed. "But I'm sure you'll console yourself well enough with the Sinton riches both in your marriage bed and out till you get her with your heir to secure things."

Abigail clapped her hands to her mouth. She wanted to storm right in to scold Tremont's friend for daring to sug-gest that her wealth had anything to do with her and Tre-mont's priceless, passionate love. But then the rest of the sky fell in.

"Law, yes," Tremont agreed vehemently. "The North-urst coffers have been pinched lately. But I'd give a big chunk of my new-won wealth to be out of this damned, dusty Kentish nunnery where the old man expects us to live. I long to return to London. As I said, gentlemen, can't wait till all this fussy folderol is over and I can get back to my mistress Sarah again...."

The men's talk and the scent of cigars went on, but everything was over for Abigail. She crumpled to the Aubusson carpet and promptly got sick on it. The next day she found strength in her battered pride and fury: she refused to see Tremont no matter how he pleaded and Grandfather lectured. She insisted the elaborate plans for her society wedding be canceled, despite the stigma.

"Tell Lord Northurst the plans for all the *fussy folderol* are over!" she told his friends who dared to come plead with her.

Regrets were sent to cancel the 340 invitations. Georgian silver and damask linen gifts were returned. Abigail did not have to refuse social invitations, for suddenly none were forthcoming. Disillusioned that she had been dropped so easily from people's lists, she soon learned the real reason why. Claiming she was going shopping in London, Abigail went unannounced to see Lord Northurst at his Hanover Square town house.

"How dare you and your coterie circulate rumors about my chastity being sullied by previous dalliances!" she had berated him. She was shaken to the core by the realization of his crassness and cruelty, but she held her ground even when he swaggered insolently up to her. "*You* are the one who is sullied by a secret dalliance, sir! You only wanted me for the money and an heir so you could run back to your common mistress!"

He had laughed in her face. It was the only time in her life she could have killed someone if she had held a gun.

"My poor little girl, it's the way of the world. That's merely expected for a man, even husbands—de rigueur, in fact."

"Not my man or my husband!"

"You pious little nitwit! You think your moneybags grandfather hasn't had his share of privately kept passions in his day? This grand protest of yours has no doubt brought the old boy to his knees, but he's laughing at you, too, just like the rest of us.''

"But why the sordid rumors? I have never even let a man so much as touch me that way, and—"

He leaped at her and clamped his hand hard over her mouth, seething with pent-up frustration and fury at her. His face contorted demonically. Before she could cry out for Janet, who was waiting outside, he bent her back over the settee and whipped up her skirts and petticoats with his free hand.

"Chaste, pristine virgin goddess, are you?" he raved as his hard hand crept lewdly up her bare thigh above her gartered stocking. She tried to thrash away, her eyes wide with hurt and shock. "My little heiress who's too proper, too good for the Northursts, for the way things are done in this town and this land, eh? You think this would be worth all your money, that I'd give up my pleasures just to plant you here with an heir? My, but you've got a good deal to learn about life!"

He was hurting her. He was squeezing her between her legs in her most private place. Angered at his insults, she bit down hard on his fingers and tasted blood. He yelped; she kicked. He jumped back and she sprawled to her knees before she scrambled up, tearing the ruffled hem of her gown.

"You spoiled little bitch!" he shouted.

She ran for the door, which Janet pulled open in that instant. But when he did not pursue, she turned back to him and pointed her shaking hand. "I don't want any part of you or your dreadful world, sir! I swear I'll tell all about your lies if I must!"

"And face everyone's stares and whispers? Go ahead, tell that poor old man to come challenge me then, if your golden honor is so sullied by a Northurst!"

But she did not do any of that. She grabbed Janet's hand and fled. She never told her grandfather about Northurst's threats or further perfidy. Perhaps she was afraid to hear from that dear man that he, too, once had a mistress and it was the way of the world, just as that viper had said. She never went back to society or court, even when the new king, William IV, was crowned six years later and she was invited to several coronation festivities. She never saw Lord Northurst again, never wanted to. She'd heard he'd found another heiress and had four sons in ten years. She made a life for herself in Kent, and was almost certain sometimes she was content and fulfilled—until she lost Janet and realized perhaps she hadn't yet lived at all.

Hadn't lived when she heard laughter on the sea breeze from the young women and had to try to draw it to stifle her regrets and fears. Hadn't lived when she had to admit to herself in the depths of a night like this that she did not lead a solitary life, but a lonely one!

Abigail Anne Rosemont drew a charming smile on the woman farthest left on her page. Then she tilted the woman's gaze as if she looked up into what would be the eyes of the man whose likeness would soon grace the very center of this paper. The next woman, a shorter reddish-haired one, she drew actually laughing up into the place where the man's face would be. But all the while she sketched smiles and laughter, silent tears ran down her cheeks to plop on her hand, holding her pen so steadily.

# Chapter Two

The two cabin-class botanists had invited him to dinner! Though the day was calm and sunny, the ship suddenly seemed to pitch and roll under Abigail's feet the minute she heard. She had been sketching clouds over the distant Moroccan coast all afternoon, and had come in just in time to hear he'd accepted the invitation she hadn't known had even been tendered. Though famished and thirsty, she almost considered playing the coward and missing dinner. But she refused to give the man the satisfaction of thinking she was still thinking of him after their absurd meeting last week!

She dressed and did her hair with particular care to appear as much different as possible from the disheveled wretch he had seen that day. She was beginning to master handling her own bounteous, naturally curly hair, though with water rationed, she longed to wash it in something besides seawater. Cold sponge baths with saltwater were already growing as stale as the repetitious diet of salt beef, salt pork, salt fish, potatoes and bland-tasting soda bread.

To think there were weeks and months yet to go! What she wouldn't give for a fresh Kentish pear or apple or a good hot tub bath. She'd been dreaming of such luxuries lately. The men aboard were fortunate to be able to bathe in rainwater collected in the sails. Mrs. Gates had told her that sometimes late at night the crew just disrobed and stood out on deck in a gentle storm. Unfortunately, women could hardly do the same. But she wondered if those six women, whose voices she heard at night, could be up on deck washing in the warm nighttime rain. If so, she'd have liked to join them, reputation or not!

With the help of Mrs. Gates's girl, Susan, Abigail donned her cream-colored muslin gown with the rose flower design and tiny tucks across the bodice. Low-cut flat slippers, ribbon-wrapped to her feet and revealed by the ankle-length scalloped hem, completed the warm-weather ensemble. The fact she'd picked one of her plainer day dresses had nothing to do, she told herself, with the sheep farmer's comment that she didn't need all her ruffles and flounces out here. Her coif looked quite controlled, she thought, as she put her looking glass back in her trunk amid her extra petticoats for safekeeping. Her heavy tresses were swept back and up from a central part into an Apollo knot on top of her head and softened with long, bouncy curls before each ear. She hadn't bothered with her false hair plaits this time.

She assured herself once again that she didn't care if she never heard the name of the man who was visiting the cuddy dining hall tonight. That would make him even more real than the drawing she'd finally done of him. But as she learned while she stood stiffly, as if at military attention, during the introductions, his name suited him perfectly because it was quite beyond the pale of propriety: *Duke* Braden. It made him sound as if he wanted to claim a title he could never hope to attain. Or it was a good name for a spaniel, like H.M., she thought, secretly amused at his expense. After all, she had almost named her dog Duchess.

"I see you can smile," Duke Braden murmured to her as they all approached the table and waited for Captain Gates to seat his wife.

"When occasion suits," she replied archly, without returning his overly intense stare.

Just then H.M. poked through Abigail's skirts to sniff Mr. Braden's leg, and Abigail could not repress a slight smile. His name and his occupation had somehow made this rather painful formal meeting so much easier for her.

"What's the dog's name?" Mr. Braden asked, evidently trying to be kinder than he had been last week when his presumptuous comments on her garments and hair had been absolutely uncalled for.

"H.M., for Henrietta Maria, King Charles II's queen," she told him. "She's a King Charles breed spaniel, you see."

"Are you certain H.M. doesn't stand for Her Majesty, Your Majesty?" he parried, loud enough for everyone to hear.

Several of those present laughed, though Abigail considered the remark another insult. Up went her guard. She hardly responded to another thing the man said all evening, though he said a great deal she found fascinating.

At the prompting of the two scientists, Duke Braden described what he called "the raw, untamed beauty of New South Wales." Cockatoos, kangaroos—though Abigail had seen those in the royal menagerie at St. James's Park years ago—gum and bottlebrush trees, the blue haze of the eucalyptus forests. She listened entranced, despite her renewed personal dislike of him.

"It's just a shame—and pure tomfoolery—that free settlers there don't up and admit New South Wales is not old Mother England," Mr. Braden declared as they all partook of claret after the meal. Despite the pointed stares of Mrs. Gates and Mrs. Graham, Abigail drank a second glass with the men when the decanter was passed around again. H.M. had been so thirsty lately, and she'd had to wash her quill pens in something besides seawater. Her ration was not stretching far enough, and when her fresh linen ran out she shuddered to think of washing her undergarments in saltwater.

"Tomfoolery in what way?" Michael Saxon pursued Mr. Braden's comment from behind his spectacles. "Nothing more tried and true than English ways, and that land is English!"

"But in the deepest sense it is *not* England!" Mr. Braden insisted and hit the table with his fist so the glassware bounced.

Through veiled eyes, Abigail studied him from across the table as she had all evening. He was so intense, so... passionate, when he expressed his opinions. His blue eyes ablaze, his square jaw set hard, his nostrils flaring. Emotion surged through him, though the other day she would have thought he had nothing but ice in his veins. The pattern of his words, so distinctly clipped from the English she was used to, seemed perfect for his personality. If native-born folk where he was from spoke like that, it was definitely not the same as England.

Surprisingly, the idea thrilled instead of worried her. Gooseflesh rose along her arms, and something strange prickled up the nape of her neck and raced along her backbone. She shifted her hips in her hard chair and clamped her thighs tighter together under her gathered skirts.

"Now take the basic matter of food," Mr. Braden plunged on, despite the sputterings and arguments he sensed coming from these prideful English folk. Back in London, he reminded himself, he'd had his fill of the warped thinking that anything different from British ways was inferior to British ways. Every time he had met with a Member of Parliament to argue the cause of freer female immigration or more rights for the aborigines or convicts, he had gotten the same blank stare, the same rigid attitudes walling off understanding and agreement. These people sitting here were no doubt not to blame, but he just wanted them to understand, damn them!

"Food? What about English food?" Mrs. Gates interrupted. "Especially out here on sea rations, one must admit English food is the best in the world."

"I must tell you, Mrs. Gates," Duke Braden went on, trying to hold his voice and temper in check, "Sydney's rock lobster and oysters are far more delectable than anything in English waters. But I'd prefer just to call them different. The point is, the Exclusives there—that's what the rich, 'came-free' settlers call themselves—don't even give a fair go to the bounty of the sea and streams and fields, not unless it's somehow 'English.' Instead, they cling to a salt-fish diet rather than the fresh, different varieties the natives eat—''

"Is it true that kangaroo-tail stew is some sort of native delicacy?'' Mrs. Graham got a word in at last.

"'Roo-tail soup, they say, is far better than any sort of oxtail, but I can't testify to it myself as I don't eat that. Too many 'roos around my place have pets' names, just like your H.M. there, Miss Rosemont," Braden said.

He wanted to diffuse the antagonistic feeling growing here. He didn't want these people—especially that spoiled Miss Rosemont—to judge his homeland before they arrived. He had hardly said two words to her this evening since his little tease about her dog's name backfired. He was now too used to his charges' easy give-and-take when he teased them. He must have been balmy to try it with that stiff-necked little redhead. Still, he'd felt her huge hazel eyes on him all evening. Felt them clear down to his loins! He'd just change the subject quickly and hope to leave all this on a less volatile note.

"I've heard almost everyone else's specific destination in Sydney, Miss Rosemont," he said, turning his face to hers. The impact when their eyes locked jolted him—and her, too, he was sure. Her gaze widened slightly and her lower lip, really not as thin and stiff as he remembered, trembled ever so slightly. He had been watching her each day from a distance, and he was certain she had been doing the same. It was quite a ridiculous thought, of course, but perhaps if they had a few private moments to chat tonight, he'd be able to get her out of his mind. Even his delightful forecastle friends hadn't really made him forget his unfortunate first encounter with this woman.

But her answer certainly ruined any thoughts he'd had of mending fences, and just as well.

"I'm going to be living eight miles outside of Sydney, actually," she told him. "With my second cousins, the Godfrey-Bennetts, in the Parramatta Valley."

Abigail was astounded to see his expectant face freeze to cold disdain again.

"I see," he said.

"You certainly don't—don't actually know them?"

"I know of them. Everyone does. As a matter of fact I know a great deal about them. Enough said, after a lovely *English* dinner," he added and, to everyone's surprise, rose abruptly.

No one knew quite what to make of that, but Abigail felt snubbed and insulted again. How dared he carry on as if he knew something secret that he would not say here but just might share with others! And how dared a sheep farmer set himself up as judge over a family as influential and generous as the Godfrey-Bennetts!

As if speaking for her, H.M. barked at Mr. Braden from behind Abigail's chair as the man said his good-nights and exited the cuddy without another glance her way. It was just as well Mr. Braden beat a hasty retreat, as she'd have been tempted to sic H.M. on him, and one nip might have poisoned the poor dog with bitterness and sour rancor!

The next week, as the *Challenge* sailed farther south along the coast of West Africa, approaching the line, Abigail decided to venture on deck to draw again. The day was sunny and balmy; she could surely manage her paper tacked to her board and her quills and ink while H.M. dozed at her feet. The dog had finally grown accustomed to the chickens, some of which were caged under the railing. And on the rails above the chicken coops hung proof of the continued water problems aboard: buckets of water, which was discolored from the barrels in the hold, were hanging in the breeze to air out. How tempting it was to plunge one's head into a bucket to drink deeply and wash one's face properly in the process!

Abigail settled herself on a three-legged stool she had borrowed from the captain's cabin. Lately, she had used the rough wind as an excuse not to promenade on deck at her usual times. The truth was, she had no desire even to see Mr. Duke Braden across the distance from the elevated stern deck to the more crowded forecastle deck. But today, Abigail had decided to brazen it out up here despite Mr. Braden and his harem—not to mention his aborigine companion, who sat hunched over something along the rail of their deck.

It didn't take long for Abigail, squinting into the breeze and sun from under the brim of her ribboned poke bonnet, to realize what a thrill it would be to draw that aborigine. She'd sketched the others of the Braden entourage both while they were on deck and from memory, though, of course, she'd seen Mr. Braden twice up close and had a better idea of his face. This fresh piece of paper just cried out to be filled with lines depicting the exotic aborigine man across the way.

So as not to be caught staring, Abigail looked sideways at her unsuspecting model as she sketched him. He was slighter and shorter than Duke Braden. His skin glowed copper in the sun, and his hair was a wavy brown with a slight dusting of silver. Like his master, he wore no hat. His limbs seemed made from flexible wire; he could contort himself practically into a ball as he sat hunched over his task. He was garbed in English clothes, but she could just imagine him in something more—more elemental. From here, she could tell his brow was broad and his nose flatter than any nose she'd ever seen. Though she was working strictly in shades of gray from ink and water washes, she wished she could know the true color of his eyes. And how he spoke. What he was doing now. How he lived. What he thought. And why he was aboard: was he some sort of shadowy valet or guard to Duke Braden?

When the aborigine stood and glanced her way, Abigail shuddered with excitement. If only she were bold enough, she would descend this wooden ladder from the roof of the cuddy to the main deck and stride over to speak with him. She would perhaps show him her sketch and offer to pay him something for posing. If Mr. Braden weren't beyond such proprieties, she might even request a proper, formal introduction.

She looked searchingly toward the forecastle exercise deck again. She had been sketching the man's outline with her ivory fountain pen before she colored in his hair and skin with gray wash. She filled the pen anew with ink from her bottle. When the man seemed to turn away, she held the pen up in the air, trying to gauge his height. Under her feet, H.M. shifted slightly as two chickens undertook a clucking disagreement with each other. Then everything happened at once.

The aborigine gave a strangled cry. She looked up. Duke Braden shouted something. Several of his women squealed. Too late, Abigail realized the aborigine had leaped to his feet and hurled at her whatever he'd been holding in his hands. A long, painted wooden object thudded off her sketch and skittered into a chicken cage to set the fowl squawking. She screamed and tried to stand, her pens, quills, ink and water precariously balanced on her board.

In a flash, the shrieking aborigine vaulted off his own platform and charged hers, fists and voice raised. Duke Braden ran behind him, shouting something she did not understand. The aborigine lunged at the ladder to her platform and climbed it. She screamed again and stepped back into the cages while H.M. went crazy barking. The water buckets on the rail tipped and gave the chickens and the back of Abigail's skirts a big bath. The native grabbed her ivory fountain pen from her hand, threw it to the deck and stomped on it. Meanwhile, others came running.

"No, Kulalang! Wait! Wait!" Duke Braden ordered as he, too, vaulted up the narrow steps to the cabin-class platform. His women spilled up after him, shouting, calling to the man named Kulalang. Kulalang reached for the sketch board Abigail had grasped to herself like a barrier, smearing fresh ink on her bodice. He wrenched it away before Duke could reach him. Ink, water, pens flew. H.M., coming to her rescue, charged the aborigine, then skirted right around him to sink her teeth in Duke Braden's ankle. Abigail screamed.

"See! See!" the dark man yelled at Duke. Duke shook H.M. away, and Abigail called her off. Ignoring Abigail now, the aborigine ripped her sketch from the board and thrust it before Duke Braden, whose ladies were ministering to his injured ankle. "See! Her make spirit! Her point the bone. Her make my dreamtime spirit! She die!"

Everything exploded again. H.M. ran in circles barking. Chickens, half-drowned from three tipped buckets, cackled and clucked. Duke dabbed at his bloodied ankle with a handkerchief, after one glance at the sketch. Kulalang retrieved from the cage the wooden piece he'd thrown and brandished it in Abigail's direction. She scooped up H.M. and prepared to flee, just as Captain Gates appeared on the scene. When he held up his hands for quiet, he did not get it at first.

"Oh, look, Mr. Braden," a big-boned, brown-haired woman cried. "She's drawn us, too, on this page under the one of Kulalang. And you, too! Oh, look at your face, so stern and gruff in this sketch. She's an artist!"

"Oh, no!" another Braden woman cried. "I've got ink all over my best gown and slippers—and you, too, Clarissa!"

"Enough!" Duke Braden roared to quiet the noise for the captain. While the captain spoke to those present, Abigail and Duke hardly heard a word he said. They glared at each other through the chaos until his leg evidently pained him and he bent to dab blood again.

Abigail wanted to apologize to them all, but her mouth wouldn't work. In the moment she had to look around her before Captain Gates escorted her down the stairs to safety, her eyes took in only two things besides the harsh look on Duke Braden's austere face. Several of his ladies had spots of ink all over their skirts. And the once fierce aborigine, Kulalang, had wilted to a distraught pile at their feet.

All that afternoon, that night and the next morning Abigail agonized over the chaos she had caused. True, the pagan had tried to hit her with that carved piece of wood, but she had obviously done something to cause the attack. The results were all bad: precious water spilled, gowns ruined, Mr. Braden bitten and Mr. Kulalang's situation uncertain. All she knew was, in the midst of all that upheaval, the native had accused her of drawing his spirit and pointing some bone! And just before he seemed to collapse at their feet, he had said she should die!

It was as if everyone aboard were imprisoned here, with the classes at war! she thought. Why did this wretched voyage have to take so long! Why were there no British steamships on this route as there were from Bristol to New York City—now a mere fifteen-day run? Even on land, steam vehicles had been able to travel thirty miles per hour for several years now. She would simply perish during this four-month voyage that seemed never-ending.

Near noon, Abigail gathered up her courage, and some garments to replace those that were ink-stained, and left her cabin to visit the forecastle women. The captain had explained to her that the aboriginal man was ill, and she wondered if he was sorry for his violent actions and threats. Her heart beat rapidly in her chest, and her legs felt brittle as she ventured out. She intended to ask Mrs. Gates or Mrs. Graham to serve as chaperon and go below deck to inquire after Mr. Kulalang, the women—and Mr. Braden. She would simply apologize and ask what she could do to help. But as she started across the cuddy to find a chaperon, Duke Braden entered from the other side.

For a silent moment they stared at each other across the bare tables, startled, frowning.

"I was just coming to fetch you," he said.

"I was coming to inquire what I might do—and ask what really happened. I didn't have any idea your man would react like that."

"Obviously," he said. "But he's my friend and not 'my man.' At least all he threw at you was the *woomera* he was decorating—his spear thrower—and not the spear itself. That would have sliced even your steely little backbone in two."

She shuddered. Her knees went even weaker, whether from shame or fear or just this man's presence she was not sure. She clutched the clothes in her arms more closely.

"Your laundry?" he asked, nodding at the bundle she held.

"Hardly, not with the water I spilled when Mr. Kulalang charged. I want to offer your women charges these things to replace those my ink ruined."

For the first time since she had known him, his features softened. Though he didn't smile, he wore a different expression from the stern look she was used to seeing, or even the avid one that lit his face when he spoke of his homeland. This look nearly staggered her. She stepped forward to lean her elbows for support on the chair back nearest her.

"May I escort you below, then?" he inquired, bowing politely with his hands clasped behind his back. He could almost have been the proper suitor, calling to inquire if she would accept his company for a walk in the park.

"But first," he went on, "I'd appreciate it if you'd come to my cabin to reassure Kulalang that you did not mean to curse his spirit by drawing his image and pointing that bone at him."

"What bone?" she asked, both intrigued and entranced. She allowed him to escort her out on deck.

"I assume he meant that ivory pen of yours he stomped to bits. When you held it up toward him and when he saw that you'd sketched his likeness, he thought you meant to destroy his spirit. You see, if an aborigine is 'boned' or 'pointed,' as they call it, they're likely to just give up, lie down and die. And so," he said earnestly, "I hope you will tell him you had no such intention. I've been trying to convince him, but he'll recover—dare I say—his spirits faster if you'll back me up."

"Oh, yes! I certainly had no notion—"

"I know. Here, just down these steps," he said.

Abigail Anne Rosemont then began to learn at close quarters what the people she had thought about and drawn were really like. She forgot it was most improper to visit a man's cabin alone; instead she began to grasp the aborigine Kulalang's beliefs and saw that the color of the man's eyes was a unique ruddy brown. Her heart was touched when Kulalang rose from his prone position on the mat next to Mr. Braden's bunk. She almost cried with a poignant pain she had never before experienced when he nodded at her explanation and apology. "Much same, you, me," he told her. "Sunset in hair. Hair like sea waves. Kulalang draw, too. See!" He thrust into her hands as a gift the *woomera* he had heaved at her just yesterday, with its strange carvings of hunters and prey.

Too shaken to speak, Abigail nodded and blinked back tears. The stern Duke Braden didn't so much as flick an eyelash during the whole thing.

She also learned that the six women in his care called themselves Braden's brides, though he claimed he did not intend to wed one of them.

He introduced his charges to Abigail in the narrow steerage compartment lined with bunk beds like shelves. "Clarissa Nye, Deanna Dill, Evelyn Chase, Cora Mercer, Grace Buck and Beth Anne Clare," he said. "Each lady is a free bounty immigrant, under a new government plan, whose husband will pay her passage over when they're wed. Each one will contribute greatly, I'm certain, to the growth and civilizing of New South Wales."

"Pleased ta meecha, I'm sure," each young woman echoed in turn when introduced, and two bobbed Abigail a curtsy.

The one named Grace Buck, a dark-eyed brunette, spoke up. "Don't have the foggiest notion who our husbands might be yet, though. When we land, Mr. Braden says 'twill be quite a dockside mob scene, eh? And quite a hurly-burly of your own yestiday, wasn't it, Miss Rosemont, with them chickens and all? And Kulalang's really ever so nice and quiet on the ordinary, right, Mr. Braden?"

Duke nodded. "Miss Rosemont has spoken with Kulalang and explained to him she had no intention of pointing the bone at him or ever cursing *any* of us, isn't that right, Miss Rosemont?'' he inquired most politely.

"Exactly, Mr. Braden," she responded. But Abigail could tell by the glint in his eye he knew full well she had certainly cursed Duke Braden himself more than once. "And now, I hope you ladies will accept from me these garments to replace those that were speckled with ink."

"Oh, we couldn't, though they's ever so fine," Grace responded, even as she shyly fingered the fine dark blue wool of one dress.

"Now, I know for a fact saltwater washes do not fade ink stains, and I want to make amends, please," Abigail protested. "Besides, I've drawn you in gowns like these several times already, and I'd like you to accept them as payment for being my artist's models."

"Well then! Artist's models! An' what you gonna give Mr. Braden then for the ink on his frock coat and his own blood on his trouser legs?" the elfin-faced Evelyn Chase inquired with a poke of her elbow in Duke Braden's arm.

There was a little lull while Braden's six brides waited to see what this fine, proper lady would say to that. Abigail started to stammer an answer, but Mr. Braden, perhaps feeling as awkward as she, rescued her.

"She's going to promise me she won't press charges against Kulalang for attacking her, when we put in to Sydney, right, Miss Rosemont? It would go very hard for an aborigine there."

"Press charges? No, of course not. Not if your friends will accept this recompense from me."

"I think I must warn you," Mr. Braden said over the ensuing hubbub, "if they take them they'll be your friends, too, and it will take the very devil to keep them from fussing over you!"

Braden's brides descended on her like excited children. They held the skirts and sturdy day dresses up to one another and passed them around, oohing and aahing while they eyed and stroked the material. Meanwhile, Duke Braden eyed Abigail so intensely she felt as if he were stroking her, too. She thrilled in that knowledge as surely as the brides did in their gifts.

"You know," he said at last to her as he escorted her back upstairs, "tomorrow's to be the day we cross the line."

"Oh, yes, the equator," she said nervously. "I hear there will be a big celebration for those on their first time across. And then, Captain Gates says, we'll head out across the ocean until we see Brazil."

"But what I meant to say," he told her with his hand on her elbow to stop her before she turned in through the cuddy door, "is that I think today's the day you already crossed the line. And quite a celebration it has been."

She turned to face him as they stood in the hot glare of the sun. Their feet seemed to be rooted in the hot tar between the deck boards. They gazed, breathless, at each other on the rolling deck. Neither looked away to break the bond suddenly forged between them. His eyes dropped to her mouth; her lips pouted in an anticipation she could not control. Her thick auburn lashes lowered as she studied his taut lips before she risked plunging into the depths of his blue eyes. Then she heard voices behind her, beyond the cuddy door, and spiraled back to earth.

"Good day then," she managed to bid him, her voice suddenly raspy.

"Indeed it is," he returned.

His hand, which they both now realized had been firmly clasping her elbow, dropped to his side. She sighed so deeply as he turned and walked away that she felt limp-sailed without him.

Once the small sailing ship crossed the equator, the days seemed to fly by. Abigail drew each of Braden's brides individually while they chatted companionably to her. Sometimes she and Kulalang would sketch side by side. He spoke little, but when he did she listened and learned. Between her and Mr. Braden, there was still something of a mutual barrier, though it was no longer covered with thorns.

She learned much about New South Wales from Duke Braden and much about England she had never known from her new steerage-class friends. She listened to the women's stories of their circumstances, so much sadder than hers that she became ashamed to tell her tale. Cora Mercer was the fifth unwanted daughter in a family of eleven children. She had been a seamstress working from dawn to dusk until the measles made her eyes go bad. She became destitute and was considering what she called "street harlotry", until someone read her Mr. Braden's advertisement from a London paper that had blown into the gutter. Grace Buck's father had beaten her in his drunken rages until she ran away to stay with friends in Southwark, who didn't want her either. Evelyn Chase was a sailor's widow who had lost two infants to "the sweats" and had believed she had no future until Duke Braden gave her a chance for a new life in a new land.

So Abigail was careful to be vague about her own past. She said only that she was looking forward to visiting her second cousins. But each time she brought that up in earshot of Mr. Braden, it seemed rain clouds hovered over her and that painfully polite, if brazenly unconventional man.

It was also driving Abigail to distraction that rain clouds of the atmospheric sort gathered almost every afternoon and night to drench the decks with soft, warm, saltless water. She was eager to wash her garments, her hair and herself in the clean rain. To a woman who had taken daily baths, the paucity of water was now the greatest burden of this voyage. The other cuddy-class women made do with a daily pitcherful, which Captain Gates had the first mate fetch for them. Abigail needed and wanted more, but hesitated to alienate the others. She didn't wish to seem some rich lady who could not bear the trials the others did or would stoop to bribe some sailor to fetch extra water. When she heard women's voices from the forecastle one night while a gentle rain was falling, she wondered if those happy girls hadn't taken matters into their own hands to bathe in the downpour. She could never venture outside like that nor climb the shrouds to scoop out water caught there—or could she? One balmy night, when all seemed still after the second cloud-burst that day, she decided to risk gathering some water for herself.

Leaving behind H.M., who had been roused by the thunder and wanted to go too, she stealthily tiptoed out of her cabin through the cuddy. She had gleaned random information from Captain Gates that between three and four in the morning the fewest men were on deck, and only the first mate and one other sailor manned the wheelhouse. She would pull on the ropes of each sail until enough water was dislodged to fill her pitcher, then she'd return to the cabin to dump it in her washbowl, repeating the operation as many times as were necessary, until she had washed herself, her hair, her clothes and her dog! And she would drink her fill of rainwater, too! In her cabin, all her soiled linen was laid out to be plunged in and rinsed.

Her plan worked perfectly, though she took a good splashing when she rocked each sail to free some water. She laughed softly; she was having a grand time. Without underpinnings and petticoats, her dark gown soon stuck to her like a second skin. On her next trip, she went barefoot on the smoothly holystoned boards. It felt so good, so free, to be out like this with the rain-washed breeze ruffling her newly washed hair. She had intended to bathe with the last water she gathered, but halfway through her mission she could not wait. She stripped off her garments in her cabin to sponge and rinse herself all over with the delicious water and sweet-smelling lavender soap that made her think of home.

She tugged her gown back on while her skin was still damp—a heavenly feeling. Just one or two more trips to get enough to wash her clothes, then H.M., and she'd pitch the evidence out her porthole. She had already harvested the trapped pools of water from the spanker and the mizzen sails, and only the main lower topsail remained to be checked. It was the farthest away, but luck was with her! She would be able to do this other nights, as long as she made certain the storm depositing the water followed another where the men would have fetched all they wanted.

She lugged her big porcelain pitcher across the softly rolling deck toward the forecastle. After nearly two months at sea, she almost felt a part of this great wooden vessel. The big-bellied topsail billowed out over her head, surely as full of fresh bounty for her to harvest as the trees at home from which she used to pluck fruit. But this sail was set just far enough off the deck that she'd have to reach its corner from near the bulwarks. She tiptoed around the shadowy protruding forecastle and grasped a line for stability. She leaned up and reached out on tiptoe, stretching her pitcher upward.

"A deliciously damp sea nymph emerged from the waves to tempt mere mortals."

That voice from behind made her jump. Duke Braden! She might have fallen or dropped her precious burden, but a hard arm came around her waist to steady her. They both clasped the handle of the pitcher out to the side, their hands overlapping. She yanked back the pitcher and he let her have it. But then she made the mistake of spinning in his arms to face him.

That move left her tipped backward in his embrace with her hips and thighs pressed firmly against him and her wet bodice stretched over her taut, heaving breasts just inches from his chest. To her utter embarrassment, she felt her nipples pucker through the soaked cotton of her dress. He was casually attired in trousers and a white, open-necked shirt.

"You startled me!" she hissed and tried to squirm away. He did not budge. She tried to pull the pitcher between them, but could not wedge it in.

"That's why I grabbed you. If you went overboard, no one would miss you for hours, you little fool. And we wouldn't want to deprive the illustrious Godfrey-Bennetts of getting their hands on you—like this—would we now?" he demanded, his voice more clipped than usual.

She knew she should demand that he release her, but the feel of his hard body against hers, his strong arm embracing her lower back, even the scent and feel of his brandy-tinged breath, racked her senses. She felt numb, though jolts of energy coursed through her.

At last, she found her voice. "The Godfrey-Bennetts will hardly have their hands on me like this!"

"Really?" he challenged, then released her. "I'm afraid you don't know their son Phillip very well, then. He'll think you and your fortune a tasty morsel." He sat down on the low rail along the forecastle where he had been seated when she'd appeared. He folded his arms over his chest and crossed his long legs at the ankles. His feet were bare.

"You've no right to talk that way about Phillip—or tasty morsels!" she insisted, clutching her half-filled pitcher to her fluttering belly. "And what do you know about my fortune?" she added suspiciously. Perhaps that was why he had allowed her to be included in his little coterie when he obviously didn't think much of her. Sometimes she had worried it was just for her gifts to his women or her kindness to Kulalang, that he abided her presence at all. It was the curse of her fortune that had gotten her in trouble with a man before.

"I believe some of your cabin-class cronies mentioned your inherited wealth. Far be it for me to keep track of noble heiresses or their fortunes."

"I am not noble, though my proper title would be the Lady Abigail, should I return to court."

He shrugged. "I'm not very noble, either," he countered in a mocking tone. "And I'd just be called Duke at court, of course." His intense gaze burned into her.

"Back to your bitter ways, I see," she accused and started off. But she hadn't gone four steps before he seized her arm and spun her back into his hard embrace.

"You ought to know. But you've buried all that to charm them, haven't you? Bribed and sketched and sympathized your way into their hearts and lives to amuse yourself later at their expense?"

"What? You mean your little harem of Braden's brides, sir? At least, some of us do have charm, though I'd not expect a person like you to recognize it if it smacked you in the face or bit your leg! At least Kulalang turned out not to be a savage, but you—"

"Drawn to savages, are you, Miss Rosemont? Perhaps that's what it will take to tame the likes of you and your Godfrey-Bennett ilk!"

She swung her free hand to slap him. He seized her wrist. He did not believe in violence or showing anger. He had not intended to goad her or touch her again, and certainly never to kiss her, but he felt his self-control lurch away. He had only gone to her at first when he feared for her rash behavior, leaning over the rail like that in a gown that clung to her hips and legs as she bent away from him. She was uncorseted and without that silly-looking bottom bolster. Other than her molded, supple body—and that sweet flower scent about her hair and skin tonight—the reasons why she shook him so deeply, when he could not stomach her type, eluded him. But now, infuriated, he clamped her to him and cupped her chin in one hand while his mouth covered hers.

He waited for a struggle, a slap, a squeal, even a bite. She seemed to go limp against him. Her mouth was stiff, though; he almost wanted to draw back and remind her to breathe. Then his relentless kiss parted her lips and softened them. And he was lost at sea.

Abigail was stunned by his sudden, outrageous move. She went all muddleheaded, then felt she would get the vapors and actually faint. His touching her, skin to skin, mouth to mouth, and his gently teasing tongue tilted her insides. She began to respond to him. She relaxed slightly, secure in the embrace of the iron band of his arm around her back.

Her soft thighs molded to his hard ones, and she breathed in unison with him. His tongue darted into the depths of her mouth; he skimmed her teeth and taunted her tongue until she responded in kind. Her breasts felt so heavy and full against his muscled chest. His hand moved from her chin to stroke the slant of her cheek upward. Then he wove his fin-

gers through the damp, curly bounty of her hair at the nape
of her neck. He cradled her head there, tipping it back so he
could deepen the kiss. He plundered her with pleasure, reveling and playing the way she had earlier in the delicious
water.

Both of them shaken and clinging together, the moment
ended slowly with his pecking two more quick kisses on her
tingling mouth.

"Crazy," he rasped so low the night wind snatched the
word.

"Insanity, indeed."

"Will you draw us like this?"

"Don't be ridiculous."

He sighed and set her back. "When I saw you there like
that sea nymph figurehead come to life—"

"Is that what she is?" Abigail tried to keep the inane
conversation going to cover the devastation of her poise. "A
sea nymph?" This man had obviously kissed women before, so she was not about to let him think he'd rattled her.

"The captain said she's Clytie, the water nymph who
loved Apollo, but he couldn't abide her," he told her, his
voice his own once more. "So, sitting all damp and disheveled on the edge of the sea, poor Clytie pined for her love,
while he loved elsewhere. She just wasted away until she
turned into a sunflower so her face could always follow her
beloved Apollo, the sun god. A pretty story for a pretty water nymph like yourself," he said, his tone sharp and goad-
ing again. "You do take the moral of the tale, I hope?"

"This water nymph loves no one, nor shall she if he cannot kiss better than that!" she blurted in her pique. She
splashed the water from her pitcher on him and fled.

He did not follow, though she half feared, half wished he
would. She heard his sharp laugh behind her and ran more
quickly. Already, she regretted her impulsive act—all of
them—tonight. She, who was usually so careful and cir-
cumspect, had really lost her head of late, and it was all that
pompous, prideful man's fault!

It annoyed her that he knew about Phillip Godfrey-Bennett being a newly eligible match, though she had considered that a liability about her visit—not an asset! Who was to say Duke Braden hadn't somehow learned about her long exile in Kent? Perhaps he had even delved to discover the rumors about her supposed indiscretions with Lord Northurst. Mr. Braden would probably believe all those stories! And if he did indeed know about her past, and her fortune, he might see her as an easy mark for his casual passions, and it would be the same tragedy all over again!

Despite the hour of the night, she slammed her cabin door too hard and had to hold H.M.'s muzzle closed when she began to bark.

# Chapter Three

The ship being stuck in what was called "the doldrums" suited Abigail's mood perfectly. One whole, airless tropical week off the eastern coast of Brazil was followed by a sudden squall, which snapped spars and rent sails. But after repairs, the breeze picked up and they cruised southward toward Cape Horn. Abigail, realizing she could not keep to her cabin without looking both suspicious and foolish, tried to be as congenial as ever to her companions of all classes aboard the vessel—except for Mr. Braden, who evidently thought he was in a class by himself anyway.

Every time it rained, however, Abigail found a bucket of rainwater outside her door, and she had no intention of throwing that in Mr. Braden's face. Instead, shyly, she thanked him. That kindness, and, in the days beyond Cape Horn, his proper demeanor toward her, mingled with her fascination of him. Perhaps he even hoped to make amends by trying very hard to play the gentleman. Though they spoke nothing of it, he obviously regretted grabbing her for a kiss that night, and she regretted dousing him with water. She admitted to herself she heartily enjoyed his company as well as that of his brides. So, despite her painful past, she chose to ignore hints that Mrs. Gates and Mrs. Graham were gossiping about how Abigail seemed to prefer the company of those women in forecastle steerage, and of that pagan aborigine—not to mention the sheep farmer who had left their dinner gathering so abruptly.

* * *

"Those grassy, grazing plains and beautiful Blue Mountains you speak of—it does all sound so wonderful," Abigail admitted to Braden one afternoon on deck amid his inquisitive charges.

Abigail probably didn't even realize that, after weeks of him bringing her along, she'd let down her guard again. Her face had gone soft and expectant and a smile lifted her lips to reveal small, straight teeth. That glimpse of her radiant beauty scattered his thoughts so he wasn't even certain what he had said last but for the word *fascinating* revolving in his brain.

"It is fascinating, I assure you," he managed and, for the first time in weeks, while she was watching, he let his eyes stray to her mouth and drop to her ruffled bodice. When he saw her eyes widen, he looked quickly away. No good to ruin the tenuous trust they had rebuilt after that wild kiss weeks ago. All this was, he thought, a strange sort of wooing, and yet he knew if he kept on with it, it could and probably would end in disaster. He cleared his throat, suddenly afraid she would read his calculating thoughts.

"Let's have a go at a walkabout, shall we?" he said quickly to his ladies. "Whose turn is it now for a jaunt around the ship?"

"Miss Abigail's turn," the clever Grace Buck put in. Duke knew Grace had been enamored of him from the first, but she was acting now as if he were no more to the women than guardian and adviser. The trouble was, like Abigail, Grace seemed to have made a study of him, and that was dangerous. But an exchange he'd overheard between Grace and Abigail last week had amused and cheered him mightily.

"Duke Braden's such a dandy man," Grace had assured Abigail. "And always in control of himself and everything. Hope all the unwed lads in New South Wales are just like him!"

"Really? Do you?" Abigail had asked, all too astounded. "Still, I don't know if 'dandy' is the word to put to him, at least considering the independent way he garbs himself. But you care for him a great deal then?''

"'Course. All of us do. Could of stuck us on this ship and never give us the time o' day, he could. But he's done ever so much to buck us up. I, 'specially, look up to him in more ways than one, if you catch my drift. Not that I'd ever tell him, 'cause for sure he'll wed a Currency lass—one of the girls born there."

"Oh, no doubt, he will," Abigail had put in.

As if she'd ever heard the term *currency* used like that before, the spoiled little heiress. Yet, Duke knew, damn it, she would learn soon enough what *Currency* and *Exclusive* meant in New South Wales!

"But, Grace," Abigail had probed, "don't you think Mr. Braden has...you know, a sort of dark, back-side element to his personality, a...well, his other side?"

Grace Buck had thrown back her head and bellowed a laugh. "'Course I think he's got a really interesting back-side, almost as handsome as his front side, Miss Abigail, but don't s'pose it's as dark as Kulalang's backside must be!"

"Really, Grace!" Abigail had protested.

Duke had had to hold his sides to keep from joining in with Grace's raucous laughter. He wasn't certain why, but he reveled in Abigail Rosemont's blushes and discomfitures.

But today he was in the mood to make Abigail like him. Sometimes he wanted the woman so desperately he was tempted to act the savage and sprint off with her in his arms to his cabin, despite the ruination of both their reputations. Opposing urges to have her or hurt her came and went, depending, he supposed, on whether or not he could forget what lay ahead for them both when they reached their destinations. In short, damn it, he alternately wanted to seduce or strangle Miss Abigail Anne Rosemont! He'd never lost control of himself before this, and it scared him. When he had finally told her the Braden farm and sheep run was in the Parramatta Valley abutting the big Godfrey-Bennett estate, she had been thrilled. "So close and yet so far," he'd added, and refused to answer her many ensuing questions on the subject.

Right now, with all those female eyes on him, he had no choice but to accept Grace's challenge. While Kulalang sat cross-legged on the deck of the forecastle and beat out a rocking rhythm with two carved sticks, Duke offered Abigail his arm, and they promenaded the deck. She religiously kept her long-stemmed parasol poised to ward off the sun, as if a few rays would shrivel her silken skin.

"With that big bonnet on," he observed without looking at her, "you could forgo that ruffled toadstool over your head. You're getting freckles from reflection off the water anyway."

"It's not proper for a lady to get brown or for gentlemen to notice," she replied pertly.

"If you mean to hint I'm a gentleman, I'm both amazed and delighted. But I must tell you, another great foolishness among the ladies of Sydney town and surrounding parts is that they refuse to ride horseback because the sun's brighter there than in England and browns their delicate ivory skin!"

"Oh, really?" She turned to meet his eyes for the first time on their roundabout. She felt a little jolt in the pit of her belly from simply meeting his gaze. "What a shame," she bemoaned, "though I'd risk a thousand freckles before I'd give up riding!"

"Nicely put, but they *will* talk about you."

She jerked her head away and stared out over the endless blue-green. "Who will? I love riding. I would wear a veil first. My hosts and their friends daren't talk about me for that!"

He liked to hear such defiance from those pouting lips. But he knew better than to believe such independent thinking would survive once she was ensconced at the Grange with the powerful, rich, sanctimonious Godfrey-Bennetts.

"Don't you think even they—" he nodded his head toward the cuddy door as they passed by "—are talking about us? For mingling classes as you've done, that is."

She knew they were, but she didn't want him to think it bothered her. She had weighed the risks and rewards; besides, this was only a few months on a ship, and she didn't plan to see Mrs. Gates or Mrs. Graham afterward.

"I hope they think only that I've made some new friends and learned a great deal about New South Wales from you and Kulalang," she told him. "Our two botanist friends ask me daily what you've said about flora and fauna, you know."

He smiled. When she even hinted at a compliment he felt himself melt, though he knew well enough the dangers of such vulnerability. "Do they? I must say I like your attitude about some things, Miss Abigail Rosemont. It will be the pity of the year if you change when we arrive."

"I won't. Age twenty-six is far too old to be changing one's personality. I've been on my own long enough to have my own opinions."

"Ah, the past you won't speak of."

"Perhaps I shall speak of it when you admit why you are so prejudiced against my cousins, the Godfrey-Bennetts!" she retorted.

He could almost see her hackles rise again, and they had barely made one circuit around the deck of the *Challenge*. But she was right about how hard it was to change one's opinions; he exploded despite himself.

"*I* prejudiced against *them*? Just let me tell you what your Mrs. Godly-Bennett will say if you get freckles or ride a horse. She'll say your face is convict-brown. That's a disgusting color to their way of thinking! It describes something unbearably awful—convict-brown!" He was shouting, but he couldn't help it. What they would do to this woman would be a disaster, and there was nothing he could do to save her.

They turned and faced each other at the rail like adversaries. He crossed his arms over his chest and jutted out his jaw. She propped one fist on her hip and the parasol swayed as if she might use it as a lance to run him through. The

thump-thump-thud of Kulalang's singing sticks came louder
to their ears.

"Are you, that is—" She began again. "I realize there are
many convicts there. You don't go about befriending crim-
inals, do you? I mean, New South Wales as you described
it sounds so pretty, but it's obviously full of prisoners."

"Damn!" he spit out. He felt furious and disappointed.
He was rid of her for good then. Once she found out about
his family—hell, found out about half the families in her
"pretty" and "fascinating" New South Wales, she'd never
want to see him again anyway, and just as well! But he
couldn't bear to say all that now.

"You know, Miss Exclusive English Rosemont, most
places, including this ship, are full of prisoners!"

"That's not what I meant and you know it. You yourself—you haven't been sent to prison there, have you?"

"No, my dear. But if I ever were, it would probably be for
tossing overboard the likes of you. So perhaps it would be
best for your precious reputation both here and there if you
didn't spend your time with such a suspicious person as
Duke Braden again. Excuse me, permanently."

He nodded his bare auburn head, with those blondish
streaks running through it, and stalked away.

After that, the days dragged for Abigail. She still spent
time with her women friends of the forecastle, for she refused to let Duke Braden bully her away from them. But he
never came around when she was there, and Abigail grieved
for that. Braden's brides noticed, too, as no doubt did those
tellers of tales in cabin class, Mrs. Gates and Mrs. Graham.
Grace Buck inquired bluntly what had happened between
her and Mr. Braden.

Abigail tried to put her off. "Mr. Braden and I have discovered we hardly see eye to eye, that's all. We're really from
different worlds—and I don't just mean England and the
colony. It's a mutually acceptable and mutually desirable
agreement, I assure you, Grace."

"Mutually desirable, a good way to put it," Grace had murmured under her breath. Fine with Grace if Abigail and Braden got on like vinegar and oil. Originally Grace hadn't cared for the two of them together at all; but now, as the last days and weeks of the voyage went by, she wished she could help the two of them out. She liked both of them ever so much. It was clear as glass to Grace they were eyeing each other, and fighting it with all their might.

Of the six women, it was Grace who became closest to Abigail. Grace liked to fuss over her clothes and was pleased when Abigail let her fix her hair. One afternoon, though it ruffled the feathers of the others a good bit, she and Abigail heated irons on the cook's stove in the galley and smoothed out some dresses that had been pressed in Abigail's trunks for weeks.

Just talking to Abigail, whom Grace found to be a wonderful listener, helped her exorcise her ghosts. For years she had been blaming herself for the fact her father had beaten her. He had a terrible temper, Grace shuddered to recall even now.

"Guess I felt like a no 'count, like sometimes I must've deserved what I got," she finally admitted to Abigail.

But Abigail assured her some men were so low they struck out at one when they themselves were at fault, and one hadn't done a thing to deserve it. Grace had been sure more than once that Abigail was going to tell her that her father had whipped her, too, or some such, but she never did.

"One time," Abigail had said though, "I crossed a man who was a villain at heart. He grabbed me, gagged me with his hand and—and hurt me. I'm sure he hated me even more because that violence showed him how low he was. Maybe it was like that for your father, too, Grace, and none of your fault at all. He really knew you were better and stronger than he, so he struck out again and again. You know, I once even blamed myself that my mother died longing for my father because I wasn't enough for her to love. But a friend of mine made me see that wasn't my fault, and I was worth someone's friendship and love. The same is true for you, and don't you forget it!''

"Oh, I shan't now you put it that way, Miss Abigail," Grace promised, with tears gilding her brown eyes. "You know, just like your friend helped you, our talks been cheering me ever so much. Now I won't be so scared the husband I end up with where we're going will be like my dad.''

"I'm sure he won't! Mr. Braden would never let you be wed to someone like that!"

"Glad you still think so highly of him," Grace had murmured.

And it was that very day Abigail decided she would have to brave another meeting with the brazen Mr. Braden after all. She was going to obtain his permission to ask Grace Buck to become her personal maid and companion during her stay in New South Wales.

"Absolutely out of the question!" Duke Braden clipped out the moment she asked him. The two of them stood alone at the rail where Grace had found him. Off the bow, porpoises and flying fish cavorted in the waves.

"It would be a good job for her," she protested, trying to reason calmly with his carved face and icy, narrowed eyes. "Of course, I would reimburse you for her passage. And it certainly does not preclude her wedding when she has time to find someone *she* favors and not be rushed into it dockside with this scheme of yours."

"This *scheme* of mine?" he repeated, his jaw set in stone.

"You see, I thought it best to ask you first, not to get her hopes up, but I'm sure it's best for her. Since her father mistreated her so, she's very worried she'll get a husband who will do the same. But you see, my other maid was going to marry and I've no argument with Grace doing that when she wishes."

"How touching that you've solved everything for her and me in *your* little scheme," he snapped.

His brown fist was much too close to her hand gripping the rail. She wanted to push him over that rail to swim with the fish below, but she kept her temper in check for Grace's sake and tried another tack.

"Grace is very skilled with gowns and hair, and I would have her also as a companion and not just some low—"

"They're all low to you and your kind!" he exploded. "And I'll not have the Godfrey-Bennetts ruining *her* life, too!"

"Too? You mean they've somehow ruined yours and you're blaming me? Is that what this is all about?"

"I mean ruining Grace's life in addition to yours, *Lady* Abigail!"

"Now look here—"

"No, you look here. Grace Buck and the others are the vanguard of free women coming to New South Wales to wed men of independent lives, who have been carefully screened. They are certainly not to become the servants of Exclusives. Such nonsense as having even one of these women go into service, while the *Sydney Gazette* will be hovering to see what happens when the so-called 'Braden's brides' go ashore, would ruin everything."

"Really? Well, perhaps Miss Grace Buck should be allowed to choose her own fate," she argued, her voice now more mocking than she intended. "You know, *women* of independent lives, sir. Of course, I should hate to ruin everything for you ashore, despite the fact that you've done your best to ruin everything for me at sea."

"The answer, Miss Rosemont, is no."

"Then goodbye and good riddance!"

"At least we agree on that!"

And that *was* that, though Abigail had half a mind to just make her proposal to Grace and let her choose, no matter how Duke Braden ranted and raved. But she said not one word, not even the afternoon she presented Braden's brides with prenuptial gifts: a tiered shoulder cape for Clarissa, who always seemed to be cold; an embroidered velvet muff to Deanna Dill, who herself was skilled at needlework. She gave Evelyn Chase a scallop-edged satin petticoat, and Cora Mercer a ruffled green parasol to keep the sun off. Beth Anne Clare received a blue bonnet with ribbons and feathers to match her eyes. And to her friend Grace Abigail gave a pair of white kid gloves for her wedding day and a carved box to keep them in—and remember her by. Abigail knew her dear, departed friend Janet would have understood these gifts and her wanting to take Grace Buck on. So why couldn't Mr. Braden see any side but his own? If he couldn't even grasp that little bit of humanity, she wanted nothing whatsoever to do with him.

And yet, in those last days past New Zealand as they westered toward the coast of New South Wales, Abigail's jumbled thoughts were often with him. When Kulalang, evidently loyal to the end to Mr. Braden, seldom sought her out on deck anymore to tell her about the wind and waves or the identity of birds aloft, she was doubly pained things had ended so badly between her and the first folks she had known from New South Wales. She felt unsettled even in the happy times she spent with the women when Duke was not about. She was relieved, at least, that the Gates-Graham gossip would no longer include Mr. Braden's name. She was amazed at herself, that she had chosen to risk and then ignore their whisperings by having Mr. Braden for a—an acquaintance. And she finally admitted she was panicked this voyage would end without the slightest hint of reconciliation between them. Horror of horrors, she realized, she missed the dratted man!

In mid-June, the hint of cooler weather tinged the sea air. The seasons were reversed in these latitudes, and autumn had begun. Perhaps the entire place would be as topsy-turvy as her churning emotions, Abigail thought. For several nights she paced her tiny cabin, four steps one way and four steps back, debating whether she should request to speak with Mr. Braden, to at least thank him for sharing his "brides" with her on the voyage. Perhaps a simple note of gratitude, delivered by Grace, would be the best approach. But the seas kicked up in a storm just as the travelers spotted on the horizon the gray line of the continent they sought. Half regretful, half relieved, Abigail took to her cabin, though her sea legs were as good as ever.

It was on the afternoon of June 20, after 122 days at sea, that Mrs. Gates knocked on Abigail's door. "The Sydney heads are off the port prow," she told her.

Abigail knew what the Sydney heads were. Duke Braden had described those promontory portals that guarded the straight yellow sandstone cliffs at the entrance to the harbor.

"We're going to make a run in before this gale gets worse! Batten down in there the best you can for a rough entry, Miss Rosemont!"

But later, with H.M. in her arms, Abigail ventured to the dining hall door on the deck to peer out.

She could see little but spray and flying foam under a boiling gray sky. A shiver shot along her spine, not for fear of the storm or of those looming gray heads they had to shoot, but because out there, in that misty gloom, lay her new life in New South Wales. She felt she was somehow a much different person from the woman who had left the security of her home and boarded the *Challenge* at Gravesend four months ago. But she had also left behind things she was glad were two oceans away. She cuddled the whimpering H.M. closer at the sight of black clouds and choppy seas. Well, she would not fear the toss of this tempest, not when she'd come this far.

But by the time she'd battened down all loose objects in her cabin and settled herself and the spaniel on the bed, conditions had worsened. Through lulls in the gale, she could hear men's shouts, strident, even desperate, through their brass speaking horns. The vessel groaned and shuddered. She hoped her forecastle friends were weathering this well and wished she had Grace here to ride it out with her. But she dared not brave the sloshing, tipping decks to go to them. Finally, she zigzagged her way across the dining cuddy to Mrs. Graham's cabin and found the captain's wife huddled in with her. At least she could tell from the looks of them that they had not been talking about her this time.

"Are we still heading in?" Abigail yelled to Mrs. Gates above the roar of wind.

"Too late to back off now!" she shrieked from her position at the end of Mrs. Graham's bunk. The Scotswoman hung her head as if she would retch at any moment. "Just pray we don't pile up on those rocks at the foot of the cliff called the Gap, just off South Head!"

That hardly gave Abigail the comfort she was seeking, but she went back to the cabin and wedged herself in with H.M. The spaniel's helpless little whimpers, as if she had a premonition of disaster, tore at Abigail's tattered poise. How she wished she knew what was really happening. How she wished she could be with Braden's brides, or the man himself—just to tell him she was sorry how things had gone between them.

The din outside grew louder. She wondered if that sound was worse than the horrid howls of dingo dogs Kulalang had described. She hugged H.M. tighter. That was the only thing that made her at all uncomfortable with the aborigine she had once feared: he had always called H.M. "it dingo," and she knew the aborigines hunted and ate dingoes! Her mind wheeled through all the things she had learned of the exotic land just across this storm—things she might never see! But to come this far and have it end this way—impossible!

She could not fathom why it was taking so long to make the security of Port Jackson Harbour, as they called their bay. Pitch-dark night descended outside her porthole, but she had long since given up glancing out. From this side of the ship, there had been no hint of land, only rolling gray sea. She held the dog and fought to keep her head from thudding against the wall at each yaw and pitch. Her table scraped its way across the floor, then back. Her trunks bumped and creaked. Her single whale-oil lantern rocked wildly on its hook on the ceiling beam throwing everything into sharp, swinging shadow. She bit her lower lip while tears prickled behind her eyelids. She thought of Janet, facing death without having ever seen the outside world she had so longed for. Longed for secretly, never sharing that dream with the woman who thought she was closer to her than a sister. At that unsettling thought, Abigail became even more afraid they were not going to make it. And then a thumping noise started, as if something had broken free or a door banged to the decks to let water pour in.

She screamed when her door flew open. A big form there, a man. Duke Braden! He dared to stride in, to close and latch the door behind him.

"Didn't you hear me knock? Are you all right? I had to know."

He had to know, he had to know. His words repeated in her dazed mind as he leaned over her bed and grasped her shoulders. Even at this invasion of the cabin, H.M., who had never really made her peace with Duke Braden, did not stir. But Abigail did. Somehow she was on her knees in Duke Braden's firm embrace, her cheek pressed to his chest and the dog caught somewhere between them.

"I was—so afraid. Is everyone all right?" she cried, turning her mouth to his ear so he could hear her over the storm.

"All right now. Yes, they have each other for comfort, but I was worried about you."

Worried about her, he was worried about her. She clung tighter and was rewarded with the firm feel of his hip next to hers, no, under hers as he lifted her and leaned back to catch his boot heels in the side rail of her bunk. He wedged himself against the wall and cradled her in his lap with the dog somehow still in hers.

"I'm fine," she managed, her eyes filling with forbidden tears at last. "Really."

"I figured it was just like you to take a little stroll about the deck in this. And then when we made port, you'd be the scandal of the town with your skirts up."

She didn't even protest his teasing nor react to the mention of scandal. She just held to him, struck by her utter amazement that if the ship did go down right now, she would somehow go calmly, fulfilled. She almost wished this night would never end despite the outer danger. And this new inner one.

His lips were in her tousled hair; he seemed to be inhaling its scent. She had washed it to be presentable tomorrow. Presentable to the Godfrey-Bennetts, whom he detested. But she didn't care about any of that tonight, only that he was here holding her like this.

When the swinging lamp guttered out, he said only, "Let it go." And then a moment later he whispered so close to her temple that his breath stirred the tendrils there, "But I can't let you go."

H.M. scrambled off Abigail's lap. In the pitching, rocking dark, Duke Braden began to kiss her, first her temples, then her cheeks, her nose, her chin, even her eyelids, which fluttered under each gentle caress in this wild storm. She lifted her lips for the kiss she had yearned for since that balmy night on deck weeks ago. Her mouth softened instantly, her right hand tucked in against the wall to clasp the nape of his strong neck and hold him closer to her. The kiss, amid the turbulence out there, went on and on.

They made their own turbulence in here, inside each other. His hands moved over her back now, caressing her trim waist through the gown and single petticoat. She had removed her underpinnings, thinking she might have to swim—though she didn't actually know how.

"I can't swim," she told him when they came up for air from a fervent, dizzying kiss. She wanted to share everything with him, tell him of all her sadnesses, inadequacies, dreams and longings.

"I'll teach you someday," he whispered hotly in her ear, before darting his tongue in it. "If we go in, I'll save you."

But he didn't save her from the desires that swept her into a whirlpool. Her need for him grew so strong it almost sucked her under. His big, hard hands were tender but insistent on her back, her hips, her bottom, to bring her closer. Then he cradled and cupped her breasts right through her gown. She tingled there; she longed to have nothing between them.

Abigail dared to go on a little exploratory expedition of her own, running her trembling hands along Duke's shoulders, clasping the hard muscles of his upper arms, and stroking, sliding down his chest to his flat belly. He moaned and would have laid her flat down on the bunk had not the terrified spaniel protested with a yelp.

"Oh, H.M.," she murmured against Duke's mouth in another searing kiss.

"Is she all right?" he asked, sounding dazed and distant. "She won't bite again?"

"No," Abigail promised as she put out a hand to comfort the dog, "but I might." And she nibbled at Duke's lower lip until he groaned and kissed her hard again.

The kisses and caresses they shared kept fear at bay. The feelings she had for this man she both desired and detested nearly swamped her more than once. His warm hand under her skirt ruffled up the hem as it crept higher. He slid up past her cotton stocking and then he clasped the warm flesh of her bare thigh there.

Even in the darkness, she knew they stared deep into each other's eyes while unspoken questions and endless possibilities stretched between them. She felt so secure, so splendid with him. His touch made everything that had ever threatened her—including his own dark moods—slip into the deep silence of the sea.

And then, breathless, clinging, they realized the storm was quieting.

"Maybe we're almost in. Maybe we're going to make it, after all," he said, his voice raspy.

"You came here because you thought we wouldn't?"

"I don't know. No. This voyage couldn't be over unless I held you," he tried to explain before his voice faltered. "At least once before everything ends, I had to."

Though she longed to clamp her legs together to keep his hand there, she didn't. He pulled it away and smoothed down her skirts. Already, the seas were calmer. They held each other yet, though the beginning of rationality—even embarrassment—came creeping in.

Duke pulled open the curtain of her porthole and peered out. "I can see the Macquarie Lighthouse beam behind us," he said. "We're in. I'd best go up on deck before someone finds me here, and you're compromised for good." He stood to straighten his clothes and brush himself off.

Abigail stood on shaky legs and did the same. "I feel we've only compromised on our differences," she told him stubbornly, though she could not pretend she didn't know what he meant, with Mrs. Gates and Mrs. Graham just across the hall. Yet, she could not let him go like this without saying what she felt. "And I do feel it was for good, what we shared. You and your brides have made me feel welcome, as if I have friends here already, and when we all get settled—"

"Your friends will be the folks you live with and their friends, no way around that," he told her.

His voice took on that hard ring again. He bent over the bed once more, his face stoic, to pet the spaniel. H.M., wonder of wonders, wagged her tail.

"But since you and your family are going to be living so close," she tried again, "surely we can visit—"

"We will *live* close, but not *be* close, Abigail. I've told you that, and you must believe and accept it."

Though she was moved to hear him use her given name for the first time, she couldn't stem the panic and anger when he caressed her cheek as he might have H.M.'s and turned away to unlatch the door.

"Then it is you who are prejudiced, Duke Braden, and not—"

"Leave it, Lady Abigail!" he insisted, one hand held up as if to ward off any arguments or pleas. "Let's just end with the way we've been tonight, because of necessity, things will be so different now." He frowned, and quietly closed the door behind him as he left.

* * *

Later, when Abigail went up on deck to watch the harbor lights of Sydney grow larger, she saw Duke Braden down the way near the forecastle in the midst of his brides, pointing out things to them even in the predawn dark. His deep voice floated to her, though she could not tell what he said. They probably did not even see her down here in the shadows; if they had, Grace at least would have come over. Feeling very lonely again, Abigail forced herself to look away, but the wall of darkness still kept her from seeing her new home.

While binnacle lamps blazed from the prow and stern of the ship, the crew called out to people ashore, who could not be seen behind the lanterns dotting the docks. At last, the *Challenge* edged into her berth with a final bump and sway. They were really here, she thought, yet she felt empty rather than exhilarated. She hugged her burnoose cloak around herself in a sudden chill. She would, of course, wait aboard until the Godfrey-Bennetts heard she was here and came to fetch her.

Right now, other than the bustle of crewmen securing ropes on the rain-swept dock, all seemed quiet ashore, an anticlimax to the voyage. Abigail was suddenly afraid of how quiet things would be tomorrow and ever after, now that she had known and lost Duke Braden and his brides. And all because of some hidden hatreds here that she was no part of. She gripped the rail harder. She leaned over and stared straight down at the water, lapping and swirling gently against the pilings of the wharf. Her knees went weak with gratitude for the ship's safety, and with sorrow that the little world she and Duke and his brides had shared aboard had now like the voyage come to an end. Stifling a sob, she turned away before they heard or saw her, and went in to try to sleep before the dawn.

## Chapter Four

Abigail's first day in New South Wales blazed bright and clear outside her porthole as Grace finished with her hair and hooked the back of her best traveling gown. Grace chattered nervously about—among other things—Mr. Braden's request that she help prepare Abigail to meet her hosts. Now why did such a kindly gesture as that annoy her so? Abigail scolded herself.

She felt more fully dressed than she had for weeks—overdressed, in fact. A dark green gown with a three-tiered lace collar over her shoulder cape and leg-o'-mutton sleeves balanced her full, padded bottom bolster, which belled out her ruffled skirts over four scalloped petticoats. Around her green pleated silk bonnet awash in white feathers, she had tied a transparent veil, which she could use with her Dunstable straw hat if the Godfrey-Bennetts protested her riding in the sun. For all she knew, Abigail thought, Duke Braden could have been misleading her on everything he'd said and implied about her hosts.

At last she tearfully hugged Grace in a private farewell, and attached a tooled leather leash to H.M.'s red-ribboned collar. Then she and H.M. went up on deck to wait.

A noisy crowd, almost entirely male, had gathered on the dock. By nine o'clock visitors began to come aboard. Abigail immediately picked out her second cousin, the fifty-five-year-old Griffin, in the crush below the hull by the gangplank. She waved to him; he lifted his tall top hat and walking stick in greeting. She remembered well the time he had visited Fairleigh before Grandfather died, but of course he looked much older now, and ruddier and stockier than she recalled. He had heavy jowls framed by salt-and-pepper side whiskers. With him stood a younger man, dressed similarly in blue frock coat, crisply starched collar, pristine cravat and black top hat, who was smoking a cheroot and trying to clear the way for Griffin.

Abigail stayed where she was when she saw the chaotic scene below. Then she saw Duke Braden and his brides promenade down the plank. At the last moment, Grace waved a wild goodbye to Abigail and shouted something she could not hear. While the noisy, waiting world stood still, Duke Braden's gaze met hers just before he looked away and led his ladies from the ship.

Abigail's eyes filled with tears at both the loss and pride of the moment. Braden's brides had decked themselves in her fashionable nuptial gifts and held their heads as high as queens. Even shy Clarissa Nye in her new cape looked as if she owned at least that fine dockside barouche carriage, which Abigail suspected held Mrs. Garnet Godfrey-Bennett, since it was emblazoned with the huge gilt monogram *GG*. Though the day was not cold, Deanna Dill sported her muff. Cora Mercer twirled her London parasol, Beth Anne's blue bonnet feathers rivaled Abigail's, and dear Grace dared to wave to the half-cheering, half-jeering crowd with her white-kid-gloved hand. Their procession stopped Mr. Godfrey-Bennett from boarding and made his wife, a petite woman in a straw bonnet buried in bows and feathers, lean far out of the carriage window to gawk.

"Braden's brides, the Currency's pride!" some men directly under Abigail's vantage point began to shout from the dock, and others took up the raucous chant. It soon drowned out the wails of "Banbury cakes and mutton pies!" from the street vendors, until they, too, joined in.

It seemed to Abigail the milling masses below formed two distinct groups: those smiling and those frowning at Duke and his women. The smiling men included, no doubt, a host of potential grooms who were obviously there to scrutinize these imported women. Then, too, as Duke had predicted, there were the men from the *Sydney Gazette,* scrambling after the brides with paper and pencils in their hands as if they meant to sketch them instead of just describe them. The rest of those whose faces clearly showed disapproval were just as well dressed as Griffin Godfrey-Bennett, who was obviously fuming while waiting to get up the gangplank. Duke had told her true, Abigail thought, but her heart fell anyway: there was a sort of war here between the so-called Exclusives and the Currency. She vowed then to learn everything she could about the conflict and not to join one side against the other unless—

"My dear girl!" her cousin Griffin boomed to jolt her from her agonizing. He and his companion had pushed their way up the gangplank and walked down the deck to meet her while her gaze was riveted on Duke Braden's entourage. She knew for certain now Griffin's escort was his son Phillip, for they resembled each other a great deal but for coloring. Griffin was ruddy and had been dark-haired; Phillip was rosy-cheeked, but paler and blond.

"So sorry those wretches ended up on your vessel!" Griffin shouted and kissed the flushed Abigail on both cheeks. "Dreadfully bad luck, what say? Such a scandal! Now, the Mrs. is waiting in the barouche, and we'll be able to get a good start on the eight miles to the Grange, eh? Been staying lately in our Sydney town house on government business, and what perfect timing you arrived while we were here!"

He seemed jovial and warm, though his perpetual squint made him look suspicious or displeased. Phillip stood first on one leather-booted foot and then the other, staring at her, his cigar smoke drifting up and away. He was a robust, full-lipped, brown-eyed man of age thirty, with a roundish face and high forehead. He looked the part of the London dandy of ten or so years ago. Though fairly stocky in his upper body, his stiff stance and trim middle suggested he wore a once-fashionable male corset, and his striped waistcoat looked narrow enough to be laced up the back in the old way. He flicked his cheroot butt over the rail without a thought as to whom it might hit below. He twirled a Regency quizzing glass in one hand as if he wanted to scrutinize her under it like some sort of specimen stuck through by a pin.

"Ah, my dear Abigail, may I present my son and heir, your third cousin, Phillip Godfrey-Bennett, a recent widower, sad to tell."

"I heard. I'm so sorry," she managed as Phillip bent under her bonnet to kiss one cheek. Then, as if she had passed that close inspection, he kissed the other.

"I'm just sorry all this rabble had to be on the same ship, coz," Phillip told her in his well-modulated voice amid the hubbub from the dock she longed to watch. "But, of course, a lady like you'd have nothing to do with those dregs of society. Currency trash abounds wherever that Braden rebel goes. Quite the black sheep. Bad luck to us, he lives too blinking close for our liking. Been quite fresh-aired 'round here the months he's been away, preaching his free-system gospel in the motherland, hasn't it, Father?"

"Quite, but Abigail's not to trouble her pretty head for any of that," he told Phillip pointedly.

She was bursting with questions about Duke Braden, but she knew she dared not ask even one, at least not until everything settled down.

"Now, my dear," Griffin went on, "allow us to escort you to the carriage and we'll see that our servants help fetch all your goods and follow us to Parramatta in the baggage wagon, what say. The Mrs. is going to be thrilled to get the news on London fashions, you know. Now, where is your retinue of servants?"

"I—due to circumstances—I brought no servants. I just used the captain's wife's girl, you see—"

Griffin's jowls bounced, and he squinted even harder. "Four months with no servants?"

"I'll be happy to hire someone to help with the trunks, of course, and hire my own staff here if need be, so—"

"No, no, that's not what I meant. Our staff is quite large enough, but—indeed, I'll let you explain it all to the Mrs., as I'm sure you have your reasons."

Since Duke and her friends had gone from deck to dock, Abigail was relieved to go ashore. But it didn't please her that Mrs. Gates had set herself up for farewells at the top of the gangplank while Abigail bade goodbye to the two old botanists and the captain.

The woman in the large carriage with the blue-liveried driver, guard and footman was indeed Mrs. Garnet Godfrey-Bennett. A petite, pale, graying blonde with nervous gestures, she hugged and kissed Abigail. She fell back onto the padded leather seat in surprise and dismay at word of no servants, but recovered quickly to fuss over Abigail's clothing.

"Nothing like dear London fashion, nothing like!" she assured Abigail as they settled their skirts and the excited spaniel. Mr. Godfrey-Bennett joined them inside, while Phillip was to ride a fine bay stallion that a servant held for him until he mounted with a flourish.

"I've brought you several things from London dressmakers I hope you will like, ma'am," Abigail told her when she could get a word in.

"Oh, how absolutely lovely. Everyone will be so thrilled!"

Everyone, Abigail assumed, meant her rather complicated list of friends she began telling Abigail about. She tried to answer her hostess's flurry of questions and take the view of Sydney at the same time. Finally, Phillip spotted her peeking surreptitiously out the window and rode his mount closer.

"Sydney's quite a town!" he boasted, and she returned his broad smile warily, grateful for the temporary rescue.

"It looks as big as London right now, considering how long I've been at sea," she admitted.

The congested waterfront with its colonial marine, wool and whale oil export ships and busy merchant houses slowed their carriage's exit from King's Wharf. Abigail twisted back for a glimpse of Duke Braden and his brides, but they were lost in the press of people and then the clutter of gigs, phaetons, stagecoaches and carriages.

As the carriage rumbled down broad George Street, Phillip pointed out to her the sights of the crescent-shaped town around and above them. She noted some small, quaint cottages with treed yards, some two- and three-story commercial buildings with white verandas, mingled with some large, foursquare sandstone official buildings on the heights sloping down to the sea. A forest of ship's masts sprouted behind them while steeples and windmills poked the cloudless blue sky beyond. Georgian harborside mansions reached northward from Sydney Cove, balanced by the greenery of the Government Domain with the Botanical Gardens on the other side. And everything was lorded over by stout Fort Phillip on the overlooking bluff.

"Can't brag that fort's named for me," Phillip said with a smile, though Abigail only nodded. "We try to make our town as much like London as we can," he assured her as he jogged along closer and leaned down from his saddle his cigar smoke drifting into the carriage. "I say, we even have a Hyde Park and a Theatre Royal. We can hear regimental music out by Dawes Battery and go hunting at Homebush, though of course the ladies don't ride."

"I ride," Abigail declared and noted with unease that her hostess began to sputter a protest before her next words cut them off. "If it's like England here, surely all the ladies ride," Abigail added pointedly, wishing Duke were here to see she was standing up for herself as he'd implied she would not. "But I must admit I don't favor hunting foxes."

"Foxes, here?" Phillip crowed and slapped his knee with his gloved hand. He dropped back as the carriage sped northward up the wide street with its busy footways on either side. "I adore shooting, but we hunt dingo or kangaroo here, coz," he shouted.

*How very English indeed,* she almost yelled back sarcastically. Duke Braden had done this to her, made her touchy and instinctively critical of these generous people who were her hosts. She vowed to be more accepting and broad-minded. It was just that she was tired after that storm last night and her lack of sleep. And this rocking carriage made her feel as if she were still at sea!

Despite her excitement at finally seeing New South Wales and despite her hostess's friendly attention, Abigail felt more and more irritable. The eight miles to the Godfrey-Bennett estate, the Grange, seemed interminable.

As they left Sydney, Abigail saw nearly naked aborigines begging at the elaborate tollgate on the high road to Parramatta, and she thought of dear, strange Kulalang.

"Oh, those poor hungry people, begging," she noted. "Can't they hunt on their lands?"

"*Their* lands?" Griffin replied as if she'd asked a question in a foreign tongue. "Like to pick those damned abos off with a gun, cluttering up this road on *our* lands with their thieving, begging ways, the lazy bastards!"

His reply shocked her to silence. She well knew Kulalang's skills and pride, and his sadness for the lost land of his Bandajong tribe, but she hadn't imagined she'd find so many aborigines in dire straits here.

Despite the low rail fence along the road, their carriage almost struck a kangaroo hopping madly across with the head of her baby—Duke said young kangaroos were called joeys—sticking from her pouch. H.M. barked madly at the mere scent, though she hadn't seen the 'roo from her position on the floor at Abigail's feet.

"You'll get used to those unpleasant pests everywhere, as thick as the hares at home," Mrs. Godfrey-Bennett assured Abigail. "Best to just ignore them."

And that, Abigail surmised, was just what the proper women of this land were supposed to do when anything offended their English sensibilities: ignore it. Ignore kangaroos, and starving "abos," too. Ignore the fact the hunt was for dingoes and not foxes. Ignore that this was not England. If you were a man, you did not ignore these unfortunate differences, but hoped to "pick them off with a gun."

And yet there was all this wild, untamed wilderness alongside the road. Bush, they called it, as if they could simply prune it or uproot it! The bush was hardly the forests of England, but she knew better than to say so and get herself off to a worse start than simply not bringing a bevy of English servants. It was beginning to look as if Duke Braden might have been right about certain things after all.

But Abigail's worst shock came when the carriage slowed to pass a group of yellow-suited men, who were repairing a break in the fence on the dipping, twisting road. Each man bore a big black number on his back. They shuffled stifflegged, hunched over, bound together by fetters as a mounted, armed guard shouted orders down at them.

"Oh, those poor convicts!" Abigail blurted.

"Not convicts," Griffin corrected. "Transportees or pensioners of the crown, we call them."

"Just don't look," her hostess advised while her husband flapped down the leather rolls at the windows to obscure the view.

"The cross we have to bear," he added and took another swig of what smelled like rum from his silver filigreed flask.

They were turning through the gate into the long drive of the Grange when Abigail persuaded her hosts to lift the window flaps again. At her request, Mr. Godfrey-Bennett had the driver rein in so she could step down and survey the grand sweep of lawn to the distant house. Rail fences enclosed herds of merino sheep, which looked like puffy white clouds in the gray-green sea of pastureland. One thousand acres of Grange land stretched out around them from this vantage point. At the bottom of the curving gravel lane stood the three-storied house, an elegant, domed pavilion. It was a muted miniature, Abigail thought, of the Royal Pavilion at Brighton, built in his regency by King George IV. A proud, pristine facade of Ionic pillars, tall windows gleaming in the noontide sun and a graceful portico greeted her gaze.

It was windy here. They stood on a gentle rise overlooking the Parramatta Valley with its ribbon of blue-gray river.

Griffin pointed out Iron Cove and the bay of the river. The haze of the distant forest framed the house, with slices of the Blue Mountains visible above the high land of the Pennant Hills.

"It's so lovely here," she told them.

"The house will be enlarged soon on the backs of those merinos over there, if you know what I mean," her host told her smugly.

But Abigail was squinting off toward a different direction. "How far away are your nearest neighbors, then?" she inquired, hoping the question sounded innocent enough.

"Not far enough," he grumbled, while Phillip, who had ridden back to see why the carriage had halted, snorted his agreement as he dismounted. "A bit of a fuss over a water hole," Griffin continued. "I bought out the old lags—that's freed prisoners—in this area, but for one. Matter of fact," he admitted as he helped Abigail back up the folding step into the carriage, "there's eighty acres over there I'll get one way or the other." He pointed to the west with his flask. "Owned by the transportee father of that rotter Duke Braden, the man on your ship with those females he intends to palm off like concubines to make some public protest—"

"Mr. Godfrey-Bennett, please!" cried his wife from inside the carriage. "After being cooped up on the same ship with those...those heathens, I'm sure Abigail hardly wants to hear his name!"

"I'm sure that's true, isn't it, dear coz?" Phillip stuck his head into the carriage before the footman closed the door. Before Abigail could answer, he went on, "Mrs. Gates, the captain's wife on your ship, as good as told me the same thing. Seems she was almost like a devoted mother to you, keeping a close eye on your doings and all."

He grinned, his large mouth flaunting big, widely spaced teeth. He dared to wink at her, obviously gloating over whatever tidbit of gossip he had pried from Mrs. Gates in such a short time. Abigail felt scandalized. She had a wild urge to mount Phillip's horse and gallop over to see Duke Braden's little farm and sheep run. She wanted to ask Phillip what vile things that woman had said. But her old fear and shame pressed hard on her to make her hold her tongue.

"Now, Phillip, you're not to tease our guest as you do those light-o'-loves at the cotillions in town!" his mother scolded.

"Let the boy be," his father said and downed another swig of rum. "He and Abigail have a lot in common. They are heirs to a proud past and rich heritage, so just let nature take its course and don't mix in, my dear!"

Mrs. Godfrey-Bennett merely sniffed. Stunned at the twist of events, Abigail sat rigid in her seat, biding her time until she could sort out the chaos of today and speak with Phillip in private.

The next day Abigail, who had not been sick one day on the entire voyage, took to her bed with exhaustion and the strange feeling that she was still rocking back and forth on the deck of the ship.

"Don't you fret, my dear. Mr. Godfrey-Bennett says it's quite a natural reaction when back on terra firma," Mrs. Godfrey-Bennett comforted while the maid brought in a tray of tea and toast. "You'll be on your feet tomorrow, just fine and dandy."

Abigail slept and slept, stumbling from dream to dream. Sometimes she was certain she was still in her little cabin aboard the *Challenge,* in Duke Braden's arms, as the ship pitched through a dangerous storm. But when she reached out for him, there was only the faithful H.M.

In the depths of her second night at the Grange, she woke abruptly from her sleep and sat up in bed with her coverlet clutched about her. She had dreamed she had turned into a sunflower, just like the nymph that was the ship's figurehead! She had turned her face toward Duke Braden and wanted to draw him, as if he were the god Apollo himself! She had wanted to sketch him the way the Greeks had done, all bare with sculpted muscles. And Duke had agreed. She had ridden over to his place to draw him. He had taken off all his clothes and kissed and held her in his lap. . . .

"Oh, no, I can't think such things," she whispered in the lovely bedchamber. "It's over, it's over."

She wrapped herself in a satin robe and padded barefoot, with H.M. at her heels, across a floral carpet to her western window to gaze out in the direction where Duke Braden lived. *So close and yet not close at all.* But that just wasn't right or fair. She wanted to know what had happened to her forecastle friends, whom they would wed, where they would live, what would become of them in this big new land. And she had to make her own way here. Yes, she felt better now; her legs were steady; her head had cleared. She picked up the spaniel in her arms and rubbed her cheek along the top of H.M.'s sleek head and the curves of the floppy ears. Tomorrow, she would deal with Phillip's apparent attempt at blackmail. And then she would begin her new life here.

Abigail had hoped Phillip might give her a tour of the mansion so that she could speak with him alone, but he had gone to Sydney so Mrs. Godfrey-Bennett showed her about.

"That boy," she admitted to Abigail, her voice proud but her face pinched, "spends so much time away with his friends there. But he just dotes on his little daughter, Charlotte—calls her Lottie, you know."

Charlotte was Phillip's seven-year-old motherless daughter, a coquettish moppet with blond curls who could not sit still at breakfast and had taken to chasing H.M. ragged all morning. But if Phillip spent as much time in Sydney society as his mother said, Abigail could not quite fathom how he doted on his daughter. Rather it was Charlotte's grandmother who doted on her, sending maids to fetch this and that at the child's whim or jumping up herself when necessary.

And, Abigail wondered, how could Phillip leave behind such a beautiful and busy place as the Grange if he were the heir and would run it all someday? She, a woman, had even helped to oversee Fairleigh's bailiff and staff and had delighted in riding the grounds to be certain all was well.

This huge house her hostess showed her seemed a Georgian pleasure palace magically transported from home, with English furniture and paintings enhancing each room. An airy, wide-windowed oval drawing room at each end of the pillared facade impressed Abigail most. Staffordshire porcelain loaded the shelves and the long table in the formal dining room, each green- and gold-banded piece monogrammed with the ornate *GG* that appeared on every piece of linen and every carved mantelpiece. There was a banquet room and a music room with a pianoforte she would enjoy. A porticoed orangery with all sorts of indoor plants—orange, citron, lemon, almond—stretched across the back of the house with its tall windows and columns reflected on the marble floor. Abigail and Garnet Godfrey-Bennett took tea there at a small table in the afternoon warmth amid the sweet scents of plants.

"I'm sure Mr. Godfrey-Bennett will be pleased to show you the outbuildings tomorrow. We don't want to overtax your strength now," her hostess said as she poured tea from a bone porcelain pot.

"I'm fine now, really, ma'am," Abigail replied, but she frowned to hear Charlotte rampaging once again after H.M. down the lines of plants. "I had hoped perhaps Phillip would show me around as he likes to ride, too."

"Phillip. Dear me, no. As I said, he's awfully busy in town. He looks after our wool exports and mutton market while he's there, of course. Really, you mustn't expect to see much of him, and as for your notion to ride—"

Her hostess's remonstrance ended in a shriek at the sound of porcelain crashing in the distance. Both women rushed to the scene and found neither dog nor child but only the shards of a potted plant around the ruins of a fig tree seedling. Both were going to fetch the respective culprits, when Phillip and his father came striding in, Phillip waving a copy of the latest *Sydney Gazette*. The scolding that ensued was not of Charlotte or H.M. but of Abigail herself.

"Why, I just can't believe this, Abigail!" Griffin blustered, pointing to a front page article headed, Braden's Brides Arrive in London Style.

"Whatever will our friends say?" Mrs. Godfrey-Bennett moaned as her husband read selectively from the article.

Lady Abigail Rosemont, cousin and guest of the well-known Godfrey-Bennett family of the Grange, Parramatta, so generously helped to outfit this first flux of female immigrants.

Mrs. Godfrey-Bennett shook her beribboned head. "This means," she said with a shudder, "that *those women* were clad in your gifts from London just as I am! And after I told some friends what you'd brought me. Oh, my, that will spread like bushfire!"

"Now, Mother, I'm sure they won't blame *you*," Phillip put in pointedly as he scraped a sulfur match on his boot sole and lit a new cheroot.

Flushing, feeling caught like the child or the dog who had broken something delicate, Abigail glared at Phillip, who looked to be enjoying her embarrassment.

Griffin continued.

The so-called "Braden's brides" responded to shouted compliments about their appearance by declaring that their fine London-made garb was donated by their friend, the nicest English lady they had ever met. At least one bride, Miss Grace Buck, was on first-name terms with the above-mentioned "Miss Abigail," Lady Abigail Rosemont.

"You, I take it—" Mr. Godfrey-Bennett floundered, hardly able to bring himself to say the words "—you also met and mingled with Mr. Braden."

"It was a small ship, sir. I met both him and his native friend, Kulalang."

"That abo!" Griffin roared. "That black Bandajong troublemaker who always hangs about our western water hole and—"

"Best watch your apoplexy, Father," Phillip cut in.

Perhaps the only good thing to emerge from this wretched beginning, Abigail thought, was that Phillip Godfrey-Bennett could hardly be interested in her after all this. It had been obvious to her that his father had been matchmaking just as heartily as his mother had been trying to ruin any such possibilities.

"My dear, I see we were very remiss not to discuss Mr. Duke Braden with you the other day," Phillip's father began, his voice deliberate but his face florid. "He's a great enemy to the stability of our country, you see, an enemy to our way of life."

"A damned rebel!" Phillip put in, only to have his father glare at him.

"Yes, that too," he said, squinting more than usual. "He is, you see, dear Abigail, quite tainted by the stain—the moral weakness inherited from his father and mother. Old Squire Braden's an evil, depraved old man."

"You're saying," Abigail asked slowly, "that Duke Braden is morally tainted because his father and mother went to prison?"

"Of course, though the old lag was released for good behavior. Good behavior!" he scoffed. "Impossible for a vile old lunatic like that. But half the colony's so infected, being descended from prisoners. And we Exclusives have to guard against any sort of dangerous mixing with the Currency—that's the widespread group the Bradens head. Currency, you see, just like cheap worthless coins that can only be spent in the colony. Just as we can't have weak stock mixing in with our sheep, you see, my dear, we can't have any sort of social mixing with the Currency. You do understand, I hope."

Her head spun with the terms and with the hatred they cloaked. "You're saying people are just like sheep and have

to be carefully bred,'' she murmured, still astounded at the
tumble of events.

''Exactly!'' Mrs. Godfrey-Bennett spoke up again. ''We
Exclusives are even called pure Merinos in contrast to them,
those mixed breeds. And my dear, if you've so much as
spoken with that abo who always tags along behind Duke
Braden...''

Abigail wanted to scream and break more porcelain pots.
She wanted to tip the English bone china tea tray over on
them all. Of course, she had realized she was stepping over
a social line in befriending Braden's brides and running
down another forbidden path by getting close to Duke Braden, but these people didn't understand. They didn't understand that on a ship everything was different. It was like
one little country out at sea where everything was new and
different. It was like—then the thought hit her and nearly
knocked her from her chair—like starting a new country
here in this raw land where everyone had to pull together.
She opened her mouth to explain that, but Phillip's next
words stopped her.

''I'm sure Abigail understands and regrets the problems
she's caused. It's rotten luck that devil and those women
were on her ship, and I'm sure she hardly said two words to
that abo, as he certainly wouldn't understand her if she did
speak to him. And as for Duke Braden, she didn't so much
as take a turn around the deck with him, did you, Abigail?
She obviously won't be seeing those women again, as they're
scattered here and there with whoever claimed them, like
newly arrived barrels of English goods. Now, let's just put
all this away and go on from here, what say.

''Dear coz, come on and walk with me,'' he challenged,
his voice dripping sweetness now, ''and we'll just hope all
this blows over. I'll introduce you 'round to proper folk in
town first chance I get, and you'll weather all this well
enough when they get a good look at you and your English
ways, eh, Mother?''

Before his mother could protest his walking his cousin off
in private, he whisked Abigail away. She suffered him to

tuck her hand in his arm long enough to escape their elders. They strolled out of the well-lighted orangery down the main hall to the front entrance where they drew a breath of mutual relief.

"Thank you for that rescue," she told him and slowly disengaged her arm from his. "I'm afraid my emotions would have made me say things I shouldn't back there."

"Not in defense of Braden, I hope."

"I see nothing wrong with increased immigration of English females brought here to wed," she blurted before she realized he stared so intensely at her. She looked away. "I did not mean to imply myself," she added hastily.

"Good. My father, I fear, has other motives."

"But not your mother."

"How quickly you have read the cards," he said. He led her into the south drawing room, and they sat on opposite sides of an S-shaped dark green brocade courting settee. He smashed his cigar butt to ashes in a china plate on the side table. "Now let me lay my cards on the table, Abigail."

Her heart beat very fast. She wanted to find out what he had learned from Mrs. Gates, but he seemed in control of the conversation now. "Do so, sir."

"I have no desire to be wed to anyone right now. I'm enjoying myself and favor my independence. As heir to all this, I've no desire to have an heiress, or any sort of wife for that matter. Mother only wants me single to keep control of me and Lottie without a wife underfoot. She adores Lottie, you see."

"I see. And I hear you adore Lottie, too."

"My father, however," he went on, as if she had not mentioned the child, "wants a second-generation heir for his fortune, a male heir to carry on the name, and Lottie's hardly that."

"I was my grandfather's heir, but—yes, I understand."

"Now that I've shown you my hand, I must tell you I do hold a trump card or two. You will be my partner and not my adversary in this little game."

"Meaning?" she asked warily.

"Meaning, that I have certain information the *Sydney Gazette* does not have yet, that you were not only friendly with Braden's brides, but with the very devil himself, strolling the deck with him, given extra rations of water by him, et cetera."

"I fail to see the crime," she insisted, ready to defend her rights.

"Oh, yes, I heard you argued with him, too, so I'll give you some credit for not losing your sanity. And as for that black abo of his, I hear he tossed a carved stick at you, and I really think it's strange you have not pressed charges—"

"It was a misunderstanding. He did not harm me."

"Damn it, coz, all of this has harmed you! And since you and I are going to be working on the same side now to keep my father from marrying us off against my will—though I am pleased to see you're quite a pretty thing—"

"Sir!"

"Just listen, damn you!" he insisted and reached over the back of the settee to seize her wrist. Suddenly he realized that though her spunky independence annoyed him, it amused him, too. Amused him to bring it out in her, just the way he loved to control the mistresses he had enjoyed in town over the years, a string of them, Currency sluts all. They deserved to be seduced, degraded and eventually abandoned. Such was his own private contribution to humiliating and debasing the low, upstart Currency. But this interfering little bitch was an entirely different matter with her family position, not to mention her vast inheritance. He calmed himself so as not to alarm her with the violent feelings ripping through him.

"Don't you realize," he began quietly, "that Duke Braden's out to get the Godfrey-Bennetts, to rub us in the dirt where he lives, any way he can? They've clung to that little slice of land that is ours by right!" His voice rose. "Duke and that hotspur brother of his have a personal vendetta against me, and he's using you—seducing you, no doubt—"

"He has not!"

"Into thinking he and his plans are noble. But the bastard's going to cause civil war with his radical preaching about equality for those ignorant, violent abos and for that morally tainted Currency! I suppose he sweet-talked you into not pressing charges for assault against that abo and even has his eye on your riches. Found out somehow you were an heiress, I've no doubt."

She wanted to berate this man for his misguided ideas, but his accusations hit her hard. Yes, Duke had discovered she was an heiress. Yes, he had asked her not to press charges against Kulalang. Worse, she had obviously annoyed, even disgusted him, just as the Godfrey-Bennetts did, and yet he had forced himself to be kind. He had tried to control her through his enticing kisses and caresses in the moments he knew she was most lonely and vulnerable. Worse, she had fallen for it—fallen for him. Perhaps he had even asked the women to befriend her to keep her quiet, to turn her against the people he obviously hated and their friends, the ruling class here. When she had offered his brides those gifts that first time, had he been kind to her so she would give them more things that could be held up for derision in the Sydney paper?

For one moment she sat slumped, devastated to her core, barely aware that Phillip still held her wrist in an iron grip.

"I dare say, coz, we have a deal," he said.

She looked into his smug face and tugged back her arm. "I assure you, I never came here to wed you. I have no intention of marrying."

She did not realize that it was her lack of interest in him that made Phillip almost regret he had been so adamant and hasty to put her off. If there was anything Phillip Godfrey-Bennett loved, it was a challenge. After all, he'd always had everything he wanted without the slightest fuss. But he had no intention of giving up his sporting life in Sydney, including chasing and ruining whatever Currency lass caught his eye. In a way, his parents even approved, though his mother was appalled that his current mistress, Catty, was Currency.

He noted Abigail looked furious now, but not at him. Slowly, he pulled his fat sterling match case from his inside waistcoat pocket and extracted a sulfur match, then another. He stroked the first match on his boot sole, then lit the other with it until they both flared.

"Abigail?" he said.

She stared at the matches, wondering what he intended. "What? Yes, we have a deal that you won't spread whatever vile gossip Mrs. Gates threw your way, and I won't go along with any of your father's plans to get us together."

"A deal!" He snuffed out the now low-burning flames between his fingers and tossed the sticks in the general direction of the dish with the other ashes. He rose and extended his hand to help her.

When she extended her hand, he surprised Abigail by turning it over and kissing her palm. She stood quickly, excused herself and hurried upstairs.

Abigail was infuriated, but not with Phillip. In one way, rather, he had turned out to be a pleasant surprise, an ally of sorts, despite his strange, underhanded ways. It was that deceitful Duke Braden she was angry with—and with herself, too, for being so taken in. The first chance she got, she was going to ride over there and tell him so in person!

# Chapter Five

To keep the *Gazette*'s implications from turning to rampant rumors, Garnet Godfrey-Bennett took Abigail into Sydney to display her very English presence at the homes of friends. Abigail made her best effort to cooperate, for she regretted hurting her relatives. She also wanted to show her ally and potential blackmailer, Phillip, that she did not intend to be the Exclusives' enemy. Still, she couldn't help speaking out in favor of befriending new immigrants, even if they were dubbed "Braden's brides." That not only raised eyebrows, but, she assumed, cut her initial whirl a bit short.

She'd gotten her ears full of the Exclusives' hatred of Duke Braden's causes—all of them. Furious with him herself, she eagerly took in all the accusations to employ later as ammunition.

After all, Abigail assured herself, the man was obsessed with his beliefs and obviously detested the Exclusives as much as they did him. So, surely he had been laughing at her behind her back. She saw the rotter clearly now, and she intended to tell him so the first chance she got. The trouble was, even when she hardened her heart against the man, she could not help but admire his goals.

Besides promoting assistance to immigrants in this new land, Duke Braden, it seemed, had also spoken out for and urged Governor Bourke to stand for aborigines' and squatters' rights. Squatters, Abigail learned, were not the portly gentlemen and their fashion-hungry wives who lolled about the lavish tables and elegant drawing rooms at Sydney dinner parties. Squatters were free settlers who yearned to move westward over the Blue Mountains to claim grazing lands for their sheep. With few exceptions, between the coast and the mountains, pastureland was mostly taken by rich Exclusives. Indeed, what could be so terrible about the ambition of the "Currency class" to own land? But when she asked that question aloud, she was stared to silence.

She also learned in her first whirl through Sydney society that Mrs. Godfrey-Bennett was actually afraid to let Phillip so much as escort her around town to meet his friends. Perhaps, Abigail thought, when she could convince her hostess that she had no intentions of snaring her precious son, she would be her ally just like Phillip. Perhaps then Mrs. Godfrey-Bennett would be willing to think in a kindlier vein of immigrants like Braden's brides and dispossessed aborigines like Kulalang!

Back in the Parramatta Valley, Mrs. Godfrey-Bennett didn't keep Abigail as close by her side. Still, it was two more days before Abigail saw her first chance to ride away from the Grange to berate Duke Braden for his selfish, smug treatment of her on the voyage over. The afternoon of June 30, while her hostess was indisposed with a headache, Abigail donned a short cape, put H.M. on a leash and boldly informed the stable's head groom that she wanted a horse saddled. She wedged H.M. in a big side pack strapped before her saddle the way they had ridden at home. Wrapping a veil around her straw hat, she set out westward, riding sidesaddle.

She dismounted to let herself out a sheep gate emblazoned with the familiar *GG* monogram. She rehooked the gate and mounted again. At first she supposed this must be the western boundary of Grange land. But beyond the next pasture, a natural escarpment of rocks and cliffs protected three sides of a quiet water hole where sheep's hooves had pockmarked the mud. Four reddish 'roos were drinking from the hole, though they bolted in great leaps when H.M. barked.

"You think you're big and brave to scatter animals that large, don't you, my girl?" Abigail asked the excited dog. She gazed about the shadowed sandstone cliffs, honeycombed with caves and rocky shelves. It seemed so peaceful here, yet she felt as if invisible eyes watched her from crevices overhead. She glanced around and shivered. She had no other companions here, she assured herself, but for one of those strange kookaburra birds laughing like a lunatic from the bottlebrush tree across the hole.

She wondered if this was the water hole her cousin had mentioned was once disputed with Duke's father, the pensioner, or the old lag, as they called him. An old lag sounded like someone who just lazed about and did next to nothing; that was how she would describe some of the Exclusives she had met in town, she thought petulantly. If this was that water hole, she must still be on Grange land. She let her horse drink while she sat mounted, then turned his nose westward again.

She rode up a gentle ridge beyond the rocks and water. Below her on a slant of land, sheep dotted blocks of grayish grassland while small stands of rye, wheat and vegetables nodded at her. Beyond all that sat a small house with a cluster of outbuildings embraced by a rail-fenced yard. Smoke trailed a crooked finger in the sky from the chimney of one outbuilding. How tiny the house looked after the grandeur of the Grange!

This house was the essence of simplicity: a single story of stone walls instead of triple-tiered magnificence. A broad roof also covered a wraparound veranda supported by slender board pillars. The windows were shuttered down to the flagstones of the veranda floor. A few fruit trees dotted the yard instead of a patterned array of clipped bushes and tended flower beds.

The pastoral scene beckoned her. It almost cooled her anger at Duke Braden until she reminded herself he must have been laughing at her like that kookaburra back there. How gullible and stupid she had been to care for him all those weeks at sea while he was only using her! He was probably reveling in the fact that the *Gazette* had held her up to ridicule and given his free-immigrant brides publicity at her—and hence, her relatives'—expense!

Determinedly, she cantered her mount down the narrow lane, past random, rippling patches of rye. She was almost to the fenced-in area when she heard a man yell.

"You! Halt there!"

She reined in, ready to give Duke Braden what for. But the man who had risen from the grain like a scarecrow was a weathered, brown-faced old man holding a scythe. He reminded her of a sketch of Father Time she'd seen in a childhood book.

"Oh!" Abigail exclaimed. H.M. barked madly until she quieted her. "Pardon me," she said, thinking she was addressing a farmhand, "but I am seeking Mr. Braden."

"You found him. Squire Braden, at your service. This is me place here. That pretty little spaniel yours?"

"Yes," she told him as he emerged from the small grain field and leaned on the wooden handle of his scythe. She unwrapped her hat veil and squinted into the afternoon sun to see better: the handle of the scythe was carved with aboriginal designs like those on the *woomera* Kulalang had given her, now hidden under her mattress at the Grange.

*So this is Duke's father,* she thought, recalling his strange name, Squire. Did all these Bradens have names that seemed to claim a rank far from their reach? Despite her hurt and anger at Duke's cruel treatment of her, she smiled at the man when he doffed his dusty, felt top hat like the most polite English gentleman. At least he, unlike Duke, strove to keep up proper appearances, she thought.

Abigail noted Squire Braden was hardly taller than she. He had silver hair cropped close to his head. His features were spare; he looked dusty all over. Yet his eyes shone as ice-blue as Duke's to testify to their kinship.

"Nice puppy." He came closer to croon to the dog, and began to introduce himself to H.M. "Jes' call me Squire, puppy, though me folks named me Simon in Dorset. That's why we call this the Dorset Downs. This me land, planted with the sweat of me brow, though me boys want to turn it to a damned sheep run when all I want the stupid sheep for is their good manure for me crops." H.M. seemed most entranced by the man's information.

"This puppy of yours," he said, addressing Abigail now, "he a sheep chaser?"

"H.M.'s a she, Mr. Braden. And I hope not, though she barks at 'roos. I'll be sure she doesn't chase your sheep."

"Don't mind if she does. Those other fool dogs Duke and Earl got just rounds them damned stupid sheep up. If your puppy chased all their merinos off, I'd be happy, long as that king of the Exclusives, Godly-Bennett, next place over don't get them. Then I'd have a proper Dorset farm to leave me boys, jes' like I planned. Like to beat all that overlanding squatter tomfoolery outta their heads, I would, but Earl'd cuff me right back."

There was an *Earl* Braden, too? Abigail thought in amazement as Squire Braden kept reaching up to the saddle pouch to pet H.M. The man's face was a leathered web of wrinkles, which aged him more than his years. He seemed too small to be Duke's father, but perhaps his years in prison had stunted his growth somehow.

"I met your son Duke on the ship en route here," she told him.

"Didn't think you's one o' his Currency lass friends from town, and those brides o' his gone their own ways now. I said to him, jes' wed one o' those and get your old lag dad a grandchild. But he's stubborn as ever, jes' like Earl. Earl says he's agoing to the Female Factory to get hisself a transportee bride, though I tell him the grade o' prisoners ain't so good no more like when I picked his ma there."

"I see. But Duke—is he here? I have something to tell him."

Shouldering his scythe, he led her down the lane and through the gate to the yard, reaching up to pat H.M. every few steps. "Earl! Earl! A lady come acalling on your fancy brother!" Squire yelled out in the yard.

Abigail jumped and blushed. She had no notion of being on display for his family if Duke were not about. And why had his father called him "fancy"? But when Earl Braden ambled out of the house and shaded his eyes to survey her, she thought perhaps it was just by comparison with Earl that Duke was fancy.

Earl Braden was the same height and build as Duke, though their physical similarities ended there. Earl's black hair framed dancing brown eyes in a round face crowded with heavy features. But she soon saw Earl could flash that Braden smile more easily than Duke ever had.

"Well, well, well," Earl said, grinning up at her. "Duke's gonna kick himself for being out on the north forty with the flock. Won't you please come in and wait for him then, ma'am?"

"No, thank you, I really couldn't," she said, more nervous now, as Earl's eyes assessed her blatantly.

"I'm gonna fetch that puppy some water," the old man insisted and marched over to the well.

As she and Earl exchanged stiff introductions, Abigail realized how foolish this crusade to crucify Duke Braden had been. She had dared to leave the Grange, and they might be looking for her. She had no idea what these men were really like or what Duke would do in his anger if she confronted him with her bitter accusations. She had as good as trespassed on Braden land when they had a feud going with her cousins. And worse, she had lost her head to come here because she was longing to see that wretch Duke Braden again—however much she hated him.

Squire Braden hurried back to lift his top hat, brimming with water, to H.M.! Abigail gawked, though Earl, who had come closer, seemed not to blink an eye. And H.M. just obliged by lapping loudly.

"See," Earl said to her, "at least your dog knows who to trust. Come in and have a cup of tea then, and I'll send a man for Duke. Come, it's safe enough. Bucky, girl, where are you?" he called to someone. "We got us a lady visitor! Over here!" Earl bellowed and windmilled one arm while steadying Abigail's skittish horse by the bridle with his other.

Abigail turned and gaped. From the cook house with its smoke coming from the roof, a dark-haired woman emerged. "It's Grace!" Abigail cried. "Grace Buck! Grace!"

She dismounted faster than Earl could help her and ran toward her friend. Grace squealed and flapped her apron while she ran hard at Abigail, who suddenly stood as if frozen.

"He—Duke brought you here?" Abigail demanded. "To wed for himself?"

"Wish't he did, Miss Abigail," Grace said and grinned saucily. "Say, wasn't that some swell newspaper with both our names writ real fine in it? I wanted you to get some thanks for helping us. But, see, the man who specially spoke for me on the wharf was a big bruiser. I got real scared and asked Duke if I had to wed him. Praise be I balked, 'cause the man was ever so furious. With his vile temper, he wanted to pound Duke right into the ground when Duke told him I couldn't wed right then. I'm still shaking thinking what would've happened to me with that one! So I guess I'm off the hook now, even though Duke says the paper will make a big stink if it finds out he kept me with him. But I'm happy as a lark, cleaning the cook house and fixing meals for Duke and his dad here. And, 'course, Earl," she added, and her warm gaze swept over Abigail's shoulder to take in Duke's brother.

Abigail knew that look. She'd seen it before on Grace's face when she gazed fondly at Duke aboard the *Challenge*. Now it seemed he'd as good as passed her off to his brother. And she'd seen that look on herself, too, in her mirror on the vessel coming over, drat Duke Braden! However kind Grace thought Duke was, Abigail knew now that kindness from the likes of him was all a cruel ruse!

And how dared he tell her she could not hire Grace for a "low" lady's maid and then make her cook and scullery maid for three men and dusty, dirty sheep hands on their little farm out here! But none of that was Grace Buck's fault. Nor maybe even Earl's, nor Squire Braden's. They seemed friendly: Earl looked a bit rough-edged, but surely Squire was harmless in his eccentricities. She'd settle things permanently with Duke, then never see him again!

Grace prepared tea for them and set out some sort of flat soda bread big as a cake called damper she was "trying to get the hang of fixing." Abigail sat bolt upright in a wooden chair in the Braden common room while Earl sent a man for Duke. But her stomach felt twisted. She could barely get the buttered bread down, though Grace proudly watched her eat each bite. H.M. made up for Abigail's lack of enthusiasm by gobbling the damper Squire gave her on a plate on the floor.

The interior of the house was pleasant enough, Abigail thought, trying to calm herself. It seemed perfectly matched to the uncluttered exterior, laid out in four equal-sized rooms sparsely decorated, with items either homemade or aboriginal. Simple, well-polished cedar furniture smelled fresh, and soft India cane matting on the floor rustled under one's feet.

"And why," Abigail asked while Earl eyed Grace and Squire eyed H.M., "did you name this place Castle Keep, Mr. Braden?"

Earl groaned as though she'd asked the worst question possible while his father launched into a long explanation of earning his pardon from prison.

"During me time as a stockman on a sheep farm fifty miles up country from Sydney town, I always dreamed of having a fine place, a castle, like I'd seen back in Dorset. Most ticket-of-leave men hated farming since they's forced to work the farms, but not Squire Braden, not even when the loss of one stupid sheep meant a flogging in those days!" he said, bending over from his chair to stroke H.M.

"But I loved the land, wanted only to make it grow good food and just mind me own business when I got out. Got me a gov'ners' good-behavior ticket-of-leave thirty-five years ago, got me forty acres of land on release, plus twenty for a pensioner wife from the Female Factory prison at Parramatta, and ten for each of the three children."

"Oh, you've a third son?" Abigail asked.

"It was a daughter," Earl put in. "Margaret."

"Queenie!" Squire corrected. "Your ma said Queenie was a good 'nuff name to match Squire and Duke and Earl!"

"Queenie died real young and Ma a week later," Earl went on with a helpless shrug of his big shoulders. "And when they did—"

"When they did," the deep voice at the door took up the story, "your hosts, the illustrious Godfrey-Bennetts, petitioned to have our ten extra acres returned to government lands. Of course, then the Godfrey-Bennetts bought the land for a pittance, taking our best water hole in the process—a water hole we shared with the Bandajong tribe your hosts shot like 'roos if they so much as set foot on what had once been their sacred tribal land!"

"Oh!" was all Abigail could manage to say, and she stared openmouthed at the furious Duke. She meant to jump to her feet to face him on equal terms, but her legs failed her and she stayed put.

Duke addressed Earl. "What's she doing here? I told you where she was living!"

Earl stood and balled his fists, looking every bit as if he were ready for a fight. Grace jumped up to take the tray of tea things and beat a quick retreat.

"Maybe I just wanted to see her close up and liked what I saw," Earl told Duke as if Abigail were not even in the room. "Besides, they can't have bent her mind too much if she's here drinking Braden tea."

"Here to gawk or spy," Duke insisted. "Allow me to escort you out, Miss Rosemont."

"I am in this house at your family's invitation, not yours!" she dared, though she had begun to tremble like an autumn leaf.

When Duke started toward her, Earl blocked his path. "She's hardly old man Godly-Bennett or his precious son," he insisted. "I can tell the difference if you can't."

"Stow it, Earl, and get out of my way. She's my affair."

"Well, since you put it that way," Earl goaded and stood aside with a dramatic sweep of his arm.

Duke ignored his brother to take Abigail's elbow.

She shook him off and rose. "I thank you, Mr. Braden and Mr. Braden," she said, nodding to Squire and Earl, "for your hospitality. And I'd like you to know if Grace Buck ever wishes to find another position, I would be pleased to take her on."

"Bet you could take on a more stubborn one than Grace and win," Earl said with a snide grin at his older brother.

"I'll trade Grace for this puppy," Squire declared and stooped to lift the willing H.M. into his lap.

With flustered apologies, Abigail retrieved the spaniel and walked stiffly ahead of Duke to the door.

"I must say," she said to Duke in a clipped tone as they stood on the veranda, "I've never been actually tossed out of a Christian home before, you rude—"

"I have. By your relatives and all their friends when I tried to reason with them. How does it feel? Not that I expect you to understand my motives." He seemed to have her full attention now. "I lose my temper," he went on, "when people want my father to talk about his past. He's not ashamed of it nor am I, but it's what he's done with his life since that matters."

"All I asked was why he called the house Castle Keep. And I liked him almost as much as he liked H.M., so there!" She put the dog up in the saddle pouch. She tried to mount before Duke helped her, but he was too quick. He did not just give her a boost by her foot, but lifted her clear up by her waist and even dared place her foot in the sidesaddle stirrup while she was tempted to kick him. Then he mounted the horse he had evidently ridden in on.

"If I was abrupt in there," he added, "it was for your own good."

"Don't lecture me like some child!"

His narrowed, blue eyes swept her, toes to top, so thoroughly she quickly retied her veil around her heated face.

"I assure you, Lady Abigail, I don't see you as a child! You know, you're amazing," he added to disarm her totally. He reached over to put one big hand on hers gripping her reins. "You like taking crazy risks, don't you, Abigail?"

"No. I don't see it that way. I came, quite honestly, because I have had my fill of the way you've treated me and meant to tell you I'm not as simple as you think."

"Of all the things I think of you, that you're simple is not one."

"And don't give me any of your insincere flattery!" she insisted and yanked her hands free to urge her horse on.

He quickly caught up with her, then passed her to lead the way. Far behind them, Squire came out on the side veranda to call farewell to them.

"You've got all the answers, haven't you," Duke challenged. "Tell me then, now that we're out of earshot of the others."

"I've no desire to ride off alone with you!" she said and reined in again. "I just wanted to tell you that I know how despicable and deceitful you have been to me!"

"I am beginning to get that message. So they've turned your head already, just as I suspected they would. And I suppose your cousin Phillip is cramming it with all sorts of vile things about me. Let's hear it then, Lady Abigail, before I deliver you back to them, more or less in one piece after this little jaunt to where we Braden devils live!"

They paused on a hill shaded with tall, gray-green-leafed eucalyptus trees oozing a strange reddish gum. The moment they halted their horses overlooking a partly wooded, partly pastured sweep of land, her long pent-up feelings poured forth.

"You might just as well have had the *Sydney Gazette* print all the rest of my foolishness for letting you get so close!"

she accused. "On deck that rainy night and in my cabin during the storm!"

"Pleased you haven't forgotten all that. I assure you I haven't, either."

"I'm sure it's been a source of high amusement for you! I know now you were just leading me on for your own reasons!"

"No doubt. But weren't you leading me on for yours?"

He turned to face her and raked his fingers through his unruly hair, leaving dust streaks on his broad brown forehead. She had to admit he smelled a bit of sheep, but, even as furious with him as she was, that didn't matter. She tried to steel herself and tried again to put him in his place.

"*I* extended true friendship, Duke Braden," she declared, hoping her voice sounded cold, "not to mention those gifts to your brides! *You* just wanted me to not accuse Kulalang. *You* just wanted some good fodder for attacking the Exclusives through ridiculing me once we arrived!"

"Now we're down to it. So you've learned that's all I do, no doubt. I rampage about the town and country causing your friends—the 'pure-bred' merinos with two feet instead of four who call themselves Exclusives—a lot of trouble!"

"And don't you?"

"As best I can!"

He threw his leg over his saddle and dismounted hastily. He reached up and yanked her down while H.M. growled at him. "And you know what, Miss Exclusive English? All I know about your family made me furious with you!" he admitted and gave her a hard shake.

"There, you see?" she insisted, glad he had confessed. "Now set me free!"

He didn't. He hauled her closer, his hands hard on her shoulders. He spoke his words quietly, bitterly, his mouth so close to hers she stared up into his harsh, devouring gaze as if mesmerized.

"You said it all there, didn't you, Abigail?" he demanded. "'Set me free!' You think the convicts—yes, I know, your friends pretty it all up with polite names for them—don't want to be free? You think the aborigines don't want to roam and hunt free on their sacred dreamtime land like they used to? You think the Currency lads who are kept from all but the lowest jobs so some of them even turn bushrangers don't want to be free to head west and own some land? Hell, they'd pay for it after a shearing or two and help build up this country with their wool exports! You think anything you want about me and my kind! But just clear off my land and out of my life then!"

She hung limp in his hands at the impact of that tirade, ignoring H.M.'s whimpering. Duke was still only grasping her shoulders, but it seemed he gripped her all over, outside and in. She didn't intend to let him lead her on and use her against her people again. And yet, she reasoned, she did not feel the Exclusives were really *her* people. It was his scattered Braden's brides she cared about. It was Squire and Earl and their little place that lured her much more than her stuffy cousins and their grand Grange. And it was this man whose touch she had longed for that still absolutely swamped her senses!

He sat her down hard on a big, gnarled root of a eucalyptus tree. He lifted the skittish H.M. out of the saddle pouch and put her on the ground. In the awkward silence following, Duke stared at the ground between his feet while H.M. settled at Abigail's side.

"I can't believe I'm here with you. I had to come." She had blurted out the truth before she even knew what she would say.

He sat next to Abigail and leaned back against the big tree, his body still rigid. This place seemed to envelop them with the most elemental aroma, emanating from the embracing eucalyptus mingled with the breeze. She cleared her throat and looked away, her face solemn, as Duke lifted his head to stare at her again.

"Perhaps you are a simpleton, Abigail. You're upset by a mention in the *Gazette* that you befriended the brides and the implication thereby you had been mixing in with Duke Braden. But if you think that rocked the establishment, don't you realize what visiting our land could mean to your reputation? Your cousins, glad as they are to show you off in town and have a chance to wed you and your fortune to Phillip, would toss you out on your pretty tail for coming here!"

"Sir! You do not know the first thing about that! And I resent your referring to my, that is, do not address me as if I were one of your—as your father calls them—your stupid damned sheep!"

He smiled tautly. "Sheep get their tails docked, and I had no like plans for you. I take it you weren't appalled by my father?"

"Hardly. He's more charming than you'll ever hope to be!"

He grinned now, flashing his straight white teeth she so seldom saw—unless he snarled. Abigail was amazed to find she had relaxed. Right at this moment, she felt the happiest she had been since that storm at sea.

"Abigail," he said, his eyes intent on her, "you are plucky and, evidently, still in command of your own brain after more than a week among your relatives. But this is pure insanity that you've come to Braden land, for whatever reason. We're all men here, and keeping an eye on Grace's reputation is bad enough. So if an apology from me for involving you at all in my struggles will keep you away from here in the future, I duly apologize."

That sort of contrition was not what she wanted to hear. Didn't that attitude also prove he didn't care for her one whit? It horrified her that she wanted him to care! Why did he always have to scramble her thinking and make her feel so jumbled?

"You mean I'm no use to you now that I'm on to you," she accused.

"Damn it, do I have to illustrate the dangers?" he demanded and reached out to drag her into his lap.

She went rigid, then started to struggle. He kissed her once, hard, and lifted them both to their feet before releasing her. Abigail stood, swaying a bit, wanting more, though she had fought him at first.

"You'll find worse than that from me—much worse, if you ever come back!" he insisted, wagging his finger at her. "Your precious reputation in ruins will be the least of what you'll get. Believe me, gossip and scandal await, enough to drive you away from New South Wales, let alone from my touch!"

He was warning her! she rejoiced. He thought enough of her to be honest and warn her! He was giving her a chance to run, to decide her own future as that dreadful Lord Northurst had not before he'd set out to ruin her with lies. But hadn't Duke always told the truth? After all, it was Grace's excited babbling to the *Gazette* that had implicated her. At any rate, she finally had to admit to herself she did care very much for him!

Stubbornly, she sat down again, her arms embracing her bent knees. "I know all about gossip and scandal, so you needn't warn me for that, Duke. I thought our friendship was worth the risk of Mrs. Gates's gossip aboard ship, and I think so here, even with bigger stakes on the line." She thought about telling him what Phillip was holding over her head to get her compliance, but she saved that for later and forged on. "I apologize for thinking the worst of you. I only did so because of what happened to me once with another man."

"*What* other man?" he snapped, sitting beside her again.

"A deceiver, who wanted my money. When I discovered his lies and cast him off, he ruined my reputation, causing me to hide in the country for years, like a nun."

She shared her story with Duke Braden while she stared down at her knees. She admitted all about Lord Northurst and told of losing Janet. When she was done, he touched her hand. She dared to glance at him. His face had gone soft and his eyes looked glazed.

"So you've carried that bastard's cruel handling of you around for years," he whispered, his voice rough. "No wonder you didn't want to share your past."

"It's over now."

"Is it? You are ready to risk being involved again? You must realize that the 'friendship' you say you offered truthfully to me is not all I want from you. I'm a stubborn, bitter, hungry man, Abigail. And not so pious I won't take something you offer that I want very badly. You'd better know before you ever set foot over here again that I want you as a woman and not just as a friend. Maybe, if we can stop fighting each other, we can manage a friendship, too. I see a glimmer of possibility. Only, *don't come back* unless you accept those terms."

She slowly pivoted to face him. Her cheeks were flushed; big butterflies beat their wings in her belly. During that last speech of his, she had forgotten to breathe. She let him help her up and, when he took her in his arms this time, she did not struggle with him or herself. She responded with a full heart and ready body to his crushing embrace and demanding kisses. Strength and energy flowed through her. She hugged him back, her arms locked around his narrow waist just as tightly as he held her. Her hat bumped back to dangle by its ribbons in the breeze. And when he finally set her back, he laughed and pointed at the dust his closeness had transferred to her dark blue riding skirt, bodice and cape.

"I'm afraid we'll have to brush you off," he said and began swiping at her thighs, stomach and breasts, right through her garments.

"Duke!" she protested and hit at his eager hands, but her voice was shaky and not angry. He pulled her hard against him again and tipped her chin up in one callused hand.

"'Duke,'" he whispered. "I like how easily you say that now. And if you set foot on Braden land again, I'm going to call you my Abigail, Miss Rosemont. No," he said and smiled down into her eyes, making her pulse pound. "I'm going to call you my Abby Rose. Because if you do return, it will only be because you want to be with me in every way, completely. And we will face whatever happens then, together. Tell me you understand."

*Abby. Abby Rose.* She had not told him in her story of Janet that Janet alone had called her Abby, and now—now there was no way she could not love and want Duke Braden, whatever the consequences! She had never dared hope for such openness with a man, free of pretense or games— or proper chaperons. Never, in her wildest dreams, could she have conjured up Duke Braden! She recalled again how a Gypsy fortune-teller had predicted she would wed a prince or a duke. It struck her as being so funny now, out here in the midst of the bush under a strong-scented gum tree with this dusty man.

"What is it?" he demanded. "What did I say that is cause for such mirth?"

"Nothing you said. Someday I'll tell you."

He lifted her up on her horse's back. "You didn't promise me you'll take my terms, but if you set foot on Braden land again, I'll know," he said. "And I'll find you. If I didn't have to send you back today, we'd seal this bargain another way besides a kiss." As he lifted H.M. up into the pouch, Duke's eyes met Abigail's and held them. Then he turned away and swung himself up on his horse. "You're certainly turning into a New South Wales woman with a vengeance," he said lightly. It was all he could manage to keep from hauling her off her horse again and kissing her senseless—for starters. "You've turned that horse into a 'roo with that pouch and H.M. riding high in it like a joey."

"I just hope you don't hunt 'roos, then," she responded as they turned their horses toward the Grange.

"Never shoot them and never eat them. Someday I'll tell you why."

"I recall you said because you've named some like pets."

"It's more than that," he told her and nodded toward the distant water hole and surrounding sandstone cliffs.

His face had gone hard again. She couldn't bear to leave him like that, but Abigail knew she had been gone too long already. Her eyes followed his harsh gaze. "Is it something about that water hole the Godfrey-Bennetts took away from your family, you mean?"

"Let's just leave it for now, leave it this way, Abby Rose," he said and reached over to tip her halfway to him for a peck of a kiss. "Remember, if you come back, we'll leave all our differences at the boundaries and just be—together. Go on now, and if Abigail never becomes my Abby Rose again, I'll understand."

Before she could answer, he smacked her mare's rump and sent the horse galloping off toward Grange land. When she was past the water hole at the sheep gate marked *GG* in bold black letters, she looked back. Only stark sky stared at her now from the horizon where he had just been.

## Chapter Six

Bundled up in the chill breeze of an early July morning, Abigail sat outside the orangery on the back portico to sketch the scene. Under a crisp, clear sky, the hazy Blue Mountains beckoned to her ink quills and to her happy heart. The range of peaks looked so far away from here, though Phillip had told her it was but thirty-two miles before the foothills began. More than longing to see them closer, Abigail was longing to escape the Grange and become Abby Rose over on the Dorset Downs today.

Two days ago, she had returned from being with Duke Braden in such a dreamy state she had hardly minded her cousin's scolding for riding so far out—for riding out at all. Abigail fully intended to go visiting the Bradens again. And she'd sketch a bit of the lovely water hole between the two estates, too, though she'd have to hide her drawings from her relatives.

The disputed water hole puzzled and intrigued her. There were things about it Duke and the Godfrey-Bennetts were not saying. Or perhaps, she mused, recalling the strange beliefs of Kulalang, the aborigine spirits still guarded the old spot; could that have been the eerie presence she had sensed there? But she was not afraid of the place any more than she would be riding over those Blue Mountains to see what lay beyond. She was, however, a bit afraid of facing Duke Braden on his own land on his own terms, though she yearned for that adventure more than any of the others she could envision here in this awesome country.

She had to admit, she still dreaded scandal. Just sharing her past with Duke had not really exorcised that fear. Duke and his world might be worth the risk, but last night she had suffered from that old nightmare where she stood naked in a room of fashionably attired people and they laughed and laughed like the kookaburra that guarded the water hole.

"Oh! Lottie, do be careful!" she cried as Charlotte dashed by with H.M. on a leash. Abigail grabbed for her inkwell and pens as the leash wrapped around the legs of her chair and jostled her wooden easel. "Lottie, you're going to make yet another mess!"

"It's your dog's fault for running so fast, not mine!" the little hoyden replied tartly and darted back around to free H.M.'s leash. The dog had obviously had quite enough of Lottie, too, and plopped at her mistress's cloak hem, refusing to go on.

"Come on, then, you little brat!" Lottie yelled at H.M., tugging at her leash. "Let's play some more!"

"H.M.'s played quite enough," Abigail told the child and put her hand on the leash to take it from her. "If you want a dog of your own, perhaps your father or grandfather will let you have one of the puppies from that new sheepdog litter and—"

"Dear me, no!" the familiar voice of Garnet Godfrey-Bennett behind her admonished. "I'll have none of those field-bred sheepdogs in my house! It's bad enough we've got government pensioners working for us who clomp around like barnyard gentlemen instead of proper servants. I really don't mind servants in the house who were simply forgers or pickpockets and know how to set silver or decant wine, but the sort we get here now—well, you understand. Oh, you draw quite well indeed, Abigail! Is pen-and-ink sketching popular at home for ladies now?"

Strange, Abigail thought again, that although she'd been living here since she was thirteen, England was still home to her cousin-in-law. She herself had thought of this new land as "home," at least for a while.

"Not really," Abigail admitted. "Riding's much more popular," she added, hoping to prepare the woman for her later request to ride again—ride right over to see Duke, though she'd have to pull some fine escape to do it. But it was obvious from the woman's animated expression that some announcement was forthcoming.

"What can I do now if Miss Abigail's dog won't play with me, and I can't have one from the sheep barn, Grandmother?" Lottie asked, posing in a preening pout.

The child knew full well some treat would fall her way, Abigail groused silently. She herself had the strangest sense of doom that she was going to be dragged from the Grange—and proximity to Duke Braden again—by another ladies' trip to "stylish" Sydney while Griffin Godfrey-Bennett stayed behind to oversee the plantation. The child obviously loved such trips: it was easier for her to ignore her tutor and she saw her father more. Besides, gifts from the Colonnade shops or the Emporium in Brickfield Hill would tumble her way like the falling bark these strange New South Wales trees lost instead of their leaves.

"We're going on a lovely week's trip to Sydney this afternoon," her cousin-in-law crowed and Lottie clapped her hands. "Now don't look glum, Abigail, as you may take your things and draw the hills and harbor there. We'll start a new rage for English ladies with your drawings! Mr. Godfrey-Bennett's coming Sunday, but I suppose Phillip will be about a bit—though we mustn't any of us keep him from his friends or business, except for dear Lottie, of course."

Lottie beamed. Even H.M. knew something was up and flopped her tail. It was obvious Mrs. Godfrey-Bennett had decided that letting Abigail near Phillip was worth the risk since Abigail showed little interest in him. Gazing westward, Abigail had to force herself to smile at the prospect of being away in big, busy Sydney, far from Duke Braden's idyllic little piece of land.

* * *

Grace Buck wrapped a hunk of mutton, a piece of cheese and a big slice of damper in a square of muslin and popped the package in her basket. She filled the small water jug with fresh water she drew from the well. Since Earl had not come in for the noontide meal when Duke and his father ate, she had decided to take his food to him. Duke had said Earl would be in soon enough, but he had ridden off the other way, and she knew Earl could be an impatient man.

Grace wiped her wet hands nervously on her apron before she left the protection of the fenced-in yard. She'd studied Earl Braden close-up and felt drawn to him. But she was afraid of him, too. He was quick to feel anger, especially toward Duke. He'd never yet turned his wrath on her, and she meant to see he wouldn't find a reason to. She liked directness in a man, though not a quick temper. Why, just yesterday, he and Duke had argued in the shearing barn loud enough for her to hear when she was passing. Earl had bellowed loud enough to make her drop her mending things all over the grass.

"You're just like the old man, you know that, Duke?"

"I'm nothing like him! He wants only to be left alone so he won't get into trouble ever again. I can understand that, but my provoking the Exclusives is the only way we're going to get anywhere around here!"

"Oh, yes, you're like him," Earl repeated. "He got seven years' transportation for complaining publicly about unjust conditions in Dorset after the Enclosure Acts there! Someone else burned that farm rick he got arrested for, but it was his speaking out got him punished. It's gonna be the same for you, damn your stubborn hide! Some idiot's gonna burn something in town or knock some Exclusive bastard like Godly-Bennett over the head, and they're all gonna blame you and lock you up! And where will Dad be then?"

"You're a fine one to talk!" Duke had shouted back. "Your solution is to *be* the rick burner, the one who knocks folks on the head. I've been telling you for years that won't work and you've got to learn to curb your fast mouth and faster fists! We've got to fight them on their own terms—fine talk, meetings with the governor and pushing Parliament in England.''

"That right, Duke? Hell, you'll turn into one of them if you're not careful! And we'll just see when we finally make our squatters' drive over the Blues whether we need my fists or your talk, won't we?''

They had evidently not come to blows as Grace had feared. She had seen them not an hour later, bent shoulder to shoulder over a sick ewe out by the shearing barn.

Now, she squared her shoulders and headed up the hill while the July wind buffeted her skirts. She gazed eastward, wondering how Miss Abigail was and how her private talk with Duke had gone two days ago when they rode off together in this very direction. Funny, but when she stood in the cook house door to watch them go, she had wished two things: that she could ride so pretty like Miss Abigail and that the man beside her on her horse would be Earl Braden, all calmed down and kind, and smiling just at her.

"Eh, Mistress Bucky, that basket for me?''

The shout behind Grace, as distant as it was, made her jump. She spun to see Earl, sitting on a rocky outcrop thirty feet away, apparently just surveying the sheep scattered below and beyond.

"If you're hungry, it's for you!'' she called to him, and her heart began a little dance inside her chest as she clambered up slowly and he came down partway to meet her. He extended his hand and helped her up to sit beside him. She took her time arranging her skirt while he pulled food from the basket. The wind whipped a strand of her hair loose from her bonnet, and she caught it and tried to shove it back in place.

"Real pretty view,'' she said.

"Especially right now,'' he replied.

He warmed her with his grin and dark brown eyes under brows lifted in unspoken challenge. "Never mind clever talk," she blurted, though she treasured his words and looks when he seemed all gentled like this.

"Duke's the one for clever talk," he said abruptly before he bit into some damper wrapped around the mutton. "It's a bit of a walk up here into this wind," he added. "You should have ridden out."

"Can't ride. Never had a horse, never did learn."

He downed a swig of well water. "Then I'd better teach you, Miss Bucky. That will be a good name for you if I teach you how to ride, even if I have to fight my big brother for the privilege."

"Oh, sure, I'd like to learn to ride ever so fine, but not if you fight Duke. And I'd like it if you'd just call me Grace."

"Grace it is, then, maybe Gracie if we get on real good. A term of endearment. Like Dad always called my mother Annie, and baby Margaret was Queenie before she died. But I've gotta admit, Grace suits you," he hurried on when he saw the confusion in her eyes at his rambling. "But then Bucky does, too."

"But it's Buck!"

"I know, but we've got to have some fun 'round here, don't we?" he asked and his eyes studied her lips while he wiped his own mouth with the back of his hand.

"Castle Keep and your family here's no fun?" she asked, twisting a handful of skirt hem around her index finger. "Why, I'd think I was in heaven if I had a family and great place like this."

He was both surprised and touched. Then he frowned and looked away. "My own great place is gonna be west of those Blues, Gracie. And I'm gonna get me a pensioner bride just like Dad got my ma at the Female Factory at Parramatta, and the hell with anyone who says I can't. I'm not ashamed of my parents being prisoners. I'll show them all, Duke included! Most freed folks are hardworking and law-abiding! My woman will make the best wife to go overlanding with me!"

Grace felt both entranced and deflated at that confession. "Your woman—you already got her picked out and just have to go get her at this factory?" she ventured.

"No, not quite that easy. It's gonna take applications and a formal ticket-of-leave. And probably a lot of ink spilled in the damned papers, which hang on everything the Bradens do because of Duke's goings-on. But as soon as we decide when we're heading over the Blues to squatters' heaven, I'll go fetch her. I'm glad you're here, to have a woman friend around for her. Meanwhile," he drawled, "about having some fun around here..."

He put the rest of his supper down to wipe his hands on his dusty brown trousers stuffed into riding boots. "Grace," he said, "Duke's gonna be out riding our boundaries all day to check the fences, then he's going to Sydney later for some sort of business. What say you and I surprise him by going in for a nice Sunday stroll tomorrow, too, maybe meet him there after church and all?"

She stopped twisting her skirt hem around her finger and dared to meet his eyes again. He was asking her to go to Sydney with him, just for the day and to church, so it would be proper enough. After all, he hadn't chosen his own Braden bride yet.

"It would be our surprise for Duke, you mean?" she asked, smiling shyly. When Earl was so sweet like this, she would just about promise him anything, even if he was planning to wed some convict girl from some wretched place called the Female Factory.

He nodded, his gaze dropping from her wide, dark-fringed eyes, to her pursed lips, to her full breasts; the sight of her just about shattered his hard-won control around this desirable woman. But he'd be damned if such temptation was going to make him change his mind about getting a Factory bride to defy Duke, Dad and the whole of Sydney!

"It will be our surprise for Duke," he told her solemnly.

"I'd love to do it!"

"Me, too."

And he leaned forward to drop a quick kiss on her mouth before either of them knew it would happen, just as if she'd asked him to.

In Sydney on Sunday, Abigail dressed in her English best, more to please her hosts than herself. Her sky-blue shoulder cape sloped to the puffed sleeves of her gown. As she walked her fully belled scalloped skirts printed with sprigs of roses on pale blue satin swayed gracefully. Though she wore gloves and a broad-brimmed, pleated silk bonnet with blue streamers and white feathers to shade her face, she also carried a rose-hued fringed parasol.

She and the Godfrey-Bennetts attended church in the private, brass-plated family pew at fashionable St. James's in Hyde Park. Afterward, she strolled on Phillip's arm amid the elegant crowds, while Griffin Godfrey-Bennett, who had come with them yesterday after all, was dragged along by the prancing Lottie. Much to Garnet Godfrey-Bennett's dismay, she had come down with one of her vaporish headaches this morning and kept to her room all day. To Abigail's relief she was temporarily delivered from the older woman's close scrutiny when Abigail and her son were together.

In Georgian grandeur, St. James's Church and Hyde Park Barracks faced each other across Queen Street and across the sweep of lawn where everyone paraded after church. Griffin and Phillip Godfrey-Bennett greeted numerous friends and, with Abigail, slowly promenaded past the barracks, which had been built by convicts and still housed the unspeakable same. Indeed, at this very moment a long line of transportees approached, being marched back from their own place of worship at St. Phillip's on Church Street.

Seeing the group of shuffling, gray-garbed men, some fine folk turned away. A few stared. Others walked in the opposite direction. Abigail's escorts hustled her and little Lottie clear across the road to a grassy, treed area called the Government Domain.

"We won't go far here," Griffin began nervously.

"And we won't tell Mother. It's a secret, do you hear me, Lottie?" Phillip called back over his shoulder to his lively daughter.

"But we thought, Phillip and I," her cousin went on, "it would be a sound lesson to you, Abigail, to see what elements might take over this town and this land if we don't keep up proper barriers. Just glance about a bit, and you'll see what I mean!"

While Lottie actually squealed and pointed, Abigail just looked, wide-eyed. But her escorts would have been shocked and appalled to know, she thought, as she surveyed these new surroundings, that the people did not repel her at all. Rather, they intrigued her.

A rich, variegated stew of exotic people stirred around Abigail on the Government Domain, with the thick undergrowth of the bush crowding in just beyond the clipped, rolled grass. "Elements from the interior beyond the Blue Mountains," as Phillip put it, stood or sat about looking like Robinson Crusoe with long, unruly beards and mustaches, woven cabbage tree hats and pipe stems or pieces of damper bread in their mouths.

"The rabble don't know a proper top hat exists," Phillip groused and settled his more firmly on his fashionably trimmed hair. He spoke without removing his cheroot from his mouth.

"Only squatters or worse eat that wretched, yeastless damper, like other native foods," her elder cousin informed her with a sniff while he paused to unscrew his silver flask to sip his Bengali India rum.

Abigail's thoughts jumped to Grace Buck baking damper for the Bradens. She had thought it tasty enough, though she hadn't felt like eating, all tied up inside waiting for Duke that day. Her mind drifted: while she was trapped here in Sydney, was he now waiting impatiently for her to return to the boundary of Braden land to be with her on his terms? How she wished there was some way they could communicate! And was Grace still stealing glances at Earl while poor Squire recalled that "nice puppy" who had visited?

"O-o-h, look, Father," Lottie's squeals interrupted Abigail's musings. "Whatever is that funny-looking dark man with the wild hair?"

"Don't know and don't want to, Lottie," replied Phillip to the girl's loud question. "Another bit of flotsam blown in from Tahiti or Fiji, I suppose. Seen enough to get our point about the dangers of a so-called free society, Abigail?" he added, and he tucked her arm in against his ribs again.

But it was Abigail's turn to gawk at someone. Surely that could not be Earl Braden coming toward them with Grace Buck on his arm! She squinted into the colorful crowd for Duke, but with mingled relief and regret, did not see him anywhere.

"Miss Abigail! Hello, it's Grace!" came to her ears. Abigail's heart banged at the thought Grace or Earl might give away that she had been to see them at Castle Keep. Her little entourage stopped and stared in shock to think someone in this place could be addressing one of them. Then Abigail heard Phillip curse under his breath as he evidently recognized Earl Braden.

"Grace, so good to see you after *all* this time!" Abigail cried and gave Grace a hearty hug as well as a little warning squeeze.

"Oh, yes, right. And this here's Mr. Earl Braden, what's a neighbor of yours in the Parramatta Valley, so's I hear," Grace told them with a smile.

Abigail was touched to see Grace dressed in her Sunday best, including the white kid gloves she had given her for a wedding that had never taken place. Abigail dared to meet Earl's blunt stare during stilted introductions made by Phillip, undoubtedly to impress her. She held her breath. Would Earl give her away because he hated her cousins so?

"Bit out of your element even here, aren't you, Braden?" Phillip inquired frostily as soon as the proprieties were over. He tossed his cigar away and blew a ring of smoke at Earl.

"Bit out of yours over here with the folk who really work for a living, aren't you?" Earl challenged back with a swipe at the air that broke the ring.

Both men looked frozen; neither moved as Grace clung to Earl's arm and Abigail to Phillip's again. Mr. Godfrey-Bennett pulled back Lottie a few steps.

"Come on then, Earl," Grace coaxed. "So nice to see you again, Miss Abigail!"

Earl didn't budge. His face just got a bit ruddier as Phillip's went even paler. Phillip tap-tapped his walking stick in one palm as if to threaten Earl with a beating, while Earl did not blink an eye.

"We're over here to show our guest whom *not* to mingle with," Phillip dared. "And that, of course, includes your bothersome brother, Braden."

"Does it now?" Earl replied and flexed his fists. Grace tried another tug and then stepped back nervously, turning her head away to scan the area. A small crowd of the curious had gathered at this obvious confrontation of adversaries. The Bradens and the Godfrey-Bennetts were well-known as figureheads of the opposing sides of the well-publicized struggles in town. And those who knew nothing of the feud were willing enough to be entertained by a free show.

Abigail tried to diffuse the explosive situation. "Please, Phillip, let's just walk back to Hyde Park! I've seen enough now."

"Come on, son, no Braden's worth sullying one's frock coat for," Griffin put in. "This one, as I recall, fights with those mutton-chop fists instead of lies and tricks like his brother—"

Grace squealed and waved to someone to keep Earl from launching himself against both men. Abigail jerked her head around to see. Duke! Oh, yes! Oh, no! Duke here, hurrying toward them, looking as angry as she had ever seen him. She dropped Phillip's arm as if it were a red-hot poker.

"What sort of double-dealing is this?" Duke demanded of his brother, but his glare stabbed Abigail. He wore a top hat and looked so very different in it, though his face was as bronze as ever. "Is this the little surprise you sent for me to see, Earl?"

"I meant it to be just Grace and me, but the stakes have just gone up," Earl told him, without changing his stiff I-dare-you stance before Phillip.

"Indeed, with Lady Abigail Rosemont on Phillip God-frey-Bennett's arm," Duke began bitterly as he shouldered the fuming Earl back a step and made himself a barrier between the two men. "I see how you've decided to do things now!" he accused, his eyes on Phillip now.

But Abigail felt Duke's words slap her across the face. Though the others assumed he spoke to his brother or even to Phillip, it was obvious to her whom his words were meant for. He implied she'd chosen Phillip and Sydney over him and another visit to Dorset Downs. He thought she'd decided to cast her lot with the Exclusives' world instead of his own. He was insisting she had rejected him!

"Look, Mr. Braden, and the other Mr. Braden, too," she began with a placating sweep of her arm, "it is all an unfortunate accident we even met at all here, and—"

"You bet it is!" Duke cut her off, and she knew he meant to reject her in turn.

Phillip and his father stepped forward to face Duke and Earl. The crowd grew larger, murmuring, pressing closer. Grace wrung her kid gloves as if they were someone's neck, and the distraught Abigail tugged the curious Lottie several steps farther away. Then what happened was even worse than the fisticuffs she feared were coming.

"Say," a burly man in the crowd cried out and pushed his way forward. "Young woman," he addressed Grace, "aren't you one of Braden's brides? And you were the one walked in here on Duke Braden's brother's arm, aren't you? May I ask if you've been with the Bradens, for we at the *Gazette* were never able to ascertain where you ended up. Am I to assume," he went on, "that Duke Braden arranged for his brother to—ah, have you? Not wed, are you, as I could not find your banns read in church like the other five women, and—''

"Get Grace out of here, Earl!" Duke ordered. Amazingly, Earl obeyed, though he elbowed Phillip in passing and almost bounced the *Gazette* reporter on his ample rear.

"It's true, isn't it?" the dauntless *Gazette* reporter asked, addressing Duke now. When Duke turned away, the man went after Abigail. "Lady Abigail, perhaps a brief statement from you would clear all this up. On the voyage over, did you ever hear that Mr. Braden had ulterior designs on any of these so-called free female immigrants for his own purposes—or those of his family?"

"Certainly not, sir!" Abigail managed before Phillip pulled her away with Lottie clinging to her other hand. Phillip looked furious. But at least he was rescuing her from the *Gazette* and from Duke's murderous expression—aimed right at her. Behind them, Griffin Godfrey-Bennett spoke brusquely to the reporter, who immediately disappeared, and her cousin hurried along behind her and Phillip. All this time, the crowd continued to buzz.

Abigail felt as if she were caught in her nightmare once again. None of this was her fault! Now Duke had berated and blamed her—though perhaps no one else knew it. It was his own brother and Grace who had caused all this mess! Surely Duke would discover, if he just asked Earl or Grace, that she had been in on none of the planning of Earl's so-called surprise!

She forced herself to breathe more slowly while Phillip hustled her along until they had crossed into tree-lined Hyde Park again. They waited there for his father to catch up to them.

"Do I have to keep *all* this a secret from Grandmother?" Lottie piped up. "The funny way those people dressed, and the way you almost got in a fight, too?"

"Yes! A secret!" Phillip roared down to silence the girl.

*Secrets*. Abigail had to keep it a secret that Phillip had knowledge of her relationship on board ship with Duke

Braden. She had to keep it a secret she longed to be with Duke. That probably didn't matter now anyway. She felt stunned and hurt. What if Duke thought she was trying to make him jealous with Phillip? What if he thought she really desired Phillip? All she wanted to do was run back there to explain to him—back there, across another of this colony's imaginary lines that divided people from one another as solidly as the Blue Mountain barrier divided owned land from open land!

They walked across the park toward their waiting carriage. She was so preoccupied with her own turmoil that at first she did not realize the look in Phillip's eyes had changed. He was no longer angry; his light brown eyes blazed with desire now. When his arm crept tightly around her corseted waist, she was jolted to her senses. She was so surprised by the raw lust on his face that she tripped, and he halted to steady her.

"No, don't, I'm fine, really, Phillip."

"Please, my pleasure!"

While Lottie skipped ahead, bargaining with her grandfather for sweets to keep her from telling her grandmother all she knew, Phillip's heated gaze raked Abigail. She halted and turned to face him down.

"I'm sorry about all that back there, but it was obviously no one's fault...." she said, but her voice quavered and began to fade. "Why are you looking at me that way?"

"You care for that Braden bastard, the one with a brain as well as fists, don't you, dear coz?" he demanded.

"Please, Phillip, don't try to make some shipboard interest a major accusation!"

"And he wants you," he went on, his features stretched taut on his smug face. "I could see it, feel it!"

"That's entirely ridiculous!"

"Yes, it is, but that's what's so damned exciting!" They began to walk side by side.

Was it so obvious then? That terrified Abigail as much as did Phillip's correct deduction.

"And you're even willing to lie to hide it," he went on. "Or don't you even realize it yourself? You know, Abigail, I'm starting to think I sold my silence to you a bit cheaply. Such passion lurking in those lovely hazel eyes of yours, just like this." A match he had hidden in his hand flared at the scratch of his thumbnail. She jumped back. He held it between them for a moment before he tossed it down and stamped it out.

"You know," he said, speaking more slowly now, "maybe Father's right. You and I should see more of each other, and I should spend less time with my friends here in town. Such feelings as you're showing should not go wasted and, with a bastard like that, they're going to be."

"Phillip," she protested, "we have a deal for your silence, and we're sticking to it! Unless you've changed your mind to wed against your mother's wishes," she dared.

"Hardly. Though things change, you know. You're so much deeper than you seemed at first, dear coz, and I'd like to plumb those lovely depths!"

Her first instinct was to slap him. But how would she explain herself to his father? She wanted no more upheaval today! She only wanted to find a way to proclaim her innocence to Duke and to escape this new predicament with Phillip! She felt trapped in these subtle wars raging in Sydney and in the Godfrey-Bennett family. She might be able to set Phillip back by asking his mother to become a stricter watchdog. If worse came to worst, and he tried to force her, she could admit to his parents the truth of her relationship with Duke Braden. That might weaken Phillip's power over her, but it would no doubt as good as make her a prisoner at the Grange. Then how would she ever slip away to visit Duke again?

"I say, Abigail, my dear." Mr. Godfrey-Bennett's voice rang out. "You didn't hear me. I said we'd best make a pact not to worsen Mrs. Godfrey-Bennett's head pain with word of any of this. What say?"

"Oh, yes, just a most unfortunate incident," she managed as Phillip helped her climb up into the carriage, his

hands lingering on her waist. Inside, on the wide leather
seat, he sat much too close, wedging her in the corner and
pressing his thigh against hers until she jammed the molded
tip of her parasol pointedly between them.

Duke finally caught up with Earl and Grace in the Botanical Gardens overlooking the sea. Despite the chill of the
season, the bottlebrush and wattles were in bloom, mingling exotic scents with the tang of salt air. Duke sat on the
other end of the secluded wooden bench where Earl sat, with
Grace wedged between them.

"You and your damned surprise!" Duke began, leaning
around her to face Earl. "You've probably ruined Grace's
stay with us as well as endangered my chance to sponsor
bringing more brides over after this next batch!"

"You mean I can't stay at your place anymore?" Grace
cried.

"She's staying, no matter what they or you say!" Earl
responded and jumped to his feet to lean over Duke, his
hand pressed to his brother's shoulder to emphasize his
words. "She stays no matter what the bastards do! Actually, I'm planning to escort her to a front pew in St.
James's next week and take her to the governor's birthday
ball! *That* will get their attention—since you can't!"

"Oh! Really, do you mean it? The governor's ball?"
Grace cried, but Earl and Duke ignored her.

"You like to rile these Exclusives," Earl accused Duke,
"but only your way! It takes you so long to get anywhere,
and you keep putting off our overlanding trip! Bet I'll get
the bastards' attention one hell of a lot faster and leave us
free to go!"

Duke leaped to his feet. They circled halfway around each
other as if they would take up the fight they had escaped
earlier. "Get their attention?" Duke demanded. "You'd
also get their opinion you're just some no-account blow-
hard to arrest or ignore. I fight them in public, legally, logically."

"Logically!" Earl snorted, and pushed Duke in the chest. "Forget logic in this lousy world and fight back with everything you've got! At least, I see you've forgotten logic when it comes to that little red-haired filly. I have never seen you lose your temper at all over a woman—"

"That's it!" Duke roared and shoved Earl so hard he did a backward somersault over the bench, just missing Grace.

Grace jumped up and backed away, her hands pressed to her face, her eyes wide with fear they would tear each other apart. "Please don't fight—please! You two—you're really on the same side, aren't you?"

Earl quickly got to his feet and vaulted over the bench to grab Duke's lapels. Duke's arms came up to shove him back. But the brothers stood locked like that, nose to nose, while Grace's question hung in the air. Then Earl loosed Duke, and Duke stepped back. Grace saw she was biting the expensive gloves that Abigail had given her for happy times. Now, she might have to leave Duke Braden's protection just because she had wanted to please Earl.

"Where will I go if I have to leave, Mr. Braden?" she asked Duke, as he brushed himself off and retrieved his top hat. "What if that rough man at the wharf who wanted me still does and—"

"You won't have to leave until we find you a good husband, Grace," Duke promised as he came over to offer his arm. "One who will demonstrate good sense and a civilized demeanor before you at all times," he said with a level glare at Earl. It struck Duke that his hotheaded brother looked humbled for the first time since Mother and Queenie died.

"I said I'd like to take her to the governor's ball, if she'll go," Earl said, but he stood where he was with his arms crossed against his chest.

"Perhaps she'll consider it," Duke countered.

"Why don't you take Miss English Exclusive to the ball, and eat a few of your own words?" Earl dared.

"Don't be absurd, and get Grace home safely," Duke spit out and transferred Grace's hand to Earl's arm before he turned away.

Duke jammed his top hat back on—he hated it and only wore it when he had to look the part of a proper spokesman—and started at a good clip toward the edge of the hill above Farm Cove. Breathing more easily now, he gazed down into the distant swirl of gray-blue sea as it crashed on sand and rocks.

Earl was right, damn him. He did lose all logic when Abigail was involved, and he could have shoved Phillip Godly-Bennett's teeth down his throat today in front of them all for so much as touching her. He'd never forget that day Phillip had picked off the 'roo he and Kulalang had been nursing at the water hole.

Phillip Godfrey-Bennett, the self-indulgent, pampered heir to the vast fortune—and to the water hole that was sacred land to the aborigines—had killed that kangaroo for more than one reason, Duke knew. He had done it to amuse himself and to impress the four Grange men with him that day, to show Duke and Kulalang that they were trespassing, to show them his utter disdain for what they valued, to let them know he would just as soon have put a bullet in them. Several Bandajong had been shot like prey in the bush there before, and the survivors hiding in elevated caves had said the "hunter" was Phillip.

The bastard's words still reverberated in Duke's brain even after ten years: "See, boys. I could have killed the two of you also and not blinked an eye in remorse," he had bellowed at them. "But it amuses me to see you staring down not only *my* gun barrel but all the other guns of the government that's going to take all your land sooner or later. You stupid, savage Bandajongs are doomed—translate to him what I said, Braden! And you stupid, savage Bradens are just as doomed, because both here and anywhere, the Godfrey-Bennetts will take your land and run you into the dirt where you tainted convict-bred Currency come from!"

His brutal laugh had echoed off the walls of the cliffs over the dreamtime spirit home of the Bandajong. Kulalang had muttered something dire in his language. They had both stood there, not moving under the glint of Phillip's gun barrel until he turned and rode off with his men.

From that moment, Duke Braden had personally detested Phillip as if all he hated about the Exclusives were centered in one man. Phillip was a lazy clod who did not even value overseeing his father's fine land; Duke and Earl had broken their backs to use each acre of Squire's allotment to them, even while they longed to go overland across the Blues on their own. In defiant protest against the hated landowning system, Earl had vowed to wed a Factory lass as his father had.

Duke, the elder, had made a vow to himself that day at the water hole. He would fight not only the Exclusives' unjust beliefs, but specifically the Godfrey-Bennetts and their ilk. He'd fight Phillip to the death if he had to, but he'd also fight their *proper* way of running the Bradens into the dirt where they tried to bury everyone else.

He'd studied like a man obsessed under the tutelage of Squire's friend from prison who came to stay with them until he could earn his passage back to England. Transported seven years for forging a private library permit in Liverpool, James Mansfield was a learned man, an ex-tutor who'd fallen on hard times. There were no books for Duke to learn from; if Squire could have afforded them, he'd not have thought them worth Duke's time or his hard-earned coins. But having taught literature, mathematics, common law, even mythology, James Mansfield was a walking lesson book. He imparted what he knew while he worked beside young Duke; before the fireplace or camp fires at night he taught Duke to read and write. In the six years it took James to earn his fare home by herding at Dorset Downs, Duke learned almost all James knew. James Mansfield was Duke's spiritual father every bit as much as Squire Braden was his physical one.

Through it all, neither Squire nor Earl had wanted any part of the fancy learning Duke thrived on. Later, when Duke spoke out for Currency causes and got some backing, he bought books of his own both in Sydney and in London. He read them, then passed them on so others would learn. Duke had even seen his old mentor James Mansfield in England last time he was there, though the poor wretch had found his family had moved away and he'd never been trusted with another teaching job there after being "sent south." But James's heritage to Duke lived on as the younger man sought to change things for anyone the Exclusives cheated and hated. Duke Braden tried to fight them with their own polished, well-honed tools of oratory and proper connections. Yet, when it came to Phillip Godfrey-Bennett, he could almost have tossed it all aside to sink to the depths of Earl's vengeful violence.

And now he was letting that Exclusive woman on Phillip's arm ruin everything. Earl was so right. He had lost his control, his logic, strayed from his path when Abigail Rosemont had come into his life.

Suddenly he was glad she was probably never coming back to tempt him on his own land again. She had not come the three days he had ridden the boundaries and waited like a besotted fool for her. She had come, instead, to town on his arch-enemy's arm. Duke cursed and kicked a rock over the cliff with his boot, watching it tumble to the sea below.

"Just as well," he spit out as if to lecture himself the stern way James Mansfield used to. He squared his shoulders. "It would all have backfired, worse than Earl's little surprise today. That woman and I—fire and powder together, so just as well. Goodbye to her and damned good riddance!"

He turned away and strode quickly back into the gardens.

# *Chapter Seven*

On their first day back from Sydney, Phillip pinned Abigail against the wall in a back corridor at the Grange. "I don't care for the way you've been avoiding me, dear coz!" he insisted. "Just one sweet kiss, and I'll let you go."

She tried to shove him away, but he leaned closer to press her against the wall. She turned her face over her shoulder to keep his lips from touching hers. He reeked of tobacco smoke.

"Let me pass! Remove yourself this instant, or I shall summon help!"

She had been on her way to visit the schoolroom just down the hall when Phillip as good as ambushed her. Reluctantly, he loosed her, realizing a cry might bring Lottie and her elderly tutor out into the hall. But he still hemmed Abigail in by leaning a palm on either side of her head, his stocky body hovering inches from hers. Gilt-framed oils of English fox hunts lined the dark green curve of hall where he'd trapped her.

Because Mrs. Godfrey-Bennett was increasingly debilitated by headaches, the ladies and Phillip had stayed a full week at the Sydney town house. Playing cat and mouse with Phillip had driven Abigail mad with cabin fever, worse than being stuck in that small cubby at sea. She had found respite from his advances only by keeping to her room. But with her hostess ailing and people paying calls, she had not in good conscience been able to remain there all the time.

So, to keep Phillip at bay as well as aid her cousin-in-law, Abigail had spent much time visiting the darkened, silent sickroom, or keeping Lottie about as an unwitting chaperon. Soon that, too, had driven Abigail batty, unless she was just sitting in on the little minx's lessons, as she had intended to this morning.

They had returned to the Grange after an article on Grace Buck had appeared in the *Gazette*. The article itself did not mention Abigail or the Godfrey-Bennetts, since Griffin had obviously silenced the reporter concerning their part in the incident after church. But Phillip had cornered Abigail to tell her in his most sickeningly solicitous tones that he knew his ill mother would hear it all too soon and be distraught about Abigail. Someone would come and read her the article and tell her all the rest that was rampant gossip in Sydney.

Even worse, she thought, the article emphasized Duke's part in what had happened. He had ordered his brother to hustle the young woman away and refused to explain why she was living at a "place teeming with Currency farmhands and sheep herders" when she was to have been properly wed. As for the Godfrey-Bennetts or their English guest being present when this "surprising public discovery" took place, Mr. Godfrey-Bennett's power had prevailed. There was no mention of Phillip's or Griffin's almost coming to blows with those "pugnacious personalities, the Braden brothers" nor of Abigail's hearty denial that Duke had any personal designs on any of the brides.

Back at the Grange, Abigail felt even more imprisoned by Phillip's avid attentions. She wanted to ride over to Dorset Downs to explain to Duke her innocence in the confrontation that had bred the unfair public comments. But now, when she'd thought Phillip was returning to Sydney and she would be free to visit Duke, Phillip had cornered her again.

"Come on, pretty coz, just a quick, quiet little kiss," he whispered. "No reason for Mother, ill as she is, to have to see the article or know all about what *really* happened." He dipped toward her and she knocked one stiffly propped arm away to duck under it. But he had one of her wrists, then the other, in a steady grip to draw her closer.

"I'll call and Lottie will hear, Phillip!" she threatened, her voice rising. "And you know your mother can't abide upsets and loud noises! I shall tell her everything! Everything, even if it means I must move to Sydney by myself!"

That drew him up short. He looked annoyed at first, but then the lechery that stained his face whenever she stood up to him glittered in his dark brown eyes. He let her go, though he still blocked her from the narrowed curve of the hall that led to the schoolroom.

"I say, Abigail, don't fuss so," he cajoled. "Young women of your rank and breed don't live alone in Sydney or anywhere else without proper sponsors and chaperons as you have here."

"I hope you don't include yourself in that august category!" she replied huffily and brushed off her sleeves as if he'd ruined them. "Besides, I lived alone in England after Grandfather died as head of my own household with only my maid as companion. I could find someone in town, I wager."

"Not with the associations you've made from the other side of the fence! Still, you and I could have a merry time there without Mother's servant spies about, but your reputation—"

"Which you obviously care not one bit for since—"

"That's not true, my dear," he went on, trying to control both his lust and his temper. He made a show of pulling down his dark waistcoat and his shirt cuffs under his riding coat sleeves. "If I have been flirting a bit too heavy-handedly, I apologize."

At those words, her mind drifted to Duke. He had apologized to keep her from risking her reputation by coming to Dorset Downs. Yet he had wanted her to return there on his terms—at least before the trouble in Sydney last week.

Abigail dragged herself back to reality as Phillip took one of her hands in both of his, his face so falsely sincere and concerned.

"And please dismiss the notion that I really believe you and Duke Braden have anything in common. It's you and I who could build a beautiful world here together if we so desired. I swear, I'll accuse you no more about that man. I realize I was sorely mistaken."

Abigail studied his face, almost wanting to believe him. He was quite right about the inappropriateness of her living alone in Sydney. Back in England it had caused talk; here in this restrictive community, it would be disastrous enough to cause her expulsion from society—Exclusive society. Her thoughts drifted off again. She would have to join the Currency, if they'd have her. She pondered that a moment, wondering how things would work out for her and Duke then. But Phillip, drat him, was right that she and Duke had nothing in common—did they?

"Upon my word, Abigail, are you even listening to me bare my heart?"

"Oh, yes. I would like to accept your apology," she managed, "and your offer of friendship—strictly friendship. And to believe," she went on, pulling her hand back and holding it palm up to stay his next words, "that we can go on with you never again mentioning to anyone things you once threatened to hold over my head. Do we have a deal on that, sir?"

"If you would not be so distant and devious to avoid me."

"I said we can be friends."

"And if you would not call me 'sir,' but rather 'my dearest Phillip.'"

He was toying with her again as a hound might with a cornered animal. "'Dear coz,' I believe, is what you call me," she replied, as icily as she could. "That will have to do."

"Then, dear coz, to seal our new bargain, you will walk with me after dinner, will you not? A stroll around the grounds, the two of us, without Lottie hanging on?"

"But if you do anything out of order, I shall tell your mother, her headaches notwithstanding," she challenged.

"But if you tell her I've become—shall we say, avidly interested in my sweet cousin, she'll be out of that bed and make this place a prison for you."

"For you too, I've no doubt."

"I'll escape. I always have. I'd die before I'd ever be imprisoned."

"Then, Phillip," she said, and dared to put her hand briefly on his arm before she drew it back, "why can you not feel more sympathy for those who are or have been imprisoned? Some, I take it, for rather minor offenses. And for their children who have not done one thing but be born to—"

Their tenuous truce exploded. He pushed her back against the wall, his hands hard on her shoulders, his pale face stained beet-red.

"It's completely different, you little fool! They've been imprisoned *because* they bear an inherent moral stain, not the other way 'round! They need complete control and constant watching, not your sugary sympathy! I swear, association with that bas—with Duke Braden and his brides—has warped your brain! And I tell you, if I ever hear you've so much as spoken with him again, I'll—"

He halted. He shook his head and his blond hair bounced on his high forehead. For a moment he had seemed to be another man, a hateful, horrid ranter. Her heart pounded as he muttered another apology and stepped back to free her. He cleared his throat and straightened his cravat. He was fighting for control, she thought, planning his next move. And she must do that, too. Even if he appeared to be on her side, Phillip was too prejudiced and proud to really be her ally unless her plans perfectly suited his.

"I didn't mean to get carried away, my dear," he told her. "It's just that Duke Braden and I go back a long way in a sort of unspoken competition, opposing heirs to two neighboring lands so to speak, you see."

She knew it was much more than that. Like the mysterious water hole between the properties, there was a great deal she could not yet understand. It only made her more con-

vinced she should ride out to Dorset Downs as soon as
Phillip left for Sydney this morning. He would never sus-
pect she would attempt such a thing after this confrontation they had been skirting for days. She felt freer already
when Phillip took two steps back and made a brief bow.

"We will no doubt have more to say to each other tonight on our stroll. Let's vow it will be on civil terms," he
told her. "I know you will not be willful or foolish enough
to involve Mother in our affairs, and I promise I shall not,
either. Until this evening, dear Abigail," he said and strode
off down the thickly carpeted hall toward his room, leaving
her standing there, staring narrow-eyed after him.

Just a few minutes later, Phillip Godfrey-Bennett went
out to the stables to mount his horse, saddled and waiting
for his hour's jaunt to Sydney. As was his practice, he would
depart with four Grange men who served to guard him from
bushrangers along the high road to town. He was planning
only a brief trip today, to see some friends and his mistress
Catty and be back at the Grange for dinner. He ordered his
men to hold up a minute and summoned one over to speak
with him alone after they both mounted.

"On our way out to the high road, I want you to double
right back here, George. I have another job for you today."

George, stalwart and slope-shouldered, was entirely ded-
icated to his master's heir. He simple nodded. Since Phillip
was sixteen, George had been a guard when "the young
master," or "boss" as he called him now, rode out on the
estate or to town.

"Lady Abigail has a passion," Phillip began to explain,
but paused at his choice of words, "a tendency, that is, to
ride out on her own. I don't want any harm to come to her.
But she'd not like it if she thought I didn't trust her. So if she
takes a stable horse at any time today, I want you to follow
and observe her for her own protection—secretly, at a distance, of course. And, when I return, report directly to me."

"You kin rest easy, boss. Fine young lady like that shouldn't be riding out. Not even on a well-staffed sheep run. With wild dingoes and all," the burly George told him.

"Exactly. Wild dingoes and 'roos. We take good care of them when we spot them, don't we, George?" Phillip asked. He patted the stock of his gun, slung through its leather straps behind his saddle before he spurred his mount away.

As Phillip led his men down the lane toward the Parramatta Road, memories taunted him of the day he could've—and should've—shot both Braden and that cursed black abo of his at the water hole where Grange sheep and men did not like to go. Abigail's obvious fascination with Braden and the fact she might have even met the abo aboard ship were trouble. While they'd been away in Sydney, the maid he'd had search her room here had turned up an aborigine carved weapon holder hidden under her mattress. It was a piece of rubbish she probably got from either Braden or that savage.

Yes, George was right she might be harmed by wild dogs—human ones who ran out of the bush and nipped and snapped at the heels of proper folks in power. That was Braden's way, especially these past few years. But now Phillip realized he'd been wrong to underestimate the bastard and his friends. Duke Braden had cultivated ties to the British Parliament and colonial Governor Bourke. He had a big Currency following and was importing new, so-called free immigrants whom he'd win to his ways. Obviously, the wretch was not just going to fade away. Worse, he had somehow snared Abigail's sympathies, if not her heart itself, to make her a potential traitor in their midst.

Phillip regretted he hadn't cleared Duke Braden off the face of New South Wales years ago with a good clean shot that he and his men could surely have covered up. Why, he could have thought Braden was another 'roo, standing so close to the one he was nursing, and, after all, he had been on Grange land. Now, soon, Phillip knew, he'd have to find another way. Especially if there was really anything be-

tween Braden and the free-spirited Abigail, whom he wanted
worse than he ever had his little Currency bitch Catty.

He might actually have to take Father's advice and get
involved for once. Only not with the boring business of
overseeing the smelly sheep and the Grange and the wool
trade, when lackeys could be hired to do all that dirty work.
No, Phillip had finally found his cause in life. He would
make his name and fortune by ridding the colony of Duke
Braden—and by possessing Abigail Rosemont. Indeed,
partly for her inheritance, but mostly because he was certain Duke Braden aspired to have her. Maybe Abigail's fortune was what Braden wanted his hands on, too. Phillip had
seen Braden eye her hotly as if he'd tear her up in little pieces
and devour each one, so Phillip judged Braden's passions
ran deeper than money, just as his own did now.

Phillip Godfrey-Bennett shifted in his saddle to watch
George pull away from the group and head back toward the
house. He shouted to his men and spurred his horse even
faster, to leave his guards temporarily in his dust. Imagine,
he thought, he had gone hard and ready for a woman just
thinking how he'd like to shoot Duke Braden right before
Abigail's eyes—and right before he showed her that her
bounty and her body would be his to plunder any way he
wanted!

Abigail rode out to the western boundary of Grange land.
She had her small drawing board, paper and pens in her
saddle pack. She had not brought H.M. along, although she
was obviously her pass to Braden land as far as Squire was
concerned. But the spaniel was out for a walk with the maid
and Abigail hadn't wanted to wait until they got back. The
moment Phillip and his men rode out, she had hurried into
the stables to request a mount.

The day was sunny and very warm for mid-July, though
Duke had told her how the seasons blurred here between the
Blue Mountains and the coast. The sun beat down pleasantly on her veiled bonnet and made her want to throw it off
to shake her curls loose. She rode faster than she would have

with H.M. in the side pouch, like a joey, as Duke had said. Why, oh, why, she scolded herself, did she always have to think of Duke Braden, however distant—and furious—he was with her?

Rather than riding around the cliffs cupping the water hole that had once belonged to Kulalang and his Bandajong tribe, she decided to ride through the area again as she approached Braden land. She paused to let the horse drink as she had before; it must be good water here despite the fact there was no source to be seen. Many of the holes here were fed by small rivers on their way down from the mountains to the Parramatta Valley, but not this one. Perhaps it glittered with rainwater from the heavens. It seemed self-contained, bottomless and so special.

Once again she felt the strange presence of something, someone here. The hair along the back of her neck prickled; gooseflesh rose on her arms. For one moment she actually thought she heard a baby wail in an eerie echo deep in the earth itself. She jerked her head around and stared up at the cliffs. Nothing. Probably just a distant kookaburra or even a dingo.

She was not really afraid. She was nervous, yes, very nervous, Abigail admitted to herself, but that was fear at the thought of facing Duke again. Despite the strange vibrations here, she liked this place the aborigines and Duke, too, must have valued once, which now seemed always deserted. She scanned the shadowy, pockmarked face of the reddish sandstone again, saw nothing and pulled her horse's head toward Braden land.

A burly, slope-shouldered man on a horse followed Abigail at a careful, hidden distance. When she paused, he paused. When she rode on, he did, too.

Three dark figures, a man and two women, one holding a baby, stirred from a shadowy cave on the high cliff face.

*"Warrang, balanda,"* one woman whispered to the man at her side in the cave's mouth. The baby was silent now.

The nearly naked man, resembling a skeleton with white paint on his copper skin, stepped toward the lip of the elevated cave and lifted his arm. The white man rode below to follow the white woman across the dreamtime place of the ancestors. The aborigine's arm cocked and launched a V-shaped wooden weapon, carved intricately from heavy mahogany. It hit the back of the man's head, neatly knocking him from his horse, but the force of the blow kept the weapon from returning to the hunter's hand. The boomerang skittered to a stop by the edge of the water and lay as still on the ground as did the man. The horse, scenting danger, ran off in the direction of the Grange.

Quick and surefooted as a wallaby, the aborigine hunter descended from his lofty sandstone perch and retrieved the boomerang. He drank a handful of the fresh, clear water that sustained his body and his soul. He looked up once at his cave and nodded in silent farewell. Then he scampered off in the direction of Braden land, but not in the same way the woman had gone.

Duke Braden sat on his horse, one knee crooked up in front of him, his elbow on his knee and his chin in his hand. He was staring at sheep, but seeing instead the assembled masses at the governor's birthday ball in Sydney next month. He was mentally revising the speech he'd like to make to them about New South Wales becoming one colony instead of two divided ones. But he'd probably never get his chance there, especially not after the latest attempt of the *Gazette* to cast aspersions on his integrity.

That was one reason he'd been careful with women before: so the Exclusives would have no stones to throw. Many of them were hypocrites, though, for Currency lasses were all the rage as Exclusive mistresses. He'd had a few passionate, lusty romances with pretty Currency lasses in town himself, but never a mistress or even one special sweetheart. And later, even when Dad had been after him and Earl to marry and give him grandchildren, he just hadn't had the time.

Then, in one simple delivery of the first bunch of Braden's brides, he'd turned his life upside down. He'd gotten romantically entangled with Lady Exclusive Abigail Rosemont, an English heiress. He'd gotten morally involved trying to protect Grace Buck from a brutal bridegroom—and from his own hot-tempered brother. Earl obviously wanted Grace in his bed, at least until he stubbornly found himself a Factory lass to marry.

Duke sighed and tried to force thoughts of the people he cared for from his mind; Abby Rose refused to budge. He pondered her entirely too much. He agonized over her especially at night when he craved only sleep, or thought he did until he found himself getting feverish and frustrated to the point he was tempted to ride over to the Grange after dark and—and actually abduct her!

"Damn them all!" Duke snapped, as if they all crowded in upon his brain right now.

He went back to planning what he would say to Governor Bourke when he met with him in a few days to urge him to speak out at his birthday gala on August 12. Duke was so preoccupied that at first he didn't even hear the strange breathy notes of Kulalang's signal.

Then it jolted him alert—the aborigine warning on the wind made by blowing through a torn leaf. It probably meant some of the Grange's men had ridden onto their land. He jammed both feet into his stirrups, then cocked his head to listen again. Yes, the sound came from up on that first outcrop overlooking the lay of the land.

"Jeffreys!" he yelled to the herder just down the way a bit. "Be right back!"

He picked his way through the sheep, carefully at first so they would not bolt or scatter. On the outskirts of the small herd, he urged his horse to a gallop up toward the outcrop, knowing Kulalang would appear from somewhere when he was close enough.

As Duke neared the top of the crest, a boomerang cut about ten yards ahead of him, looped and swung back to the hand that threw it. Duke reined in and waited for his friend as he emerged from the shadow of a stringybark tree just below the rocky outcrop.

"Sunset-hair woman come again," Kulalang told him and pointed northward. "And man behind her. Boomerang—" he lifted the weapon straight up "—did put man face in ground."

"He's not dead?"

Kulalang shook his head. "But man not touch sunset-hair woman, or him gone finish," he boasted proudly. "One of young boss mans, same man come day young boss shoot *malu*. Him face in ground," he repeated.

For as long as Duke had worked with Kulalang to teach him English—while Kulalang taught him some of his language, such as *malu* for kangaroo—the aborigine had steadfastly refused to call anyone by his or her name. So Abigail was sunset-hair woman; Phillip Godfrey-Bennett was young boss. Though Duke was allowed to call Kulalang and other tribal members by name, speaking names was taboo among the Bandajong. To their way of thinking it was just as impossible as that they should ever have to leave the sacred water hole tied to their *malu* totem. Occasionally over the years, Duke had had a little trouble understanding some of Kulalang's ways. But he understood quite enough of Kulalang's message now, and he galloped off in the direction his friend indicated the unsuspecting Abigail had ridden.

Abigail had meant to charge right down toward Castle Keep and demand that someone fetch Duke, but instead she halted on the rise of land where she had first beheld the Braden farm several weeks ago. More men were there today. They were funneling sheep toward some sort of narrow, board-lined run that led to a trough, to give them a bath. She unwound her veil and let her bonnet hang by its strings down her back as she had wanted to do all the way over. She was wondering which of those men might be Duke when she heard hoofbeats behind her and twisted around in her saddle. Her heart thundered in her throat. At the mere sight of Duke Braden so close, she froze right where she was.

"You've taken quite a chance to come back here!" he began when he reined in next to her, so close their knees almost touched.

"Once, you said I was invited."

"What if they had you followed?"

"Why do you ask?" she demanded, as all her rehearsed beginnings flew right out of her head. She looked back the way she'd come. "Did you see someone?"

"No."

"Well, then. I don't doubt you're just regretful I got past your border guards."

"My border guards are invisible to human eyes," he told her cryptically, "so don't worry about them. But you always have all the answers, don't you, Abby Rose, even when you don't really know the questions?"

Duke had meant to meet her with disdain and just toss her troublesome little tail off the Downs. But her passionate defiance made him feel as though he'd tumbled from his horse. He wanted her so badly in every way, he felt he could almost have dragged her into his embrace in the dust to kiss that prissy, pristine look right off her face! But he controlled himself as his carefully hooded eyes slowly surveyed every inch of her.

"More fine hospitality from the gentlemanly, illustrious Duke Braden, I see," she said, her voice dripping sarcasm she had not intended. It scared her how much she wanted him to just pull her into his arms on his horse, even though he was being such a nasty brute! She only meant to say she was sorry for the mess the other day and get away from here! But once again, the place and the man lured her to stay.

His devouring gaze both panicked and annoyed her. Was that the sort of look Phillip had so easily noticed? And was she, too, staring at this cold, rude man in much the same way? When Duke's taut lips moved to speak in that commanding tone again, she almost jumped straight out of her saddle.

"I think I'd best take you right back where you belong."

He reached for her reins but she slapped his hand away. He swore softly and reached for them again, though she'd left a long scratch on his wrist. He pulled the reins from her so she had to hang on to her horse's mane as he led her away from the hillside.

"If you want to fight me, I'm willing!" he yelled back over his shoulder. "But if you want it to be strictly physical between us, I'll win."

"Strictly physical? Strictly verbal is what I had in mind! And I don't need your scoldings or your threats, Duke Braden!" she insisted, bouncing along. "I came simply to tell you I had nothing to do with the fact your brother almost took on the Godfrey-Bennetts the other day! And to tell you I'm sorry the unfair implications about Grace and you got in the *Gazette.* You know, I was right from the beginning! If you'd just let me take her on as a companion, none of the insinuations about her reputation, and yours, would ever have hap—Duke!" she cried as he urged their horses to a harder gallop in the opposite direction from Grange land. "Duke! Stop this moment!"

He led them northward, toward the mountains. Then he slowed the pace so they could pick their way around and down into a tiny hidden glen. She heard the trickling of a small waterfall the minute he reined in and jumped down to lift her to him. Tall eucalyptus trees made a natural screen here by a small, clear pond speckled with sunlight. He slid her to the ground, her body slowly scraping his all the way down.

"Duke," she began. "I did not come here to argue—and most certainly not to take you up on those things you said before about meeting on new terms."

"That's fine," he said, though he spoke through nearly clenched teeth. "Besides, we're arguing, so I don't see any chance of new terms."

"But you said," she protested, shaken to her very core by the feel of his hard body so close to her softer one, "there would be a few times when we could be friends."

"Curse it, Abigail! Please tell me you only came here to berate me! To hit at me and scratch me! To throw my terms for our affair in my face! Please convince me you don't really want me too, or I swear I don't know what will become of us!"

His breath scalded her face and throat. He was so close, still holding her. His words, harshly spoken though they were, lured and caressed her. She knew he wanted her. He was afraid she would not fight him, and they would both tumble into—into something neither one could control.

The bottom half of her body pressed against his, thigh to thigh. Surely her legs were just shaking from the bouncing ride, she told herself. Looking up into his eyes, the color of that clear pond behind them, she thought she might drown right now, standing on dry land.

"I'm sorry if I hit or scratched—" she got out before his mouth descended.

They plunged together into a single, endless kiss. Her fingers wove through his thick hair. His hard yet gentle hands lifted her against him, then clamped her to him full length, like iron bands, first on her back under her short green cape, then around her waist. Then he cupped her bottom as if she could lean back in the sweet seat of his hands to savor the taste and touch of him forever.

His tongue ravaged, played, and she answered each challenge. When they both gasped for breath, he outlined her lips with the tip of his tongue, then he moved down to her arched throat, up around her earlobes and into the cup of her ear until she laughed with joyful pleasure. She returned the favor while his hands moved to her full breasts and cradled them carefully, then fervently.

Suddenly, he turned away to yank a rolled blanket from the pack behind his saddle. He walked her deeper into the grove of gums encircling the water's edge and flapped the blanket open on the ground. He unhooked the frogs of her cape; she shrugged it off. Hidden by an overhang of limbs, he pulled her down and sat beside her with his eager hands on the small buttons at the back of her gown.

"Oh, Duke. We can't!"

"We couldn't from the beginning, but we did!" he countered as her bodice gaped away in front. "Too late for us to ever stop now, my Abby Rose!"

## Chapter Eight

Duke speckled Abby's throat and the hollow between her collarbones with kisses: she had never felt such grandeur. Lying here next to him in the grass while the world spun by was wonderful! She gazed up dizzily: Duke's face looked taut; his hair was mussed. His lower lip trembled the slightest bit the way she did all over. Suddenly, she was helping him peel her gown down to her belted waist and loosen her corset ties and stays.

"I told you the first time we met," he said, his voice ragged, "you should not wear all that stuff."

She giggled as if he'd made the wildest joke, but it was the warm touch of his hands right through her cotton stockings that made her giddy now. She began to dot his hard jawline and the sinews of his neck with kisses while her skirts crept higher. He dared to untie garters and peel her stockings down. He ran his hands over her legs as if he were rubbing scented lotion into her skin. She asked him between kisses, "Mmm, what are you doing, taking my stockings off, too?"

"Maybe we're going swimming. I told you I'd teach you how to swim," he murmured, his head buried between her naked breasts. "You'll have to get all wet and kick these beautiful legs."

She felt the slightest rasp of his day's beard against her flesh and closed her eyes tightly to revel in that and each new sensation. Desperately, as she never had before, she wished she knew all about this sort of thing—exactly what was coming next and how to please him. He could not mean it about the swimming, she thought. They weren't going to swim in that water, really. They were only going to swim in each other's desire and love.

Love! Her eyes flew wide open when his hand stopped stroking to grasp the naked flesh of her thigh. In that same moment he had kissed his way to the tip of her breast, the nipple puckering against the slight breeze and the wet, insistent heat of his tongue. But none of that had jolted her as much as the realization that she loved this man. And not just because of what was happening. It was because she could not get him out of her mind and heart that she wanted him in her body, too. It was because she admired all he stood for and tried to do. It was the very essence of his exciting masculinity she wanted to tame and yet never tame.

"Oh, Duke!" she cried when his tongue began to flick and caress the pink tip of her breast.

His other hand stroked even farther up her bare thigh. She clamped her legs together reflexively, then slowly separated them for him. He was soon even closer to her very center, touching some place she had never imagined that—

"Oh, Duke!"

He settled harder against her thigh so she would realize that this was all real, that there was so much more yet to come. She was bold and yet naive, he thought, deeply touched. He was grateful that wretch who had betrayed her back in England had evidently not taken her this far or turned her against lovemaking.

Abby felt the thrust of his desire against her thigh. Slowly, deliberately, so he would think she really knew what came next, she pulled his shirttail from his heavy work trousers and spread her palms flat on the hard-ridged muscles of his naked lower back. His skin radiated heat.

Duke shifted his weight to his elbows on either side of her head. He knelt between her legs and stared down into her face. Then, taking his time as if to allow her to say no, he reached down to fumble with his trouser buttons. He pushed her knees apart to open her even more to him. The breeze stirred cool on the dampness at the juncture of her thighs where his skilled fingers had teased her until she'd been desperate for more. After he lowered his trousers, she felt the rasp of his hairy legs between her smooth ones.

Her breathing became quick and shallow while her senses grew more keen to everything around her: the pungent scent of eucalyptus, the splashing sounds, the cool grass and the rough texture of the woolen blanket under her buttocks and back.

"I desire you desperately, always have, sweetheart," he whispered. "I'm trying to keep my head, but I think we both want this. I'll be careful, but once we start, there's really no way back!"

She clung to him. "I don't want to go back, ever! Not to England, and not back to *them!*"

He lifted his head to gaze down, narrow-eyed. That wasn't exactly what he meant, and yet it was. He hesitated, actually afraid now to possess her. She was more to him than just a stiff, snide woman who had blossomed on board ship and come to full bloom in this raw land like a sunstruck morning glory. She was his Abby Rose and she moved him to his very soul.

But she did have to go back to *them,* or he'd have a battle on his hands that would ruin all his plans for a civil protest at the governor's birthday ball. She could never really be his, he mourned. Not as helpmeet and companion and wife throughout the struggles that lay ahead until he got what was right for the Currency she could be no part of. He was just endangering both their futures here. Yet if she wanted this and came to him, he could not hold back. Kissing her, pressing closer, he made his decision to love her now even though he lost her later.

Just before he fully possessed her, Duke was startled by a familiar sound. He froze, listening. The aborigine warning again? Surely not his imagining or the wind in the leaves above! He'd had no idea Kulalang had followed them, and wondered why he was warning them now.

"What is it?" she asked. She looked so dazed, so disappointed. He was almost tempted to take her quickly in case they never got this far again. Perhaps then he could rid his mind of her. But he could never take this woman that way. She deserved tenderness and care, a soft bed and a fine home and security— Stifling a curse of regret, he quickly swept her skirts down to cover her and rolled away to cover himself.

"Why did we stop? What did I do?" she asked.

He pulled her to a sitting position in the shelter of his arm and helped her tug her bodice closed. He struggled with buttons on her back while he explained hurriedly, "I hear Kulalang's danger signal. It was nothing you did wrong. You did everything just right to make me lose my head!"

He stood and walked stiffly from their shelter up the path a ways while Abigail scrambled to regarter her stockings and straighten her skirts. She stood, feeling almost dizzy, both sorry and yet strangely relieved they had stopped. She had wanted more, wanted him totally, and had been so swept away, so outside herself that she had not given one moment's thought to the consequences. She gave her skirts a final shake as she saw Kulalang, his half-naked body painted with white clay, emerge from a distant bush and speak to Duke near the horses. On shaky legs, she knelt to retrieve her bonnet and the blanket and joined them.

"Kulalang says the Bandajong men have started to gather for a *corroboree*," Duke told her. "That's a nighttime religious dance under a full moon to commune with the spirits of their totems—spirits of earth or animals where they believe each person gets his power. And he's afraid your being here so long and his knocking out the man following you—"

"His what? What man? Not Phillip, he's—"

"I don't want to even hear his name here!" Duke cut her off. "And we don't need his hair-trigger Grange garrison using you as an excuse to take target practice on the Bandajongs gathering at the water hole! I blame myself for not sending you right back."

"But you said before that you saw no man following me! If you knew, why did you allow me to—to let myself—get literally carried away—"

He took her elbow to turn her toward her horse, then boosted her and positioned her foot in the single sidesaddle stirrup. He pulled the blanket from her grip and heaved it over his horse's rump. "Let's just leave it that it was my mistake and it won't happen again. I'll make sure you get back without any further interference," he said tautly and mounted in one fluid movement.

Kulalang just nodded as if he knew full well what they had been doing, Abigail thought. She felt heat prickle her throat and cheeks again, and quickly retied her bonnet and positioned her veil. After all, maybe it was a good thing Kulalang had come along to stop them. She, too, had lost her head—if not quite completely her virginity—to a man who... Oh, heaven help her, to a man she had to admit she loved beyond all reason!

They rode out of the hidden valley and galloped back toward Grange land. Duke's face looked set and worried now, and she cursed him for being able to turn off his feelings—if he had any to match hers—so easily. Neither of them had spoken of love or a future. She felt so confused and afraid, but she could not bear it if they parted angry again. She had to admit she'd wanted him as badly as he had evidently wanted her.

"Are you going to let the Bandajong have their... collaborate at Castle Keep?" she said to break the unbearable silence between them.

He almost smiled at that as he sighted the water hole and its protective cliffs. "*Corroboree,* Abby Rose. No, it will be held here at *kuri kuri* in the dead of night. The aborigines name all their water holes, as they're even more precious than people. *Kuri kuri,* the name of this water hole, means home. It was home to them once. All of the Grange was, but especially this sacred source of life before the Godfrey-Bennetts took it from us and them."

"Duke, I'm sorry. But how can the tribe meet here when Grange men may come calling?"

"It's a terrible risk every time they do it, but it's life to them to be here and living death to stay away. So, they dance around fires under a full moon and make themselves perfect targets, and nothing I can say stops them. I've tried. I should never have told you, because in case something happens, I'd worry—"

"Not that I'd tell them at the Grange! I never would! I'm not really part of them even if I live among them, Duke. Less and less all the time. I'll prove that to you someday."

At the edge of the water hole called *kuri kuri,* Duke reined in and Abigail stopped, too. "What we almost did today, Abby Rose, proved enough to me about your sincere intentions. But intentions are not enough, and I don't want you hurt in the cross fire of this war. I have to put myself in the middle of it, but not you. That's why it was wrong that I wanted to make you mine today."

She pushed aside her veil to see him better. She was suddenly very afraid he was going to tell her it was over, that she would never see him again. "You're regretting what we did—almost did?" she asked.

Duke sighed and his big shoulders slumped. He turned to face her squarely, squinting into the afternoon sun. "I'm regretting it as thoroughly as I am that we didn't finish it and aren't starting it over again right this minute."

His gaze seared her, singed the air between them. She began to tremble with deep longing as if he touched her everywhere again, intimately.

He went on, "Each time you're here I know it should be the last time. It's best that you go back, and keep this place, as well as what we have shared, an eternal secret."

"But how can this place be a secret?" she asked and craned her neck to look around. She sounded as shaky as she felt. She would feel terrible if anything more happened to Kulalang and his people. "Everyone at the Grange knows about this place, and if some man was knocked out here today and wanders back to tell them—"

"I mean, keep it a secret that this is the place for the *corroboree*. Anyway, it's a cursed, deserted place as far as the Grange hands believe. I don't think even Griffin or his son have set foot here for years, despite its crystal water. And if they think it's haunted, perhaps they're right."

He nodded toward the upper cliff face behind her. Just then, Abigail turned to look. Two dusky figures emerged from the mouth of one shadowy cave. Two women, one holding a baby.

"Do you know them?" she asked.

"Kulalang's two remaining wives," he told her.

She gasped, shocked, picturing wives in the hundreds, perhaps all those aborigine women begging with children along the Parramatta road. How little she knew about Kulalang and his people, even though she wished them well. She glanced through her thick eyelashes at Duke and rewrapped her veil around her face. Perhaps she didn't really know him, either, and that thought terrified her. But before she could ask him one more question about Kulalang's wives or admit to herself the stunning realization that she would give anything to be Duke Braden's *only* wife, he smacked her horse on its rump and sent horse and rider back toward the *GG* sheep fence on the rim of the Grange.

That evening Abby could not bear to face a private walk after dark with Phillip, so she claimed dizziness—it was not far from the truth after what had happened today—and kept to her room with only H.M. for a companion. Her maid, Sally, finally brought up tea and toast at eight with a message that Phillip would call on her first thing in the morning to see personally to her "welfare."

Still, Abby spent most of the evening recalling what had passed between her and Duke today, with hardly a thought for Phillip. She loved Duke Braden, and that was that. What would become of that love she could not guess, but it was too late to change things now. She lay in bed long after dark, staring at the ceiling, remembering every word and touch she and Duke had shared today. Again, even without his presence, she felt the aching for him only he could somehow ease. When she finally did doze, she had the strangest dream.

It was like the old nightmare where she was left naked by Lord Northurst, everyone pointing and laughing at her. But this time, the room was crowded with women who were all married to Duke—Currency brides—standing in shadowy caves along the ceiling of the room, watching her, laughing, pointing, knowing that Abby Rose could never really be his. Duke was swimming in the water hole called *kuri kuri*. Floating, sweet-smelling roses filled the water. She wanted to be with him, but she could not swim. A fence marked with a big black *GG* kept her away from him as his many brides just kept whispering. And all the while she heard a steady rhythm....

She stirred from the dream and opened her eyes to a dark room. She heard H.M. growl over by the window. She wondered what had disturbed him, then she heard the droning beat of distant drums. The sound was real! It was not just in her dream!

She donned her silk wrapper and hurried to her western window, which overlooked the distant stables in the direction of Braden land. A full moon bathed the scene in pale light and soft shadows. She shoved open the casement and breathed deeply of crisp night air. Then she heard the sound again and knew it must be the Bandajongs' *corroboree* celebration just across the fields at *kuri kuri*. But if she could hear it, would not others here hear it too, and realize the aborigines were "trespassing" on Godfrey-Bennett land? And if it drew any attention after she had told Duke she would keep their secret—

She gasped as her worst fears came true: a string of lanterns appeared near the stable doors. Men already mounted, a good number of them!

She jammed her feet in mules and threw her burnoose over her wrapper. She picked up the restive H.M. and fastened the leash on the dog's collar. If those men were going out there to make target practice of the tribe dancing around the fires under this full moon, they had to be warned or stopped. She had no doubt any Godfrey-Bennett men would just as soon shoot an aborigine as a 'roo; she had heard as much from Griffin the first day she arrived!

Frenzied, she rushed down the dim hall and the sweep of staircase. She put H.M. on the floor and pulled her along by her leash. Heedless of propriety or danger, Abby tore across the dew-dampened grass toward the stables.

"What's happening? Where are you going?" she called to the men.

"Glory be! That you, Lady Abigail? Mr. Phillip, sir, Lady Abigail's here!"

Damn! Abby cursed silently. But perhaps Phillip was the one to stop this madness. "The noise woke me," she began when Phillip strode out of the stables, leading his saddled and bridled mount.

His eyes gleamed at her in the lamps' glow.

"You mean that savage drumming out there somewhere on our property? A bunch of abos, I'll bet, and we're going to clear them out." He approached her and she backed up slightly, holding her burnoose tightly around her. The nervous spaniel soon managed to wrap the leash around her ankles but she stood her ground, ignoring the growling dog.

"Phillip, it's too dangerous. Please don't go."

"Your regard for me is touching. But look what you've done—" He bent down to unwrap the leash from her legs, his touch lingering on her legs. Then he rose and moved closer, though he had her already pinned against the stable door. "If you're so concerned for my safety, dearest Abigail, what's it worth for you to keep me here? Perhaps I'll send the men on without me, and you and I will await the head count of the hunt inside the nice warm, freshly strawed stable, hmm?"

His voice and touch and implication sickened her, but she was more frightened for the Bandajongs. "Hunt? Head count? Phillip, you're demented! This hatred of these people has got to stop!"

"My pious little sweet, you don't know the first damned thing about it! Or do you?" he asked and shook her hard.

"I believe you and I have a great deal to settle later." H.M. yipped, but Phillip had already loosed Abigail. "You know, I almost think you're misguided enough to offer me something really sweet to call off my pack, but I intend to have you anyway. We're fated for each other, Abigail. And I'm going to dedicate my life to your great joy in bearing both my name and my son! Men, let's go!"

"You're demented! Never!" she called after him, but he didn't hear. The beat of ten horses' hooves drowned out her shouts and the distant drums. She had to dart after the barking dog to keep her from being trampled in the mad dash toward the sacred water hole. She knew that by the time she got a horse to tear after them to warn Kulalang and his tribe, it would be entirely too late. Tears tracking down her face, she headed back into the house. Shaken with fear and fury, she hurried to her room to wait and hope and pray.

She spent what seemed like an eternity sitting at the window, staring out and cursing herself for not having wakened sooner. Finally the riders returned. It took every shred of her fragile self-control not to tear downstairs again to demand of that demon what had happened, but she had no intention of being trapped alone with him again.

Later, after all was quiet, she saw Phillip's dark form cross the yard through the big block of moonlight. She heard his father's door down the hall open and close. Perhaps with her ailments, Mrs. Godfrey-Bennett had slept through it all. Barefoot, leaving the skittish H.M. behind this time, Abigail opened her door and padded down the hall. She froze when she heard Griffin's voice.

"If you wouldn't ride out of here hell-bent, but instead sneak up on the savages, you'd get a few, son."

"It's always like they smell we're coming. Just bonfires again and lots of tracks, but no abos!"

Abby wilted against the wall in relief. They had found no one there!

"I've a good notion to poison that hole," Mr. Godfrey-Bennett went on, "but we can't afford to take the chance some of our flock would drink there or we'd get runoff when the spring rains came down from the mountains. Still, as you said, we can't have our men getting mysterious bumps on the head while out looking for stray sheep over that way, can we?"

"That's exactly what I mean. Something's got to be done. At the ball, I'm going to talk to the governor about coming down harder on abos sneaking back on land that's no longer theirs. I'll just bet Braden's been bending the poor man's ear lately. And as for Braden—" Phillip lowered his voice "—I'll find a way to ruin that tricky son of a convict bitch if I have to chase him all the way across the Blue Mountains!"

Their voices seemed closer now and Abby dashed for her room before they turned into the hall from the staircase landing. She leaned against her closed door, shaking, furious but flooded with joyous relief Kulalang's tribe and "his remaining wives" were temporarily safe.

But after what she had just heard, she would now have to reconsider her refusal to attend the governor's birthday ball on Phillip's arm. As much as she detested Phillip, if he meant to pour his poisons in Governor Bourke's ear, she was going to cling to him like honey, until he dared to try to turn the governor against everything Duke stood for. Then she would get her chance to put in her say to help Duke and the Currency causes!

Strength ran through her now. With H.M. at her heels, she began to pace back and forth and make her plans.

"Hey now," Earl said to Grace as he poked his head in the cook house door the next morning right after breakfast. "Not gonna be bent over that stove all day, are you? It smells real good. But I was thinking of giving you your first riding lesson so we don't have to burden my horse overmuch next time we go into Sydney."

"Why, I thought you had ever such a good time with us riding together like that!" Grace teased. She grinned and turned to face him, studying his guilty smile. From now on, she knew, her heart would flutter every time a shadow fell across the door while she worked in the kitchen. Earl's nonchalant ease despite his formidable size always surprised her. Now his dark brown eyes caressed her in the small room, warmed by baking bread. He looked suddenly tongue-tied and shy, not like a man who was governed by temper and fists. Bad luck, but she cared desperately for this stubborn man, though she was still a bit afraid of him.

"I told you I was going to bake you some real English bread, Earl Braden, if I got some white flour and yeast. It's just done. It should set a while, but I'll let you taste it hot if you can hold up a minute. It's ever so good!"

"Bet it is," was all he could manage as he sauntered in. Ordinarily he would have scoffed at someone fussing over English bread rather than good solid damper, but he often found himself unable to form more than a short sentence when he got this close to Grace and took a good look at her. Right now her sweetly rounded bottom and the trim ankles he glimpsed when she bent over like that almost drove him to distraction. He'd been through this sort of thirst for a woman before, but he'd always slaked it soon enough. Duke said he couldn't so much as touch this one, and playing shepherd over her was making it worse. Yet, with Gracie, it was more than just lust, and that was what rattled him.

He even enjoyed the sound of her voice. He looked forward to hearing her quick footsteps when she brought his food to the table. He couldn't wait to see her when he rode in at night or anytime. He felt like a guilty schoolboy, sniffing at the sweet scent of her rainwater-washed hair when she cleared dishes or trying to get a glimpse down her bodice when she ladled stew on his plate. He loved to hear her laugh. He had a terrible itch to buy her things, though all she'd accepted so far was some danged yeast and white flour when they were in town. She was always telling him he should buy presents only for his Female Factory bride when he got her, but she was always deliberately swishing her hips near him and hanging on every word he said and touching his arm and gazing up like some kind of moony calf, too! Curse the woman, but she got to him! He leaned against the pile of stove wood, appreciating her clean, quick moves as she cut him a hunk of bread.

"Here," she said, "want some of that honey on it your dad found?" She broke off a piece of the gooey comb from a plate on her worktable and spread it on the bread with her fingers, then licked them. Some honey dripped down his chin as he ate the bread. She swiped at it and he caught her wrist in his hand and licked the tips of her fingers thoroughly.

She jumped back, yanking her hand away as if he'd burned it. "Oh!"

"Sorry. It's real delicious. The bread, I mean, even if it is English."

"Now, that's right," she said. She hoped her voice was strong enough to let him know a gentle scolding was coming his way. She felt her heart beat very hard in her breast behind her canvas apron, tied tightly around her tiny waist. "You're the man wants only what's got the New South Wales convict imprint on it from the Female Factory—even if the lasses there were all English-born, just like me. Well, hope you find yourself one that can cook your damper and put up with your temper!" she taunted, amazed she dared go this far. She'd never found the grit to rile Earl so directly before.

Gulping down the last of the bread, he stood and pulled her to him. "I like a woman with sass, but one who knows her place, too. And I've got a good way to show you what your place should be," he added, narrow-eyed and tight-jawed.

"Earl, no, don't!" she cried in fear, thinking he would hit her. Visions of her father's attacks on her—even of that muscle-bound bully who wanted her for a wife on the docks that first day in New South Wales—racked her. But Earl only tugged her closer and bent his mouth to cover hers in their first real kiss.

Yet the impact of that shocked her, too. She'd been wanting Earl's touch and kiss for weeks now, even though she knew Duke did not approve. But Duke had actually slept in today for once, after having been up all night with some of his hands, guarding the dancing of Kulalang's tribe over to the east somewhere.

"Gracie, Gracie, I want you so bad," Earl breathed against her cheek when the kiss finally ended. "But I gotta hold to my dream."

Surprised she was hugging him back so hard, she pulled away just enough to look up into his eyes. "Well, maybe I got myself some dreams, too, Earl. And loving someone with a temper like yours who's always spoiling for a fight is sure not one of them!"

He gaped at her. "Loving? You mean—"

"Not a bit of it! I'll love only the man who cares enough to wed me, and Duke's gonna find him real soon, too!"

"The sooner the better, I see," came the stern voice from the door. Duke strode in and stared down Earl's defiant look. Earl loosed Grace and took a step back.

"Maybe you just better marry Mistress Buck yourself, brother dear!" Earl taunted. "The old man's just as eager for a few Braden brats from you as he is from me!"

"I don't believe we're discussing me here, Earl, because—"

"Because if we did, we'd have to talk all fancy about the 'pure merino breed' redhead I hear you rode off with more than once on, what's a good word now, real *exclusive* terms?"

"Drop it. I just wanted to tell Grace I'd like some breakfast and that I intend to introduce her to several fine young men with good trades and calm temperaments at the governor's ball. And to facilitate that, it would be best if you don't escort her there and I do."

Earl shouldered Grace back and rounded on Duke. Grace scrambled to cut another hunk of fresh bread for Duke's tray, but her eyes did not leave the two men.

"I've already asked her and she's accepted, isn't that right, Gracie?" Earl asked over his shoulder.

She looked at Duke before answering Earl. Duke had done so much for her; Duke was her savior. But Duke was just as stubborn about Miss Abigail as Earl was about her. They were cut from the same cloth, these two Braden brothers. She couldn't help loving Earl.

"I told Earl I'd go with him, and I want to ever so much, with your permission," she said to Duke, but her gaze locked with Earl's when he spun around to face her. "I can still meet those lads, can't I? I mean, it's my dream to be wed to a kind and loving lad, so it would be my last time with Earl anyway, as he's so set on getting hisself a Factory lass before you two set out overlanding this autumn."

Earl, she thought, should have looked triumphant at her siding with him against Duke, but instead he looked shaken. When Earl nodded and strode stiffly out without another word, Grace felt the flush of victory.

"Grace, I hope you know what you're doing with Earl," Duke said, not budging from where he stood. "If you goad a ram too long, he eventually charges and can trample anything in his path. Especially to get to a ewe he fancies."

"I take your meaning. Earl—he's real bitter inside 'cause of losing his mother, is that it?" The question spilled out before she knew she'd dare to ask it.

"I think the fire in his belly is not from our mother's death or even our baby sister's the same week," Duke said. "I think it's because Squire handled his grief by walking right outside and going back to work, and Earl thought he didn't care. I don't know, maybe Earl felt his dad was ashamed of our mother because she was a Factory lass. I don't know what he thought."

Grace looked thoughtful for a moment. "Earl's not all brawn and quick temper. Maybe more often we should ask him what he thinks, even though you're the one with all the clever talk and smart head to go with it. I mean, even you prob'ly can't figure out all your own feelings and what you should do sometimes."

Duke's eyes narrowed; his jaws clenched. He looked away from Grace, astounded she'd not only read his mind, but maybe given him the way to reach Earl, too. "Sometimes, I don't feel a bit smart-headed, Grace," he said and took the tray from her hands to spare her the trip up to the house with it. At the door he turned back. "And I have to go into Sydney on business until tomorrow, so I won't be back for dinner. When Squire retires early, you just keep an eye on Earl now."

She shook her head and smiled as she watched him walk back to the house with his tray of good English bread and tea and New South Wales butter and honey.

Duke crossed the veranda of the narrow stone town house on Cumberland Street in Sydney and pounded the brass knocker on the door. He had known for years where Phillip Godfrey-Bennett kept his string of Currency mistresses, but he had never had the slightest urge to venture there. But the young woman Phillip had been keeping in his Exclusive style lately was one whose family Duke had long known. Her father, Charles Collister, oversaw the warehouse where Braden wool was stored before being shipped to the hungry English mills. Compared to the number of pressed bales exported by big runs like the Grange, the Braden trade was minimal, but someday, when he and Earl staked out their big run across the Blues, they would expand and flourish.

He banged the knocker again, hoping Catherine Collister, called Catty, was here without some gun-happy guard from the Grange. Only a few weeks ago, Catty's father had hinted to him that the pretty blond girl was not happy, however glorious the fine carriage, clothes, money and perverted prestige had once looked to her. It was then the idea had come to Duke of inviting her to the governor's ball to stand proudly with her old Currency friends there, and by so doing, to take a stand against the way the Exclusives used and then discarded women like her.

No one answered the door and he knocked again. Women really took the brunt of things in New South Wales, Duke thought, as he tried to see through the lace curtains into a darkened parlor but caught only his own reflection. With so few women here, compared to the numbers of men, they should've been treasured instead of knocked about. Currency women were fair game to be used and abused by bastards like Phillip, who'd gone through six or seven in the years Duke had known him. That was why Duke wanted to import the brides, to set a high standard. Maybe then even Currency lads would take the hint not to be so free and easy with their women, let alone how some Exclusives like Phillip treated them.

With a sigh he turned away. Obviously, Catty was not there.

But as Duke started down the steps, he heard the door open behind him. He turned back, expecting to see a maid. Catty, her face pale, stared at him through the crack of the door. Her hair was loose to her shoulders; she was dressed but looked disheveled.

"I saw it was you," she said. "Come in then, if you dare."

He stepped into a tiny foyer with twin brass lanterns and a gilt mirror. She closed the door and leaned against it. Then he saw the bluish bruises on her face and the dark circles under her bloodshot eyes that made her look strained and old.

"Catty, what happened to you?" Duke asked, appalled.

"I don't want to say. What're you here for?"

She did not budge, but leaned against the door as if she had no strength to move. He remembered her as a lovely, laughing girl. It had galled him when he came back from England to hear the name of the man who had taken her into his so-called care.

"If he beats you—even if he doesn't—you should leave him."

"Listen, I know there's real bad feelings between you two. Everyone does. So don't go getting him in trouble," she said in a monotone.

"I'm thinking of the trouble you're in, not him." He regretted not telling her the truth, that he had come to ask her to help him best Phillip.

She wrapped her arms around herself and hugged tight. He had the urge to comfort her just that way, but he held himself back. If Phillip had done this to her already, Duke wondered what he would do to her if she betrayed him by appearing at the ball.

"Listen, Catty, I'm sorry I'm upsetting you. Just remember your parents want you back and love you."

"Love me! Oh, sure, I know it. I thought that was what I'd get from him, see, and I did for a while. But now he always wants me to play at fighting him, struggling, but when I do like he wants, he just forces me and then—then he still hits me—" Her torrent of words dissolved into a strangled sob. She buckled at the knees, but Duke caught her before she hit the marble tiles.

"Come on," he coaxed, as he held her. "You've got to leave him. Get some things together, and I'll take you home right now!"

She shook her head wildly, her hair whipping her shoulders. "He said I can't take a thing if I ever leave before he wants me to."

"You could take your independence and your pride!"

"Pride!" She spit out the word. "After all this! After Phillip Godfrey-Bennett? Who from the old days would ever want to be seen with me now?" She half laughed, half sobbed. He fumbled for his handkerchief and offered it to her. She crumpled the square of linen to her mouth as if gasping for breath while he still supported her. Silent shudders shook her.

"I came to invite you to the governor's ball next week, Catty. I'd be proud to take you, but with the bad blood between Phillip and me, it was obviously a crazy idea. But I know several stout Currency lads who'd be proud to have you there to stand with us. There's a big public confrontation coming over everything, and it's likely to be there. I just thought—" He floundered for words as he helped her to a chair just inside the parlor door. "But it was wrong of me to ask it of you. Please, just let me take you home."

"Nothing for me there," she choked out. "Eight younger ones and three rooms. I thought there was something for me here. He promised fine things, till just lately when he don't seem to care no more and just wants me to play being someone else and even says he wishes I talked fine English and had red hair—"

"What?" Duke demanded, his voice suddenly so harsh she jumped. Was Phillip wanting this poor girl to help him pretend he was beating and bedding Abigail? He knew Phillip was dangerous in some ways, but he had thought Abigail's relationship to the Godfrey-Bennetts would keep her safe from that lecher. Yet, who could not desire Abigail?

"Land sakes, don't scowl at me so, please," Catty went on, wondering at his anger. "It's so strange, but even if I do what he says, he's still angry, you know, after he's done with me...." Her voice trailed off.

Duke patted her shoulder awkwardly. If she had been Phillip right here, right now, he could have shaken the life out of him. He stayed a few more minutes, wanting to carry her home, but finally realizing she would not go. He worried for her as he finally let himself out, convinced he had to do something to help her. But more than that, he had to stop that maniac Phillip. He couldn't shake the certainty that Phillip was forcing Catty to play out how he wanted things between him and Abby until he got his way. He stopped and stared about him; he'd been so absorbed in his thoughts he'd taken a wrong turn toward the docks. He'd go on then and tell Catty's father what he'd learned and hope the man wouldn't dare to face Phillip over his daughter. She had made her own bed and now...

"Damn Phillip Godfrey-Bennett!" Duke cursed. He still believed Abby was protected from Phillip while she lived with his parents, but he couldn't bear her being in the same house with that man and his perverted thoughts. And if Phillip was the one who had had her followed onto Braden land, that was trouble. Worse, there was no way he'd get through the governor's ball if Abby appeared there on Phillip's arm! If he warned her, she'd probably take Phillip on about his mistress and that would endanger poor Catty, who was evidently too downtrodden to try to leave him.

"Damn him!" he repeated as he rounded the corner toward the docks. "I'll stop him any way I can if it's the last thing I ever do!"

# Chapter Nine

The Godfrey-Bennett barouche pulled up in the line of carriages before Government House for the governor's ball in honor of the king's birthday. Cannons peeked over the protective walls into the park as if to guard folk flowing through the big central doorway to the lighted two-story building. Mrs. Godfrey-Bennett turned to Abigail and fanned herself faster. It was the first outing she had made for weeks because of her headaches; despite the cool breeze, she seemed to think it helped to fan her face at all times, especially with the fan Abigail had brought her from London.

Well, Abigail thought to buck herself up, even if these folks insisted on pretending this was England, she intended to focus on New South Wales tonight. She had come to do battle against the problems she saw here, so she allowed Phillip to help her descend from the barouche. Her plan was to stick close to his side, and when he tried to prejudice the governor against the aborigines or the Currency, she would speak her mind no matter what!

As she alighted, many Exclusive ladies stared and little whispers began about "dear London fashion." She had worn her finest evening gown, of emerald silk with an embroidered skirt and bodice. The off-the-shoulder neckline exposed her bare throat and the ivory slant of her shoulders. Her puffed sleeves were gathered at the elbows, and she wore long white kid gloves to properly cover her arms and hands for dancing. Her only jewelry was her mother's large pearl-and-emerald drop earrings and a headband to adorn her upswept, looped tresses. From the delicate chain-link headband, a large pearl dangling from an emerald graced her forehead. The entire ensemble made her hazel eyes look very green.

Adroitly managing her full skirts in the crush of people in the reception hall, Abigail recalled how Duke had teased her that she had "worn too much stuff" and someday would dress more simply in this land. She wondered what he would say or think when he saw her tonight, and she wished—

"Abigail, I'm expecting the first dance—and every one thereafter," Phillip said, interrupting her musings.

His words jolted her back to reality, and she looked around as they entered the council chamber, which had been transformed into a ballroom, adorned with potted trees, ferns and trelliswork with silk roses. Lanterns and festooned chandeliers lighted the big room. Chairs and benches lined three sides, and food tables, decked with white linen and silver candelabras, stretched the entire length of the fourth. And there were two orchestras, one at each end of the long room, which she thought rather a clever idea, no doubt so folks could better hear the music when they danced.

"Perhaps the first dance," she replied. She begrudgingly laid her hand on Phillip's proffered arm, hoping they would meet Governor Bourke soon. But still she could not bear to be his partner, not when she knew Phillip had set out after the aborigines with guns—and how Duke had reacted once when he came upon her merely strolling in the park with Phillip. At least tonight, her cousin seemed on his most decorous behavior. He was elegantly attired in embroidered waistcoat and a shirt with a stiff wing collar. If only she could stall until they spoke with the governor, perhaps Phillip would not want to dance with her afterward at all!

"Do you mind if we stroll a bit first?" she asked. "That food looks intriguing."

"Of course, my dear. Anything your heart desires."

The reply almost turned her stomach against the food as they walked past the expanse of tables. They all looked very much the way Abigail remembered the displays of food during her long-past London season. Here, platters were heaped with pickled pigs' trotters and spuds, and slices of roast mutton, ham, chicken and corned beef. Plates of sweets were plentiful. Punches and creamy wine syllabubs swirled in sterling silver bowls.

Nothing but a cool drink truly appealed to her, but she had to eat something to put off for as long as possible the dance with Phillip. While he filled two small china plates for them, her eyes scanned the room for Duke. At least both the Currency and the Exclusives had been invited here by Governor Bourke, and she prayed that a sense of community rather than conflict would come from that.

"Here, dearest, try this goose," Phillip said, handing her a plate of food.

"Goose, really? More shades of England," she said and managed a laugh. She forked the slightest bit of it and its breaded stuffing into her mouth. "But it tastes like mutton."

"It is," he told her as he passed her a cup of punch. "Colonial goose—shoulder of mutton highly seasoned and stuffed, of course."

His eyes were hot on her bare shoulders as she choked down the food while still stubbornly scanning the crowd. "And where is the honorable Sir Richard Bourke?" she asked.

"Upon my word, I'm glad if that's who you're looking for!" Phillip told her testily and took the plate from her. "I'll introduce him to you—after the first of many dances, of *all* the dances we will share tonight."

Abigail had long ago wearied of Phillip's attempts at blackmail, but she'd call his bluff as soon as she could. She acquiesced to his request and was led onto the dance floor when couples began to form squares for a quadrille.

Where was Governor Bourke? Where was Duke Braden? she wondered. Nervously trying to keep her disgust at Phillip's touch under control, she remarked, "Just think, two orchestras to choose from."

Phillip laughed as they joined three other couples in the square. "We don't choose the orchestra, dearest Abigail," he whispered. "It's chosen for us. The one at the far end of the room is for the Currency, just as their food is on those tables there. Our people will cluster here with this orchestra, and only the governor and his lady will go between. I see he's down there right now probably getting his ear bent, unfortunately. But he'll be with us most of the time, if he knows what's good for him and this colony!"

As the musical introduction began, Abigail froze. Even here under the governor's watchful eye, such social separation was condoned and promoted. It wasn't right! Duke had been justified all along in his bitter anger and passionate desire to fight this! To fight *them*, the Exclusives with whom she lived on such intimate terms! She pulled back from Phillip and shrugged his hand off her back as the first set step began. Startled, he seized her wrist and pulled her toward him to make the first turn. She yanked back and stalked to the side of the room.

"What in the devil is the matter with you?" he demanded as he followed her.

"It's abominable—two orchestras! Two separate colonies! Phillip, that is ridiculous!"

"Of course it is!" he blazed and pushed her over behind a potted tree for a bit of privacy. "If we didn't have a fence-sitting governor whom the likes of Braden can pander to, we'd never have Currency at the same damn ball in the first place!"

"I just cannot abide this anymore."

"Now you listen to me! When Mother catches wind of this little episode, you'll knock her right back into her sickbed!"

"*I?* She said just the other day when I visited her there—which you never do, of course—that she'd feel much better if you'd spend some time with her and Lottie!"

"Lottie has nothing, but nothing, to do with this!"

Over Phillip's shoulder, Abigail saw Duke enter. He had Earl and Grace with him! She might have shoved Phillip into the tree to rush to them, but she saw Duke had a delicate, pretty blond woman on his arm. Her already knotted stomach fell to her silk-slippered feet.

At the stricken look on her face, Phillip turned to gawk. "Curse that little bitch!" he gritted out. "I'll kill her for this, him, too, burn all he has and—"

To Abigail's amazement, Phillip seemed to choke on his words. He strode toward his parents, seated across the way, as if he'd forgotten she were there. Abigail felt elated to see Duke, but shattered that he'd brought another woman. Her mind skipped to that first day she had gone to visit Castle Keep: Squire had said she didn't look like Duke's Currency lass friends from town. How blind she had been! Of course, women would adore him, and he, like Earl, would want a woman of his own kind he could wed.

"No," she muttered. "No!" It was wrong of her to think of someone as being Duke's "own kind." That made her as bad as these proud, powerful Exclusives. *She* was Duke's own kind, just as much as that woman. *She* wanted Duke Braden's love and approval—public approval—and she would earn it!

She watched as the Braden entourage—there were more couples who had come in behind Duke and Earl—made its way through the clustered, chatting Exclusives toward the far end of the room. For one moment Abigail thought they would defy convention by joining the Exclusive quadrille, but they did not. Still, people gave the Bradens and their Currency coterie a wide berth as if they were untouchables. She saw Duke stop to speak with a balding man and his plump wife, the same man she had seen greeting others. She decided he must be Governor Bourke. Then she made her move.

Abigail Anne Rosemont sailed right through the murmuring crowd toward the Braden group. Unescorted as she was, she was going to speak to the governor, whatever the consequences. And she was going to show Duke Braden and the rest of New South Wales what she thought of two orchestras and the implications therein.

Grace saw her first. She looked pleased, then awed as if she might even bob Abigail a curtsy. Abigail pressed a quick kiss to Grace's cheek, just the way the Exclusive women greeted one another. Earl grinned and Duke gawked. Duke looked so handsome, so gentlemanly. Imagine, Duke Braden in pearl-gray waistcoat with a frilled edge to his shirt under a silk bow tie!

"I'm so happy to see my friends from the voyage!" Abigail declared, momentarily ignoring the woman Duke escorted. "It's a lovely ball," she added with a nod at the governor, "except for the unfortunate enforced separation of people who should all be getting on and working together."

Her gaze met and held Duke's for the first time that night. Pride flared in his blue eyes. Despite the woman on his left arm, his right hand reached out to clasp Abigail's briefly.

"Abigail, may I introduce our governor, the Honorable Sir Richard Bourke and Mrs. Bourke," he said. "And, sir and ma'am, may I present Lady Abigail Rosemont." Then formal introductions flowed all around. The blond woman clinging to Duke was named Catherine Collister, called Catty.

"I've read and heard of you, I must say," Governor Bourke told Abigail, lifting heavily thatched eyebrows as he surveyed her. "I believe my father knew your grandfather, Lord Sinton, years back in London. So you think there's an unnatural separation here tonight?" he asked with a swift perusal of the room. "Then I thank you for coming, anyway, as I do the Braden brothers. We're working on things for the future, aren't we, Duke?"

"On improved conditions for aborigines and on squatters' rights, too?" Abigail inquired.

"Indeed!" the governor remarked, amused. "No one told me she was such a firebrand!" he added in a stage whisper to Duke.

"Perhaps no one knew," Duke managed to say as the governor wished them well and moved on to greet others. Duke turned to Abigail. "I think it's better if you don't get so involved tonight, Miss Rosemont, though I appreciate your support," he told her. "As long as the governor and his lady were here with us, your presence would perhaps pass, but to remain here with us alone is a serious breach of behavior."

"I never took you for a coward," Abigail challenged, unflinching.

"But I did know you were a risk taker," Duke countered. "Look, Abigail, I've promised the governor there will be no disruption tonight. Besides, he's vowed to introduce a licensing system, for squatters to pay fees to hold their sheep runs west of the mountains. That will be a blow to those who think they hold divine rights to all that land!"

"Like the Godly-Bennetts," Earl put in. "Why didn't you tell me, Duke? Something like that's all I been waiting to hear to put a few plans in motion!" Grace's face fell. She looked away and bit her lower lip.

"You look beautiful tonight with that forehead emerald and pearl, like a painting I saw in London of some empress in India," Duke told Abigail suddenly.

His voice had gone soft, his face, too. It was as if they stood alone in the vast room. If he complimented her like that in front of this Catty, Abigail thought, stunned, perhaps there was not so much between him and the pretty lass.

Then Duke broke the spell. "You'd better hightail it back to your relatives or, believe me, they'll never take you back, empress of India or not!"

"I don't care if they do," Abigail insisted. "I've gotten to the point I have to make a stand!"

"They'll drive you away, Abby," he said, using his pet name for her.

"They won't!" she declared.

Suddenly, Earl turned to his brother. "Shall we go ahead with it then, Duke? You can take Abigail if I find someone for Catty. What do you say?"

"What are you going to do?" Abigail asked.

"No!" Duke argued with Earl, ignoring Abigail's question. "Dancing with us would be social suicide for her, as if her chatting with us out here isn't bad enough!"

"Duke Braden, I won't be dismissed by you!" Abigail insisted.

"You're a fool if you back down now," Earl told Duke and darted off with Grace, while Duke, with Catty on his arm, and Abigail stood in the middle of the room.

Duke explained that they had merely planned to dance on the Exclusive half of the floor. That didn't seem so bad at first, but suddenly Abigail began to realize the price she would pay for her defiance. She almost wished she were hidden behind a potted tree again. She knew she was being stared at, but stood her ground, waiting to dance with Duke and his friends. The haunting memory of her dreaded recurring nightmare surfaced briefly, but she fought it back. Let them all stare! She was protesting for things she believed in and with the man she loved!

She gasped as Phillip and his father suddenly joined them. Both were obviously furious.

"You cheap Currency baggage!" Phillip began, addressing the cowering Catty. "I ought to—"

Griffin cut him off. "I said, not here!" He turned to Abigail. "Abigail, we demand you quit this present company and come over with us. Mrs. Godfrey-Bennett is going to be very ill!"

"I hope not, sir," Abigail told him sincerely. "But, you see, I've been getting very ill myself with all the unfair treatment of the Currency and native aborigines I've seen, and I cannot stand for more, so—"

Phillip interrupted her. "I'll ruin you, both of you—*all* of you for this outrage!" His brutal grip smashed the half-smoked cheroot he held in his fingers and the pieces fell to the floor. "You knew a gentleman could not protest publicly, didn't you, Braden, though you haven't a gentlemanly bone in your damned, seducing body!"

"Are you coming, Abigail?" Mr. Godfrey-Bennett demanded. "Now!"

"I've asked Abigail for the next dance," Duke said, "though, of course, it's up to her."

At that, Phillip looked as if he'd like to strangle her. Abigail glanced at Duke. His hands were balled fists, his tensed body looked ready to spring. "And I've accepted Mr. Braden's kind invitation, sir," she said to Griffin. She dared not look at Phillip again. "Just a dance to show everyone that neighbors can get along in this land."

Phillip looked as if he would have an apoplectic fit. She was afraid he would try to drag her off the floor, but his father restrained him.

"There are other ways—" Griffin whispered to his son, and dragged him from the floor.

Earl came back with not only a partner for Catty, but another of Braden's brides, Beth Anne Clare, with her new husband in tow. Grace would obviously be Earl's partner.

"Oh, Beth Anne, so good to see you again!" Abigail cried as she hugged her.

She was relieved that the woman Duke had brought was partnered with another man. But had Duke only asked her to dance to make a political protest? Or strictly to bedevil Griffin and Phillip? Catty was an endearing name—just like Abby Rose—so perhaps Duke cared for Catty, too.

The small group moved to the other end of the room and formed their square for the cotillion. The Exclusive orchestra refused to play. After a few tense moments, the more distant Currency orchestra struck up a tune. Currency folk straggled down the room to watch and applaud while Exclusives glared and even hissed. As she curtsied to Duke's bow, Abigail realized their square was the only one to commence dancing!

All eyes were on them. Earl danced with surprising grace, Abigail thought as she watched him and Grace. Grace looked both thrilled and wary. Beth Anne was wearing her London blue bonnet with bouncing feathers, Abigail noted, though this was hardly the proper place for it.

Oh well, she scolded herself, banish all such thoughts of proper old ways tonight. She was dancing publicly in New South Wales with the man she loved! She was risking her reputation as she never had before, and she was reveling in it. At first light tomorrow, she might feel devastated, but if so, it would be because Duke went home with this Catty he seemed somehow to have taken away from Phillip. Whoever could she really be? Despite all her questions, right now Abigail's heart soared.

She tried to talk to Duke between turns and twirls. "I want you to know I didn't tell Phillip about that *corroboree*."

"You didn't have to," Duke replied. "The wind was wrong and carried the sounds. But my guards warned the Bandajongs in time."

"What's Catty to you and Phillip?" she dared, half-afraid to hear the answer.

"I've known her family for years. You've got to steer clear of Phillip, Abby. He's more violent and brutal than you know. Catty's been his mistress in town and—"

Abigail missed a step, but Duke kept her from stumbling. Lord Northurst, she remembered all too clearly, had had a mistress he couldn't wait to return to. Phillip had one, too—no wonder he spent his days in town. Well, good for him, Abigail thought, except she pitied Catty.

"Listen to me, Abby," Duke was saying. "Catty's left him, and we're going to protect her. She's going to live with someone where Phillip will not find her, but you may be endangered, too. That's why I wished you hadn't pushed me to this—but I am so glad you did. I've never been happier or prouder!"

Abigail felt such joy she could have flown. Surely, Duke loved her in return! She had learned not to trust men once, but surely Duke was different! After tonight, their friendship was public. And when he asked her to marry him, their love would be, too! She could help him over the years just as she had tonight by speaking up to the governor.

Too soon the dance—and her ebullient confidence—
ended.

"We've made our point. Let's go," Duke said abruptly.

"Should I go, too?" she blurted to him, her hand still
linked through his arm while she caught her breath. At that
moment she would have gone with him anywhere, propriety and society be damned. The rebels walked to the far side
of the room and she went with them. No one else was doing
anything but gawking and whispering.

"Go where?" Duke asked her. "Hardly with us. We're
going to hide Catty up-country now that she's helped us put
your precious Phillip in his place."

"My Phillip? He's certainly not—"

Grace's loud voice cut Abigail off. She was addressing
Earl, "If you feel that way, forget anything between us! If
you still want a convict bride, go ahead and be cursed!"

Earl spun on Duke. "Did you tell her if I danced with her
publicly here, I'd have to wed her?" Earl demanded.

"No, Earl," Duke answered calmly. "I told her if you
cared for her and brought her here tonight, you'd be a fool
not to wed her. Otherwise the *Gazette* and everyone else will
see her reputation permanently in ruins. You told me to stop
playing her shepherd, so I was trusting you to do it. But if
you don't care a fig for her, just go to the Factory and—"

"I will, damn you! You tried to trick me, both of you!
And *you* should talk about ruining a woman, you fool!" he
shouted and pointed at Abigail. "I have my goals and vows
and dreams, too, Duke, and don't try to change them!"

Grace rounded on Earl and shoved him back from Duke.
"Just leave your brother alone, Earl Braden! I'm just ever
so glad this happened tonight, so I know we're quits. Stupid of me to fall for a rough, selfish lout when I know well
enough what they're like. Go on then, go ahead and wallop
me, just like my blackhearted dad!" she challenged. But she
took several quick steps back from Earl. "Mr. Braden, if
you don't mind, I think I'll just stay here at the dance, down
at that end, with Mr. Melvin Mott you invited here for me
to meet tonight. He, at least, seems ever so kind and

thoughtful and looking for a loving lass to wed." She turned and marched over to Mr. Mott's side. Catty came back and clung to Duke.

Abigail stood stunned. Earl had been using Grace and had no intention of wedding her. And Duke—surely, he had done this tonight partly because he wanted her to be part of his world now. He had, after all, warned her about Phillip and the possible danger to herself. He had let her dance with him in public tonight because he cared for her, didn't he, despite how Earl had betrayed Grace's trust?

"Duke, I can't go back to them," she told him as Earl swore and stalked off.

"I can't hide you away on some small sheep run like where I'm taking Catty," Duke muttered, without meeting her eyes. "I don't doubt the Godfrey-Bennetts will be protection for you against Phillip until you decide what to do."

"But after this," she said and seized his arm in a crushing grip, "they'll never let me out to come see you!"

His eyes, narrowed harshly under his furrowed brow, met hers. "It's best, Abby," he choked out, turning to her so only she could hear. "When you visit me, it's dangerous for you. For you *and* for me. Because of what almost happened between us before..."

"You're as bad as Earl!" she told him. "Worse, you're like these Exclusives who won't mix outside their class!"

"Abby, this isn't the place," he said, trying to control his anger, while quiet Catty waited for him. "We—we would never work. It's for your own good, believe me—"

"No!" she said and yanked her hand back. "I will never believe you again!"

Her cheeks burning, she walked slowly to the other side of the room. She took a glass of punch for herself, while barbed stares and whispers pierced her. Damn Duke Braden! Damn this new land! She had loved him and been denied and ruined again! The scandal and rumors would plague her now, just as they had before, but she had no Fairleigh to run to, no dear Janet's shoulder to cry on or

Grandfather's power to protect her. She downed two good gulps from the cup, but the cool liquid burned her throat.

She jumped at a man's voice behind her, but it was not Duke. When she turned around, Griffin Godfrey-Bennett stood before her. "We'd best leave now," he told her. "Phillip's long gone, but the Mrs.'s head is hurting."

She dared to meet his eyes. "Yes, of course. My head hurts, too. Are you sure you still want me to go home with you?"

His face looked hard. "The Mrs. does. Can't do without your sickbed visits, she says. For her, yes, come on home."

Walking stiffly at Griffin's side, Abigail traversed the long room and long hall to the waiting carriage. Home, her cousin had said. But the Grange was not home, and never could be. Where was home for her after this rejection and desertion by the second man she'd trusted and thought she loved? Home, she told herself, as she straightened her back and climbed into the dark carriage, was wherever she and H.M. would live. A little spaniel, that was all she had now to love. Her victory had turned to dust. She bit her lip hard to keep from sobbing as Mrs. Godfrey-Bennett patted her hand and the carriage rumbled away from the blazing lights of Government House.

Abigail decided to keep to her room the next day. But when her maid, Sally, told her that "Master Phillip" had not returned from Sydney and was not expected for several days, Abigail ventured out to take H.M. for a walk on the windswept lawn between the house and stables. She needed some time to think without being cooped up in her room. Thinking was all she had been doing since last night, but she still couldn't seem to come to a conclusion about her situation with Duke.

She felt, in good conscience, she could no longer stay here at the Grange. She had compromised her cousins' beliefs and insulted them and their friends, however misled they were. Her reputation, at first so polished by the very fact she was English, was now thoroughly tarnished.

She had been through such circumstances before when she was young and foolish, and had survived. Then, she had been hurt by a selfish, shallow man not worth the pain. Now she was no longer so young or so foolish, and had been hurt by a man very much worth the pain. She wanted Duke, despite their different worlds.

Abigail sighed. She stopped walking and gazed westward while H.M. sniffed at some new discovery in the grass. The Blue Mountains beckoned to her from the misty eucalyptus haze. Her anger slowly built, replacing the hurt.

How could Duke have set her aside so cruelly! How dared he reject her offer to help him, to be with him—and in public? They had shared so much—especially in that little hidden glen last month. At that memory, her fury was reduced to frustration. How she treasured each thought of him, each touch and word she carried in her heart. She knew now, unless she sneaked out from here in the dead of night, she would never set foot on Braden land unwatched again. Kulalang might not be there to throw his boomerang at her pursuer, or if he did, Phillip's men might shoot him this time! No, it was too great a risk to visit the Bradens and Grace, not as long as she lived at the Grange.

Since her reputation was full of holes anyway, perhaps she should move to Sydney and let a town house there. She absolutely refused to entertain the possibility of booking herself on an England-bound ship. She was not defeated yet! In Sydney, she could hire someone to send for Grace to live with her, now that a Braden brother had let her down, too. Yes, perhaps with Grace as a companion, she could live in Sydney for a time to decide if and when she should go back to England and her inheritance at Fairleigh. In Sydney, she would try to benefit the causes she had come to believe in, even if they were ones Duke Braden also spoke out for. Perhaps Duke's next batch of brides could live with her until they found husbands of their own choice.

She tugged H.M.'s leash while the wintry August wind pulled at her skirts. Had she found Duke Braden by chance or by Providence that windy day on the deck of the *Chal-*

*lenge?* How she longed to start over again with him from that moment! How she wished she were just one of his brides, without her money, clothes and background, because then he might have loved her enough to make her his only bride.

"Abigail! Abigail!"

Abigail started and turned around, then lifted her skirts to hurry back to the house. Mrs. Godfrey-Bennett stood outside on the front veranda, motioning to her. Surely, the way the woman's health had been these past weeks, something must be wrong for her to be out of her room, calling like this.

"What is it? Are you all right, ma'am?"

"Yes, my dear, yes. I was startled when I saw your room empty, that's all. Come inside for tea, won't you?"

Perhaps the woman had gotten up to give her an ultimatum about leaving, Abigail thought. Last night Abigail had sat stiffly in the dark carriage all the way back to the Grange, while Griffin Godfrey-Bennett sulked and swigged his rum. But Garnet had sympathetically patted Abigail's gloved hand more than once.

Abigail was surprised to see the servants had tea all laid out in the south drawing room, yet not one stood by to serve it. "I sent Lottie up for a nap so we won't be disturbed," Garnet told her and poured the tea. This seemed to be a new Garnet Godfrey-Bennett, Abigail mused. Lottie hated to be sent upstairs for naps and her grandmother always obliged the child's whims. Abigail's interest was piqued.

"I do sympathize with your agonizings, my dear," Garnet began. Abigail looked up, wide-eyed. "Ah, I see you are surprised. But I'm not so far removed from a young girl's memories that I can't recall how things are in the flush of youth, you see."

Abigail put her hand to her cup and saucer but did not lift it. "I am twenty-six, ma'am."

"But you are unwed, my dear. It's being wed that really gives one experience in things of the heart."

"Things of the heart," Abigail repeated. "But I—"

Garnet raised one lace-gloved hand. "Just listen, please, dear. You see, I watched your face as you danced with that man last night. And I recalled how you craned your neck in the carriage that day we met you at the wharf, as if you sought someone even while Phillip spoke to you. I realize how distracted you have been here. And, of course, for you not to fall head over heels for Phillip, especially now that he seems to be warming to you, would not have been possible unless your heart hoped elsewhere, even misguidedly."

Abigail gaped at her cousin-in-law. She was amazed that this woman, who had seemed the merest flibbertigibbet, adrift in her passion for fashion and society, had guessed her secret, just as Phillip had. But then, she realized, Earl had evidently also guessed it. And, oh dear, Grace too. Now, all of Sydney was talking!

"There, there," Garnet comforted and reached over to pat Abigail's hand as she had last night in the carriage. "Now just let me tell you a bit of a tale before we talk more. There was a young English girl who came with her family to live in Sydney when she was thirteen. If you think there are few women here to the number of men now, you should have seen it then! This young girl could have had—did have—her choice of many wealthy, eligible young men. But would you believe she lost her heart to a young man who had been freed from prison to tutor her brother? Specials, we used to call educated servants like that, specials. Anyway, this special had been transported for forgery, and he was terribly handsome and clever at flirting with young women. Young women who were but fifteen and didn't know better."

"Oh," Abigail said, before she realized she should not talk.

"Yes, well, nothing along the lines of—of complete ruination occurred, fortunately. You see, once, the same morning he had been—well, kissing her, she came upon the wretch in a highly compromising position with her sister! She was hurt and shocked, but she wished—" Garnet's shrill voice grew quiet "—even years later, that it had been she locked in that man's embrace instead of her sister! She told on them, and they were both punished. The special was flogged and shipped off for hard labor in Van Diemen's Land, and her sister did not speak to her for years, though she's dead now.''

"I'm sorry—for them." Abigail put down her cup and twisted her napkin in her lap. She understood well enough who that young girl had been. But did it mean Garnet sanctioned Abigail's feelings for such a man as Duke?

"You're sorry for them," Garnet repeated Abigail's words. "It doesn't really matter. There was no way the young woman's heartsick feelings for that man would have survived. It just didn't do! But back to you, Abigail," she declared and blinked tears from her eyes. "I have been pleased to see that you realize Phillip is still in mourning for his dear, departed wife and should not wed again for years—"

"Ma'am, how can you be so truthful one minute and then in the next fail to see that Phillip is not a man I would consider?"

"But I see he cares for you!" Garnet insisted.

"Cares!" Abigail jumped to her feet and sent H.M. rolling off her hems. She faced her hostess across the back of her chair. "If he 'cares,' it's in the wrong way for the wrong reasons. And if he didn't spend so much time in Sydney, that's where I'd go to live straightaway so as not to burden you and Mr. Godfrey-Bennett anymore with my wayward presence here!"

"But, my young lady, it just won't do if you care for Duke Braden." She managed to spit out the name this time. "That's what I meant to illustrate by my story. You must denounce him and his ways, publicly, after what occurred last night. If you have any hope that Phillip would ever consider you even for a friend, then—"

"*Please* understand! I want no part of Phillip in my future life! You may love him, but I do not! We are unsuited by temperament, interests and ethics!"

There, she thought, she'd done it now. However many sickroom visits Abigail had paid, however much time she and Garnet had spent talking, this woman would surely demand Abigail get out now, on her own. She would have no choice but to move to Sydney and risk facing Phillip's bizarre behavior.

But Mrs. Godfrey-Bennett was not done with surprises yet. "My dear, it does my heart good to hear you so settled on your unsuitability for my Phillip—and vice versa, of course. Come, sit again. As long as I know you've no designs on my boy, let me tell you about my elderly widowed friend, Mrs. Cranbrook, who lives with a spate of servants in her big seaside house in town. I'm certain she would like a long-term houseguest. She's deaf and hardly pays a bit of heed to goings-on in town anymore, if you catch my drift. But best yet, she won't let a man set foot on her premises—and that includes Phillip—so you'd be quite safe from any sort of scolding he'd deign to give you. And, of course, that way the town will know there's no way that vile Duke Braden—you simply must admit to me it just won't do, my dear—would bother you, either."

Breathless, Abigail sank back into her seat. Now that her cousin-in-law knew she did not have her sights set on her precious Phillip, she intended to be her ally. Perhaps in Mrs. Cranbrook's house, she could take in Grace and salvage what was left of *her* reputation, too. And then, just maybe, together, they could go visiting the Braden brothers.

"Abigail, what do you say?" the woman asked anxiously.

"I say I owe you my thanks, ma'am. Your head pains have certainly not harmed your thinking."

"Then you'll do it? Phillip will be most annoyed at me, I know, but I'll take to my room and weather it out."

Abigail thanked her hostess again as troubled thoughts swirled through her mind. After all this, she knew only one thing for certain: if Duke Braden thought he was tossing her away after last night, he had "another think" coming!

# Chapter Ten

Two days later, Abigail moved into the large sandstone Georgian mansion of Mrs. Sarah Cranbrook along the shore of Sydney Cove. Surrounded by trees and spacious lawns, guarded by a tall iron fence, Cliffside House stood in a line of elegant homes of the rich and powerful.

Sarah Cranbrook's deceased husband had been a colonial officer who made his fortune in the Rum Corps, the group of military men who once held a monopoly on trade. When the regiment was recalled to England, many of these newly wealthy men chose to stay in the land that had profited them so handsomely—Griffin Godfrey-Bennett's father included. Mrs. Cranbrook's only son had visited England and stayed there with the heiress he wed, and so been promptly disowned by his mother.

Evidently mistrusting men in general, the eccentric Widow Cranbrook allowed none of them at Cliffside House; all the many servants, including grooms and carriage drivers, were female. Friends like Garnet Godfrey-Bennett had continued to call on the widow over the years, though now in her late seventies, Mrs. Cranbrook was quite a recluse.

Abigail, too, soon felt like a recluse, except for an hour every afternoon when the widow liked to have her come "calling in for tea and a chat." Her voice grew hoarse from that daily hour of shouting into Mrs. Cranbrook's brass ear trumpet.

In her first few days at Cliffside House, Abigail busied herself exploring the mansion and grounds and making plans. Her suite of five rooms pleased her, not for their size and ponderous furniture, but for the very different, inspiring views from the windows. The house was built around a quadrangle, so out one side Abigail could see inner sheltered gardens, fragrant with the aromatic leaves of peppermint bark trees. The courtyard was busy with yellow-breasted robins hunting grubs and the startling flash of occasional bluebonnet parrots; walks there helped to soothe her anxious moods.

But out the other side of her suite—this view better suited her frame of mind, she thought—Abigail could look down to a rocky cove edging a white sand beach crested by deep blue, whitecapped water. And on the first sunny day, despite the nip of the season, swimmers came to challenge the breakers and ropes of seaweed.

"I saw swimmers down in the cove!" Abigail shouted into Mrs. Cranbrook's speaking trumpet at tea that afternoon. "They go so far out!"

"Swimmers? Public bathers, you mean. Yes, yes," the old lady responded with a nod that bounced her lace cap. "My underparlormaid, Rebecca, has been down there. I scolded her for it, too! A dangerous climb down, and then those waves! But Currency lasses swim like dabchicks, just like the men. They shouldn't be down there, but Rebecca says the waves are wildest there. There are police proclamations against it and fines for it, but there they are! There used to be legal public bathing for the Currency near Campbell's Wharf and on the west side of Woolomolo Bay, but I tell you, they're stubborn to have those big wild waves. More tea, Lady Abigail?"

As she gazed down at the swimmers again later that afternoon, Abigail pondered what Widow Cranbrook had told her. Duke had teased her about learning to swim; he'd said he'd teach her. In a way, she was certain she would fear going out in waves like those below, and yet—if she were with Duke—to please him, she would do it. "The waves are wildest there," Widow Cranbrook had said, and Abigail could see snares of floating seaweed. Yet that sort of defiance of danger, the challenge of being part of this wild land, suddenly seemed worth the risk to her. She laid her forehead against the cool window glass and stared down at the dots that were swimmers' heads in the foaming waves.

She tried to clear her mind of daydreams; she had been wasting time. What had happened with Duke or Phillip was not going to make her a recluse here, imprisoned in this free, wild land. She knew what she wanted, whom she wanted, and she was going to make decisions and move ahead. She was going to jump in and learn to swim, only not in the ocean!

She sat down at her drop-leaf secretary and penned a quick note to Grace Buck. That very afternoon she sent two housemaids out to hire a Currency lad to ride the Parramatta Road to deliver the note to Castle Keep on Braden land. And she requested that one of the carriages in the mews be cleaned for her use, as she would be going out and about in the near future.

The very next day, Grace came to live as Abigail's companion at Cliffside House.

"You saved my neck, I can tell you that, Miss Abigail!" Grace cried as they hugged. "Earl was like to grab me and haul me off in the bush, and trouble was, the way he kept looking at me, I wanted him to ever so much, the blackguard. And all the time I knew he was still set on getting himself a Parramatta Factory lass, even though he wants me as much as I do him, I just know it. Why's a man have to be like that when he wants a woman who loves him back?"

"Because they're sometimes too proud and stubborn for their own good, Grace," Abigail replied. "But that doesn't mean we can't fight back any way we can!"

"Fight back? Oh, no, wish't I could, but Earl'd be like to haul off and cuff me good if I pushed him too far."

"Has he ever hit you?" Abigail demanded.

"Well, no, but he's got a temper to beat all."

"But not to beat you, not with his fists and not in this life, that's my guess, my friend. I've seen how he looks at you, and that's not anger on his face! I think we've got to fight for what we want in this land, ride the rough waves even if a bit of danger's involved!"

"Ride the waves? But how are you—are *we* gonna pull off something like that with Earl the way he is?" Grace demanded, her big brown eyes wide. "Besides that, you and Mr. Duke Braden are not exactly treading some smooth primrose path!"

"We'll see!" Abigail declared with a sideways glance out the window at the waves challenging the beach and cove. "We've got to go to town to hire guards and a driver for that carriage I've borrowed from the widow. We're going to take a little jaunt up the high road toward Parramatta, and then we'll just see!"

But two days later, just as the women were planning their first trip out of Sydney to call on the Bradens, a surprise visitor called on Abigail and Grace.

"A lass who says her name is Catty Collister, Lady Rosemont," the Widow Cranbrook's stiff-as-starch butler, Mistress Penrod, informed Abigail.

"Yes, please show her in!"

The three of them shared an awkward little reunion.

"Can't stay, but just wanted to drop by to see all was well with both of you. I'm cleaning and cooking for Mr. Squire Braden out at Castle Keep now," the pale blond told them the moment she was seated. "I want to thank you for giving up that job for me, Miss Grace."

Grace and Abigail exchanged a quick look, then turned back to Catty. "Came to town to buy goods with four strapping shearers for guards," Catty chattered on, "in case Mr. Phillip got wind I was here or where I'm staying now. But I feel safe enough out at Castle Keep with all them men around even if it is next to Phillip's country place. It's so good to feel—well, clean again, out there, even with all the dust, if you know what I mean," she confided to them in a low whisper.

"I do know." Abigail found her voice at last, surprised the shy, quiet Catty was quite the chatterbox now. She had been liberated indeed. "And knowing Phillip Godfrey-Bennett's changeable moods as I do, I'm glad you've gotten away from him, as I have, too."

"I thought so!" Catty said and nodded sagely. "Anyhow, Duke wanted to know how you two are getting on."

Abigail's heart caught. Perhaps he did care!

"And Earl—not a word from him?" Grace asked expectantly.

"Not *from* him, exactly. But he's been a reg'lar storm cloud since the ball, snapping at folks and all, growling around the place and almost coming to blows with his brother."

Abigail saw Grace grip her fingers so tightly in her lap they turned white. "Maybe he's just nervous, getting closer to his dream of overlanding this summer," Grace suggested, her voice shaking slightly.

"Or maybe he realizes he's made a grave mistake, letting you slip away!" Abigail put in and reached over to cover Grace's clenched hands with her own. "His temper's always been quick where you've been concerned, but I think it's because he's angry with himself."

"You know," Catty put in, her voice so small, "after Mr. Phillip being so rough on me and all, I tell you, I don't really think Mr. Earl's like that. Mr. Phillip had two faces. One minute proper as you please, and the next a raving lunatic to—to mistreat a woman who cares for him. I think Earl Braden always says just what he means and wouldn't harm a lady ever. I sure hope not, 'cause some poor woman he's going to fetch home tomorrow is sure to have a rough row to hoe if I'm not right and—"

"Tomorrow?" Abigail and Grace demanded in unison.

"Him and Duke—to the Female Factory at Parramatta. That's another strange thing. Earl went to lots of trouble to get ticket-of-leave papers for his bride, and then he wadded them up once and had to unfold them. Asked me to iron them wrinkles out just like on a shirt! Guess I said all I had to, so best be running. And thanks again, Miss Grace, for leaving Castle Keep so Duke could give me the job there. I don't think, with what Mr. Phillip thinks of the Bradens and all, he'd ever dare to set foot there.''

"Please, stay for a while and I'll ring for tea," Abigail managed, though Grace sat like a statue. But Catty had to be on her way back as her guards were forced to wait outside the fence of this no-man's land.

When Abigail came back from seeing Catty out, Grace remained in her chair, her hands clenched, head bowed.

"I've lost him. I didn't really think he would do it," she whispered as Abigail put a hand on her shoulder. "I thought he might come after me here. I thought I could change his mind, but now—''

"But now, we've just one more chance, so we've got to make it good. And you've got to be strong to do this.''

Grace lifted her head. "Do what? Tomorrow, he'll get his own Braden's bride, just like Catty said.''

"Maybe not. Maybe not if he sees the woman he really loves at the last minute. After all, how would an English lady like me know she had to have special permission and something called a ticket-of-leave if she went to that Parramatta Factory looking for a lass to be a maid?''

"What? With all these female servants already here at Cliffside House? And that Factory has got some reputation! Currency men go there to look for brides and the Exclusives send there for special servants, but you—we—couldn't just—''

"Nonsense, Grace! You sound like Mrs. Godfrey-Bennett. Besides, Catty said Duke's going along, and I have a bone or two to pick with him. And if this doesn't work, you won't be one bit worse off than you are now without Earl, will you?''

Grace's mouth hung open. "Well, no.''

"Then it's settled. And we'll just see if the two of us can't settle down those Braden brothers. You need a husband and

I'd love to announce to that wretched *Sydney Gazette* that Earl Braden is Buck's bridegroom!''

The next morning Abigail and Grace took the carriage and the guards Abigail had hired to the Parramatta River ferry slip in Sydney. Leaving the driver and guards with the carriage, since she had hired them only to protect her in town and on the Parramatta Road, they boarded the steamship's first of four daily runs upriver. Grace, who had never been on a steamship, was so nervous she looked dazed.

Abigail had made Grace take inordinate care with her hair and clothes today, including a ruffled rose shoulder cape and bonnet from Abigail's London wardrobe. Abigail had gowned herself in a cheery yellow cotton gown and green cape. Her attire would not flaunt wealth or status and yet Duke could not possibly miss noticing her.

They disembarked in the bustling market town of Parramatta by midmorning and hired a cart to the Female Factory.

"To *where,* missus?" the driver demanded when they were perched on the plank seats facing each other. "You don' mean there! Tha's where them women inmates make clothes, but not for purchase, you know. Sewing garb for other prisoners, tha's what they make there, and ever'one of 'em's a prisoner fresh off a boat from the homeland.''

"Yes," Abigail insisted, "I *do* mean we wish to be delivered there and quickly. We're meeting someone, you see."

The long stone building behind the walls looked innocent enough, Abigail thought as she climbed down from the cart upon arrival. She tugged the trembling Grace after her. Abigail paid the driver and asked him to wait, then marched Grace up to the sentry box before either of them changed their minds.

"Lady Abigail Rosemont and Miss Grace Buck to meet Duke and Earl Braden here," she said to the guard in a commanding voice, her grip hard on Grace's wrist.

Obviously surprised at the sight of two proper ladies, the guard frowned down at a piece of paper. "They's not come in yet, neither of 'em," he grunted.

"Well, that's fine," Abigail told him. "We're perfectly content to wait inside, since I want to see about getting a servant here, too."

"Fine ladies just sends for 'em and the matron picks 'em out," he insisted, shuffling out of his little roofed house.

"I like to choose my own. Just like choosing a husband, right, Grace?" Abigail ventured with a quick shove in the small of Grace's back to move her on.

Grace nodded numbly. Her eyes, gone wide as saucers, were obviously scanning the entrance and the street behind for Earl.

Reluctantly, the guard took them in and introduced them to the matron, a stout, stern-looking woman all in black with a large bunch of keys jangling at her belt. Abigail almost shrank under the woman's grim glare but launched into her explanation of wanting a maid. When the matron learned Abigail had not obtained the required ticket-of-leave, she seemed ready to turn them out, until Abigail explained they'd be glad to wait until their friends, the Bradens, arrived.

"Of course, perhaps I could still select a maid today," Abigail told the frowning woman as she walked them to a bench in the corner beyond the matron's office, "and then get her leave papers in Sydney tomorrow."

"Law," Grace whispered after the matron's footsteps died away down the hall, "what pluck you got!"

"Desperate situations demand desperate measures," Abigail declared, but her heart was still hammering and her legs shook. "I'm just thankful we weren't too late."

After waiting for what seemed an eternity, Abigail got up to look out a window over the central courtyard. She gasped as she heard Duke's voice echo distantly down the corridor. They were here! Meanwhile, out the window, she saw female prisoners dressed in gray duffel with white mobcaps.

And each one of them had her hair cropped so short it barely covered her earlobes!

Grace darted over to grab Abigail's hand, crying, "I hear them. We shouldn't have come! Earl's gonna skin me alive, and Mr. Duke—eh, now, what you doing?" Grace demanded as Abigail untied the ribbons to Grace's bonnet and lifted it off.

"Get the pins out of your hair!" she ordered Grace. "Shake it loose and hurry!"

"What? But—"

"Those poor souls out there all have their hair short, and we want Earl to see the difference, don't we?" Abigail insisted. "Now, quick!"

They'd fluffed her long brown hair loose down her back and popped her bonnet back on as Duke and Earl came down the corridor with the matron. Both brothers stopped in their tracks when they saw Abigail and Grace.

"What in damnation?" Earl bellowed as Duke just stared at Abigail.

"I wanted a maid, you see, now that I've left the Grange. And I heard you could get them here," Abigail began. "Grace is my companion now, so of course I brought her along," she added, and forced a bright smile at Duke. He looked as if he were about to strangle her. "So, we'll just go along with you while Earl picks his mate—it's all arranged."

"No way in hell!" Earl put in.

Abigail's eyes silently pleaded with Duke for help. His sharp gaze swept Grace, standing there trembling with tears in her eyes, her luxuriant hair wreathing her shoulders. He sneaked a glance at Earl, who looked stricken to his very soul.

"It's fine with me if you two tag along to see how it's done," Duke said to Earl's obvious chagrin. "I'm sure Earl won't mind, either, will you, Earl?"

"I couldn't care less if they even decided to live here with the inmates!" Earl blustered.

Earl started down the corridor at a good clip. Duke noted Abigail almost had to drag Grace along in Earl's wake. He could not help but admire her cleverness and courage to try to bring Grace and Earl together before it was too late. Damn, he should have thought of this himself when Grace told him how much she loved Earl, then fled to Abigail in Sydney!

As for Abigail's leaving the Grange and becoming much more independent, it both bolstered and bothered him. He could sympathize with Earl's loving Grace but being stubbornly committed to his dreams. After all, he himself had always planned to have a proud, strong Currency lass at his side. If he ever married an Exclusive, no matter how alluring or admirable she was, he would have to publicly eat crow from all his ranting and raving against the Exclusives through the years. He cursed under his breath and hurried after the two women.

In the courtyard the matron spoke to a guard, who bellowed commands to the prisoners. "Order! Take your places in the line for review! Shake a foot now or else!"

"Or else what?" Abigail whispered, but Grace was not listening. When she saw these pale girls and pasty-faced women with their short, ragged haircuts and demeanors ranging from listless to pugnacious, she seemed to come out of her daze.

"So, how've things been since I've been gone, Earl?" Grace asked and dared to rest her hand on his stiff arm a moment before she drew it back. "Catty bake damper good as mine?"

"Catty's known how since she's been knee high," Earl said gruffly without looking at her. "You're just learning."

"Can't fault a lass for just learning, not if she really wants to learn," Grace crooned. "And here now I'll never get another riding lesson from you!" she bemoaned.

Grace was so melodramatic, Abigail almost laughed despite the situation. She was astounded at Grace's transformation from shy violet to thorny rose. Abigail stepped back and bounced off Duke. His hands steadied her waist before dropping quickly away, but even that slightest touch made Abigail go as weak-legged as Grace had been moments ago.

Earl dared to look at Grace even as the prisoners fell into line across the exercise courtyard. She was shaking her head and her curls and the feathers of her hat bobbed about her face.

"I do know you pretty well, Earl Braden, so I'll be glad to help you choose," she volunteered sweetly. "A person really ought to choose a mate freely, so you just take your time here, don't you think so, Mr. Duke and Miss Abigail?" Grace asked over her shoulder, her big brown eyes never leaving Earl's face. "I mean, that kindly Melvin Mott I met at the ball is probably going to be the one I'll choose. Such a fine man and surely does know his mind, too!"

Abigail watched Grace in action. Earl looked thunderstruck. And Duke, standing so close, made her tremble. She jumped when the matron began shouting orders.

"You baggage stand up straight and get off those mobcaps, case he wants to check for lice! An' show the man your teeth if he wants a look! Searching for a good helpmeet to work with a sheep drive and setting up a run over the mountains is what he's planning. So there'd be no chance for any one of you he picks to do no bolting or there'd be nothing but bush to run to!"

"I don't know why a woman you'd pick would ever do any bolting, Earl," Grace dared and pointed to a stocky, surly-looking brunette across the way. "Now that one looks like she might be able to stand up to your bad-tempered rages and—"

"That's it, that's *it!*" Earl roared so loud the line of convicts jumped. He grabbed Grace's arm and half dragged her out of the courtyard to the corridor while Abigail and Duke hurried along behind them. In the dim hall, Earl lifted Grace by her shoulders in a hard grasp until only her toes dangled on the floor. Abigail made a move to help her, but Duke pulled her back.

"You think I need your meddling in all this, one of the biggest days of my life?" Earl roared at Grace. "Made my-

self a promise the day Ma died and my dad just turned away
to go back to work his damned fields that I'd never be
ashamed of my Parramatta wife someday!''

Grace's voice trembled, but it was strong. "Mr. Squire
wasn't ashamed of her, Earl! He picked her, didn't he? She
gave him three fine children, and they worked hard together to make a home. It was just his way of dealing with
the pain of losing the one he loved. I know about that, see,
'cause if it wouldn't have been for my friend Miss Abigail,
I might have just throwed myself off a cliff into the sea after I lost you!''

"But—you didn't try it, did you?''

"No, you big brute, and you're hurting me, so let go. I'd
never do away with myself like that—not over the likes of
you. But you as good as wanted to rid yourself of me, didn't
you?''

"Grace, I—no, Grace, I never meant—'' Earl swept
Grace into his crushing embrace as the befuddled matron,
keys rattling, entered the hall to stare aghast at the passionate scene before her. "Grace, Grace, it's been hell without
you, and thinking I wanted—I had—to do this,'' Earl muttered into her hair. Grace's London bonnet slid off and
dangled by its ribbons.

"My darling,'' Grace murmured. She fluttered kisses on
Earl's chin and cheeks until he clasped the back of her neck
to hold her head still for a sweeping kiss.

"Well!'' Abigail declared, feeling moved to tears.

"Earl promised his father a wedding, day after tomorrow, and it looks like he'll keep his word,'' Duke told her
and wiped away a tear from Abigail's cheek with his finger.
"So I hope you'll come, Abby Rose, and bring the bride.
After all, you're the one to thank for this. We're real busy
getting ready to shear, and there's some lambing going on
that should never have happened this time of year. The place
is a mess, but Earl and I can sleep with the shearers and you
and Grace can have our room if you'll stay the night before
the wedding. After all, any woman who has been on my arm
at the governor's ball and then taken on the Female Fac-

tory is surely ready to stay the night on Braden land in my
bed, even if I'm not in it.''

That little speech set her to trembling again with longing
and love for him. But she had to keep her head this time.
She would make him realize he needed her more than anything.

"I answer to no one but myself now," Abigail told him,
trying to keep her voice steady. "I am not an Exclusive, nor
a Currency lass. I am not even English anymore. I am just—
myself."

"Earl told Grace he's missed her," Duke said, his gaze
steady on hers, his hands rotating his hat brim through his
hands. "I've missed you, too, Abby Rose."

She almost melted. She had to lock her knees to stand
straight. "Then I will come out—for Grace and Earl," she
replied as crisply as she could manage. "And with H.M. to
please Squire."

That hint of challenge lit Duke's eyes, but he nodded and
stepped away to try to calm the fuming matron. Abigail
quickly wiped away more tears with her cambric handkerchief, then went to congratulate Earl and Grace. Grace
threw her arms around her friend's neck, then hugged
everyone, including the matron.

Abigail turned from them to take one last look out the
window at the poor souls imprisoned here, none of whom
had been granted their freedom by Earl today. She suddenly felt very sad, despite her joyful companions.

As the four of them left the Female Factory, Abby rejoiced for Grace, but could not help wondering about her
own future with the elder Braden brother.

In the side yard of Castle Keep, under two greening fruit
trees, Duke and Abigail stood with Earl and Grace as sup-
porters for their wedding. It was a lovely early September
day; spring was coming to New South Wales. Noisy sheep
were penned and ready for the beginning of shearing tomorrow; the herders stood, hats in hands, behind the tiny
wedding party while the cleric read the vows. Just behind

Abigail, Squire held H.M. in his arms, with Catty sniffling beside him. The sun beat down; the breeze was sweet; and Earl's beloved Blues beckoned across the fields and beyond the foothills. Standing so close to Duke, as if the two of them stood here to be wed, Abigail realized how much she, too, longed to be a Braden bride. Her gaze locked with Duke's, his eyes bluer than the mountains or the sky.

"Now our Lord Himself dearly loved sheep and spoke of Himself as a shepherd," the cleric, who had ridden out from Sydney, was saying. "So it is an honorable profession Earl Braden follows. And he must take care of his wife better than any shepherd ever did a precious lamb, just as the Lord cares for each of his beloved flock."

It struck Abigail with cold reality for the first time that Grace and Earl would be leaving before the cold weather came to the mountains next fall. Grace had said they would travel over the mountain road and settle near a new rural town called Bathurst to stake out and clear a vast sheep run. Abigail listened distractedly as the cleric recited the familiar words of the Twenty-Third Psalm. Still waters, somewhere over the Blues, Abigail thought, so different from the wild waves of the coast and the turbulent lives of the Currency who defied those waves. But she would gladly face either waves or still waters with Duke at her side. Whatever loss and pain might come her way for her decision, she vowed to do anything she could to earn Duke Braden's love!

When the ceremony ended, Kulalang, his wives and child and several other aborigines materialized as if from the earth itself, bearing carved gifts for the wedding couple. Some starved-looking dogs trailed at their heels, and Squire immediately rescued H.M. from a possible confrontation. The wedding guests shared a feast laid on plank tables on the veranda while the Bandajongs sat in the yard to partake of the mutton steamer, poultry pie made from the Australian cockatoo called galah, beetroot salad and rich treacle cake. Though Grace and Earl protested, Abigail insisted on helping Catty and several of the men serve. Her hand brushed Duke's when she ladled currant jelly on his mutton steamer.

"Catty and the lads can do that, Abby Rose," he told her quietly.

His continued use of her pet name thrilled her. She wished desperately she could read his thoughts, especially about their future. When her eyes met his again she felt a little jolt. She realized she was standing there just staring like a ninny.

"I want to help," she replied. "And tomorrow I want to see how a sheep is sheared."

"It's a dusty, dirty business for a lady," he protested, but his voice held promise and not denial.

"Out here," she told him, "it's more important to be a woman." Let him chew on *that,* she thought and turned away to serve the Bandajongs as Squire scraped back his chair to propose a toast from the keg of rum they'd all been pulling from.

"I been through a lot of days, some sad, some proud," Squire began while the noisy table slowly quieted. "Always tried to be what we old lags used to call a pebble, meaning a strong man who don't break under hard times. See, a sandstone—that's just the op'site, the man who crumbles. Even when times was worst and I lost me beloved wife and little daughter, I tried not to be a sandstone. But how I wish me wife and little Queenie could be here today to see how proud I am of Earl and Gracie, and Duke, too."

Earl hugged the teary-eyed Grace closer to him. He looked teary-eyed himself. "But today," Squire went on, clearing his throat, "I got a tear or two in me eye. Been after me boys to get themselves brides and make old Squire some grandsons to live on here at Castle Keep after I'm gone. But Duke was always busy with his causes, 'portant as they be, and Earl got his dream to overland 'cross the Blues, so he'll be moving on—"

Squire's voice faltered. Evidently not trusting himself to say more, he simply lifted his cup stiff-armed and Duke took up the toast, which everyone else joined in his or her own way.

"To Earl and Grace! To the bride and groom! To Braden's bride!"

Grace beamed and Earl almost blushed. Duke smiled to flash those straight white teeth he so seldom showed. H.M., now back on Squire's lap, added her bark to the noise. Lady Abigail Anne Rosemont, overcome with both loving and longing, couldn't say a word. Never in her days in England had she felt such joy or riches or belonging. Never had she so yearned to stay plain Abby Rose forever in a place she felt was home.

That night Abby lay in Duke's narrow bed while he slept out another night with the hands. Catty, just as she had last night, lay in heavy slumber on Earl's bed across this small, spare room. Squire was outside, too, telling stories of the old days, and Abigail had let him keep H.M. on a leash for the night. The dog was as excited as the rest of them. Men's loud voices drifted into the house for hours, betraying the effects of rum after a day of celebration.

Besides the usual herders and hands, two extra shearers had been hired on as well as several more boundary guards. Duke hadn't wanted to say why at first, but he had finally admitted to her that Phillip Godfrey-Bennett had hired a small army of bullyboys from town so he wanted to be prepared. And she had been certain more than once that she heard distant Bandajong skin drums and that strange torn-leaf whistle of Kulalang's on the breeze. How could Catty sleep through all this!

Abigail was tired, but so tense she could not sleep. Thinking about Grace and Earl on their wedding night in Squire's small room at the back of the house didn't help. Grace had been so excited and flustered when it came time to wave good-night to everyone and go with Earl.

She had hugged Abigail and whispered in her ear, "I owe it all to you. And somehow, someway I'm gonna help you get Mr. Duke right where you want him, too!"

That and everything made Abigail think how much she longed for Duke's touch. She flopped over again restlessly, making a hopeless tangle of her bedclothes. Her merest memory of Duke's look or touch today sent shivers up her spine. His auburn hair with its sun-bleached streaks had been tousled by the breeze. Those tiny, endearing squint lines at the corners of his clear blue eyes had crinkled when he smiled. The sun-browned skin of his high forehead had furrowed when his brows lifted and he gave her that challenging look that rocked her to her toes. When she took his arm or his arm crept, even lightly, around her, she felt the molded strength of his muscles and yearned for so much more.

She wanted to be gathered on his lap the way Grace had sat on Earl's today—just the way she herself had ridden out the storm aboard the *Challenge* with Duke! She yearned to be crushed to that wiry, powerful body for a searing kiss again. She wanted to be pressed down on a rough wool blanket in the grass, the way she'd been that day they had almost, almost—

"Oh!" Abigail muttered to the dark room and sat up to press her face in her hands. She scolded herself for such yearnings and threw herself back down.

Tonight, when Duke had so politely bade her good-night, she had wanted him to kiss her. But he only squeezed her shoulder and went out, to leave her standing in the lighted doorway gazing after him. How she would have loved to run off into the darkness after him! She'd share his bed outside or in a pile of straw in the barn! Tomorrow, he had said, he would show her the shearing and the lambing before she headed back to Sydney. But she didn't want to head back to Sydney, not if Duke remained here!

She sighed and turned over again on the hard mattress. She thought of all the nights Duke had lain here, thinking, dreaming. She was starting to feel drowsy when she had an idea how to make Duke explode to possess her just the way Earl had Grace. She'd convince Duke to love her more—and without Kulalang's interrupting them this time!

She drifted through dreams, seeing Duke posing for her as she put pen to paper.

"Why don't you draw a wedding portrait of us, too?" he asked. He smiled at her, leaned back on one elbow, his booted foot on the fence rail.

"My dearest Duke, my beloved bridegroom," she heard herself murmur seductively, "let me draw you undraped, a naked Greek god, like Apollo." But, she thought, spinning deeper into restless sleep, Apollo had not loved the nymph who had turned into a sunflower in her longing. Now she was only a wooden, painted figurehead on a ship, challenging the waves alone. Still, Abigail would draw Duke's sleek muscles and his bronze skin all uncovered, and then—then—

She heard a man's distant laughter. Was she awake or asleep in Duke's bed? She yawned and stretched; her eyes watered from exhaustion. She knew her final prayer was quite profane, but she couldn't help it: when she put her plan into action tomorrow, Duke would be bedding with her!

# *Chapter Eleven*

After a hearty breakfast early the next morning, Duke kept his word to take Abigail out to see the shearing. Squire trailed along with H.M. in his arms.

"Can't let a little princess like this get bothered by me boys' sheepdogs," Squire explained.

"I'm afraid H.M. is rather spoiled," Abigail admitted. "She's been pampered all her life and doesn't know what hard work is."

"That's the trouble with things," Duke put in without looking at her as he gazed over the busy scene just beyond the fenced yard. "However badly H.M. might want to adapt to being a sheepdog, with her pampered past it just can't be done."

Annoyed, Abigail tucked her drawing board and pouch of pens and ink tighter to her side. She got Duke's point, though Squire seemed oblivious. "I don't think you're right about that, Duke Braden, but I'll not persuade you just with talk," she told him.

"I admit actions speak louder than words," he said as the three of them halted on the far side of the first shearing pen, "but I hardly think you're up to this sort of life—especially what Grace is facing on the journey west."

Abigail hated things getting off to such a bad start when she meant to convince Duke once and for all that he needed her—and not just in bed. She truly found the prospect of life in the country exhilarating. She was a wealthy woman; with her money poured into a place like this, they could build their own vast spread someday, and she'd revel in every minute of it with Duke at her side.

"Never could see what me boys saw in these animals," Squire grumbled under his breath as they watched a shearer seize the next noisy sheep in the fenced trough and keep back the others by closing a gate. In his own little pen, the shearer swung the sheep on its hip between his legs and bent to separate it and its fleecy coat with the hand-shears.

"I don't do shearing," Duke told her, "but the secret's in learning how to hold the sheep right where you want it." He turned to study her again, then looked away. "I've learned that much over these years when Earl and I insisted we take on a flock of Polwarths here as well as Dad's crops."

"And done all right too, I s'pose," Squire admitted, "but this here's meant to be a farm like where I grew up, and they never had so many of these blasted sheep there, no sir!"

Abigail smiled at Squire, and he nodded back. In a way, she thought, the stubborn old man was just as tied to England as the Exclusives who detested him. It was the next generation, men like Earl and Duke, who were the future of this land. She herself, in finding and loving Duke, could set her English past aside. She welcomed the change. Now, if only she could convince Duke of that!

"The shearer's boots are so shiny," Abigail noted.

"You do have an artist's eye for details," Duke replied. "That's from the lanolin in the wool. And they say shearers have softer hands than a lady. Come over here and I'll show you how to skirt the fleece."

They left Squire and H.M. behind. Duke led her to a rough board table where men spread the fleece and removed hunks of wool colored or stained by dust, mud or burrs. She watched for a moment, then tried it herself. "Oh!" she said as a burr stuck on her finger on her first try. She yanked it out and watched a crimson drop of blood form on her fingertip. "I'm sure I could learn to do this without dying your wool bright red!"

"You're so eager to please," he said, his voice suddenly quiet and intimate, so only she could hear. "I should put you and your men right back on the high road to town, before this goes any farther between us again."

"I'm not leaving until I see how all this is done. Besides, I want to complete Earl and Grace's nuptial portrait before I go. And," she added, hoping her voice sounded nonchalant as she tugged loose another puff of muddy fleece, "I thought I'd do a sketch of you."

"Of me? And sell it to the *Gazette* to accompany their next lambasting of me, you mean?"

"I intend to keep it for myself," she said and smiled at him. "For throwing darts at from time to time."

He chuckled, and she realized how seldom she had heard him laugh. He escorted her to the woolshed where Earl oversaw the classing and the pressing of the fleeces into big bales branded D. & E. BRADEN, PARRA.

"And how's the new bridegroom today?" Duke asked Earl and clapped him between his shoulder blades.

"Still sleepy, tell you that!" Earl managed with a wink at Abigail before he swung an armload of wool into the next bale. "How about you two?"

"I slept like a baby!" Duke teased. "I'll be back in to help you shortly."

That last comment disturbed Abigail. Did he mean to send her away already or end their tour soon so he could help Earl? She had thought it would take most of the day to see the shearing, that maybe he'd even let her help. They needed to talk. She needed to get him off alone!

"Duke," she began as they strolled back outside, away from the noisy, busy scene, "perhaps I could help you and Earl—or at least do some sketches while you work."

He turned to her and leaned back on the fence to the yard with one boot heel hooked on the lowest rail. "Abby, I promise I will come calling on you in town when shearing's over, but you'd help me most now if you'd leave the premises."

"The Widow Cranbrook doesn't allow male visitors—you know that. Besides, I—"

"Damn it, why do you have to keep getting in the way?" he snapped so loud she jumped. "Eve loose in the Garden of Eden holding out the shiny apple to Adam! And he wants a big bite of that apple real bad, Abby, but it might ruin things for him."

"You sound like Earl did just a few days ago! You know Grace is good for him, and—"

"It's not the same! Yes, Grace was good and right for Earl, but they didn't really come from two different worlds, sweetheart. Damn it, don't you see what you're driving me to! I can't concentrate on anything but you!"

She relished that admission of her small victory. But why did he have to be so stubborn? She was certain that if there had not been so many men around Duke would have grabbed and kissed her on the spot. Instead, he turned away and ran to meet an anxious young fellow who had ridden in from the west.

"What is it, O'Brien?" Duke yelled up at the boy.

"Those ewes the stray ram got to are starting to drop lambs, Mr. Duke, and some having a bad time of it. With all that's goin' on, I'm the only one up there! I hated to leave! Anyone you can spare I can use!"

"I'll come myself!" Duke told him. The boy nodded, wheeled around and started right back out. Duke ran for his horse and pulled it unsaddled from the small stable while he fastened the bridle and reins.

Abigail tore after him, shouting, "I can help! I've helped birth calves on the estate in Kent. I know how!"

Duke sprang up on the horse's back and glared down at her. She was certain her plans for showing him she could thrive in this life were ruined. He would just ride off and leave her in his dust. But he cursed under his breath and reached down for her. She found herself, still holding her sketching supplies, sitting sideways before him as he urged the horse away from the farm.

Abby clung to her things and to him. She was getting her chance! After all, she had told him the truth about observing and even helping birth several calves who would have been stillborn without the dairymaid's help.

"This lecherous big merino ram we call King Henry VIII got loose on a flock of ewes five months ago," Duke told her as they rode. "He was in sheep heaven, tupping every damned one of them. Then he paid his dues by collapsing for a week."

Abby felt herself blush hot, even though he was just talking about sheep. "How many ewes?" she asked.

"Twenty-two," he clipped out. "And every single one took! We can't even shear them until they get through this alive. We'll need every sheep we can get to start fresh over the Blues, Abby. I don't know how it is for cows in England, but most of these are first-timers and some will be bearing twins, so don't pull too hard."

Pull too hard? she thought. With just her hands? At Fairleigh they had the latest device, brass tongs to reach inside the animal to help. And she'd always had the milkmaid there, who knew what she was doing. Why did Duke make it sound as if she'd be off by herself? Wouldn't he be with her? But she prepared herself to learn and help any way she could.

In a flat, short valley with a stream bisecting it, O'Brien was already off his horse and leaning over a sheep. Duke reined in at the opposite end of the valley. He swung Abigail down by one arm and then dismounted. Sheep dotted the area, evidently guarded by one clever, quiet dog who made occasional outruns on the perimeter to bring in nervous strays. It suddenly seemed like hundreds, thousands of sheep to Abigail, but Duke had said only twenty-two. She could see that a few had already dropped their lambs and were nudging them to their wobbly feet. She put her things under a bush and nervously wiped her hands on her brown day gown as she approached the first skittish ewe that was grunting and straining in pain.

"Take that one first!" Duke ordered, pointing to it. "That's Quick Step and the one just beyond is Feather. Talk to them to calm them so they don't kick or run." Then he turned and ran to the next cluster of ewes.

Abigail sidled up to the wide-eyed ewe called Quick Step. They named and recognized all these sheep? They looked the same to her—every last one of them! "All right now, hello there, Quick Step. I've come to help. Are you sure you won't do this yourself? Well, all right then. Just let me see back here. Oh, it looks like you're—ready."

Abigail took a breath to calm herself. She had told Duke she would help and she meant to! But she was so nervous she probably felt worse than this poor sheep! Then she saw the frenzied look in its eyes. She tentatively stroked its soft back and gasped when she saw tiny hooves protruding from the birth opening. Don't pull too hard, Duke had said, so he obviously meant for her to pull gently and with no brass tongs.

Holding her breath, Abigail did what she had to do. Dripping with sweat, speaking to the ewe to calm her, she soon enough pulled out a wet, wriggling lamb who fell onto the grass. She was elated!

"Duke, look, I've got one! How will I know if it's to be twins?" she called. He seemed so very far away now.

He did not look up but called, "Just keep an eye on her and go on to the next."

She did as he said, and then went on to the next after that and the next. Her back ached, her hands were sore and chapped. One feisty ewe had stepped on her foot, so she was hobbling. But she had conquered her fear and ignorance, and she was so proud!

"How many?" Duke asked and came over to rub her shoulders. She realized with a look at the sun it was no longer early morning but early afternoon.

"Eight, I think, counting two pair of twins, but that one you called Feather won't let the little thing nurse and keeps nosing it away. She's likely to kick it next!"

Duke hurried over to rescue the lamb. "I've got one that died whose mother's looking for one to nurse," he told her. "If Feather doesn't want it by now, she never will."

Young O'Brien came back through, herding the new mothers and their brood together with the dog's help while Abigail followed Duke over to his baaing, lambless ewe. Abigail stared aghast as she held Feather's rejected lamb; she watched Duke skin the one that had been born dead. Abigail closed her eyes.

"You aren't going to faint on me now, are you, Abby Rose?" Duke asked lightly. "Hold that lamb tight for me now, while I put on its new coat."

She did as he said, but she was trembling again, exhausted to the bone. She watched while Duke fitted the tiny rejected lamb in the bloody fleece of the dead one, right over its own curly wool.

"You see," he told her, "the ewe will nurse this little one, but only if she smells it first to assure herself it's hers. And with this coat of the dead one, she'll accept it as her own. A trick of sorts, but a justifiable one to save a life."

"Yes, I see," she told him. She had, after all, thought of her own plan to convince and seduce Duke in much the same way, she thought wearily. A trick only of sorts, a justifiable one to save their futures.

When O'Brien came along to gather up the ewes they'd worked with, Duke took Abigail's filthy hand in his filthier one and led her down to the creek. They scrubbed their hands and faces and sat, tired, side by side, not speaking for a moment.

"You were wonderful, Abby Rose."

"Thank you. I wanted to help. I'm glad you let me."

"It's turned out to be a warm day," he said with a slow look that covered every inch of her, perspiring and dusty as she was. "Hot."

"Yes."

"This stream comes from a pond. Not the same one with the waterfall," he added hastily. "Let's wash off more there. Maybe it's time for your first swimming lesson."

If he thought she would balk, he was mistaken. "Yes," she acquiesced at once. "Just let me get my things."

They rode his horse along the streambank into a copse of gums and dismounted. Grass grew right up to the edge of the small pond; water tumbled over a few rocks cleverly piled to dam up the pond before the stream rippled away.

"We water the flock below this, so the water's clean," he told her as he lifted her down and took her things from her hands. Their gazes met and held. "I love this time of year before the streams flood or bushfires come," he rushed on, as if he had to fill the air between them with words. "In the spring weather of September and October, it seems we're always right on the edge of new possibilities."

He led her down to the sedgy bank of the pond. Duke hopped on one foot, then the other to pull his boots off. Abby discarded her shoes and slithered out of her petticoat. "If we get in dressed, there'll be so much to dry," he said, leaving the decision up to her whether they disrobed or not.

"But our clothes need washing, too," she responded and then could have kicked herself. After all, getting both of them undressed had to be part of her plan, and here she'd reacted instinctively to scuttle it.

"All right then," he agreed pleasantly enough and picked her up to stride into the waist-high water.

She didn't squeal or protest. She just took the opportunity to put her arms around his neck and sink her head onto his shoulder. She loved the touch and scent of him. Then he lowered both of them slowly into the water.

"O-oh, a bit cold!" she said, laughing.

He bounced her and swirled her, making big ripples that sent water splashing everywhere. She clung harder, kicking her feet. She felt so wonderful suspended in his arms as if she could float and drift here with him forever.

"Time for your first lesson," he said.

He turned her over on her stomach, so that she balanced on his hands, and taught her how to paddle her cupped hands and stiffen her legs to kick. Her sopping skirts were heavy about her legs but she managed anyway. She laughed when he held his breath, thrust his face under the water and blew bubbles. Her hair got soaked and heavy, so she took out the pins and let it hang loose.

"Now," he declared at last, "swim on your own over here to me and don't panic if your face goes down. Just hold your breath."

She held it until she thought her lungs would burst, but she made it over to him. He hugged her hard, then lifted her clear out of the water with his hands on her waist. Rivulets poured from her sodden hair down her dress, which clung to her curves. Slowly, he lowered her until, breathless at their antics, they were nose to nose.

"Now we're going to have to take these things off so they won't give us a chill while we dry," he told her. "We can hardly go back drenched with all those men there."

"Hardly," she agreed.

"There are blankets in the shed just over that hill. And with O'Brien busy with the ewes and everyone else back at the shearing—"

"Yes," she said and nodded, not quite sure what she was agreeing to. But anything with Duke was right and good, she told herself. He was more than falling in with her plan: he was making it so much easier. All those come-hither comments she had rehearsed to convince him to pose for her undraped—naked— She evidently didn't need any of them! she thought as she tried to dry her hair with her discarded petticoat.

In the tiny herdsman's shed, Duke closed the door on the sunstruck afternoon and held a blanket high in front of his face so she could disrobe behind it with some privacy. Trembling, goose bumps on her skin, Abigail fumbled with her belt and buttons. "All right," she said at last as she dropped everything and grabbed for the corners of the blanket, "I'm ready."

He laughed and, to her mingled relief and regret, wrapped the blanket around her like a cocoon.

"Ready for what, Abby Rose?" he asked and flapped open another blanket for her to hold up like a curtain for him. "Or will you just turn your back like the lady you are?" he teased.

This new, playful Duke melted her bones. She felt inebriated, when she'd had nothing but a long drink of pond water. "I'll not look if you don't want me to," she said and spun about so her back was to him. "But I must admit I thought it might be great fun to draw you—well, you know, *au naturel.*"

He was silent at that, and she feared she'd overstepped. Then his hands on her shoulders turned her slowly to him. His waistcoat was gone and his shirt was unbuttoned to flaunt crisp, curly brown chest hair.

"I would think," he said, his voice shaky when he noticed her slow perusal, "that getting a man to pose *au naturel* costs an artist quite a bit. Are you willing to pay my fee?"

Panicked by the smug smile on his lips, she almost begged her way out of this mess she'd gotten herself into. This was what she'd wanted, only she hadn't thought it would be so easily accomplished. And out here alone with him, she realized she hadn't given enough thought to the danger of his reaction. In her dreams last night he had seemed so much easier to control! Getting him to know he needed her and wanted to wed her was one thing, but this lightning and thunder that crackled between them both terrified and enthralled her.

"I am willing to pay if I know the fee," she replied, her voice very breathy.

"That you pose for me, too, that's all. And the artist gets to pick the pose of the subject."

"You draw me, you mean? I didn't think you could!"

"Don't cloud the waters. A bargain or not, Abby?" he asked and removed his hands from her shoulders to tug his shirt out of his trousers and off his muscled arms; then he undid his belt. He threw the shirt and belt behind him without breaking his stare. His hands dropped to the buttons on his trousers, and the left corner of his mouth lifted in the slightest hint of a devilish grin.

Drat the man! He was calling her bluff, playing with her! If she refused, he'd probably pack her off in her carriage for Sydney before nightfall. Maybe that was just what he wanted! It would be weeks before she might see him again. He'd never get past the iron gates at Cliffside House. She certainly could not be running out here all the time, no matter how often Grace and Earl asked her, or how much Squire wanted to see H.M.! She'd just have to show this man how much he needed her, and for all sorts of reasons!

"Absolutely, a bargain," she declared. "And I'll draw first." She busied herself propping up her board and pens so she had a reason not to watch him disrobe. She sat cross-legged on the floor and dared another glance up at him. He had unbuttoned his trousers but stood stock-still now with hands splayed on his naked hips. She bit her lower lip hard. From his chest, a V of hair pointed straight down over his flat belly into his trousers. She could see he was aroused. She'd never get through this one way or the other, she thought, panicking.

"Well?" she asked.

"You, too, at the same time. I need a little down payment so I know this is all in good faith," he insisted outrageously. "Besides, you'll draw faster if we're both chilled, and we can get on to my turn."

She opened her mouth for some tart retort, but she knew her hands trembled too much to draw him now. Surely, he was just bluffing about drawing her. She didn't know what to do now. Words, ploys, plans flew out of her head. She didn't know anything except she loved and wanted this man now and forever. She shoved her sketching board aside and stood. She unwrapped her blanket and dropped it at her feet.

He heard his own sharp intake of breath. He gazed at her a moment without moving. He felt both awed and amazed she had done it. And he was deeply moved by her beauty, even as the surge of his deep desire for her staggered him.

He let his gaze wander slowly over her. She stood proudly before him, unflinching but for the tremor of her graceful limbs. Her skin looked alabaster in the dimness of the small shed. She glowed as she blushed under his perusal. Her skin seemed to reflect the crimson of the tumbled, dampened tresses that dusted the curve of her shoulders. Her curly hair had never looked more provocatively wind-tossed, even in the shelter of this shed. The globes of her small, high breasts were tipped by pert rosy tips that reflected the strawberries-and-cream of her coloring. Her nipples were puckered from the chill, but he'd take care of that soon. And at the juncture of her shapely, graceful legs, the reddish thatch pointed to the secrets between her thighs. He tugged his trousers down and off.

It was her turn now to look. How blatantly ready he was for her frightened her, and her bare bottom bumped into the slatted side of the shed as she backed up. He came closer. He spoke at last.

"Not a very good place for our first time. You deserve so much more. You're so strong, so special. And so much help today, and—"

She was in his arms clinging to him, and they both felt the shattering impact of that. "It's a wonderful place!" she told him. "You're special, too, so special—"

He kissed her so hard her head spun. He tilted her back in his arms and swept down her jawline to her throat, ravaging her flesh with kisses. Special, he was so special. That was what Mrs. Godfrey-Bennett had called that man she had loved who betrayed her. But this was so very different from that story.

"Oh, Duke, I love y—" she managed before his lips took hers again. She found herself sprawled across his lap while he sat on her discarded blanket on the ground. She kissed him back, discovering to her delight she could make him forget what he was doing and just freeze to drink in her kisses and caresses. She could make him frenzied with the tip of her tongue in his ear. She could nibble little kisses

across his shoulders and knead his lower back and make
him—

"O-o-oh!" she squealed as he twisted them down and
over on the ground. Flat on her back, she stared up at him;
he hovered over her like a protective second roof. His hands
were everywhere, stroking, grasping, invading so deliciously she felt dizzy.

He knelt between her legs and spread them wider. She
clung to him, trusting, as his tongue plundered her mouth.
He settled more heavily over her, pressing her down, causing her to take in little breaths over which she seemed to have
no control.

"You're so ready, my sweetheart," he whispered hotly in
her ear. "Will you draw us like this later? I want that
sketch—damn, I want the real thing and I always have!"

He kissed her hard again. Into her very woman's core, he
pushed, paused, then plunged. Her quick cry of surprise at
the pain was swallowed in his kiss, but the hurt passed immediately, doused by the growing circle of liquid heat in her
lower belly. She held to him with both arms and legs, as he
momentarily stilled. She thought how dazzling it was. If
there was nothing else later, she had loved every moment of
this time. But then, he began to show her there was so much
more than they had already done.

"Look at me, Abby Rose," he whispered.

She stared up into his blue, blue eyes, thickly fringed and
narrowed in passion.

"You're so beautiful, so special—"

He began to move over her, in her. She gasped at that
startling ride. "I didn't know—all this—" she tried to explain to him, but his increasing pace against her and within
her drowned everything in the cresting waves in which they
swam together.

He was so moved by her honesty and naiveté, her trust in
him, despite everything that had kept them apart. Swept
away, he murmured erotic commands in her ear. She quickly
showed him she knew what he meant. She moved with him

now, tentatively at first, then in a rhythmic motion that made him feel she rode him as fervently as he did her.

"My Abby Rose!" he cried out and feared that he would never find a way to control his life again.

"My darling!" she answered and clung to him.

An hour later, they gathered their still damp garments and reluctantly tugged them back on. How wonderful it had been just to lie in Duke's arms, trusting, unspeaking— though that had not lasted long and they had soon tumbled together again. This time he had not even turned her to him but had joined her from behind and had his hands free to pleasure her all over until she had cried out so loud, she was certain she would cause a stampede among the distant sheep. Now, as he pulled her up behind him on the horse, she still felt she floated.

"We'd better get that Earl-and-Grace newlywed look off our faces before we ride back in," he told her, his voice gone serious now. "One glance and everyone will know."

"They will not!" she insisted and held to him with her free arm. "It's our secret for a little while."

They rode back around the ewes and their new lambs. "One hundred and eight percent increase from these twenty-two ewes," he said more to himself than her. "We tried hard to keep from having new lambs while heading west, but now these young ones may have to be carried horseback most of the way. With a small flock, we need every last one and just have to hope the dingoes and other dangers out there don't get them. At least the damned bushrangers know herders with a flock make bad pickings, but Earl and Grace will need all the help we can give them."

She was touched by his continued concern for his brother and his new wife. He had shared so much with Earl he still referred to his dream trip west with the plural "we," as if he were going, too.

"You know," she told him solemnly as they rode out of the valley, "not all my money is tied up in the estate in England. If there's anything Earl and Grace need for the trip west, I'd be happy to—''

"Your wedding gift to them was very generous, Abby. I'm sure most of that will go into supplies for the trip."

She pressed her cheek to his muscular back, savoring the last moment of their closeness before they rode in sight of the others. Though his shirt and waistcoat were still damp, he radiated warmth. She longed to have him hold her again. Once they rode back to Castle Keep, he'd probably not even put an arm around her until they got everything worked out for their future. Since no men came calling at Cliffside House, she'd just have to meet him somewhere in Sydney or ride out here, so they could make plans.

"I'll miss Grace terribly and Earl, too," she told him, still reveling in the afterglow of their intimacy. "You'll be awfully busy here after they're gone on the drive, but I'll be glad to come out and help."

"If you bring your guards and H.M., I'm sure Dad would appreciate it," he told her, his voice darker and more distant now. "But Abby, there's obviously something you don't understand. I'm making the drive in just a few weeks with Earl and Grace."

She jerked bolt upright; her sketch board slid away. "What? But they're going permanently! You can't—you have things here, and Squire—"

He reined in on the crest overlooking the busy shearing scene and house below. "I'll only be gone a few months, four or five, I don't know for sure. I'll probably be back here for half a year after that."

"But—you didn't tell me. Even just now when we were so close, you didn't tell me, and all the while you knew you were leaving, after we—we—!"

"Earl and I argued over it, but I decided it's too important and he needs me. Besides, it will help my arguments in Sydney about squatters' rights to land if I'm a squatter, too. Please understand, Abby."

But Abigail was hardly listening to his explanation. Four or five months? Four or five months! Whatever would she do without him, especially when they were ready for permanent commitment after today! And then she knew.

"I want to go, too, Duke. Please. I showed you I can help and learn today. You know I'm an excellent rider, and I can cook damper or whatever. I'd be glad to invest, I said, maybe buy a big piece of land there for—"

"Absolutely not! Impossible! The last thing I want out there is some rich Exclusive buying up land when the point is to open it to those who need to work their way through to buy it! If *you* purchase some big hunk of land, why not the Godfrey-Bennetts and their ilk, too, and that would push folks like us right off the Bathurst plains! Besides, a woman of your background and breeding out there—"

"Damn you!" she cried and swung a fist at his back. She slid off the horse and stood glaring up at him. "You intentionally didn't tell me you were leaving—deserting me—so you could get what you wanted! Just tup a woman like that big stray ram and then leave her!"

"Damn *you*, Abigail!" he shouted and jumped down after her as she picked up her drawing board and started toward the house on foot. "I wasn't even sure I was going until lately, I said!" He grabbed her and swung her around to face him. When she tried to swing her board at him, he hit it away. "You were just as interested as I to get in the hay today when I warned you to leave! Did you think I wouldn't take what you were so obviously offering?"

"Just let me go! I—I—" she choked out before he threw her board to the ground again and hauled her hard into his arms. She clung to him, while he rocked her against him on the windy hill. She managed to relax a bit. After all, she thought, she had a few weeks to convince him she should go along. She'd ask Squire to keep H.M. for her. Earl and Grace would be on her side when they heard. Even if she could not convince Duke to wed her by then, she most certainly had no intention of staying in Sydney at Cliffside House, only going out with guards to keep the possibility of facing Phillip at bay. Four or five months without Duke?

But that was as long as the entire journey to New South Wales! She had to find a way to go along. He had to let her!

"I'm sorry it came out like this that I'm leaving," he said, his voice soft now.

"You should have told me earlier, that's all."

"You mean it would have made the difference today, that you would have turned me down? That you would have fled back to Sydney right after the wedding yesterday?"

"Never mind," she said, and pulled away to brush herself off, as if he'd wrinkled her already ruined gown. "You don't tell me things that affect both our lives, so perhaps I shall follow your example."

He pulled her back. "What are you thinking? You're not going, and that's that."

"It's a free country, Duke Braden," she insisted, glaring up into his stern face. "That's what you're fighting for, isn't it? I mean, I'd like to see the Blues up close, and pastoral Bathurst sounds intriguing."

"You're not going!"

"Not with you, perhaps."

Stiff-armed, he picked her up off her feet until her toes dangled on the tips of his boots. His eyes chilled her; his breath burned her.

"I won't have you hurt. Sure, there's a road, but it's a long, hard, dangerous drive, Lady Abigail, and not everyone you meet out there is real friendly. You will stay here, waiting for me, and we'll decide things between us when I get back! That's that."

She glared at him so defiantly, he put her down. "That's your *that*, not mine!" she told him as icily as she could manage. "I have no intention of waiting with bated breath for your possible return. And thank you for all the lessons about fleecing sheep today!" She bent to retrieve her board and pouch. She turned her back on him and marched away down the dusty path to Castle Keep.

She cried silent tears all the way, but she stiffened her shoulders so he wouldn't see them shake. She had felt frightened, furious and betrayed at first, but now she was only determined. Somehow, some way, she was going west with the Bradens. And he was going to admit how wrong he'd been and thank her for it, too.

At that moment, from the side of her eye, Abigail caught a glint from the rocks of the eastern outcrop, a flash of late-afternoon sun that was soon gone. She wondered if it were some aborigine signal, but doubted it. She blinked in that direction and saw nothing more. She marched on, ignoring Duke when he brought his horse to ride beside her as if to escort her in.

Stretched out on his belly, secreted on the outcrop of sandstone, Phillip Godfrey-Bennett lowered the tubular eyeglass he'd been using to spy on the shearing at Castle Keep. At first he could not believe his eyes that Abigail was here, here on Braden land and walking down out of the hills with Duke Braden! The slut! She had betrayed him in public *and* private with his worst enemy when she knew he wanted her! His mother had told him she was living with old Widow Cranbrook, so he'd been temporarily biding his time before either courting her or destroying her, but now it was different!

Though Abigail walked back and Duke Braden rode, they had obviously been off somewhere together! And it was true that his little whore, Currency Catty, was down there, too, serving the shearers drinks when they paused at their work. Maybe Braden had been enjoying her charms, too! He banged his fist against the stone and vowed again he'd make them all pay.

He'd poison the water hole where the damned abo friends of Braden's still hid, even if it did threaten to contaminate the runoff to the Grange's sheep! He'd get Catty alone somewhere, or pay to have her abducted, despite the extra guards Braden had hired on. He'd had to slip through them today by coming on foot out here before dawn broke. But more important than all that, he was going to make that bastard Braden pay for all he'd done over the years. Murder—that was it! He'd make sure Braden went to prison just as his father had, only for a much more heinous crime. That would prove once and for all that the moral stain was in these Currency!

And since Abigail more than any of them—for she was Exclusive—had defied and rejected him, she would pay the price that traitors paid. Yes, it was Lady Abigail Anne Rosemont that Duke Braden would be charged with murdering. Phillip knew he only had to find the way. Perfect justice on them all!

He crawled back in the cleft of rock where he'd hidden most of the day. Expectation surged through him like lust. He'd have Abigail for his own, groveling at his feet in front of Braden's eyes before he arranged for Braden to "kill" her. He'd like to pick them off from behind the rocks right now, the way he killed 'roos for fun, but that would be too good for them and not prove his righteous point to everyone in New South Wales.

Phillip fumbled for his flask of water hidden in the rock and took a swig. He scratched a match against his boot sole to light a cheroot, and breathed the calming smoke deep into his lungs. Just think, he'd only planned at first to start a bushfire after dark tonight to ruin their grasslands, hopefully burn that pitiful little house and those ramshackle outbuildings down there, and stampede their meager herd. But with Abigail's mixing in, the stakes were higher now. The tart-tongued little bitch had absolutely upped the ante. After all, when she died, at least some of her fortune would come to her relatives, the Godfrey-Bennetts.

He drew deeply again on his cheroot and thought of enjoying Abigail, of her pleading for his mercy, begging him not to kill her. He pictured Braden's eyes wide with fright just before he saw Phillip pull the trigger, knowing he would be blamed for Abigail's sad demise. In his shadowy hole in the rock, Phillip Godfrey-Bennett grinned and drank a toast to his perfect plan.

# Chapter Twelve

The third week of September, Abigail stood on Castle Keep's veranda with Squire as the Braden brothers and their men assembled for the sheep drive west. Squire held H.M. in his arms, as Abigail watched Grace dismount and come toward them. She hugged her father-in-law and turned to bid her friend farewell again. Squire wandered off around the corner of the veranda to talk to some men while the two women huddled together, holding hands.

"Don't you take our leaving so hard now!" Grace comforted. "Duke's gonna come back to you, you can bet on it! And next time he heads west to visit us, I just know he'll bring you, too!" Grace's voice sounded strong, but tears trickled from the corners of her big brown eyes.

"That's just not good enough, Grace!" Abigail told her bitterly. She held her tongue; she must say no more. She had not even told Grace her scheme, for she knew well enough Grace kept nothing from her new husband, who might tell Duke.

Grace and Earl's marriage had fulfilled them both. Grace had bloomed with beauty and confidence. She had told Abigail that Earl was as gentle with her as he was with the new lambs. In learning to trust him, Grace had put to rest her fear of men.

"I'm ever so sorry to see you sad, Miss Abigail!" Grace said with a glance over her shoulder as Duke pounded up toward the house on his horse. She turned back to Abigail hurriedly and the words spilled from her: "I'll never forget all the good you done for me! And Earl and I are gonna hang that fine wedding drawing you did of us right over our mantel, soon as we build a house out there over the Blues!"

At the foot of the steps, Duke boosted Grace back on her horse, then joined Abigail on the veranda. She fought tears again at the fact Duke had stubbornly refused to allow her to go west with them. Even now she refused to give him the satisfaction of looking into his eyes. Besides, he might read something there. Her secret plan was to join this drive in the mountains when it was too late for him to send her back!

"Grace," she called to her friend before she rode away on Earl's wedding gift to her. "From now on, next time I see you, you're to call me Abigail or Abby and not Miss Abigail—if you please."

Grace's face lit up in a lovely smile and then she was off.

"I take it this icy reception means I get no sort of final goodbye kiss," Duke observed warily.

"I think a *final* goodbye kiss is a fine idea," she replied, still not meeting his gaze. She couldn't resist bedeviling him since he was leaving her. "After all, I may be living back in England or even back at the Grange when you ret—"

"Don't even say that!" he ordered. His hands shackling her wrists, he pulled her around to face him. "I told you I care for you deeply, but we have a lot to work out after I sort things through."

"Meanwhile, of course," she flared, "I'm to languish in voluntary exile in the Widow Cranbrook's prison, watching life go by and shouting into her ear trumpet over tea!" She tried to pull away, but only found herself drawn into Duke's firm embrace.

"I know it's not fair, Abby, but life isn't—"

"Indeed, it is not and *you* are not, either! I've shown you I can work with sheep, the lambs at least! Oh, never mind, we've been through this argument a hundred times in the past few weeks!"

"Damn it, Abby, if we ever do decide to spend our lives together, it's not going to begin for us on a hard, dirty,

dangerous sheep drive over the mountains. You and I—
we're not Grace and Earl. I tried to think of ways for this to
work for us, but I have to go west to help get Earl settled and
to make my own political point about squatting. When I
return, everything I say will make people listen better—''

''Not me! I'm not going to listen to any of your words
again, not after you can just ride off like this!''

His fingers snagged her thick hair under the back of her
straw bonnet. The broad brim bumped forward, then the
whole hat tipped back as his forehead knocked it off when
his mouth took hers. Despite her desire to be strong, to fight
him, she melted against him, returning the kiss and caress
desperately. Let them all look! Besides, Duke would probably be rather put out for the first few days after she joined
the drive. She had to treasure this now until she could win
him back by showing him she could handle anything they'd
meet out there—together.

He loosed her slowly. ''Steer clear of Phillip, like I said,
though the coward's evidently content to just sulk,'' he said,
repeating the advice he'd given her for weeks. ''I will be
back. I do love you, whatever happens, Abby Rose.
And—''

Earl's voice cut in from a distance. ''Duke! Give Dad a
shake goodbye, and let's go!''

Duke had just said he loved her, Abby thought, as she and
Duke both ignored Earl. He had said that, and yet he was
leaving her!

''You love me, and *what?*'' Abby prompted, clinging to
his arm despite herself.

''And then we'll decide things,'' he muttered lamely,
squinting into the sun under the overhang of the veranda.
He patted her bottom through her skirt, went down the steps
and swung up on his horse. He leveled a long look straight
across at her as she came to the top of the steps. ''Abby, I'm
sorry some things weren't different for us from the beginning. But since we feel the way we do despite the impossi-
bilities—''

''Duke!'' Earl shouted again.

Duke tipped two fingers to his brow in a sort of salute, then wheeled his horse along the veranda to lean down to shake hands with his father. He patted H.M. on the head. Then he urged his horse around the gathered wagons and disappeared from sight.

It was only then Abigail came back to reality. She walked over to stand with Squire as the crowded area slowly emptied of wagons. For the first time she noted Kulalang, without his family, sitting with the driver on the high front seat of the last wagon. Duke had said nothing about Kulalang's going along, but perhaps he was only traveling partway with them. Then that wagon, too, was swallowed by the morning mist and swirling dust as, beyond, dogs and mounted men began to drive the flock toward the road that led to the foothills of the mountains. In the cloudy, moving mass, Abigail could no longer pick out Duke.

"Good boys, both of 'em and got a right to their dreams," Squire said and hugged H.M., who licked the old man's chin in reply. "Guess an old lag jes' can't expect 'em to have the same dream I did. I got Castle Keep and me Dorset Downs farm here till I die, and Duke's gonna come back and forth, that's what counts."

"Yes, that's what counts," Abigail echoed sadly. But right then, she decided, her mourning for what might have been was over. She had to hurry back to town to start her journey, too. She didn't want the sheep drive to be more than one day ahead of her. Pulling her mind back to the present, she turned to Squire. "Mr. Braden, since you two are such fine friends, I was wondering if you would be willing to take care of H.M. for a while."

The leathery, bronzed face crinkled into a smile. "Leave her here with me, you mean? Why, sure can! Long as you want!"

That made her feel a bit better; the hardest part of all this was leaving H.M. behind for four or five months until she returned with Duke. But she had no intention of some dingo getting H.M. out in the bush, and the spaniel and Squire had adored each other from the first.

"You're going to be me dog for a bit, puppy! Aye, and we'll have us a reg'lar good time, won't we?" he promised H.M., but then he looked at Abigail. "Could use someone to talk to right now, and thanks for thinking of an old lag like me."

She wished, she realized as they stood there on the porch watching the dust cloud shrink and the occasional glint of gun or harness glitter, that she had only been thinking of Squire. She had a note written for him, trying to explain what she was doing, which would be delivered here in a week. She only hoped Squire, and someday Duke, too, would understand.

Phillip Godfrey-Bennett sat mounted among his men on the westernmost hill of the Grange, watching the distant parade of sheep and men head west toward the Blue Mountains.

"Damn those Braden bastards to hell!" he clipped out. "I can't believe they got the loan of funds from that new shearing of theirs. I tried to block it to keep them from doing this!"

"It's a piddling small flock," his stalwart guard George noted and spit on the ground. "We kin ride along in them hills and pick us off a few sheep or horses before they find us. And never kin tell about stray shots from some drunk bushranger picking off a mounted man or two," he added and chuckled.

"No," Phillip said calmly, though he was furious at being foiled again. It was bad enough the Braden brothers were going to establish a big squatters' run they didn't have the money for. But just when he thought he'd found a foolproof way to set up Abigail's demise and Duke's subsequent arrest for her murder along the Parramatta Road, Duke headed hundreds of miles west! He'd had no idea that loudmouthed Currency orator would take a break from haranguing Exclusives to make the trip, too! Granted, it left Abigail and the Braden spread more at his mercy, despite the armed guards still on the boundaries, but it wasn't what

Phillip had just spent three weeks planning and bribing officials in Sydney for!

His stomach churned. He shifted on his horse so violently his saddle creaked. Perhaps, out there in the bush and the mountains, he had a better chance. He could covertly abduct Abigail from Sydney and enjoy the "pleasure of her company" until he could somehow catch Duke off alone, maybe even after they staked out their spread beyond the mountains. Then there'd be less chance of interference or witnesses. He and his men could even burn the Bradens' new run out there much more easily than this puny pastureland here, at least if this dry spring weather here held over the mountains too.

Then everyone here in Sydney would see him as their savior when they heard Duke Braden had been jailed in Bathurst for the heinous crime. Abigail's death would be seen as a scandalous murder that Phillip Godfrey-Bennett, as the poor victim's cousin, had bravely tried to stop, by following the poor woman whom Duke had seduced or abducted. Public opinion would swing the Exclusives' way— he and the Godfrey-Bennett money and influence would see to that. Duke Braden's Currency causes would be crushed.

Then, even Phillip's father would have to halt his eternal flap, calling him "boy" and implying his only son did not amount to anything. Lately, he'd ridden him hard for missing his chance to wed a wealthy, proper English heiress. But he'd stand up and notice when Phillip managed to ruin the Bradens' reputation and their stand for squatters' rights in the process. Phillip had had to admit to himself, though, he had never before now had the urge to so much as approach those towering Blue Mountains, let alone cross them.

"It has to be done!" he declared so loudly his men turned to him, thinking they might be ordered to charge after the distant sheep drive below, after all.

"We gonna give them a run for it? Try for a stampede instead of burning them out later, boss?" George asked.

Phillip nodded decisively. "We're going to do all of that, my man, but not here and not today where anyone will be able to tell about it. Boys, we're going westering. And we've got a lot to do, because I don't want to be more than three or four days behind that damned, doomed drive. Let's go."

*Let's go.* His own command bounced through his brain as he led his men back toward the Grange at a quick gallop. His thoughts raced, too. He'd have to delay sending a couple of men over to Dorset Downs in the dark to bring Catty to him in one of the outer Grange barns so he could teach her the lesson of her life. He'd have to face his mother's wailing when he told her he was going to visit Bathurst for a while. Hell, she'd be sick in bed the whole time he was gone, though his father could be made to understand. As to little Lottie, it didn't really matter what she thought or felt. But no one—no one!—would know his personal, private plans for Duke and Abigail until he and his boys hauled her dead body and Duke's bound one into some ramshackle little gaol in rural Bathurst.

His heart pounding inside him at his own desperate daring, he dug his spurs into his horse and sent him flying down into the valley toward the Grange.

Abigail had never been so excited or so certain that what she was doing was right. She had hired four guards who knew the bush; two of them had once traveled to the pastoral area around the two-year-old town of Bathurst on the far side of the Blues. She admitted to herself this trip was a risk in several ways. But, right now, just cutting through some fairly open bush west of Sydney, the lure of adventure beckoned like the hazy mountains beyond. Her guide had said that the road through the mountains was convict-built, two carriages wide, the only way up and through. It was there, where that road began, she alone would leave her men and join the Braden drive.

They rode along with her in the bush now because she had decided not to ride the Parramatta high road where someone might recognize her, despite her disguise. After all, she was doing something she would never even have dared to dream about at home.

But somehow, in this free, wild land—especially only hours out from the protection of Sydney—dangers and impropriety seemed not so frightening at all. Besides, in the bush, who was there to be scandalized but lizards and dingoes and some random 'roos? She was garbed as a man and rode astride, though anyone up close would see the woman's form and curly red hair thrust up under the broad-brimmed cap. Duke had teased her that she would someday dress more simply in New South Wales, and so she had.

She smiled grimly, jogging along. There seemed to be no shadows here; everything stood out stark and clear, just as her future did. She felt dusty, and perspiration trickled down between her shoulder blades and breasts. But that did not matter. Her bottom and thighs felt sore already, but she did not mind. She was going to join Duke, to carve out a new, adventurous life with him. Still, she wondered what those who knew her once in London or Kent would think if they could see her now. And worse, what would anyone—including dear Grandfather and her beloved, departed friend Janet—think of a woman who chased after a man she wanted right across the country, guarded by four other men!

"It feels like being in another time and place out here, Sam," she told her guide, Samson Reilly, who rode ahead of her and the three other men. Sam was in his forties, a grizzle-haired, seasoned veteran of the bush, so he'd said.

He'd brought in the others who were accompanying her on what she had promised would be, for them, a ten-day trip out and back. Two of her escorts were young, including Clemmie Collister, one of Catty's six brothers. He smiled a lot and spoke with a stutter, but didn't hesitate to use a gun if he had to. The other lad was Frank Fencer, a peachy-faced blonde who did too much sleeping in the saddle to suit Abigail. The fourth man, called Tibbets, was unshaved, eagle-eyed and quite the silent type. He was the sort who kept his tweed cap tugged down over his eyes, and Abigail could hardly recall his face once she looked away.

Three of the men pulled laden packhorses behind them. The animals were loaded not so much with supplies they would need to overtake the drive, but with goods for Abigail's later journey with the Bradens. She wanted them to see she meant to be a help and not a hindrance to them. She had shopped long and hard in town for suitable clothes, cookware and foodstuffs to contribute to those supply wagons ahead on the road.

The money she had with her was strapped flat around the bare skin of her waist in a leather money belt that made her perspire more there. She trusted these men, yes, and had promised them the other half of their pay when they got her safely to the sheep drive in the mountains, but she couldn't see being overly trusting, even though one of them was Catty's brother. Most of Abby's goods and almost all her clothes were back at the Widow Cranbrook's, whom she'd told she was leaving to visit friends. If the old woman assumed that meant the Godfrey-Bennetts and she found out different, Abigail would just have to explain when she came back wed to Duke. Surely, Bathurst was not too primitive to have some sort of cleric to perform a marriage!

"Well, lookee here," Sam called out to them, reining in and gazing at the ground. The others rode over to examine his discovery. "Looks by the footprints one o' those black fellows been through here and recent, too."

Abigail stared down at the characteristic aborigine nighttime fire, a small, carefully arranged one unlike the big blazes the whites built. "Why wouldn't an aborigine be through here?" she asked. "All this land was theirs once and, to their way of thinking, still is."

Sam exchanged glances with the other men, and he shook his head at her obviously crazy ideas. "Sure," he told her, "and they used to think birds and animals was once human and a bunch of other cock-and-bull things, too. Let's head on, and keep your eyes peeled, lads. We don't need nothing like stumbling on no black fellows no more than we do anyone else till we deliver Miss Rosemont here safe and sound."

They all jumped at a noise. Tibbets and Clemmie drew their pistols. A ribald laugh, a cry and a swoop from the sky.

Abigail ducked as a shadow whipped by her. A kookaburra had a black snake in its beak and proceeded to knock the life out of it against a rock.

"Ugh!" Abigail said and looked away.

"Worse than that goes on out here day and night," Sam said.

"If the aborigines think birds and animals were once human, maybe I can see why," Abby told them as they rode on. "That's probably just about the way the whites here jumped them and took their land!"

"Well, now, we got us a real sermonizer here," Sam told his men and chuckled. But her first day out felt tarnished for Abby; the glory of the moment and the place seemed not so special now. A depressing thought swooped on her as suddenly as that bird had on its victim: what if Duke had decided to go on the drive partly to get away from her, to break things off? What if—

"Let's get us back on the road for a while through here," Sam interrupted her musings. They were just beyond Braden land where the drive had begun only yesterday. "Dingo brush is too thick here, though there's some risk on the road too, I s'pose. We got hours till we spot that big cloud of sheep dust, even if they have to go at a crawl. Let's ride."

In the dark of night, Phillip Godfrey-Bennett paced the stretch of iron fence above the cove at Cliffside House, waiting for old lady Cranbrook's underparlormaid, Rebecca, to return. Behind him, two cloaked accomplices held ropes, a gag and the big gunnysack with which to remove Abigail covertly from the house. Angered at the long time the girl was taking to come back to let them in, he muttered curses under his breath and calculated all the bribe money he'd gone through so far with meager results. Next he'd probably have to grease the palms of some rural boors in Bathurst to get Duke Braden promptly arrested, arraigned and executed there.

Finally, he heard the girl's dragging footsteps. She lagged on the other side of the gate and made no move to open it.

"Well?" he demanded.

"Gone, sir. I din't know."

"Gone? Stepped out to town this evening, you mean? At this hour?"

"No sir. Gone, her maid said. To visit friends. Honest, I din't know and gotta get back inside now."

"To visit what friends? At the Grange, did she say?" he hissed and quickly scattered some loose coins through the bars of the iron fence.

The girl halted and edged her way back. "Don't know to what friends. But had four hired guards she met outside the front gate and them all on horses, her too. And climbed right up on it astride, she did! Wore a big cloak and a hat with her hair all pushed up under it, so's I heard." Her words came muffled now as she stooped to fumble in the dark for the coins.

"Damn her!" Phillip cursed. "She's gone with the devil!"

"What, sir? Been kilt and gone to hell, you mean? Should I tell the Widow Cranbrook?"

"Keep your mouth shut, you stupid trull, and there'll be more coins for you later," he told her. He turned away and pressed back against the iron grillwork of the high fence as if he were being roasted on a grate. His mouth gaped open; he breathed in quick, hard breaths. His plans had been upset again! But had Abigail actually thrown her entire reputation away by running off with Braden—or, since he was a full day and night out, running after Braden? He stood there so long, his mind racing, that stalwart George, who held the horses, came up and touched his arm.

"We not going in after her, boss?"

"What? No. No, we're going *out* after her, out there," he said and gestured with a wide sweep of hand at the western darkness. He yanked his horse's reins from George, touched his rifle and grasped his pistol as if to reassure himself he was ready. "Let's go," he ordered. "At first light tomorrow. We've still got a lot of riding ahead." Then he added under his breath, "She's crossed me the last time. Now I'm going to take pleasure not only in having her, but in killing her!''

The third day out, the Braden drive reached the edge of the foothills. Duke, riding at the front left of the flock, tried not to count the slow accumulation of miles, miles closer to the Blues but farther away from Abby. He worried about her, even back there in so-called civilization. He'd made her promise that if she went out on the high road, she'd take guards and if she wanted to visit Squire and Catty she'd send for some of the extra men he'd hired to watch the boundaries of Dorset Downs. But she always had a way of getting into trouble, and that thought hung over him like a rain cloud on this clear, sunny day.

He heard fast hoofbeats behind him and twisted in his saddle to see Earl ride up. Sheep darted inward from the fringes of the flock to give him a wide berth.

"Trouble?" Duke called.

"Not for us. But the lads back on the other flank came upon a pair of fellows that four bushrangers waylaid and stripped clean yesterday. Must have liked the look of their clothes as well as their horses, coins and watches, too, 'cause they left them stark naked. I gave them water, blankets, a horse and some of Gracie's damper to share to make their way back. Told them to send the horse back to Dad when they reach Sydney. It's the least we could do. And Kula-lang's appeared from nowhere again and is rubbing cook fat and ashes on their skin against the sunburn, as one of them's nearly roasted raw. I tell you, with an aborigine tending to them like that, they're probably more jumpy than when they got held up."

Duke shook his head at the men's plight, but he'd heard worse stories about bushrangers preying on folks along the road. "One good thing about passing through with lots of men and sheep is that the most these thieves will take from us is a sheep for dinner. They know they'd find no riches here. But I'll keep my eyes open just in case."

"They've probably dropped back into the bush behind," Earl admitted, stiffening in his saddle to scan the area. "Kulalang's going that way too and said he'd look for them. So, how're you doing up here, just you and your thoughts?" he asked when he sat down in his saddle again.

Duke glared at Earl. "Just fine, little brother."

"Missing her already, I s'pose. It'll get worse on these long, cool nights to come."

"She'd be a disaster on this drive, so just stow the talk."

"What are you gonna do with her when you get back—you know what I mean," he amended quickly when Duke shot him another black glare. "If you'll excuse a poor ignorant lad compared to the illustrious spokesman for the Currency, I was thinking, you know, your marrying Abigail would be the best argument for social equality you ever had."

"Hardly. I'd sacrifice all I've been fighting for."

"Naw. See, you're not so smart, after all. Make a Currency lass your bride and you show we oughta stay put with our kind, despite your fancy words. Wed an Exclusive lass, 'specially one who sees things pretty much our way, and you've broken down the highest fence someone like old Godly-Bennett could ever build to keep us out."

Earl said something else and dropped back, but Duke heard nothing beyond that. He sat still as a stone on his horse while sheep shuffled by. He was astounded that Earl had said such. He had never looked at it that way himself. But would they say he had married her just to make a point and not for the woman herself? He would never want anyone—especially Abby—to think he wed her for politics or for her fortune. Damn, there was so much at stake here besides just the two of them!

He groaned and gripped his saddle tighter with his hard thighs. He had a long, long time to think about it. At least she was back there, safe and sound. Maybe after all this distance and time between them, things would not feel the same when he returned. But he refused to let himself spend his days longing for her like this! She'd be a detriment, Lady

Abigail Anne Rosemont, out here, he assured himself. She'd be nothing, he lectured himself as he jogged along again, but trouble and temptation.

Abigail sensed trouble before anyone moved. The birds, even the croaking frogs, went suddenly still by the small water hole a hundred yards off the road where she and her men had stopped to rest. It sounded and felt different after two days riding out here through the bush. Her hands still on the billy tin she'd been making tea in over the fire, she opened her mouth to ask the drowsy Sam if he heard anything. She had let her hair loose under her hat, and the last normal thing she recalled was that it tickled her face when she turned to talk. But when four mounted men charged in from nowhere pointing gun barrels, everything exploded.

She screamed. Her men, caught off guard, went for their guns. The mounted men shot first. Tibbets went down flat on the ground, gripping his belly. Frank Fencer fell back in a rag doll heap as his gun puffed noise and smoke. Sam and Clemmie dropped their guns the moment one of the invaders yelled, "Stand and deliver or die!"

Still stunned, Abigail just gaped openmouthed at the scene. This couldn't be! So quickly, so quietly, from nowhere, when she had four well-paid guards, the same number as these men. And then she realized two of her men were shot, and turned toward Tibbets, writhing on the ground.

"Stand, I said, ma'am!" one of the thieves bellowed. It was just as well. She was so frightened her feet had not moved when she willed them to.

"Not a thing of value here," Sam spoke up at last.

"Not a bit of truth in that with such a fetching lass in lad's clothes," another thief answered with a clear lilt of Irish brogue. "You know, we stripped the last two we met in the bush jaybird naked, and I can see the advantages here, gentlemen."

A general snicker went up from the bushrangers as they eyed Abigail. Furious and afraid, she studied these men for the first time. Two seemed mere lads, but the two who had spoken had black beards and looked dirty and dangerous. They were all dressed in mismatched, fancy garb, evidently taken from their various victims. They had watches and rings, which glinted in the late-day sun, strung haphazardly on their horses' harnesses.

"Please, if you've any mercy at all, let us help these two you've shot," she dared, fighting not to flinch under their harsh gazes. "We'll give you what we have, and you can be gone."

"Fair enough," said the brutish-looking man who had spoken first. "After all, what you have, ma'am, is sure of interest to us, eh, lads?"

"Now look here!" Clemmie tried to intervene by stepping between Abigail and the men. The burly spokesman spurred his horse forward and sent Clemmie sprawling with a kick to his jaw. Abigail screamed and ran, only to be scooped up in hard hands and thrown over a saddle like a sack of grain.

"Grab them goods and them horses!" her captor shouted. "Real nice pickin's for the day, so let's not press our luck. And a lass talks fine as a lady to fix us a spot of tea, eh?" He bellowed a laugh and smacked her hip hard.

Abigail squealed at the suddenness of it all more than at the blow to her bottom. This nightmare could not be happening! But the ground went by faster, faster under the horse as she heard shouts behind her and then more pounding hoofbeats. She was certain she was going to be sick down the horse's flank and on this brutal man's leg, but she wasn't. Still, the slap, slap of the saddle against her stomach made her hurt all over. She could hardly draw a breath. At last in growing evening shadows, they halted.

"'Twas not such a good idea bringing her along," the Irish voice protested to the brute. "Bailing up's one thing, but not abducting and—and—"

"And ravishment?" the brute put in for him. "I just couldn't resist the red hair or the defiant look in her eye, Bolter Bob. Besides, since the rangers hang us in Sydney town for bailing up, what worse could happen for requesting a lady's company? My name's Gentleman Jack, my lady," he said, fondling her bottom, "and if you behave, perhaps I'll just keep you for myself and not share, eh?" He smacked her again and the horse galloped on.

She felt sick to her soul, but her stomach did not empty. Only her tears dribbled down the saddle and fell into the choking dust.

That night, when darkness swallowed the bush, Abigail huddled by the bushrangers' fire with one of her own blankets wrapped over her man's garb. She still felt stunned; her brain refused to work. Each time she tried to think her way out of her predicament, she could only envision horrendous possibilities. Ravished, ruined, left injured or murdered. At the least, left out here to die the way they'd left her men behind, bleeding and horseless. The blackguard she thought of as Brute, despite his sobriquet of Gentleman Jack, had already found her money belt and taken it, after grasping her breasts in disgusting ways. But the other one, Bolter Bob—Irish to her—wanted her, too, and they were tossing dice for her across the fire.

That thought jolted her more alert. Tossing dice for her in the dust! For her, Lady Abigail Anne Rosemont of Fairleigh, who only wanted to be reunited with her friends and the man she loved. Tossing dice for her, Lord Sinton's civilized English heiress, who only wanted to have a fine adventure out here in this bright, warm land she had come to care for so deeply.

But now, the night was cold. The stars stared down uncaring and the yowls of distant dingoes threatened from the bush if she ran out there. Still, wild dogs would be preferable to the human ones here. No wonder Kulalang's people had once thought birds and animals first walked the earth as human.

She hugged her knees tight to her chest and scanned the area without turning her head. Tall box thatch called dingo brush surrounded this hidden campsite. She'd never find her way back to the road even if they let her go; dingo brush was as labyrinthine as a castle maze. She wasn't even sure from what general direction they had come. The guard they'd told to watch her, the one they called Lag Along, glared at her now with eyes gleaming from reflected firelight. The pistol in his lap glinted dully at her before he tilted up his bottle again with his other hand and gulped from it.

She saw no hope of escape or rescue out here. Her only chance was that they would drink themselves into a stupor or perhaps end up fighting for her and hurt one another. Or at least distract one another long enough so she could scramble into the bush to hide out with the animals until these four spread out to look for her at first light. Her stomach twisted and her foot hit the plate of bread and cold mutton she hadn't touched. She hugged herself very, very tight as the two men who'd gambled for her approached.

"I have the honor of the first dance, my lady," Brute announced. A row of crooked teeth leered at her through the mat of beard. The others laughed. She stared up. She did not move but for an icy shudder they could not see.

"'Tis only 'cause the damn dice were loaded," Irish complained under his breath and took a swig from Lag Along's bottle. "But then, I'll wait my turn, long's I get it."

"Now see here, you have my money belt and all my goods," Abigail dared to say, though each time she had tried to reason with them earlier, she'd been ordered to shut her mouth. "But I have much more than that back in Sydney if you'll just deliver me there. Now wouldn't ransom be better than—than—"

"Not with the likes of you!" Brute bellowed and reached to haul her to her feet. "You won't need this blanket, 'cause I got one o' my own, and I'll keep you nice and warm!"

The stench of liquor on his breath paralyzed her a moment. "Please, I—please, just a moment to myself first," she pleaded as he hauled her behind him by one wrist to the fringe of the firelight where he'd put his things. He'd made a defined area of his own, lined with her men's captured saddles. He sat down hard there and pulled her into his lap. Surely he didn't intend to just do things here with the other

men so near, staring! Surely she could grab something to
strike at that horrid face besides raking it with her nails! By
just throwing dust in his face, she'd never get away from the
others.

"Come on now, come on, I'm gonna have you put on one
o' the dresses you had in your things, and then you're gonna
take that off and give us all a nice show!" he muttered,
pawing at her shirt and the belt to her trousers. "Don't
wanta bed no boy!"

Time! She could stall for time! She could pull out her
hairbrush, hairpins, anything to use as a weapon against this
man, if she got in her saddle packs to take out the three
gowns she'd brought to please Duke. Duke! He seemed so
unreal, so far away! He might never know what had happened to her here and how much she had loved him and
wanted to be only his!

"All right, yes, I'll put on a gown!" she cried. He tumbled her off his knees, and she got shakily to her feet.

While Brute gawked up at her and the others came closer
to stare slack-mouthed as if they'd never seen a woman before, Abigail slowly, carefully drew out her blue ruffled
gown and managed to hide a single long hat pin with a pearl
top in the palm of her right hand. She pulled her shirt the
rest of the way out of her belt and dropped the gown over
her head still clothed beneath it, despite their boos and
hisses.

"Leave her be!" Brute warned everyone. "When the
gown comes off, everything else does, too!"

To play for more time, she kicked off her trousers under
the gown. She almost dry-heaved when Brute licked his lips,
but she forced herself to stay calm. Just one pin, and perhaps then she could grab his gun. She'd go for his eyes and
shoot the first man who lifted a gun to her. She'd—

"I'm tired o' this game!" Brute announced and lurched
to his feet. "Hold her hands behind her back, Bolter, and
I'm gonna finish the job for her."

Her delicate weapon fell from her grasp when Irish tugged
her hands behind her back. Brute put one rough hand down

her still unfastened gown and squeezed her breast while his other hand whipped up her skirts. All she could hear was the men's horrid breathing so close and the crackle of the fire. She bit her lower lip, too desperate and proud to scream. She tried to blot out the man's lecherous look with the memory of Duke's dear face. Her arms felt torn from their sockets behind her.

Then she heard another sound on the breeze, a whee-whee sound, an eerie but wonderful sound she knew. Aborigines out here? If she screamed now, would they come? And what would her fate be then if they, too, raided travelers sometimes as her guards had said? But the men did not notice. Brute lifted one of her bare legs to his hip, then reached for the other.

"Not a sound now, not a sound but to ask for more," Brute mumbled.

His face was raspy against her throat. Supporting her weight from behind, Irish laughed, then nuzzled her neck on the other side. That sound came to her again on the breeze as she opened her mouth to scream.

# Chapter Thirteen

A whirring boomerang neatly cracked into the back of Brute's skull. He dropped Abigail's legs and slumped to the ground. She tumbled back on Irish and they both fell.

*"Balanda! Ba-lan-daaaa!"* An unearthly shriek pierced the darkness to turn the scene to utter chaos.

Abigail froze, then tried to wriggle free from the man's harsh grip.

With frenzied shouts, her two other captors leaped to action. She gasped as a spear thudded through one man's chest to pin him to the ground right next to her.

"Shoot 'em! They're all around!" Irish roared and shoved her away. Hunkered down, he shot wildly into the bush. Then he rolled away to get another gun.

Abigail cowered next to the speared man as bullets whizzed over her. She stared unbelieving for one instant as a big crimson stain bloomed on the man's chest where the spear had entered. His wide eyes stared straight up at the stars. She smelled gunsmoke and death. With a terrified yelp, she scrambled away.

She made it to her knees, then her feet, amid bullets and screams. She felt a nip of pain in her ankle. Had she twisted it? Been shot? She had to run! She plunged away from fire-light into the cool outer darkness.

The maze of surrounding dingo brush stopped her headlong flight. She limped now, in pain, afraid to touch her leg. She hobbled this way and that to get farther away. She felt she had run for hours. Behind her, guns and shouts and hoofbeats seemed to chase her. Then all sounds softened; sudden silence swept the bush but for her panting and guttural groans of pain. Sapped of strength, flooded with fear, she embraced a big stringybark tree as if it were her last friend on earth. Taking her weight on one leg, she slid down it to the ground and put her hand to her slippery ankle.

"Oh, no!" she muttered and snatched back her hand, dark with sticky blood. Then, in the darkness, she heard something howl.

She shot straight up to her feet again, her back pressed tightly against the rough tree trunk. Her left ankle, her whole leg felt cold, then hot. She began to tremble; her teeth chattered. She had to find a limb or rock in case that animal came after her. She had to find her way to the road and hope any bushrangers who survived that tribal attack back there would not find her. She had to live through this to find Duke!

Holding her breath, she heard the barest rustling in the brush—paws shuffling carefully forward? She broke off a dry limb not far over her head. It cracked incredibly loud. She held the stick before her like a staff. But what good would it be against an attacking dingo? Closer, closer something came with almost soundless steps. She bit her lower lip; tears trickled down her cheeks as she squinted into the blackness to make it out. What if it were one of the survivors of that gang stalking her—or a hostile aborigine—

"Sunset-hair woman?" a voice asked.

She jerked her head around. The footsteps had not been from the direction she stared! "Ku—Kulalang?"

"Two bad mans gone finish. Two run. Mans no hurt sunset-hair woman now," he said matter-of-factly.

"Oh, thank God, it's you! Is Duke with you, or Earl? Where are your tribesmen?"

His form materialized before her. She saw he had retrieved his boomerang and his spear with its tip still shiny wet. He was nearly naked, barefoot and smeared with ashes in patterns to make him look like a walking, talking skeleton.

"Only Kulalang," he told her, surprised when she collapsed at that announcement. He bent over her, but did not touch her. "All right now," he told her. "My friend, your man, Kulalang go walk get."

Words tumbled from her, though her teeth still chattered. "You mean, they took all the horses? But I can't walk. How far is Duke? You can't leave me or those dingoes will get me, and I think I have a bullet in my leg."

"Wait up tree. Dingoes no climb. My friend, your man come by time sun there and not stars," he assured her and pointed straight up to the heavens with his bloody spear.

She had no choice. She kept nodding, nodding. Kulalang had saved her on his own when she had been certain there were at least ten aborigines. He would bring Duke. She would see Duke. She would have to face Duke. The pain was not so bad now; her ankle just felt numb. Her mind felt fuzzy. She hurt just as badly inside for her precious plans being ruined. But to wait up a tree when she felt so lightheaded—

Kulalang removed his headband and tied it tightly around her calf for a tourniquet; she tried to ignore that it had animal teeth hanging from it. She babbled on to him, though he said nothing more.

"I even brought gifts on the packhorses, you see. Something for you, too, Kulalang—a lovely carving knife—when I saw you'd gone along."

He bound her ankle tightly in strips she tore shakily from the ravaged blue dress, which hung on her unhooked and unbelted with nothing under it but a torn man's shirt.

"Now, everything's gone, my money, too. Duke will just skin me, won't he—oh! That hurt. But I'm so glad I didn't bring H.M., because those men and all these dingoes touching me would hurt him," she rambled on and on.

She hardly knew how the wiry, little man did it, but he had her wedged up in a big Y-shaped crotch of the stringy-bark tree. She was hot now, so hot though there was no sun, and the breeze felt cool on her forehead. She held tightly to the tree, wishing it was Duke. She realized someone had somehow tied her to the branch with strips of twisted bark. But those ties on her were like Brute's hands, and those men, those men—

"No!" she cried.

"No talk!" a man's voice warned from below her. "No talk, sunset-hair woman. Watch for sun high in sky!" she thought he said before his footsteps faded. Then she was alone with only her fear and loneliness and the vastness of the deep, black night. Still, she clung to the tree, wishing and pretending it was Duke.

When she drifted back to earth, the sun was high overhead, just as Kulalang had promised. She was sore all over and her leg— And then she heard men's voices.

Her eyes shot open; she tried to sit up. She was not in the tree but on the ground. Duke! Kulalang had brought her Duke!

"Lie down and rest!" Duke told her.

She watched his mouth form words. She wanted to kiss him and hold him, but his lips closed in a firm line and his arms pushed her back down on a blanket. She was lying in the shade somewhere with two horses cropping scrub grass just beyond. She did not see the big tree she'd evidently spent the night and morning in.

"You've had a fever," Duke told her. "But I think it broke," he added.

His voice was so cold and controlled her heart almost broke, too. Why didn't he just sweep her into his embrace and tell her everything was well between them? Now that she had faced harsh trials, even death, she knew the value of each moment they had together, even if he did not! She almost told him so, but the words wouldn't come.

As Kulalang bent over a small fire, Duke put a wet, cool cloth on her forehead again, then dabbed at her cheeks. With a silent sigh she relaxed under his ministrations. He did care deeply! He had said so more than once! She was so glad to see him! The events of last night seemed a horrid, distant nightmare with him here now, tending her, protecting her like this. Yet, his square jaw was set hard and she could clearly see a steady beat in his neck artery that stood out when he was very angry.

"I'm sorry, Duke, but I had to do it," she ventured.

"I'm sorry, too, but we'll talk about it later. And I'm sorry you woke because we're going to have to move you from here in case your two captors who escaped return. The bullet just grazed you, Abigail, but you've lost a lot of blood."

"I can't thank Kulalang enough."

"That's right, you can't," he muttered. "You tried your best to get killed by disobeying me and not respecting the bush and all its dangers, and you're just damned lucky you're not dead!"

She propped herself up on her elbows and shoved his hand with the wet cloth away. "I didn't *try* to get killed! I had four armed guards who—"

"Who were stupid enough to let you be taken by bushrangers," he interrupted. "I swear, I could almost kill your guards with my bare hands as much as I could those sons of a bitch bushrangers! Not to mention you for pushing me to such things! I can't believe you dared come out here where you weren't wanted!"

"You ungrateful wretch! I only did it to be with you, to help you on the drive!" she shouted, though her head banged like a drum.

"Help me?" he mocked and bent his furious face so close to hers she lay back flat on the blanket again. "It was bad enough falling for you, then worrying about you back in Sydney. But out here—"

"I'll be fine out here now that I'm going on with you. And I'll pay you back for anything I use on the way and work my way along!"

"You just bet you will!" he thundered, no longer keeping his voice down. "Or next time you get out of line, I don't think I'll be responsible for what I'll do to you! This is a whole new world out here, Abigail, one you don't know. And it can ruin everything, if you're not careful!"

"Spare me your all-knowing lectures! And we'll just see!" she replied, furious now she had ever cared one bit for this man. Why wasn't he so ecstatic she was alive and with him that he was shouting for joy, not rage? "Besides, you told me the same thing about Sydney on the ship, and I managed there, didn't I?"

"Did you?" he challenged. He stood over her with his legs spread stiffly, wiping his hands on his narrow hips. The rough stubble of his beard and dark shadows under his narrowed eyes gave him a forbidding look. "Depends on whom we ask, Lady Abigail. And for once, I might have to agree with the Godly-Bennetts that you've made a royal mess of things!"

Anger at him robbed the remnants of her strength. She felt dizzy, just glaring up at him. How dared Duke, whom she loved, berate her like this when she had been through so much and was probably still bleeding! She'd show him that she didn't need him at all!

She struggled to sit up, but pain knifed through her left leg and she lay stiffly still. Just a moment more and she'd get up, she thought, but her heavy eyelids closed. Well, as soon as her leg stopped throbbing and she was reunited with some sane folk like Grace and Earl, she'd show him she could fend for herself! And if he ever even hinted that she came out here because she couldn't do without him and wanted him in—in all those ways they'd shared before—he'd learn otherwise fast enough!

She sighed and tried to shift her position. He'd ask her forgiveness before she was through with him! And as to hoping he'd wed her out here, ridiculous. Perhaps she'd never want to be a Braden's bride at all now. Unless he begged and begged, she didn't want him after this cold, cruel behavior, when she had planned such a different reunion. Her fury faded to exhaustion. She had to admit she'd miscalculated the dangers out here. But she'd show Duke Braden, if it was the last thing she ever did, that he was very wrong about her, too.

She heard the men fussing over things, perhaps preparing to move on. A harness jingled; Kulalang said something to Duke in that nasal, singsong voice. She had so many things to say to Duke. She had to thank Kulalang again. But all this had just made her so floaty...that was Duke's fault, too, floaty feelings so she wanted to be in his arms. But no more. Not until he realized how much he needed her, even out here, out here...in his arms...

"Hold my horse while I lift her," Duke said to Kulalang. He carefully lifted Abby in his arms, grateful she slumbered heavily enough so the jostling would not hurt her. He balanced her on the horse, then mounted to pull her sideways in front of him, against his body. Even that jolted through him a sharp stab of desire for her that fueled his anger. Kulalang, who detested riding as much as horses detested him, insisted on walking, leading the other mount, but it was just as well they went at a slow, walking pace.

"Me find water for horses out there," Kulalang assured him and gestured into the bush he had just told Duke was devoid of other water holes for miles. "Water hole back there cursed by dead spirits of mans Kulalang finish for took sunset-hair woman."

Duke cradled Abby even closer, gazing down at her flushed face. The mere thought of what could have happened to her back there—what almost happened—staggered him with a terror that drove his fury. She breathed with her lush lips parted and looked so pale. He knew another day of rest would do her so much good before linking up with the drive. And then they heard the distant but familiar thump, swish, thump, swish, coming closer, louder.

"'Roos, a lot of them," Duke told his friend as he reined in.

"Many *malu*," Kulalang agreed, nodding. "Sacred totem we share not hurt us. Our brother *malu* come see us," he assured Duke and smiled.

Years before, Kulalang had watched from the caves at his tribe's water hole as the twelve-year-old Duke nursed an injured young 'roo back to health. That had forged their bond of friendship and trust. Kulalang, whose sacred totem was the kangaroo the aborigines called *malu,* had seen a brother in the young man who loved and did not kill the way the "young boss" on the Grange liked to do.

Since then, their trust in each other had grown enough for Kulalang to travel the ocean road to England and back with his friend. But the aborigine had still vowed he would not go all the way over the mountains with the Bradens. As soon as the road began to drop down on the other side where Kulalang's eyes could no longer look far back toward his people's dreamtime land, he would go home to await Duke's return there.

The mob of 'roos stirred a cloud of dust in this unusually dry spring. But Kulalang was always right about life in the bush, Duke thought. The mob of fifty or so 'roos parted, and went around them as if they respected those who honored them. The red-gray giants took the brush in some six-foot-high leaps, as if something had spooked them. Awed anew, though they had seen the sight before, the black man and the white man steadied the horses and watched them pass.

The bush quieted. Abigail stirred and put one hand to her head as though she thought the noise had been pounding inside her. The dust settled, but Duke's confused feelings were still anything but settled. He could not yet calm his heart toward her.

Damn, he cursed silently, he was even angry with himself for scolding her back there, but he hadn't been able to help it. Would she never learn to do as he said? And he'd been worried just for her reputation back in civilized Sydney! Not only could she have been raped and killed out here if Kulalang had not been scouting water holes, but some aborigines themselves had a custom that any woman out wandering alone—even of their own tribes—was fair game. Thank God, it was Kulalang who found her. And if she'd escaped somehow with that hat pin trick she'd been babbling about when he'd lifted her out of the tree—a hat pin against four armed lawless men, for heaven's sake!—the dingoes could have attacked her in the brush or she could have just died wandering out here as many others had before.

He cradled her as they jogged along. Sweat beaded her upper lip, and he hoped it wasn't fever again. "Kulalang, I think I'm going to rest her more and then catch up later. Will you stay with us or go on?" Duke asked.

"Me come. Me go," his friend said. "Stop there," he added and pointed his spear toward a stand of silver-blue gum trees a short distance away. "Get water there, but no water hole."

Trusting Kulalang's judgment, Duke turned his horse's head, and then decided. He could not pass up this chance to teach a lesson to Lady Abigail. Wounded, rescued, bedraggled and dizzy, she was still so certain she was right to have come out here. And she was still so alluring either defeated or defiant that she curled his toes right in his boots with desire for her.

She'd pay her way, she'd said. All he needed was her flaunting her Exclusive wealth or Godfrey-Bennett ties in Bathurst! She needed to learn respect for the bush and some of the things about it Kulalang had taught him over the years. Yes, that was it! That would make her admit she had to stop ignoring his wishes and the bounds of rationality just to have her own way.

Besides, it terrified him that she would get her own way, get him right where she wanted him so he'd have no choice. Even right now, just holding her like this with her hip jog-jogging against his lap, he wanted her. He had buttoned her tattered, dirtied gown up the back, but she made him want to take it off her, even after what she'd been through with those bastards back there. Where had all the control in his life gone since she crashed into it?

"Damn!" he snapped. She jumped. She slitted her eyes and snuggled against him to tighten his loins even more before she sat up more stiffly in his arms.

"You don't have to hold me. I can ride."

"Not likely."

"Where are we?"

"Partway back. We're going to stop early. We haven't come far," he admitted.

"I think I dreamed I heard a lot of drums coming closer. I dreamed I was at a *corroboree* celebration."

"It was a mob of 'roos," he told her, trying to avoid those hazel eyes that took in all the colors of the green valleys and blue foothills so intensely as to make the grass and sky seem pallid by comparison. Her vibrant, loosened red tresses whipped in the breeze and into his mouth, so he almost tasted her. He sucked in a quick, involuntary breath as she shifted in his arms and her bottom slid right across the distended crotch of his trousers as if to caress him there. It goaded him how quickly and powerfully his body responded to hers when he wanted to stay so aloof and strong, at least until she admitted this was not the place for her. No better time than now, he decided, to set the stage for the schooling she had coming from him out here.

"If you had been alone facing all those 'roos," he warned darkly, "they might have flattened you like damper smashed by a skillet."

"After learning to put up with you, I doubt it," she replied tartly, despite how weak she felt. She grasped his wrist and removed the hand he had splayed across her thigh over her thin gown.

And then, he knew, the battle of the bush was on.

Abigail slept all afternoon, but felt better when night fell, except for Duke's brusque attitude and Kulalang's continued silence. They had camped in a ring of ghost gums that looked silvery-white in the moonlight. The eerie howl of the distant dingo had begun again, but Abigail trusted the fire and the two men to keep them and other dangerous things at bay.

"You see," Duke began in that sonorous voice he'd used with her today, "you've got to learn to respect the raw land out here."

"I think it's lovely in its own way. Even with all that's happened, I do care for it," she told him stubbornly as she took a sip of water from his canteen, annoyed that she needed even that from him. "I'm sure I could learn to survive out here just fine if it weren't for this leg," she insisted.

"But that's just it," Duke said as he spread mutton drippings on a piece of toasted damper for her. "The bush does unexpected things to you—you might suddenly be without water, or a horse breaks a leg in an animal hole, or there's a flash flood or a bushfire, or other hostile elements."

"Like a hostile man furious with a woman he wants to detest, but can't," she put in.

Duke glared at her, then added, "You need me, Abigail, admit it. You're dependent on me right now for this water and food, for your very Exclusive, money-pampered life."

"I'm dependent on you for nothing, Duke Braden!" she flared, her voice on the edge of a sob. Whyever did he have to be so rough out here, just because she disobeyed him to come along? "I've—I've got Kulalang to help me!"

"But only because he thinks of you as my woman, right, Kulalang?" Duke asked. The man shrugged, too wise to get into this match between the two of them. "But," Duke went on, "since you feel that way, just ask Kulalang to share his water and his food with you."

"Fine, I'll just do that. He's not too proud to accept thanks and an honest promise he'll be repaid later, are you, Kulalang?"

Another shrug. Duke didn't hand over her toast with drippings, but leaned back against his saddle to eat it himself. He wedged the canteen they had been sharing between his thighs, as if to say, if you want it, try to take it from here! He yawned and stretched, so obviously bored that Abigail could have strangled him. For one moment the rage coursing through her almost made her forget the throbbing in her left ankle.

"Kulalang, the Lady Abigail would like to share your dinner and will pay you handsomely when—and if—she eventually finds her own way back to Sydney and mother England. What are you eating tonight that she'd like, my friend?"

Kulalang pointed to a yellow pudding mass on a leaf. It didn't look so bad to Abigail, something like custard à la bush, she supposed. She'd love to eat it right down to show Duke Braden what she thought of his baiting her.

"Ah, looks delicious," Duke went on. "Want some, Abigail?"

"I'm not that hungry," she lied. "What is it?"

"It does take some adapting out here," Duke said in his I-told-you-so voice again. "It's fat, yellow tree grubs, all smashed up. If you were by a water hole he'd fry you some tadpoles or mix you a drink of green ants that he and his people have lived on in the bush for centuries. I've eaten all those things and they're really quite good—"

"I, no, thank you, I'm fine, Kulalang," she told him, trying to ignore Duke's smug face when Kulalang extended the leaf to her. Why was he treating her like this? She stood and hobbled on her Y-shaped tree-limb crutch Duke had made her to her pallet and wrapped herself in the blanket. She sat with her back to them, hunched over, beyond remaining stiff-backed anymore. Suddenly, the night was very cold. She was hungry, thirsty and hurt in more ways than one. She bit her lower lip as unshed tears prickled her eyelids but did not fall. She did not turn back to look as the men spoke quietly to each other or when footsteps approached.

"Abby, here," Duke said.

She looked back over her shoulder to stare up at him. The fire behind him gilded his big silhouette. His shoulders looked so broad, his hips so narrow. He extended something to her that resembled a drainpipe.

"Is it a limb for me to ward off dingoes or more—more hostile men?" she asked and her voice broke.

"It's a cup of fresh water inside a slice of gum sapling, and I'll get you more this way to drink or wash if you want.

I know you're tired and in pain. I didn't mean to set that up back there at your expense.''

"I think you did," she said, but she took the hunk of sapling and tipped it to her lips. The water was sweet, fresh and cool.

"I just want you to learn that you can't depend on anything out here. It's a far cry from sending a butler for more tea and cakes at one's mansion in merry old England.''

"If I didn't know that, I'd go back to England. But I'm telling you I'm not afraid to face things out here. Not one bit!''

He hardened his heart again. Why he continued to desire this woman so much when she was more vinegar than honey, he didn't know, but he wanted to halt these dangerous feelings she roused in him. Earl's advice that marrying her would be the best political move he could make kept eating at him. He feared it might be true. Yet it still seemed wrong even to think of wedding her for any sort of cold, political reason.

Besides, this woman's mere presence made him feel he might as well be lying in that fire over there. He wanted to caress her, to keep her. To hold her and have her. If there had been a cool water hole nearby, he'd have jumped in it to douse those other parts of him she roused besides his temper.

"Congratulations on not being afraid of *anything* out here," he said sarcastically, "but if I were you, I'd come closer to the fire. It will help ward off both dingoes and snakes.''

"Snakes?" she said and got up quickly with the help of her crutch.

His hands were on her instantly, one around her waist, one holding her free hand. Then he stooped to pick up her blanket, feeling justified at having got some quick compliance out of her.

"It's cold at night out here anyway, and the fire will feel good," he added.

She let him lead her toward the little fire Kulalang had since vacated. Shadows danced in the bush around the small flames. She wished she didn't feel so confused. She wanted to be strong and defiant to show him she could be, yet she wanted to be soft and desirable in his arms. But she just bided her time and settled her blanket and herself across the fire from him.

"Where's Kulalang?" she asked.

"Gone off to sleep by himself," he said. He leveled a look at her. "His idea, not mine."

"Right here across the fire from you will be fine for me," she said airily.

"At least this lack of rain keeps the blowflies down," he went on.

Was he still trying to impress her with all his knowledge of the bush? Perhaps, she thought, if she just lay down, exhaustion would conquer her body's hunger for food and for this man. She watched him suspiciously as he uncoiled a length of rope and made a circle all around his blanket and saddle.

She hated to give him the satisfaction of explaining the ritual, but her curiosity got the best of her. "I take it that is not some aborigine superstition?" she ventured.

"The rope? No. Blowflies don't like spring droughts, but snakes don't mind. They won't crawl over something rough like this, but don't worry, the poisonous ones are in the minority out here."

"Do—do you have another rope for me?" she blurted, all intended nonchalance gone.

"Sure," he declared, flashing a smile. "Let me wind it around your blanket since your leg is sore."

He had won some little skirmish again, she thought. But she refused to admit defeat. After all, Kulalang was out there somewhere, and he would surely rescue them if anything really terrible happened.

"Here," Duke told her as he finished his task and settled back down across from her, "you'd better finish up this bread or it will be moldy by morning with these rich mutton drippings on it.''

Despite herself, she got on her knees to reach across the fire for it when he extended the big hunk of damper. And then, as their fingers briefly touched and their eyes met in the flare of the flames, she realized how she could fight back if he insisted on this game. He could outfox her in the bush; he had lived around it all his life and Kulalang had taught him well. But she had the advantage in a better way. Just now in his eyes she had seen rampant desire for her. Yes! He still wanted her, but he was trying to make her apologize for being the foolish woman he thought she was. He was trying to get her, but only on his terms of surrender! Well, there was absolutely no way that was going to happen, not until he apologized for being such a coldhearted ruffian to her!

Hoping he could not tell what she really intended, she took a good long time eating the bread and licking her lips and fingers. ''Mmm, it's delicious, thank you,'' she murmured, aware of his eyes, hotter than the fire, from the shadows beyond. She wiped her fingers on the grass and then combed her wild hair with them, knowing he stared. She shook and tossed her thick tresses so they danced copper in the fire glow. She stretched her arms over her head and chattered on to him about the beauty of the night, ''the sensuous wonder of it.''

His voice broke more than once when he responded. He sat still as a Greek statue until she told him she was still cold. He heaved her another blanket, flopped down at last on his and wrapped himself in it. She heard his saddle creak as he bumped his head and shoulder against it.

''If you hear scraping sounds, it's probably just a colony of bandicoots a ways off,'' he murmured huskily.

She had no idea what a bandicoot was, but she had no notion of letting him scare her again with another trick—not when she had the firm upper hand right now. She could almost feel the warmth and need for her he exuded. The trouble was, it had her insides tied up in knots, too, but she had to be strong.

"Bandicoots don't bother me," she told him, praying he had not just made them up—or should she wish he had? The name sounded entirely ridiculous to her. "Good night, Duke."

"How does your leg feel now?" he asked, as though he couldn't let her go.

"Actually," she told him, rubbing her leg slowly, "it feels stiff and swollen. It's throbbing some, too. I wish I had something to soothe it, if you know what I mean."

She heard him turn over on the hard ground with his back away from her. She held her breath.

"Yes," he said tightly. "I was shot once."

And about to be again, one way or the other, if you don't admit you need me, Abigail thought. She felt both strangely elated and quite guilty to be using such sensual weapons on him. But she was in a struggle for what had become most dear to her: this man, this country, Earl and Grace, life here where she could be Abby Rose and not Lady Abigail, unless that helped Duke's cause. Her cause right now was winning this little war they waged.

The only thing was, she thought as she turned over carefully in her cocoon of blanket, she felt all fiery inside for him. If she did much more of this—this intentional teasing—she didn't know what would happen. Or she knew what would, but was afraid that afterward he would still be as stubborn as ever. So she couldn't bend, just couldn't!

She forced herself to lie very still, and at last, tumbled off to sleep.

Though she didn't know it, Duke stayed awake for hours, listening to the velvet night, listening to the fire crackling and Abigail's even breathing. He was coiled with tension set on a hair trigger. One more even innocently seductive word out of her and he would have been over there—if she had let him. It was so quiet out here without the noisy, restless flock he was used to, without the intermittent waking to take a turn on duty, that he couldn't fall into a deep sleep. But when he had finally drifted off, he was awakened by her scream.

"No! No! Blood, on my leg. That man, that man!"

He vaulted the low fire and had her clasped in his arms before he realized he shouldn't have. "No! No!" she cried and hit at him, raking fingernail tracks down his cheek before she woke up and realized she was having a nightmare.

"Abby, it's Duke! It's Duke," he cried, hoping that would still her. He loosed her slightly so as to alarm her no further, but she blinked at him and then threw herself headlong into his arms.

"Oh, Duke, Duke, I thought—"

"It's all right. I know."

She clung to him and he to her. "When it all happened, I—I was so afraid I'd never see you again!"

"I'm here, sweetheart, I'm here. I won't ever let that happen to you again," he vowed, before he realized what he had pledged. "Not while I'm around," he amended. "Tomorrow, we'll catch up with Earl and Grace, and you can stick close to Grace and the guards."

"I'm sure Grace and Earl will appreciate that during the long, cold nights like this one," she said tautly, back to reality now.

Awkwardly, at once, they released their desperate hold on each other and sat back a bit, though their hands still touched.

"It is cold," he said. "I'll build up the fire. No, I've got a better idea."

If he had asked her right then to lie all night naked with him, she would have done it. She wanted more than anything to feel the strength and security—and love—of that muscular body next to hers. But he was digging in the ground with the tip of her crutch, making a long trough, then another not quite as long, side by side just a foot apart. He worked diligently; a light sheen of sweat glistened on his brown skin. It was then she wondered if he was digging to make her warm or to keep from making her warm the way he really wanted.

"Whatever are you doing?"

"Another aborigine trick. See, we bury the hot ashes here, cover them with a layer of soil and then lie on top of that. We can even carve the contour to fit our backs and legs for greater comfort." He scraped the glowing ashes into the trenches—more on her side—and packed the loosened earth over them. He built another fire from the few remaining ashes and helped her into the little half cave he had made for her.

"Mmm, it is warm," she told him, smiling up at him. "Very toasty."

His eyes swept her. "The only thing is you'll get a bit dirty, but it's worth it."

"Oh, yes," she said as he draped two blankets over her. "I'm sure I'll sleep with no more bad dreams now."

The new, leaping flames etched his profile as an artist might have. She longed to reach out to sketch him all over with her fingertips, too. Then she remembered for the first time the art supplies she had brought along to draw the mountains and the land for Squire were lost. There was silence but for the hungry crackle of the flames.

"Thank you for taking care of me out here," she whispered.

"When you let me," he countered and leaned low over her.

Abigail stiffened expectantly. She was certain he was going to kiss her. She offered a little smile. She saw him waver. The potential of her power to sway him coursed through her. Then he shattered it all.

"And you're going to do what I say to stay out of trouble or else!" he snapped at her.

She could hardly turn away in this body-hugging cavern he'd dug. She could hardly demand to know, "Or else what?" in this position. She closed her eyes and her mouth. She could almost hear him clench his jaw and grit his teeth when with much ado he settled into his own little pit. They lay there side by side, half-buried in the earth.

It was a tiny truce, she told herself, and that was all.

She looked so good, he thought as he settled into the warm soil. Tousled and tattered with her beautiful hair in the dust, she had actually looked content! He was overwhelmingly grateful that she had not been really hurt back there by those men—

He stopped his thoughts so anger would not capture him again. The trouble was, she had captured him and he was not certain there was any way out, here or anywhere. But he had to fight it to see—

He was jolted from his thoughts when her hand reached the little distance between them to touch his leg. He tensed his stomach muscles to raise his head and shoulders to look at her. She seemed to be asleep, and yet her fingers had settled on the very top of his thigh, near his crotch. He'd never sleep now, never. But near morning, even when the new fire finally settled to ashes, he did.

## Chapter Fourteen

Late the next afternoon, Duke and Abby spotted the Braden camp and quickened their horses' pace. When Grace saw them riding in, she ran out from the line of wagons, waving wildly.

"Earl! Earl, they're here!" she shouted back over her shoulder. "Kulalang told us everything! Oh, Miss Abigail—I mean, Abigail, it's ever so good to see you!"

Earl loped out from behind the wagons, stuffing his shirt in his trousers. Before Duke could dismount and help Abby down, Earl lifted her off her horse.

"Watch her left leg," Duke ordered as Grace and Abby hugged each other with Earl still caught between them. Duke stood stiffly outside their circle, then shook his brother's hand.

Abigail blinked back tears. She was so grateful for their warm welcome. Duke had been even more restrained and formal than ever as they rode to catch up with the drive. He'd been furious at himself for letting them sleep until midmorning. After that, he'd hurried her along, with his gun drawn, making her fear that they might meet bushrangers or something worse. If only Duke had welcomed her like this with hugs and happiness! Now, his face was unreadable: it seemed to Abigail both sun and storm flitted across his fine features before he turned away to speak with Earl.

"It's just terrible what happened!" Grace cried as she helped Abigail toward the wagons.

"It's more terrible what could have!" Duke called so loudly after them that the women stopped and turned. Limping, Abby started away again and Grace hurried to keep up.

"It's most terrible what's going to happen if that man and I don't come to terms!" Abigail told Grace as she sat on a sawed-off keg Grace offered. She briefly recounted her horrible attack by bushrangers and her sorrow at being forced to leave her dead and injured guards behind. "Duke said the two left will probably find their way back to the road and someone will pick them up. But, just in case, Kulalang's gone back to look," she said with another silent prayer for their safety. Then she told Grace about the tumult raging between her and Duke, worse than any before. "I've been brought down in other ways, my friend," Abby admitted. "This filthy, ruined gown and these shoes are the extent of my possessions out here now."

Grace was shocked by the recital of Abigail's trials. "Can't quite believe it, with you a real lady and all," Grace admitted with a shake of her head. "Still, after all, wasn't the clothes that made you a lady, no sir, not when I got to know you. But one thing about that makes me glad, if you'll forgive me for saying so. Now I can help you just the way you been helping me from the very day we met on the *Challenge,* when I got ink all over my skirt and you gave me a new one. I'm a bit shorter than you so a gown o' mine's really gonna show some leg, but I got just the dress to do. Besides, a turn or two with your ankles showing around that cranky brother-in-law of mine might be just the thing, even if one of them is all wrapped up in a bandage."

Like an excited child, Grace hiked herself up into the single covered wagon and jumped back down, shaking out a rose-hued, ruffled gown. "This one will go real fine with your copper hair and all."

"My hair ought to be gray right now, Grace. I feel I've been taking dust baths."

"But look, I've got two barrels of water just for cooking and washing strapped on the wagon from the last water hole Kulalang found us. And it won't take both of us much time to wash you and your hair before I have to fix these lads their supper, eh? Why, I remember all that fuss back on the ship about no water for washing hair and you and Duke managing to get your own!" Grace rambled on as she poured a big pan of water from the spigot of one of the kegs and helped Abby climb into the privacy of the wagon with a bowed canvas top. "And 'member how you dared ask Duke once if I could be your lady's maid, and now here we are—"

"Not my lady's maid, but my friend, Grace Buck Braden!"

"Why, sure, that's what I meant. Friends for life, that's us, so—"

God bless Grace, Abigail thought as they talked and washed the dust from her. Through both hardships and good times, they had become the best of friends. Now, she fumed, as Grace toweled her dripping hair with a petticoat and then combed through its tangles, if only she and Duke could come around from arguing and battling! Sometimes she wasn't sure they'd made any progress at all from when they crossed two oceans together to now when they were going to cross the Blues. Out the end of the covered wagon, she could see that mountain curtain hanging between the camp and the clouds. Unmovable, standing there, just daring her to cross, just like that big barrier between her and Duke Braden.

Grace's sweet voice interrupted her agonizings. "You just rest then, 'cause I've got to make up some damper to bake for supper."

"No, I couldn't rest just now, Grace. I've come to help in any way I can. And baking damper's a good way to start!"

Duke walked through the small circle of wagons a half hour later, spurs he hadn't worn in the bush jingling loudly as if to announce his arrival. He eyed Abby, bent over a makeshift plank table with Grace. She turned to catch him studying her, her bared ankles and calves in particular. Grace saw him, too, and stopped chattering.

"Don't stand on that hurt ankle too long. I'm glad to see you using it, though," Duke said, nervously rotating the coil of rope he held in his hands.

He did not come any closer, but the mountains beyond made his eyes bluer than ever. "I told you I intend to earn my way," Abigail managed after an awkward silence. "I'm going to bake damper, but my real skill lies in riding, so I'm going to tell Earl I'd like to help keep the sheep in line."

"Too dangerous when we get up on those sandstone cliffs," Duke insisted and started to turn away. "Men do that out here."

"The men do a lot of things out here I don't approve of and intend to change!" Abigail shouted. She hadn't meant to lose her temper when she wanted to show him she could fit in here, but the man was completely unreasonable and impossible! "Starting with changing some of your attitudes, Duke Braden, spokesman for equality for all!" she called after him as he disappeared.

"Oh, dear," Grace murmured behind her. "I wouldn't talk to Earl like that, even wed."

"Oh, damn!" Abigail muttered and hit her fists into the big pile of damper dough. "He infuriates me! He's out to show me I don't belong, and I—"

"You love him so bad you can hardly breathe when he's near, that's all," Grace finished softly.

"I love him so *bad* is right!" Abigail moaned and turned back to smack the mass of dough again and again with her fists.

The beating Abby gave the damper dough was only the first mistake. Grace came to explain how to tend to it while it baked, but Abigail was so upset she hardly listened. She finally managed to divide her dough and flatten it into four big, round loaves with the bottom of the heavy iron skillet. She'd never done anything like this before, but she recalled the alluring smell of yeast bread from the big ovens in the kitchen at Fairleigh. She stopped a moment, her mind darting back to the place she'd once called home. Duke Braden had never been there, and perhaps never would be. So, she picked up the flat slabs of dough and prepared to bake them, wishing she had at least one of Fairleigh's cooks here to assist her when Grace was so busy with everything else.

Relieved to have some help, Grace scurried about her other tasks, overseeing the making of mutton stew in a big, three-legged pot over the fire. Perched on her keg, Abby helped her chop dried fruit and lay out tin plates and cups on a plank. The men would pass through when they could get breaks for food and cider or tea.

Meanwhile, Abigail's damper baked deep in the ashes, but when she tried to dust the ashes off the loaves as Grace instructed, they clung as if they were embedded.

"Whatever went wrong, do you think?" Abigail asked as she showed Grace.

"Oh, no, done in spots and gooey in others, see?" Grace said. Abigail was so frustrated she'd ruined the first task she'd boasted of to Duke. Now he would have another way to ridicule her as "the helpless, hapless Lady Abigail," and in front of everyone!

"But I put the knife into it just as you said, and it came out clean," Abby protested with a groan.

"But not in a wet spot, I bet. Probably went wrong in the mixing somehow," Grace muttered with a shake of her head.

"But can't we just substitute something else for it tonight, and I'll try again tomorrow?" Abigail pleaded.

"Wish't we could, but flour and salt's measured out real close," Grace whispered as if the very wagons had ears. "Besides, these lads want their damper. We'll have to bluff it through and just tell them it was accidentally overbaked or something."

Abigail's stomach knotted as she sat on the sawed-off keg behind the plank table to ladle out stew as groups of herders arrived. She broke into a nervous sweat as she cut off hunks of the gray, mottled, bumpy damper that should have flaunted an even, two-inch-high beige crust.

Sure enough, the first men through noticed right away. "Someone using this damper for target practice today, Miz Braden?" one man asked Grace.

"Mebbe those two feisty ewes we chased been dragging these back and forth through the bush well as us, Joe!"

"And you and Earl had such a nice marriage agoin', and no doubt all 'cause of your good damper, Grace!" another man teased.

"Grace didn't make that damper tonight, gentlemen," Abigail announced, wadding her apron in her hands. Before Duke arrived, she felt she should make public penance standing on this keg as if it were some dratted confession box, but her foot was throbbing now as much as her heart. She heard murmurs, whispers, and a few muffled guffaws from the men. Two of the most playful started to toss their pieces of damper like a ball, and her ears caught part of a joke about poisoning the next dingo that took a sheep. Others just glared at her. She hated to think of them going hungry after a long, hard day. She was mortified, but her pride kept her from fleeing to the wagon. She was going to see this through, apologize to all of them—except Duke when he dared to criticize her publicly—if that was what it took to be accepted and given a second chance here.

But Duke and Earl came through the line together before she could say anything else. They eyed their plates strangely. Duke's gaze lifted to Abby's defiant glare. "Did you do this on purpose?" he asked.

"I did my best," she countered.

"Once again, out here, it wasn't enough, was it? And don't think you're the only one getting ribbed. I've been taking a beating all day about these scratch marks on my face."

That kept her quiet, but she still could have heaved his stew at him and run sobbing to the wagon. She did neither.

"It took Gracie more than once to get the hang of it," Earl murmured kindly, but she could tell he, too, was embarrassed and annoyed at the dinner he had waiting after a grueling day. He sat cross-legged on the ground next to Duke and shoveled in his stew while it was still hot.

"Men, I have just one thing to say!" Abigail called to them, her voice trembling. "I'm sorry if the damper's not what you're used to. I know I'm not what you're used to out here, either, but I'd like to help by herding sheep up through the Blues. I can ride astride and want to help—please."

Almost everyone stopped eating and turned to face Duke. She bit her lower lip just waiting for the cold, cruel, clever-tongued public thrashing she knew was coming. She tried to build a wall so it wouldn't hurt, but from Duke, she knew it would.

"This damper's not so bad," Duke said. He bravely chewed and gulped a piece, then cleared his throat under everyone's rapt stare. "Mmm—the little pockets in it make it good for scooping up the stew gravy. Besides, we've been eating dust so long on this drive I can't even taste the ashes here, can you, Earl?"

Earl exchanged looks with his wife. "Got to give new-comers a fair go," Earl said. "Not so long ago we were all newcomers to this life. And, over the Blues, we're all gonna be worse than babes for a while!"

Tears of relief and gratitude flooded Abigail's eyes. Her face was too stiff with emotion even to smile. She wanted to say something, but couldn't summon her voice. She clasped her hands so tightly together her fingers went numb. Earl and his men had not been so bad at all over this, and as for Duke... Her eyes shining, she managed a shaky little smile at him.

"As for herding the flock, only if someone else is with you," Duke put in. "Besides, that would mean Grace has to handle the damper by herself."

Everyone laughed; the tension was broken. Grace hugged Abigail. Duke, evidently not to concede too much, bent back over his food. And when the men returned the plates, not a bit of damper came back. But, then, perhaps in the dark fringe beyond the firelight it had been hurled to the bandicoots and snakes and dingoes.

The hard drive up the twisting mountain road began. If someone wanted to pass the flock on the two-carriage-wide road or if a wagon came down toward the Sydney plain, the nervous sheep had to be edged over close to rock clefts, gullies or ravines. The first day exhausted them all, though Abigail was thrilled the men accepted her riding without a grumble. Keeping ewes in line or fishing stray lambs out of crevasses with long crooks or loops of rope seemed easier to her than baking damper. Yet she still helped Grace lay out the meal at night when they found a plateau or turnabout to camp on.

Kulalang had rejoined them with word that Catty's brother Clemmie and Samson Reilly had made it back to the road and were headed for Sydney with a supply convoy. Kulalang still came and went, but never slept with the drive at night. Meanwhile, after each day's work, by the two whale-oil lamps burning at the heart of the supply wagons, Abigail worked on preparing a surprise for the men. At the end of one day, in the drizzle of the first rain they had seen for weeks, Abigail huddled over her paper, squinting in the wavering light.

"That's a good sketch of Joe," Grace said, lifting the small square of paper to the light. "O-o-oh, ever such a funny face on this one of Herb!"

They had asked Earl if he could spare two pages from his account book and some ink for Abigail to do a few small sketches. She had turned each page into eight small squares. Though she ached all over from riding and bending today, she had to finish just a few more before she turned in. After all, day and night, Duke drove himself harder than they did the herd to keep each precious sheep safe. This was the least she could do, and she wanted all the drawings finished when they came down the other side.

At sunset the third day in the mountains, still climbing, they stopped on a high plateau near the crest where they could try to keep the sheep contained for the night. Below them in the crystal-clear air lay the foothills and the gray-green stretch of bush, and beyond that were the distant river valleys from which they had begun their journey. For the first time in days Abigail and Duke had a moment alone as he came up to stand beside her. He looked so very tired and tense. Beard stubble shadowed the high angles under his lean cheekbones to make his features look as craggy as the sandstone clefts.

"Kulalang's turning back here," Duke told her without a greeting, but his gaze moved over her at a leisurely pace he had forgone days ago. She did not know it, but catching a glimpse of her astride or at night was the thing he most treasured each day, despite how stiff they still were with each other. Besides, he told himself, he had no time for her now. They would settle things on the other side of the Blues, for if he was ever really alone with her now when he hungered for her so, despite how he exhausted his body—

"I didn't know Kulalang was even here still," she said.

"He comes and goes like some guardian angel watching over us."

"How I know that! I'd like to say goodbye to him and thank him again then," she added.

He nodded and took her arm to lead her safely around a jag of sandstone where Kulalang sat on a jutting escarpment. He was partly clothed in someone's shirt, shoes and trousers, a concession to the cool air. He had a canvas traveling sack slung over his shoulder and his boomerang and spear stuck in his shoulder belt. Beyond him, as if framing him in an artist's picture, precipices rose ringing densely wooded ravines. Green-blue eucalyptus trees filled their view, exuding the peculiar blue haze that gave the mountains their name. Above them sounded the muted rush of a distant waterfall. Straight overhead, when she looked, Abigail saw a rainbow.

"Look up!" she said, and Duke and Kulalang did. "Good luck for the future!"

"Hunter boomerang in sky," Kulalang said. "Means danger, not good luck."

"No talk like that, my friend," Duke told Kulalang and grasped his shoulder. "Just a few hard times ahead on this drive yet," he went on, then let his voice trail off. Silent, all three of them scanned the grandeur of the darkening scene with the sweep of far vistas still sunset-lit. Duke hated farewells. But it was the beauty of this moment with his old friend Kulalang and this special woman at his side that made his throat close up and tears tickle the backs of his eyes.

Abigail couldn't bear to have Kulalang talk of danger, not when she had learned to trust his judgment so. "I want to thank you again for all you've done for me, Kulalang. When I return to Sydney, I want to do something to help you and your people. But right now I have this for you."

From the little pile of drawings in her trouser pocket—a pair of Duke's she had to cinch in and roll up to have them even resemble a fit—she extended to him the tiny drawing, made from one of the squares carefully cut from Earl's record book. Kulalang's sketch was not like those of the herdsmen, but showed him in full battle garb with the skeletal pattern on his skin, his spear and boomerang poised.

"You saved my life," she told him. "I can never thank you enough."

"This much good," he told her with a nod before he stuffed it in his pack. "Give to my wifes."

In one fluid motion, the aborigine stood. He clasped Duke's shoulder as Duke had his and lifted one hand as he walked away, down the rock and to the road they had climbed today. He quickened his stride and did not look back.

Stunned by the suddenness of his departure, both Duke and Abby stood there unspeaking, gazing at the place he had just been.

"You want to do something for his people," Duke said at last, "maybe you can buy an advertisement in the *Sydney Gazette* to urge better protection of their lands."

"I don't suppose your desire to help the squatters comes into conflict with other tribes' lands out here," she said as the thought struck her.

He shot her a sidelong look as they stood on the stone. "If I ever found out that the land we wanted for a sheep run was sacred dreamtime land to some tribe, I'd move on clear to the western sea to find some they didn't claim."

"Too bad you're one of a kind, Duke Braden, but then again, I guess I'm glad."

He turned to face her fully now. "You too, Abby Rose, one of a kind. And as soon as we get our woolly future fortune through these jagged passes, we'll get back to us. Come on before I start something I can't finish right now."

Several quick rejoinders flashed through her mind, but she didn't say a one. Still, her insides flopped over as he took her hand and pulled her off the rock and back on the stony trail the short distance to the camp. At least, they were not fighting. At least, he had seen that she could help them on the drive. He had promised they would "get back to us," but did that mean at the impossible impasse where they'd left off? She struggled to keep from intentionally stumbling into him or brushing her shoulder against his. Yet she yearned for a kiss, however quick; for a caress, even if a controlled one. But she had to hold in the desire just as Duke did, to meet him on his own terms.

Back at camp, Duke immediately mounted the horse Earl held for him. "Most of the men will have to be out and around all night," Duke said down to her. "Too many places for the nervous nellies to fall off tonight. Tell Grace we'll both be by for something to eat later." Earl moved on, but Duke lingered a moment longer.

She tingled; every nerve leapt alive with longing at his look. "Stay with Grace tonight, please, Abby Rose," he told her as he turned his horse away.

She had wanted to hear, "I love you and want you right here, right now, and forever." Yet, shaken, sighing, she vowed to do, for once, what he had said.

\* \* \*

At dawn's first light the next morning, Phillip Godfrey-Bennett and his men broke camp about six miles behind the sheep drive. Phillip had been jumpier than ever for the past three days, for here in the mountains, with the rain and rocks, he had no cloud of dust to follow at a leisurely distance. He held his men back a bit, so the next turn in the road would not put him up against the back of Bradens' drive to tip them off. This morning the wind whistled chill, right in their faces. The men were anxious to ride on, at least until they discovered the place the Bradens had camped last night. Phillip was adamant about actually getting a glimpse of Abigail with the Bradens, to prove once and for all to himself she really had defied him and deserved to die.

But just as he and his six guards were about to mount and ride from their hidden campsite back to the road, his man George raised a hand and whispered, "Wait."

"What is it?" Phillip hissed. "What?"

George had another man hold his horse and inched up on a rock that overlooked the road just below. Then he sidled back down.

"You won't believe this, boss," he murmured, "but I swear that's Duke Braden's abo friend comin' down the mountain. Dressed like a white man, but I've seen him a time or two and—"

Phillip elbowed George aside and crawled up on the rock himself. "I think you're right, but if you're not, what the hell? A little good target practice is in order for later."

Phillip gestured for his rifle and another man jumped to obey. George crawled up beside Phillip. "It's the wind in our faces that keeps the wily bastard from sensing us," George whispered as Phillip settled and sighted the gun. "I swear them abos kin smell and hear a white for miles around."

Phillip surprised himself by hesitating for a moment, finger curled to the trigger. His wrist was actually shaking. It wasn't, he assured himself, from getting a chance to shoot this thieving, killing animal so easily. His mind jumped to doing this to Abigail later. Abigail, under his gunsight and hair-trigger finger like this, about to be justly punished for desertion and treason. And Duke Braden would be sent to gaol to make Phillip Godfrey-Bennett the savior of the Exclusives and his father's hero—

At the last moment, he waited too long. As if his target sensed something, he turned and looked, just as Phillip fired. Kulalang fell down on the road, his body twisted.

"Got him, clean as dropping a 'roo!" Phillip boasted and fanned at the tiny puff of smoke. He jumped down to mount his horse with the others. "Before someone comes along, let's go get a look, men!"

They funneled out of their hidden camp and down to the road, still slick from last night's showers. Phillip reined in; his men halted. There was no dead or wounded man anywhere up or down the road.

"What in hell—" Phillip began.

They all craned their necks and got up stiff-legged to twist in their saddles. "It's always like that with them," George whispered, awestruck. "You think you see them, you think you got them, then they vanish into thin air."

"Don't be an ass!" Phillip accused, but his voice was shrill. "There, there, look in the road! Blood and some sort of pack he dropped! A trail of blood to the edge of the cliff! I got him, men! Fan out and find him to be sure he's dead!"

His guards searched on horse and on foot while Phillip dismounted and rifled through the pack for any sort of proof the abo had been the one George said. They all looked much the same to him. Among the food in the pack his hands touched a small piece of paper. A sketch of a warrior with a spear and boomerang and that savage skeletal pattern painted on his dark skin with ashes and smeared fat! And then he gasped.

He knew this pen-and-ink style. He knew the artist. But even if he had not, down in the lower left-hand corner there was a small, neat rendering of the initials he had seen on other drawings at the Grange: A.A.R.

"Abigail, you bitch!" he muttered. "Drawing Braden's abo, living with the enemy! Guilty, guilty! And worthy of the just execution I will carry out!"

"What, boss?" George asked as he got back on his horse. "I swear, we kin find no trace of him, even where that blood trails to the edge. 'Course there are crevasses and rocks below where we kin't see a damned thing, but—"

Phillip, shaking with excitement, pocketed the sketch and heaved the shoulder pack off the edge of the cliff. "If he's rolled off there, he's a goner," Phillip announced as another drizzle began. As much of a goner, he thought smugly, as both Braden and Abigail were going to be.

"Come on, men, let's ride," Phillip shouted as they heard the rumble of a wagon and travelers behind them. "Just another week or so and we've got a real hot party to attend, eh?" He mounted and wheeled his horse away, noting the others were only too eager to get away from this spot. He had told his guards only that they were going to burn the Bradens off their new run near Bathurst. He could not wait for the double demise of his ultimate enemies, and how sweet that victory would be. Sweeter than just picking off one lower-than-life abo for target practice on the road.

Phillip tossed back his head and exulted with a half laugh, half shout. But he made very certain that no one rode so fast that the horses might stumble and throw off their riders.

The drizzle stopped at noon, and after that the sheep drive made good time. By late evening they camped near the big waterfall they had heard booming all day as if to lure them on. Roaring over the high rock face, water crashed like churned cream into a series of pools. Some of the water rushed away over the westward mountainside, but much of it rippled down to the camp. Though there was little grass here—perhaps other squatters had come through already this spring, Earl said—there was a natural place to enclose and water the sheep. With fewer men on guard and the late-day sun bouncing off the wet cliffs, everyone free from duties celebrated by going for a swim in the pool closest to the falls.

Even in the sun the water was cold, but the lure of it was too much to ignore. Fully clothed, people ran into the water to wash themselves and their garments. Grace and Earl splashed and played like children. The herdsmen hooted and sputtered and got ten days of dust and sweat washed away. Duke dived under, then came up to watch Abby swim back and forth, just the way he'd taught her. He could see she was keeping an eye on him, so he plunged in again and swam over to her; he emerged like a fish leaping from the sea.

"Oh!" she cried. "I wondered where you went!"

"Would you have saved me if I were drowning?" he asked and shook his wet hair much as H.M. would have.

"I admit you do need saving," she told him and floated on her back.

"From you?" he asked. He moved toward her to buoy her up with one hand between her shoulder blades and one just below her waist.

She looked straight at him. Around his wet, disheveled head a halo seemed to hover from the spray and the sun, but Abigail knew Duke Braden was no angel. Still, she could not let this precious moment pass. She had been doing so much thinking lately, so much planning.

"You need saving from yourself, Duke Braden," she dared. "I might admire your causes, but why should you sacrifice your own happiness to them when you could have both?" She squirmed off his hands in case he intended to let her go under. He looked very surprised at what she said. "If you don't face up to the fact we love each other and should be together, you've become your own cause, and I won't have that!"

"You've always had all the answers, haven't you?"

"Hardly. For the longest time, I didn't even know what the questions were, but now that I've been out here and seen this part of this colony's future and proved—"

"Mr. Duke!" a man screeched from across the water. "Mr. Duke, it's Kulalang, and he's been shot real bad!"

Duke lurched toward the shore with Abby right behind. The caller was Herb, one of the older hands; he gestured to them, then ran back to camp. Dripping water, Duke and Abby, then Earl and Grace ran, too.

Duke fell to his knees beside his friend, who was lying on the ground. The shirt Duke had given him was now bright red across the belly and down into the brown trousers.

"What happened?" Duke demanded when he saw Kula-lang's eyes were open. "Where? Earl, get something!"

"He packed the wound himself with mud, Mr. Duke," Herb explained. "When I found him stumbling up the road at the back of the drive—"

"Up the road?" Earl cut in. "Wounded like that? Duke, I'll ride back and try to find out who—"

"He said I could tell what he told me," Herb cut Earl off. "He thought he was gonna die right away, I guess." Duke put his hand to Kulalang's trembling shoulders to steady them. Pain had never so much as made Kulalang blink, but he was heaving to draw each breath.

"Talk," Duke ordered Herb.

Abigail tried to warm Kulalang's limp, cold hand with both hers; she was half-afraid to touch him and yet wanted to hold him in her arms.

"He said he hid in a crack or something while his attack-ers searched for him," Herb told them. "Then he come on and went around the seven men to reach us. He said, Mr. Duke," Herb concluded, "that someone he calls 'young boss' shot him."

Duke's head jerked up. "'Young boss'! But that's what he calls Phillip Godfrey-Bennett!"

"Phillip? He couldn't be clear up here!" Abigail pro-tested as she met Duke's narrowed gaze.

"If he is, if Kulalang wasn't out of his head with all this pain and blood loss, I'm afraid I know what he's after—besides all our lives, starting with Kulalang's!" Duke said bitterly.

"Phillip's nothing to me!" Abigail began, but this was no time to argue. She knew deep inside that Phillip was quite capable of shooting Kulalang.

Duke bent over Kulalang again. "You were brave to come to warn us, my friend," Duke whispered low in the man's ear.

Kulalang's mahogany eyes slitted open and moved from Duke to Abigail. "Me gone finish now," Kulalang rasped. "Not good die here at Katoomba. Want die Bandajong water hole—" he managed, and began to wheeze.

"Don't talk, just rest!" Duke insisted. "I will take you home, as soon as you're well!"

With the tattered remnants of his once formidable strength, Kulalang shook his head and crunched his brow in pain.

"And I'll get whoever did this," Duke choked out as if he, too, were in agony. "I'll get the bastard for this!"

Abigail saw Kulalang's lips move.

"Bones!" he rasped out. "Bones at *kuri kuri*—home."

"Duke, I think he wants you to take his bones home to the Grange water hole—" Abigail began.

Kulalang tried to nod again. A hint of a smile came to his lips. He looked gratefully back to Abby's face. The frown on his forehead faded. Then he was gone.

They stared down at him silently. Duke still clasped his friend's shoulders; Abigail held his hand. Duke bit his lower lip, racked with silent sobs. She sat stunned, tears dripping down on clothes she recalled now were soaking wet from their swim. But she felt hot with grief and anger, not cold, even though she was shaking.

"He predicted danger," Duke said at last. "I thought he meant for us, getting through the Blues. But if that bastard Godfrey-Bennett's really on the road behind us—"

Duke stood. His eyes met Earl's. Earl nodded. "We've got two hours of daylight left!" Duke bellowed. "We're moving on in honor of Kulalang of the Bandajong tribe! And in honor of his people's customs, we will never say his name again!"

Abby gasped and stood stiffly. She grabbed Duke's arm. "But we have to bury him and then take his bones back when we pass through again. And to never say his name again as if to forget him—you don't believe those aborigine things, do you?"

"No, but my friend did. He believed the spot he died should be deserted and his name not spoken in order to free his spirit to ascend the star path to the heavens. Besides, if your murdering cousin's on the road behind us, I'm going back to settle with him right now!"

"No, Duke!" Earl cried. "You'll come with us now and we'll both face him later! If I lose both you and Ku—our friend, I don't know what I'd do. If Phillip heads for Bathurst to give us trouble when we claim our run, we'll settle with him there. Promise me, Duke! Later, we'll face him together!"

Reluctantly, Duke agreed. It began to rain again, but they were all soaked from before, and it didn't seem to matter. Abigail's teeth chattered as she insisted she help Duke dig a hasty grave for their friend until they passed through again toward Sydney and took his bones. When earth and leaves covered the aborigine, Abigail was surprised to see Duke tie a piece of rope to make a two-branch cross and stick it in the top of the little mound.

"I thought we were doing everything the aborigine way," she said quietly.

"I told him all about Jesus and heaven just like he told me all about the dreamtime star road," Duke said, staring down. His words sounded broken and so tired. "I'm going to miss him so. In a way, I had two fathers in this land besides the Squire. The man who taught me how to read and reason and then—this friend. My aborigine father made me love and understand the land in a way Squire never could, fine farmer that he is."

"Yes, I see. Duke, I'm so sorry," she said, knowing any words were inadequate. She touched his arm, though he did not seem to notice.

"Your damned Exclusive cousin's going to be the sorry
one!" he muttered and pulled her away from the grave. He
wrapped the blanket Grace handed him around Abigail and
hiked her up on her horse.

Sadly, Abigail looked back over her shoulder at the place
her dear aborigine rescuer and fellow artist and friend had
called Katoomba—this place where they had begun in joy
and ended in such agony.

Please, dear Lord, she prayed silently as she made an
outsweep to move the sheep along, don't let it be the same
for us when we get to the Bathurst plains. Please, let there
be no presence of enemies there! Please don't let Phillip destroy any more lives!

Fighting her fears and her tears, she urged her horse after the first ewe she saw that darted off the westward trail.

# Chapter Fifteen

The beauty and openness of the rolling Bathurst plain silenced them all when they first beheld it. The entire day before they descended to the western foothills, they caught glimpses of it spread before them like a rich carpet. That last night in their mountain camp, for the first time since Kulalang's death more than a week ago, people smiled again in expectation of arriving on the plain tomorrow. They had done it! They had crossed the Blues!

Abigail took advantage of the jubilant mood to distribute the small double sketches she had been hoarding as gifts for each fellow drover. On one side of the page was a hilarious line drawing of the man's face when he first tasted her damper: eyeball-bulging, neck-grasping, tongue-hanging shock. The other side showed each one as he looked, dignified and able, riding with the flock. All the herdsmen were pleased, some raucously amused, others shyly touched. They ended up giving Abigail three "hurrahs" that echoed in the lower ravines of the Blues.

"I saved yours for last and for private," she told Duke later, standing next to the wagon where she slept and where he had come to say good-night. She extended the small square of paper to him.

"It's too dim here to see it," he said, his tone light for the first time since they'd lost Kulalang. "But if it's half as good as the one you did of Earl, I thank you. For all the help you've been over the mountains, too. And for understanding how busy and bereft I've been.''

"I was just grateful you let me do what I could to help. And to be myself, Abby Rose," she added.

"Say," he said as the thought hit him, "this drawing of me isn't the one you threatened to do before, is it?"

"Threatened? I believe you were going to draw me in return! No, not since you evidently have no interest in posing for it anymore," she countered, but she knew her voice trembled right through her brazen banter.

He pulled her to him and kissed her good-night. He hadn't done so on the whole trip; now it surprised her. The kiss was determined and possessive, and it took the starch right out of her legs. She held to his broad shoulders. Her head spun. She wanted this kiss to go on and on and for him to climb right up into the wagon with her. Too soon, he released her and walked toward the fire, probably to see the drawing. On one side it showed him riding herd, but on the other she had done a miniature sketch for him of Kulalang sitting on that escarpment the last time they saw him before the tragedy. She stood there a few moments, hoping Duke would come back. He did not. Her heart heavy, despite the joy of giving her gifts and the nearness of their goal, she climbed up in the wagon to sleep sadly alone.

Even living between two wagon beds tipped into a V-shaped hut with a makeshift canvas roof and front, Abby felt she was home on the expansive new Braden run. The spread was nearly the acreage of the Grange back in the Parramatta Valley, stretching from the foothills of the Blues to the meandering Macquarie River. Another boundary ran for miles along the only dirt road to the ten-mile-distant town of Bathurst.

Though the women had stayed put, some of the men, including Duke and Earl, had been to town for supplies and wood planks; the Braden brothers had even come back with presents. A new brown riding skirt, ruffled shirt, straw bonnet and short cape for Abigail, as well as paper and ink and pens. A gown for Grace to replace the one she'd given Abigail and material for curtains for a cabin that was weeks away from being built. But the news from town was bad: the men had reported that Phillip Godfrey-Bennett and a bunch of men had been through before heading out again. Reluctantly, Duke and Earl pulled even more men off herding to ride the broad boundaries as guards. Later that day Abigail overheard Duke discussing Phillip with Earl.

"Phillip not only killed our aborigine friend, but he's come over the Blues to cause us more trouble!" Duke told Earl behind one of the wagons. "We've got to watch the flock every minute. That bastard could poison our water just like he threatened to the *kuri kuri* water hole. And he'll have done more damage to squatters' rights back home if this endeavor fails!"

"I can't believe that belly-crawling lizard had the gall to come out here," Earl muttered. "Maybe he's just out to retrieve his rebellious cousin Abigail to save the future of Exclusive womanhood from the likes of us Currency. Maybe he wants her for himself!"

"Damn it!" Duke exploded and slammed his fist into the wagon wheel. "Don't mention Abby in the same breath with that devil! If I thought for one minute the Exclusive cousins cared the slightest bit for each other, I don't know what I'd do. As it is, I've been thinking that what is right and just is to haul that murdering bastard into court in Bathurst and accuse him of killing an aborigine, but I'll have to find him first." He gritted his words out through clenched teeth. "I tell you, Earl, I could jump him and kill him with my bare hands!"

"Now, you're talking!"

"No, don't you see? I've got to control myself. That's what I've always demanded back in Sydney. The courts have got to be made to protect all lives here, even if a Godfrey-Bennett is the criminal!"

"You and your stupid trust in governors and courts and the moral rights of all men! It's gonna get you killed, Duke! Bad enough in Sydney to think you were gonna win social justice, but out here? You think they'll believe your word about a dead aborigine's final ramblings against Godly-Bennett and his men! Now, look, we go into town in a couple of days, find him and beat the son of a bitch with fists and not words before we haul him in, that's the way of it!'' he roared.

"We can't both leave the camp," Duke insisted.

"Riding hard, we can be in town in an hour. I've been wrong to insist we should wait him out and just watch things here. I swear, I can feel those teeth and jaws crunch against my knuckles right now!'' Earl said, an unholy gleam in his eye.

Abigail was startled when Grace came to stand beside her. By the stricken look on her face, she had evidently heard Earl's words.

"His temper and his fists," Grace whispered as the two women walked away arm in arm. "I thought with loving me, that was all past for him. Well, I'll just be sure never to rile him then," Grace said sadly.

"Grace, they're speaking about Phillip Godfrey-Bennett, and I'm the one they'd turn on first over him, not you!" Abby soothed her friend.

Right then, Abigail decided she had to do something to keep Phillip away from the sheep and the Braden brothers. Duke was right. Phillip should be accused in a court of law for killing Kulalang. Surely a judge could be made to believe her, if not the Bradens, about that. So, first chance she got, she had to ride into town. She would find a magistrate and give evidence to have her cousin arrested. She grieved for what it would do to Mr. and Mrs. Godfrey-Bennett when they heard their son was a criminal, but Phillip had overstepped the bounds of civilized law!

Grace interrupted her thoughts. "Abigail, you're frowning. Duke won't turn on you neither no matter how many worries he's got, sure he won't."

"Come on then," Abigail told her. "Let's go up on the hill and work some more on that surprise we have for them. Let's get our guard just in case Phillip ever would come out here where he isn't welcome. When we've finished the dam, that will lift Duke and Earl's spirits!''

Abigail had told the men she was working on a drawing of Grace, sitting on a hill with the valley and sheep run spread out below. It was true, and she intended to take the sketch back to Squire to show him the lay of the land. But that was only half the truth.

The still melting snow from the mountains and the late-spring rains had tumbled some soil down where a little stream cut toward the Macquarie River far below. The men had spoken of trying to find time to arrange stones in a little dam to divert the stream and save the hillside. Recalling the stones in a stream back on Braden land in the Parramatta Valley, Grace and Abigail had been rolling or hauling one or two rocks each day to make the barrier to divert the stream. And today was the day they thought they would roll the final rocks in place and then proudly display their handiwork to the exhausted Duke and Earl.

They put Abigail's art supplies under a scrap of tarp and labored over the last big stone. They knew Joe, their guard, should stay alert, so they never accepted his daily offer of help. He had vowed to keep their secret. He sat on a rock with his rifle, watching the women and the land below dotted with grazing sheep. Off a ways to the south of the flock, men were working on ringbarking box shrubs to clear potential pastureland that the shrubs sucked dry of water. With less rain than usual, even the grass was tinder dry in spots, reaching right down to the river. Each day before Abby sketched, they had washed in the cold stream so the men could not tell they had been up here sweating like laborers. But today a welcome drizzle began again, so Joe had moved under his rock and the women would hardly have to take a bath afterward.

This final big rock, along with a slight rearrangement of the earlier ones, would cut the single, eroding stream into two smaller rivulets. One would run far along the hill before going down. Both could eventually be diverted to ponds to water the sheep or to run them through before shearing next autumn.

With their skirts hiked up in knee-deep water, the women strained to roll the big rock in place. "Too heavy!" Abigail said between sharp breaths. "The snowmelt and this rain today, of all days—ugh—let's let it go until some other time!"

"I know, but I wanted to show Earl today—to make him happier with all that yelling and those threats down there!" Grace grunted. "Oh, Ab—I think this rock is just going to go—I can't stop it!"

They squealed in unison as the rock rolled. It bumped and took several others with it, then all of them, releasing the water it had been holding back and the hillside they had sought to save. Abigail grabbed for Grace as they both went down in the sudden torrent. Clawing for what had been the bank, clinging together, they managed to hang on as rocks and water crashed over and down toward the sheep and the more distant wagons that formed the Braden camp.

"Joe! Joe, help!" Grace screamed.

"Look out below!" Abigail shouted. She cupped her hands and moved as near as she dared to the disappearing hillside. She shouted again.

A brown gush of water, hill and rock swelled the stream. More land went in a rumbling tumble. Joe and the women raced along the brow of the hill. They watched in horror, then scrambled down another way as, below them, sheep went swimming and wagons and wooden items floated across Braden land.

"Oh, no! Oh, no!" Grace kept saying. "They were so proud they got us here with only six sheep lost! Earl will be furious at me. Oh, no!"

Down below, men on horseback waded after terrified, swimming sheep. Earl hooked a floating wagon with a long shepherd's crook and dragged it over to the new bank of a rushing creek where Grace had started a garden that went under. The precious salt lick nearest the site for the cabin shrank, toppled and disappeared. Abigail saw Duke on horseback in the melee, saving sheep, his horse flank-deep in swirling water. Out of breath but desperate, she waded in after several of the younger lambs she had helped to birth back at Dorset Downs.

"Here, Cloudpuff! Here, I've got you!" she cried, though she went down in the raging mess more than once. Duke rode up, hauled her out and deposited her by the bedraggled, sodden Grace and some bleating, mud-drenched lambs. Slowly, the initial gush of dammed-up water and muddy hillside subsided.

"Any more to save?" Earl gasped as he rode up, exhausted. He looked down at the women and almost fell off his dripping horse. "What's this Joe told me, though I had to put a good fist in his jaw to make him spit it up?" He strode right at Grace and yanked her to him. He shook her once. "You did what up there!" he roared. "You could have been killed right along with the sheep and the rest of us with this stupidity!"

In the face of his rage and roughness, Grace froze in fear. Abigail realized she was probably reliving once again the buried agony of her brutal father's beatings.

"Earl, don't!" Abigail cried and slipped her way over to them. "It was my idea, I talked her into it. We tried to make a little dam to divert the water, and then it just happened!"

"But Gracie, you—I could have lost you!" Earl cried and nearly smothered her in a hard hug.

Grace hung there a moment suspended and then hugged him back, sobbing out the words, "It was my fault, too, Earl, but only 'cause I love you so. I wanted to help. It was my fault, too, not just Abigail's!"

Earl bounced Grace up into his arms and sloshed away through foot-deep mud, but Duke spun Abby to face him. "And I thought you were really here to help!" he accused. "I should have known it couldn't last!"

She was sobbing now. She couldn't tell her tears from sweat and rain. "What couldn't last?" she choked out. "That we could trust each other or be together? That I could help you, help you both here and back in Sydney? Or worse, that you could love me? Or that you couldn't stomach keeping me around when you—yes, *you!*—decided I was not your kind, that you were too damned good and *exclusive* for me! I was just trying to help like Grace said and for the same reasons, Duke Braden! Because I love a Braden brother and want to be a Braden bride, fool that I am! But don't worry, it won't happen again! You can just cuddle up to your causes and keep so busy you don't have time to 'get back to us' as you promised, and see if I care!" She was nearly hysterical now, panicked by defeat and loss. "See if I care when I stake out my own special spread here and make it the finest these parts have ever, ever seen!"

He stood staring, openmouthed in the rain as she slogged away from him through the mud, retrieving random pieces of beached debris as she went.

He stood rooted in the muck. He felt that tirade and that hellfire look in her hazel eyes slice clear through him. He had to admit he had been avoiding her. Because he was ready to surrender. He wanted her. He wanted to marry her. To Earl's way of thinking, it had been so simple and so clear that Duke should wed Lady Abigail Anne Rosemont. But it wasn't simple to Duke to think of desiring with such desperation that he lost his self-control to his beautiful, wild, strong Abby Rose.

He was still afraid he would either sacrifice everything he'd spent his life on, or end up taking on a whole new array of problems if they married. Her fortune, which, no doubt, would be reason enough for many to choose her, scared him stiff. And here he had been dreaming just last night of how wonderful it would be to wed her in Bathurst because she would have to let him pay for everything. But he had to go there first to settle with Phillip. He was crazy to be following Earl's initial plan to let the bastard show his hand or come to them. He wanted Phillip out of his and Abby's life as soon as possible!

Cursing the landslide under his breath, cursing himself, he trudged up and around the slippery hillside where the flash flood had now gone back to one wild stream. When it quit raining, maybe he and Earl could somehow dam it up right instead of the way the woman had devastated the whole thing, including him!

Even after dark, while the men toiled outside by lamplight to reclaim things mired in the mud and patch the dam as best they could, Abigail prepared for what she knew she had to do tomorrow. She washed her muddied riding skirt and ruffled shirt and let them dry in the tree all night when the drizzle stopped. She tried to sleep, but everything kept going through her mind. How she had to settle with the man she detested to have any chance with the one she loved. At dawn, she pinned her curly, flyaway hair under her muddy drooping straw bonnet. She prayed hard she was doing the right thing, not only to go to town to get Phillip arrested, but to take without permission the extra gun Duke had left in Earl and Grace's wagon.

She hadn't fired a gun since her enforced hunting days with Lord Northurst years ago, and then only at targets since she refused to do more than ride at the hunt. But after having been seized by bushrangers, she would take no more risks, not even with guards. Besides, she dared not ask one of the men to take her or they might tell Duke and he would stop her.

Instead, for safety's sake, she was going to wait at the bottom of the lane to be certain she joined and blended in with some travelers on the road to town. She would go directly to the authorities, and then testify to Kulalang's murder, which Duke's men had already reported.

As for handling Duke when he discovered what she had done... She hoped he would be grateful for her evidence toward getting Phillip arrested. She prayed Duke would see finally whose side she was on. If he didn't want her with him even after that, she was going to send for her money and invest in a place of her own out here. Without Duke at her side, there was nothing for her in Sydney; out here, she would become Earl and Grace's neighbor and hire some men to help her establish a run of her own. And, of course, send for H.M. so she had something to love besides a flock of sheep! As for Fairleigh so far away in that other life that had once been hers, she would either lease or sell it and make her own beloved Fairleigh here someday, perhaps naming her fine, future sheep run Kulalang.

She helped Grace with breakfast as always, hoping her trepidation did not show on her face. Everyone seemed tense and glum despite the sunshine and sprightly breeze. Their wagons had been bumped around and some supplies water-logged or lost. Two drowned sheep had been buried. Fortunately for her this morning, it was Duke's turn to be out riding boundaries, and Earl had departed with four men to finish mending the stone dam on the ruined hill above.

She waited until Grace went out to hang wash on the limbs of a dying cedar tree. She scribbled her a brief note, telling her what she intended and that she would return by nightfall. What did it matter what Grace told the men after she got a good start? She put the note in Grace's mending basket that she would not get to until much later. Hiding Duke's gun in her single saddle pack, she strolled away from camp and saddled her horse in a copse of golden flowering wattles. She mounted, hoping Grace would think she was out helping to herd.

Abigail quickly rode out to the road and waited under a tree for someone to come along the ten-mile stretch to Bathurst. Her stomach was in knots; she waited for what seemed an eternity. The first passersby were two squatters and their wives on a jaunt to Bathurst, though Abigail soon regretted joining such a merry crew. She was hardly up to a happy chat.

"What a perfect place for those Braden bastards to end their squatters' dreams and their lives!" Phillip Godfrey-Bennett mused to himself as he again surveyed the tiny town of Bathurst. Just a stretch of stone buildings, convict-built, and a splatter of wood or small stone houses. A lowlife, ramshackle place, so appropriate for the Currency! Bathurst's streets were not paved, and it had nothing fine or grand or cultured about it. But, he thought with a smug grin, the rough gaol would do fine for the likes of Duke Braden. And the main square looked just perfect for a frontier-justice hanging.

George interrupted Phillip's thoughts. "Boss, us buying up this whole barrel o' whale oil's caused a bit of a stir in this danged so-called emporium here, even if I did bribe the man what sold it to keep his trap shut."

Phillip shot a disdainful glance at the only supply store in town. He'd refused even to cross the threshold with that jumble of mediocre goods in there. "Hasn't the blasted country bumpkin ever heard of burning out a clump of dingo dens?" Phillip asked and struck a match to light another cheroot from one of the boxes he had brought along.

"That's a good one, boss," George chortled. "Dingoes. But he said it's been a dry spring despite the recent rains and we better watch ourselves."

"Indeed," Phillip muttered and clipped off the end of the cheroot with a sterling-sliver cutter. "Indeed, we will."

He drew the smoke into his lungs and exhaled slowly to try to calm himself. He'd had his bellyful of this wretched life in the wilds, camping outside of town after a few nights in a lumpy bed here in Bathurst, just waiting for the Braden brothers to ride into town or lighten the watch on their borders. But now, he was going to act. Now he was going to flush them out, to draw their guards so he could seize Abigail and settle with Duke in the hellfire chaos that would devour their grasslands, their sheep, and trap them all in a holocaust of his hatred for them and their ways!

Today, quite simply, was the day he made his dreams come true. Abigail, the traitress, ravished and executed. Duke, shamed and arrested to be hanged. Braden Currency causes completely crushed. Their squatters' model sheep run incinerated. Then he, Phillip Godfrey-Bennett, the victorious savior of all that was righteous and precious back in Sydney, could return to civilization at last! He trembled in expectation and exhilaration as he turned to mount his horse in the main street of Bathurst.

Then he gasped and froze still as a statue. As if a sacrificial lamb were being offered him by whatever Fates ruled the world, he saw Abigail ride by with a group of strangers and head right down the street to the government building.

"Boss, it was her, Lady Abigail, wasn't it?"

"Yes, yes! Go around in back of the government building with my horse, and send the boys out of town with the oil. I'm going to get her before she tries to ruin everything as usual. Go on, damn you!" he cried and darted after her in the shadow of the crude verandas so Abigail would not spot him.

When Abigail's riding companions left her at the government building just off the tiny park in Bathurst, she felt a moment's indecision. She was very nervous. And she was not certain whether to take Duke's gun inside with her. She decided to unstrap and carry in the entire saddle pack so she would not alarm anyone. But then, before she could do that, a pistol flashed before her face and she jumped back in shock.

"Not a sound, traitress, or I swear, I'll gladly use this!"

She gasped and spun to face Phillip. How dared he accost her with a gun right outside this government building! But this was not the Phillip she had once known, she realized as she stared up into a face twisted with hate.

"Not a sound!" he repeated through clenched teeth. Hiding his gun against his left arm, he gestured with it. "This way around in back for a little chat!"

He left her horse—and her gun—there and marched her away with the muzzle of his pistol jammed into her ribs, his grip tight on her upper arm. Just behind the building, along another sparsely settled street, a slope-shouldered man waited with two horses.

She tried to calm herself. Her heart beat so loud, she was certain he would hear it too. "I know you wouldn't really shoot me, your cousin—" she began.

"You've betrayed me, betrayed us all," Phillip muttered. "Up on my horse now. One wrong move and it will be your last!"

"Phillip, you can't mean—"

He yanked her around with one hand in her hair to knock her straw bonnet askew. He pressed his gun barrel under her chin to make her stare up into his wide eyes. That look—it reminded her of those men out in the bush who wanted her, who threw dice for her, who would have killed her. Phillip shoved her so hard against the horse it neighed and sidestepped away before he pulled her back.

"Don't fret, dear coz," he murmured, leering down at her. "We're going calling on your lover, Braden, or rather he on us."

That pronouncement gave her hope at first. But this was the man who shot 'roos and aborigines for fun. This was the demented wretch who had killed Kulalang!

"Phillip, please, for your parents' sake—" she began.

He slapped her face with his other hand. "It's for my parents' sake, and the future of us all, you deceitful little bitch. And you're only getting what you so richly deserve! Now get up there!"

He boosted her up so hard, she almost toppled off the horse's other side. Her face and scalp stung. She knew with certainty that this nightmare was only beginning.

Duke rode back to the wagon campsite at late morning. He had tried to wait until evening, but he had to see Abby. He had been nasty and brusque with her yesterday after the stream and hillside went, when she had only been trying to help. For weeks he had been hiding from her and running from her—and from the irrefutable fact he not only loved her but needed her. Even out here, her strength and love had not crumbled. She was no sandstone, as his father used to say, but a sturdy, loyal pebble. He had to tell her how much he admired and adored her, and see if they could not somehow come to terms before it was too late.

"Where is she then?" he asked Grace when she told him Abigail was "out."

"You know her," she said with a shrug. "Helping with the sheep somewheres, doing anything she can to lend a hand," she added pointedly as she sat on a board bench in the sun by the wagon and propped her mending basket on her knees. Earl's shirt had taken a good tear in the scramble to save sheep the previous day. "Pro'bly she's taken to talking to sheep 'cause she wants something gentle to chat with instead of being bit at by the man she loves," Grace dared. To her amazement, Duke hung his head and looked a bit sheepish himself.

"I know, Grace," he admitted, scuffing a rut of mud with the toe of his boot. "I need to talk to her about a lot of things. You know, that little landslide you two arranged yesterday did us a real favor by showing us this isn't a safe site for the cabin even clear down here. I'm going out until I find her then. I just hope she and I have a lot of plans to make."

He mounted his horse and called back to her, "Tell her to stay put if she rides in from herding, Grace. Tell her I'll be back!"

Grace sighed and shook her head as she watched Duke tear off. She wished ever so much there was some way to get those two together permanently, like her and Earl. Then she opened her basket and saw the note on top of the thread and needles and scraps of cloth. She grabbed it and read it.

"Oh, my," she muttered. "Oh, my!"

The basket flew as she ran for the rough-built corral of horses. Duke had to get some men and ride into town to find Abigail, just in case Phillip Godfrey-Bennett heard she was there. This would make Duke show his true feelings for Abigail! He might be a bit angry at her, but he'd tell her he loved her and wanted to marry her now for sure! He had to, he just had to!

No time for a saddle, just a bridle, but Grace's hands shook with that. She pulled her horse over to the crude fence and scrambled to its back. If Abigail had just waited! Earl said he and Duke were going looking for Phillip. Grace urged her horse to a gallop in the direction Duke had ridden.

"I'm certainly not writing the Braden brothers a note telling them I started a bushfire!" Abigail snapped to Phillip. Tied to a eucalyptus sapling, she tugged again at her ropes but they did not give. She had to do something, anything to put off her ruination and that of the Braden run!

Phillip and his man George had brought her just beyond the southern edge of Braden land to a rocky rise that was a spine from the foothills. He had other men waiting here. In the distance Abby could see the brow of hill where she and Grace had tried to dam up the stream yesterday and a forlorn finger of smoke from Grace's cook fire. Here and there below, between the gray-green hills and the blue ribbon of river, she could see white puffs of grazing sheep she now knew by sight and name. How she had come to love this life, this land, as well as Duke Braden! Tears blurred her gaze. She could not quite yet discern all of Phillip's twisted plan, but she knew he intended to use the warm afternoon winds sweeping from these hills to send a bushfire racing down to trap the sheep and men and then tell Duke she had caused it. If only it would rain a bit today as it had yesterday!

"They would not believe it of me anyway!" she declared to Phillip. But fear devoured her defiance. After yesterday when Duke railed at her for causing the mudslide, and after the way he'd flown into a rage when she was with Phillip back in Sydney, who knew what he'd believe of her out here with all the pressure he was under!

"They're going to believe much more of you than that and soon!" Phillip threatened. "Anyway, this will draw them out of their holes, and we won't even have to send for Duke. But he and you and I have unfinished business, so we're going to have to be very sure one of my men brings him up here for a private visit when he appears to fight the fire. And the wind's just right. My destiny again, Abigail.

First you just appear on this day of judgment and now the very forces of nature are on my side!''

"You're demented!'' she cried, but he cracked her across her cheek again to spill her hair loose.

"All right, go on!'' Phillip's sharp command rang out to his men below. He signaled for them to dribble whale oil along the ground just below their perch where the grasslands and scrub of box shrubs began. "As soon as we start the blaze, you and I are going to make a fire of our own, dear coz,'' he told her. He was staring glassy-eyed at the obscene wet line of oil threatening the pastoral scene far below.

"All right, Phillip,'' she told him to stall for time, "if you want, I'll write the note to Duke!'' Slowly, shaking when George untied her, she sat down on a rock under Phillip's glare and gun and wrote the note he dictated:

I have decided you must pay for your deceit and cruelty to me and those I love, my family at the Grange and those folk who would keep Sydney and New South Wales pure and moral and just . . .

She almost balked, but went on at Phillip's gruff urging while he peered over her shoulder and caressed the nape of her neck with his gun barrel.

No one who cannot pay has the right to come here to rob this land from those who deserve what they have. It proves once again the moral taint of all you Currency. And I can never forgive you for seducing me away from those who truly cared for me.

"Sign it,'' he ordered. "It's enough.''

"Duke will never believe it!''

"It's not for Duke. It's for the magistrate in Bathurst at Duke's rather hasty trial.'' He snatched the note from her. He had decided not to risk trying bribes with these rural magistrates. No, the way he was going to do things, he would not even need a judge under the Godfrey-Bennett thumb. He jammed the note in his waistcoat pocket and removed a cheroot and a sulfur match he had there.

"Duke's trial?" Abigail floundered. "They won't accuse him of burning his and his brother's own place! And there were witnesses he didn't kill Kulalang—"

She regretted throwing that at him. Under his brutal questioning of why she'd come to town she had told him only that she wanted to stake her own claim here on the Bathurst plains, not that she'd come to accuse him of murder. But he seemed not to hear, even when she mentioned Kulalang. That infuriated her. The fact he'd shot the man was less to him than picking off a snake. For the first time, she became absolutely terrified for herself.

While George seized her at Phillip's barked command and held her arms behind her, Phillip strode down to the wet, waiting line of lamp oil. Abigail bucked and screamed. But he struck his match on his boot sole and, with a flourish, tossed it on the line of oil.

Whoooosh! Red-orange flame flared high. It raced the length of the line. It darted to grass and scrubs. The sporadic rains had not moistened them enough to withstand the blast of heat and fire. Phillip's sharp laugh, like a dingo's ugly howl, rang out once. Then he turned to start back toward her with his gun drawn. He pointed it right at her and nodded to George to loose her. Staring aghast at the wall of fire fanning down into the valley, she gaped right past the gun at first.

"Move, Abigail, over behind those rocks where I have the blanket spread. And do everything I say, or you won't even be here to see that defiling Braden bastard when my men bring him up here."

"Please, Phillip. For our family ties, at least—your parents, little Lottie—"

"You've ruined all that. Oh, don't look so sad, my dearest. I promise you you're going to enjoy this greatly for a while, much more even than you did the times you whored for Braden! Now move!"

## Chapter Sixteen

When Grace found Duke and handed him Abigail's note, he yelled to the two nearest herdsmen—Joe and Herb—and thundered off for the road to town with them close behind. Skittish sheep scattered, though they did not ride right through them.

Abby had said in the note she'd be careful, Duke assured himself. But there was no being careful with that devil Phillip loose out there. He'd obviously been hiding out, but Abby might be just the drawing card he'd need to show himself, even on the streets of peaceful Bathurst. Especially if word got around she'd gone there to testify against him about Kulalang's murder, let alone perhaps to claim a sheep run of her own as she'd mentioned yesterday! And it was ten long miles to town!

"What, Duke?" Joe yelled to him as they caught up, pounding along the dirt road toward Bathurst.

"Lady Abigail in trouble—again!" Duke yelled back.

Joe just nodded, but Herb called out, "She's worth saving more'n once, that one!"

Duke bit his lower lip hard until he tasted blood. So simply, eloquently put, probably what Earl would have said. And he, the so-called golden-voiced orator for Currency rights, had been so damned stupid and stubborn and tongue-tied! Now, he was terrified he would not be able to convince her he was not afraid to love her beyond belief, beyond all reason!

"Look, Duke!" Herb shouted and pointed up the valley toward the shadow of the hills. "That glow—ain't that a fire an' comin' our way?"

Duke squinted where Herb pointed. A long line of fire, descending to the valley, chewing grass and scrub and everything to glowing red!

"Circle on back, both of you! Find Earl and get men up there to make a stand. Damn, the wind's in our faces. And tell Earl why I had to go to town. I'll send men back to help! I'll check the line of it when I ride by! Go on! Hurry!" he ordered and spurred his horse even faster.

The two men dropped behind and wheeled back. All he intended to do was ride a bit closer to get a good look at it so he knew what to tell them in town. He'd bring help not only to Abby but out here to fight the flames. A brushfire in this dry spring could burn out not only the Bradens but the entire valley of hardworking, hard-dreaming squatters! At least by riding closer to the hills here he could not only view the fire but also cut off the big loop the river road made to town.

Ab-by-Rose, his horse's hoofbeats seemed to beat the message into the very land lying new and naked under this new threat. Ab-by-Rose, Ab-by-Rose. Whatever befalls, I love you and I'm coming to town to tell you, Abby Rose!

"You're lower than a thieving, raping bushranger!" Abby berated Phillip as he forced her around a rock where he had spread a blanket on the ground. "Talk about a moral taint, an inherent stain of character in the Currency! I think—"

He shoved her hard. She went down on her knees, her hands caught in her loosened hair when she pushed herself up on her haunches to face him. She was almost desperate enough that she didn't care if he did beat her the way he had poor Catty—even shoot her. Just so he didn't touch her the way those men out there on the other side of the Blues had. But then Kulalang had saved her, and Phillip had killed Kulalang.

"I had originally planned to let that brazen bastard watch our fun, but the bushfire's going so well, we may be pressed for time," Phillip announced. "So get that riding skirt—everything—off and get down on your back on the blanket."

Her mind raced for ways out. Do as he said, perhaps, then grab his gun when he came close? Turn it on him, throw dirt in his face? It was worse than the nightmare of being trapped by those bushrangers. She began to shake all over. She had less than a hatpin here, less than—

"Boss! Boss, you won't believe who's riding up this way!" George's voice came to them as the man sprinted around the rock. "Duke Braden. If you want us to just get him—"

To her mingled joy and horror, Phillip grinned and crowed his exultation to the sky. "Perfect, so perfect, all of it! Fated! Fated!" he shouted. "Yes, fetch the bastard, as I've something to show him!"

Abigail shook so hard she felt the earth heave under her feet the way the deck of the *Challenge* had during those months while it brought her here. How had it all come to this? How had Phillip become this crazed soul? And how had she and Duke been trapped like this while Earl and Grace's dream went up in flame and smoke like hers for her own happy future?

"Duke! Duke!" she cried when the man named George brought him in at gunpoint with his hands on the top of his head. She longed to run to him, no matter what, but the point of Phillip's gun held her back.

"You want his gun, too, boss?" George asked.

"Oh, yes, I've need of his gun," Phillip said, his wide-eyed face split in a big grin. "It's going to be another damning piece of evidence against him. Then tie him up over there so he can watch."

"Abby, he hasn't hurt you?" Duke demanded as if Phillip had not said a word. They dragged him back a ways as he spoke. She was flooded with relief that he obviously believed she had not fled to Phillip nor helped to set the fire.

"Not really," she called to him. "It only hurt me when I thought I'd lost you."

"No more. Never again, sweetheart," Duke assured her.

"Shut up, both of you!" Phillip roared. "And gag him, too, because—"

A crackle of gunfire sounded very close on the other side of the rocks. Phillip spun. George looked up. And Duke, for the first time since he'd been a boy sparring with Earl, attacked with his fists. His knuckles cracked George's jaw. He kicked his gun away and dived low at Phillip, feet and fists flying. They went down at Abigail's feet, rolling, grunting, punching. She screamed and scrambled for George's gun before he could right himself.

"I'll shoot you, I swear I will!" she told George and leveled it at him. "You helped kill my friend Kulalang! I swear I'll shoot you!"

Duke pummeled Phillip into the dust with blows to his jaw and belly. He banged his head on the ground. But when Earl and Joe and Herb burst at a full run around the rock to grab George, the ravaged, gasping Duke dragged Phillip Godfrey-Bennett to his feet. He promptly collapsed in a pile in the dust.

Earl assessed the scene and shouted, "I'll put a bullet in him by accident for you! He started the fire with lamp oil, and it's spreading fast!"

"No bullets! He's going to stand trial for that and more!" Duke insisted as he dragged the bloodied Phillip over by the back of his shirt. "Go, Earl, fight the flames. Dig a trench down by the camp. If you've got the rest of Godly-Bennett's hired hands, go, and I'll be right there!"

"They've scattered. We won't see the likes of them again."

Earl and his men sprinted away. Duke hauled Phillip, now on his face, back around the rock and hog-tied him with his own rope. Abigail followed, carrying Phillip's gun and the blanket to help beat out the flames. But she knew better when she got a good look. Catastrophe and chaos reigned below in the inferno of Phillip's hatred. Yet they hardly smelled smoke here, for it swept away from them on the dry wind toward the Braden run.

"He didn't hurt you, did he?" Duke demanded, turning her to him by her shoulders. He looked so eager, yet afraid to really touch her.

"No. I—I just didn't want you to think I had any part of this. He made me write a note to you that's in his pocket—"

He nodded jerkily. His sweaty face was scratched and dusty. He tried to wipe away the blood streaming from his nose with his sleeve. He tugged her to him for a hard, quick hug. "The only things you've been part of all along is teaching me how much I need you, how much I want us together always. But we've got to go down now to help Earl save what he can before the fire sweeps into the heart of the run."

He heaved the trussed Phillip up behind his own saddle. Duke mounted his horse and pulled Abigail up behind him. Phillip was moaning, half-unconscious, and he almost tumbled off when they started away. It was then the idea came to Abby.

"I know how we can stop the flames just beyond where they are, Duke! The dam we let loose yesterday! If we could just tumble those stones loose you and Earl put there to patch it up—"

But Duke had already urged their horses to a quicker gallop along the brow of the hill, with the limp, beaten body of Phillip Godfrey-Bennett bouncing along behind.

They rode up the hill just ahead of the flames. In the choking cloud of ash and smoke, they had to slow. They dismounted near the stream just above the dam. Duke tore off scraps of blanket, and they tied them around their faces. Already they looked like aborigines with blackened hair and faces. Abigail thought of Kulalang again and how he had saved her life. Perhaps it was for this—to try to save Grace and Earl's land, but probably it was so she could keep loving Duke forever.

Standing in the stream, huddled over the new boulders and rocks Duke and Earl had put in the streambed, together they moved their little mountain.

"Back! Back, it's going!" Duke cried and grabbed her arm to haul her out of the stream. With no rain today, the buildup of water was not as much, but it rushed and tumbled down, spreading to the other rivulet that traversed the brow of the hill and descended farther on. Both streams gushed flame-dousing water and mud to make the fire halt its path clear to the river far below.

Abby cheered and sucked in a huge gasp of smoke right through the wool blanket. She coughed and coughed and cheered and cheered. Jubilant too, Duke banged her on the back, then hauled her into his bruised, sopping arms. She clung to him, hardly believing in this world of flood and fire that this could be real at last. As if they were two bandits with bandannas over their faces, their teary eyes met and held.

"Marry me, please, Abby Rose," he choked out, his voice raspy from smoke and cheering. "Here or back across the Blues in Sydney, stand by my side and be my Braden bride!"

"Yes," she cried and tugged down both their masks. "Yes, always!" she added, just before they kissed.

"A flood, a mud slide, a bushfire, an arrest and a wedding all in our first few weeks here," Earl teased Duke as they stood on the main street of Bathurst waiting for Grace and Abby to join them from inside the emporium. "And I'm not sure which of those means more trouble."

Duke grinned tautly, but he was too nervous to respond. He felt tongue-tied. He didn't like coming from hearing Phillip Godfrey-Bennett arraigned for murder and "unlawful incendiary actions"—he wasn't certain which was worse to folks out here—and then going right to his wedding. But it couldn't be helped that both happened today.

The news that Phillip would be going to prison for his crimes would get back over the mountains to Sydney soon enough. Even the fact Duke would not be there to read the

*Gazette* or see the amazement when the citizens of Sydney heard that the scion of Exclusive propriety was going to be a convict did not bother him. It was only that he had wasted too much time not marrying his Abby Rose to put it off a day longer. He should have made her his Braden bride the moment they stepped off the ship. He'd wanted her that long! And he couldn't wait to see how the money he had given her and Grace to spend for Abby's wedding dress would make her look. Perhaps after all the beautiful London fashions she was used to, she would be disappointed and he couldn't bear that. He wanted to make up everything to her, make her so happy from now on!

She took his breath away when she came out of the Bathurst Emporium and Sundries Supply Store with Grace. Abby was blushing and looked tense, too. A little breeze lifted her sky-blue ruffled hem to remind him of that day he'd first seen her, skirts blown skyward, on the deck of the ship. The gown was perfect, he thought. An oval-necked tiered collar with a scalloped edge enhanced the elegant sweep of her throat and trim jaw. The small, close-fitting bonnet sported white ribbons and feathers to balance the dark blue ribbon woven through three tiers of scalloped skirt. Even in his best blue trousers and waistcoat he'd brought west, he felt he couldn't hold a candle to her.

"They had four gowns to pick from, but I chose the color of your eyes," she told him shyly as he took her hand. His eager gaze still drank her in: the tiny belted waist, the graceful puff of her sleeves above the elbow where her slender arms were bare. "I decided not to spend money on gloves, though. I'd rather put it toward replacing that salt lick that went in the flood—the first flood."

He grinned and nodded; he was still not certain he could speak. He was so grateful everything had turned out well. Only the southern acreage had burned and the fire there had cleared off the stubborn box shrubs they'd been working to ringbark for days. Phillip was to be locked away for years, a great victory for the Currency argument that crime was not something passed down through the blood, since anyone in any social class might be capable of crime. And he and Abby Rose were facing life together, really together!

The four of them stood in the small, stone Anglican church that convicts had built, as they had built so many of the sturdy structures of New South Wales. Abby's eyes glistened with grateful tears; Duke, the smooth-voiced orator, stumbled over her name and his "I will." But they were wed, and Lady Abigail Anne Rosemont was a Braden's bride at last.

Back at the run, they celebrated with food and drink the wedding party had brought back from town. Abby had long ago removed her hat and her flyaway hair had gone loose in wayward tendrils in the breeze.

"Ever so nice, just like the day Earl and me got wed," Grace said and hugged Abigail again amid the dancing that went on after dark to one herdsman's tinny harmonica.

"I just wish Squire and H.M. were here!" Abby said as Duke took her hand to whirl her around in another improvised dance. The herdsmen weren't shy. If they couldn't partner the bride or Grace, they cavorted raucously with one another. Abby had never been so happy.

She and Duke danced under jeweled stars finer than she had ever seen on any London lady's throat during her one season long ago. No, she thought as she held more tightly to Duke's strong shoulder and his big, warm hand, *this* was her season. This was her life and land now and she was ever grateful, even amid the smell of dust or distant sheep. She came down from her hazy joy at being spun dizzily in Duke's arms only long enough to bid herdsmen hello or farewell when they drifted in or out from their rounds. And then Duke tugged her hand and whispered, "Time to go."

"Go where?" she asked, surprised. "I thought Grace said we could just borrow their covered wagon until you found a good place."

"I have a good place," he assured her with a kiss that lingered so long everyone began to hoot and whistle. "Earl

and I arranged it today, and he's sworn to me he'll not lead
anyone there to visit in the dead of night. Come on!''

They bade farewell to everyone. Grace hugged Duke and
Abby, sobbing for joy. "I told you we'd manage to tame the
two of them somehow," she whispered in Abby's ear, "but
we don't want them too tame, do we now?"

Like a fairy princess in a book with gilded drawings she'd
read as a child, Abby felt herself lifted in Duke's arms and
set sidesaddle on his horse. He mounted behind her, taking
along no supplies. Probably he and Earl had attended to
that, too, she thought. Lifting a torch Earl handed him with
a rough-voiced jest, "God bless you both, my old brother
and my new sister!" Duke clucked to the horse and they
started off into the bush.

"We're surely not riding over the Blues just so we can
sleep in Squire's extra room tonight," she teased as she
leaned back against his warmth.

"By the time we head back over the Blues, Abby, we'll be
old married folk—maybe a month from now. But first,
we've got a lot of time I lost for us to make up."

The horse climbed up, up along the brow of the hill, and
she realized at last where they were going. Near the rustling
stream that had both devastated, then saved Braden's Run,
Duke led her to a lean-to he and Earl had made, nestled
back in a copse of eucalyptus. He passed her the flaring
torch, then got off to lift her down. He took the torch and
touched it to a small aborigine-type fire already laid, then
doused the torch in the stream with a sizzling hiss.

She went into his arms, savoring the security of him. But
soon their rampant need for each other challenged their
slow, deliberate tenderness. He pulled her closer, ravaging
her earlobes and throat, tugging the gown off one shoulder. "I got warm dancing," he whispered so close in her ear
he bounced the wayward corkscrew tendrils Grace had labored over. "Just a quick dip in the stream for me."

"But I want to go with you everywhere!" she told him,
hoping he could hear her words over her pounding heart.
"The stream will do fine for starters."

"And then Castle Keep and Government House in Sydney and the houses of Members of Parliament if we return to London. I've got to see your Fairleigh, then maybe we'll build our own Braden's Run near Bathurst—"

"But any shearing shed or bit of bush in this land will do," she finished the jubilant, rambling list for him as they scampered for the stream bank.

"I asked you once if you wanted to swim with your clothes off or on," he said, but he hardly waited for her answer. His hands were quick and sure on his waistcoat and the buttons on the back of her gown. "And I believe we owe ourselves a sketch of all that's coming tonight."

"So this is to be my third official swimming lesson?" she teased. But she was trembling all over already in her eagerness. She surrendered to his touch as he removed her clothing, kissing and licking and sweetly tormenting each patch of bare skin he uncovered. In turn, she tugged his shirttails from the waistband of his trousers. He slowed his movements for one moment then.

"There's a lot I'd like to teach you, but somehow, my sweetheart," he whispered as he cradled her face between his shaking hands, "it turns out you taught me how to love."

The next kiss lingered, then deepened desperately again. He slanted his mouth over hers as she held to his narrow hips to keep from tilting off balance into the stream. The mere presence of the man—her husband—made her so dizzy.

They laid her new gown and petticoats carefully on the grass, but threw his garments to the wind. Cold waters tumbled down from the Blues, but they did not notice. They waded in. Hands laved water, caressed slick, wet flesh and even drank from it. They made their own waves, turning, pressing, twisting, as if they swam in the wild, whitecapped ocean. Firelight gilded curves and angles of skin, and the blur and brush of hair. Soon, but not soon enough for her growing impatience to belong completely to him, he lifted her in his arms and carried her to a pile of blankets over a soft bed of fragrant eucalyptus leaves.

The very essence of the land crinkled and released a rich aroma to mingle with their love and racing passion. His mouth and hands were everywhere along her breasts, her belly, her limbs. Stunned anew at the rush of sensation, she savored it. She caressed his neck, his shoulders, his lower back. She nibbled along the strong sinew of his neck, then licked him there as if to apologize.

"Oh!" She sighed their first word in the longest time as his tongue teased her body and her senses endlessly. She could not hold still. She moved her hips in little circles; she moaned and pulled him closer to her, closer.

"My sweetheart, my sweetheart, tell me how you feel," he murmured against the satin skin of her flat belly.

"Feel?" she asked, dazzled, as if those stars she could see beyond the black roof of the lean-to were whirling down toward them. "I feel so happy. Astounded every time you touch me. So in love. Swept away."

"I too, my wife, my exclusively beautiful wife. I used to be so afraid when I felt myself losing control of my life with you. But now you are my life. From now on," he said and knelt almost reverently between her legs to open her to him, "I shall enjoy losing my control—with you and in you!"

She meant to smile, even to laugh in exultation, but desire overcame her. Her wide eyes met his and held. She tugged him down and moved to meet him. She could tell her eagerness pleased him. The wonder of their union surprised her anew as he moved slowly inside her, then began a plunging, pulling pace to take her with him, higher, higher. All the long nights of yearning and days of waiting for him exploded in her. All her desires spun around like stars bursting through the black night as she clung to him and rocked with him and merged with him in mind and heart forever.

Later, as the night grew cold, they lay in each other's arms on their sides, wrapped in blankets.

"Chilled?" he asked and nuzzled her neck with his lips.

"Never again. I don't need a little pit with smoldering ashes under it when I have you!"

He chuckled. The feel more than the sound of that vibrated clear through her.

"And you *do* have me," he declared. "We've come a long way."

She nodded, lightly bumping his chin. "The ocean, the city, the bush, the mountains, the plain," she said.

"I mean, to put two such different lives together to be man and wife."

"I know. And I was thinking maybe our old friend is up there on his spirit star road looking down on us and smiling."

His arms tightened around her. They both gazed up at the sprinkle of stars. Her tears blurred to molten silver that stunning sky she'd like to sketch. She snuggled back even closer against the angle of his warm, hard thighs, his hipbones and belly. His hands moved closer to caress her.

"And our dear friend is hoping for a fine future for us and for his land," he said, his voice tremulous with emotion.

She meant to say something else then, but the words caught in her throat. Besides, talk wasn't necessary now. Her deep inner calm amazed her, even as he began to make hot love to her again. He had asked her earlier how she felt. She felt part of this man and this land. And she had never felt more at one with herself, never more content or perfectly whole, Abby Rose, a Braden's bride at last in deed as well as dreams.

# Author's Note

The next year, 1836, was an important time for New South Wales. Governor Bourke, who had been listening to both Exclusive and Currency spokesmen, made great strides in attempting to solve social injustices.

He allowed a licensing system protecting squatters' rights so that the majority of the land would not be owned by a minority. For a fee of ten pounds per year, squatters could legally retain use of their sheep runs. By 1847, they could buy their land at a mere one pound per acre. A practical man, the governor realized the prosperity of the colony depended increasingly on wool produced by squatters. Spokesmen for Currency causes helped him to realize that such settlers possessed initiative, independence, drive and ambition—just the qualities that make up the Australian character today.

The early championing of social justice by Currency spokesmen of this era produced other positive changes in the colony, once firmly controlled by a few rich men for their own benefit. A British commission condemned the cruel treatment of aborigines and appointed protectors, although the dispossession and abuse of these native Australians continued for years under this paternalistic system.

Immigration became very open in the 1830s, especially for unwed British women who were not convicts. (Transportation of convicts to New South Wales was ended in 1840 and to Van Dieman's Land—present-day Tasmania—in 1853;

however, the practice continued in Western Australia until 1868.) And, as more Currency made their mark in business or other endeavors, the old notion of an inherent moral taint in the "convict class" began to lose sway. Today, many Australians are more than proud of their convict ancestors' determination and hard work.

These changes, in turn, had a civilizing influence on the predominantly white male population of this raw land. The thrilling days of the Australian gold rush, which made peaceful, pastoral Bathurst a boomtown and those who owned land around it fabulously rich, lay ahead.

*     *     *     *     *

# COMING IN 1991 FROM
# HARLEQUIN SUPERROMANCE:

Three abandoned orphans,
one missing heiress!

Dying millionaire Owen Byrnside receives an
anonymous letter informing him that twenty-six years
ago, his son, Christopher, fathered a daughter. The
infant was abandoned at a foundling home that
subsequently burned to the ground, destroying all
records. Three young women could be Owen's long-
lost granddaughter, and Owen is determined to track
down each of them! Read their stories in

#434 HIGH STAKES (available January 1991)
#438 DARK WATERS (available February 1991)
#442 BRIGHT SECRETS (available March 1991)

Three exciting stories of intrigue and romance by
veteran Superromance author Jane Silverwood.

SBRY

## Coming soon
## to an easy chair near you.

**FIRST CLASS** is Harlequin's armchair travel plan for the incurably romantic. You'll visit a different dreamy destination every month from January through December without ever packing a bag. No jet lag, no expensive air fares and *no* lost luggage. Just First Class Harlequin Romance reading, featuring exotic settings from Tasmania to Thailand, from Egypt to Australia, and more.

**FIRST CLASS** romantic excursions guaranteed! Start your world tour in January. Look for the special **FIRST CLASS** destination on selected Harlequin Romance titles—there's a new one every month.

NEXT DESTINATION:
**THAILAND**

 *Harlequin Books*

JTR2

You'll flip . . . your pages won't!
Read paperbacks *hands-free* with

# Book Mate · I

The perfect "mate" for all your romance paperbacks

**Traveling • Vacationing • At Work • In Bed • Studying • Cooking • Eating**

Perfect size for all standard paperbacks, this wonderful invention makes reading a pure pleasure! Ingenious design holds paperback books OPEN and FLAT so even wind can't ruffle pages — leaves your hands free to do other things. Reinforced, wipe-clean vinyl-covered holder flexes to let you turn pages without undoing the strap . . . supports paperbacks so well, they have the strength of hardcovers!

Pages turn WITHOUT opening the strap.

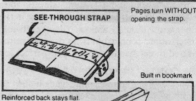

**SEE-THROUGH STRAP**

Reinforced back stays flat.

Built in bookmark

BOOK MARK

BACK COVER HOLDING STRIP

10" x 7¼", opened.
Snaps closed for easy carrying, too

Available now. Send your name, address, and zip code, along with a check or money order for just $5.95 + .75¢ for delivery (for a total of $6.70) payable to Reader Service to:

Reader Service
Bookmate Offer
3010 Walden Avenue
P.O. Box 1396
Buffalo, N.Y. 14269-1396

Offer not available in Canada
*New York residents add appropriate sales tax.

BM-GR

# COMING NEXT MONTH

### #63 THE SILVER LINK—Patricia Potter
American army scout Tristan Hampton sought adventure in
New Mexico, but he found much more in the arms of fiery
Spaniard Antonia Ramirez. Their hearts told them they were
lovers; their people told them they were enemies—and bitter
hatred threatened to destroy their perfect love.

### #64 CONTRABAND DESIRE—Lucy Elliot
Union officer Quinn Erskine made it clear that a refugee slave
camp in war-torn Tennessee was no place for the refined
Elizabeth Whitley. But Elizabeth's undaunted determination
to help the refugees was a light in the darkness of war, and her
love was a fire in the darkness of Quinn's heart.

### #65 HIGHLAND HEATHER—Ruth Langan
Spirited Brenna MacAlpin swore never to marry an
Englishman, despite Queen Elizabeth's orders. But her English
captor, the ruggedly handsome Lord Morgan Grey, soon had
her longing to exchange one vow for another.

### #66 FORBIDDEN FIRE—Heather Graham Pozzessere
Marissa Ayers already regretted being a party to the deceit she
would bring to Ian Tremayne's household. Still, when she'd
pledged to masquerade as her friend, Marissa never dreamed
that Ian was not expecting a ward . . . but a wife.

## AVAILABLE NOW:

**#61 BRADEN'S BRIDES**
Caryn Cameron

**#62 MOONWITCH**
Nicole Jordan